Blink Factor

a crime thriller

Steve Barry

 **Plain View Press**
1101 W. 34th Street, STE 404

http://plainviewpress.net
Austin, TX 78705

ISBN: 978-1-63210-091-7
ebook ISBN: 978-1-63210-092-4
Library of Congress Control Number: 2021943870

Cover Design by Steve Barry

This is a work of fiction. With the exception of some known historical events and figures, all characters, places, incidents, and dialogues are a product of the author's imagination or are used fictitiously, and any resemblance to actual persons, living or dead, is entirely coincidental.

We Find Healing In Existing Reality

Plain View Press is a 36-year-old issue-based literary publishing house. Our books result from artistic collaboration between writers, artists, and editors. Over the years we have become a far-flung community of activists whose energies bring humanitarian enlightenment and hope to individuals and communities grappling with the major issues of our time—peace, justice, the environment, education and gender. This is a humane and highly creative group of people committed to art and social change. The poems, stories, essays, non-fiction explorations of major issues are significant evidence that despite the relentless violence of our time, there is hope and there is art to show the human face of it.

to JB

with thanks to
Albert Noyer and Pam Knight

PROLOGUE

Monday, March 23, 1964
Upper Park Avenue, Manhattan

In the shadowy world of Frank Riley, clandestine operations are stock-and-trade, but tonight's meeting with Doctor Broder demanded the utmost discretion. Leaks circulating in the press mentioned marginalized New Yorkers abducted from mental institutions and halfway houses. Ongoing investigations alleged bizarre experiments, leaving victims more disturbed than they were before. The reports endangered Riley's operation—a consequence he could ill afford.

Riley ran Subproject 8, part of a covert CIA testing program called MKUltra. Approved by President Harry Truman, its larger initiative, Operation Paperclip, drew former Nazi scientists stateside to work for the government's various mind control experiments.

Specific to Subproject 8 was the investigation into memory enhancement, and Riley hinged his last years with the agency on its success. The project was winding down and the middle-aged operative was eager to make his mark while he still could. There was nothing Riley feared more than riding a desk into obscurity.

All his hopes rode on this evening's meeting with the Neuropsychologist, Martin Broder. It was the doctor's unorthodox research into Clinical Pharmacology that brought him to the attention of the CIA. Broder found his assignments so engrossing, he turned one of his consulting rooms into a laboratory. Behind its steel door, he concocted experimental mind-altering drugs, LSD derivatives for Riley to administer to his unsuspecting subjects. Tonight, the neuropsychologist would offer a candidate of his own—a college student who might ensure the success of Riley's operation and his own future with the CIA.

Located in the same building as Broder's Park Avenue apartment, his consulting rooms provided a dedicated entrance off the street. Visiting the doctor after office hours would pique the curiosity of the building's doorman. Riley moved down the opposite side of the street and, crossing over to the traffic island, doubled back to slip unseen through the doctor's entrance.

Broder was in his office, a bottle of Haig & Haig Pinch and two tumblers set out on the desk. As Riley entered, the doctor looked up, poured two scotches and handed one to the agent.

"Thanks." Riley took a sip and retreated to an upholstered chair opposite the desk. He sat with his hands clasped behind his bullet-shaped head, the receding nut-brown hair, coupled with his hawk-like nose and circular eyes, accentuating his birdlike presence.

"Did you see my wife hanging around outside as you came in?" Broder asked.

"No, but the doorman was there—I made sure he didn't see me."

"Good," said Broder. "The doorman snoops around for my wife. She's a real meddlesome bitch. Imagine, I'm doing important work for my country and all she worries about is whether I'm fooling around with another woman."

Tall and handsome, Doctor Broder had the milky complexion and high-domed forehead of a fatherly, all-knowing academic. Yet, looking beyond the straight nose and arched eyebrows, Riley noticed emotionless eyes and a dour mouth that hardly ever smiled. It was no wonder Broder's wife was unhappy. He felt sorry for the doctor and gave him an understanding smile before broaching the subject of their meeting.

"You found a subject for me?"

"That's right," Broder replied. "And as I mentioned over the phone, this one could be the crowning achievement of our collaboration."

"Just in time," said Riley. "The project's getting a lot of press. Risks of the government's involvement are outweighing the benefits. A suitable subject might extend the timeline, though. Who is it?"

"A twenty-two-year-old college art student named David Greenberg," Broder said. "He's my stepdaughter's current boyfriend, so I know him better than most of our subjects."

"Greenberg huh?" Riley responded sarcastically. "So you're sacrificing one of your own?"

Broder laughed. "He may be Jewish, but he's a nobody and I don't want him hanging around Nina. He's a fortune hunter."

"Okay, okay," Riley said. "What can you tell me about him?"

"Nina met him three years ago. At the time he was shy and retiring, with no socialization skills. In short, a wimp. Since then, there's been a drastic change in both his appearance and personality."

"How so?"

"He's put on some muscle and is a lot more sociable. On the surface, he seems to be an ordinary young man, but looking through a clinician's eye there are some behavioral markers."

"Which are?"

"He has a habit of staring off into space as if he suffers from absence seizures. But because the episodes are followed by blinking and an extended period of eye closure, I speculated he was concentrating on image retention."

"Why would he do that?" Riley asked.

"Well, every artist tries to fix objects in their mind to develop a visual alphabet. When I first noticed the blinking, I put it off to some eccentric quirk. But I quickly realized he was engaging in strategic blinking. Intentional blinking is task related. It suppresses the visual information stream and enhances memory.

"In short, I believe the young man has extended powers of perception bordering on the paranormal. By blinking, he purposely records images to access later, and when he does, it's recalled with great accuracy."

Riley drew his legs back and leaned forward, "Is there anything to back up this belief?"

"Yes, 'The Blink Factor'," the doctor said.

"'Blink Factor'," Riley repeated. "What are you talking about?"

"Several weeks ago, I hosted a dinner party attended by a colleague who works for Bell Laboratories out of New Jersey. When Greenberg walked in to pick up Nina, my friend recognized him at once. It seems three years ago; Greenberg was the subject of a research project headed by Dr. Max Bruckmann. Sometime later, Bruckmann published an article entitled 'The Blink Factor', in which a 'Subject X' demonstrated an ability to store and retrieve massive amounts of visual information at will."

Riley was hopeful. "Well, that's something the Soviets don't have. Oh, they have their mnemonists, but nothing like what you describe."

The doctor nodded. "That's not all, Greenberg is now back at Bell Labs. Their computer scientists are mapping his memory process—using it to develop protocols for the collection and retrieval of digital images."

Riley stood and placed his empty glass on the desk. "Let's say you're right and this kid's a human camera who can harvest images and recover them later. How accurate can his memory be?"

"According to my source, image detail is precise," Broder said. "I'm telling you, this is the closest we've come to finding someone with mind control. Snag him and we're way ahead of the game." He handed Riley a folder. "This is all the information I have on him so far. Drop by tomorrow, I'm expecting a copy of 'The Blink Factor' article then—further details will be inside."

The agent took the folder and left. The scotch mellowed him, but the information he heard was nothing less than his salvation. Nailing the Greenberg kid was now top priority. Within the week, Broder's stepdaughter would find her boyfriend heavily into drugs.

Riley was awfully good at his job—David Greenberg wouldn't have a chance.

CHAPTER 1

Day 1
The Foretelling

It was eerily quiet on the Upper West Side of Manhattan. The usual pre-dawn din of commuter traffic from the Hudson River Parkway seemed muffled, the intermittent wailing of sirens strangely absent. Across from Riverside Park, the scattering of birds was silent among the tree-lined side streets.

In a pre-war apartment building along West 88th Street, David Greenberg looked out from the second-floor window of his grandfather's kitchen. The cars, sidewalk and buildings were shrouded in the semidarkness of early morning. Less than a block away, a low fog from the Hudson River crept across Riverside Drive and meandered down 88th Street toward his apartment building. Fascinated, David watched the thick mist fill the empty space of the no parking zone across the street. It gathered itself around the fire hydrant like a buoy floating in a troubled harbor.

Unexpectedly, a pair of headlights broke through the fog and advanced down the street. As it came closer, its headlights traced bright arcs over the darkened walls of the kitchen. When the car reached the fire hydrant, its headlights died, and David retreated to the edge of the window. The car crawled into the restricted space, its tires crunching against the red curb. Then, the engine cut out and everything went quiet.

David's long-held fear of discovery returned. Hoping to dismiss his anxiety, he moved away from the window and started on breakfast. He put the kettle on for his grandfather's tea, placed a few prunes in a bowl and boiled some eggs. But inside he was numb with fear. Part of him thought it was a whacky notion: a young man with an indelible memory kidnapped by government agents for secret research. It was a crazy scenario straight out of the movies.

And then, a flashback from three and a half years ago played out like a slide show on the backsplash of the stove. The move to his grandfather's apartment; his first weeks at Columbia; an impacted wisdom tooth; the pain that sent him to an oral surgeon and the needle to put him under. There was no choice but to tell the truth—he was epileptic and on medication.

The surgeon understood and knew how to handle it. His son was epileptic. "Who is your neurologist?"

"I have none," David told him. "Haven't seen one since I was twelve."

"Not so smart," the surgeon replied, and gave David the name of his son's neurologist—made the appointment right there and then.

Two weeks later David was examined. The neurologist said he didn't believe it was epilepsy—he thought it might be Peduncular Hallucinosis. A rare form of hallucinations that revolve around people and places familiar to the patient. He sent David to Dr. Max Bruckmann, a vision specialist at Bell Laboratories.

Months of weird tests showed no epilepsy; no Peduncular Hallucinosis. The new diagnosis—Persistent Visual Recall.

David was an Eidetiker.

He left the research facility with assurances—no publicity and no one would know his secret but Dr. Max and the Bell team of Perceptual Scientists. Yet during this past month, he couldn't shake the feeling he was being followed. As he dropped some bread in the toaster, he recalled his last conversation with Doctor Max.

"You know how I get these intuitive flashes?" David said.

"Yes," said Max, "quite remarkable, but we could never explain them."

"Well, every once in a while I get the feeling someone's watching me."

"And you're worried about what?"

"Well, I was at Bell Labs for months—all the research was supposed to be secret—I don't want to be used as a guinea pig—you know that."

"We're not watching you David. We monitor your ability once or twice a year—that's it. All results are confidential. You've got a feeling, that's all. Feelings are tricky—don't get obsessed—it'll drive you nuts."

"You think I'm crazy?"

"No, in simple terms, you're so concerned about this, your imagination is working overtime. Relax, no one's out to experiment on you."

"So I should simply ignore the whole thing?"

"That's it. Leave it alone, and it will leave you alone."

At the time, David thought Dr. Max was right. After all, despite the double life he led, there was little evidence anyone unearthed his secret. As an art student, he hid it from his professors for over three years. As hard as they tried, they could never explain how, at the age of twenty-one, David mastered skills of an artist twice his age.

In his secret life, David was a part-time illustrator working for several of New York's top magazines and ad agencies. To the art directors who knew him, he was an enigma. They wrote paychecks made out to David Asher not realizing it was a variant of his real name—David Asher Greenberg. Meanwhile, Columbia University was preparing a diploma for David Greenberg with no idea he was the illustrator, David Asher.

David set his grandfather's breakfast on the Formica table along with some utensils and glanced out the window. The black Buick was still there. His angle of sight from the second-floor apartment afforded a limited view of the occupants of the car. The driver was wearing a dark blue suit jacket. His arm hung outside the car window; the shoulder pad of the suit bunched up and wrinkled. In the passenger seat, another man was gesticulating as if arguing with his companion. On the dash David could see a coffee cup and a pair of binoculars.

Dr. Max is wrong. The surveillance is all too obvious. I'm tagged as a person of interest. They're finally making their move.

Across the street from David's apartment, Christopher "Chip" Giamarco arose from his bed and stood in the cramped space between the mattress and the only window in the one room basement apartment. Wrapping a blanket around himself, he turned and leaned a forearm on the slimy sill. During the night, rain puddled under the partially opened sash and mixed with an accumulation of soot from the street. Chip wiped his forearm off across the front of his undershirt and moved the curtain aside.

Fucking shit...

A black Buick pulled into the no parking zone in front of his apartment. A Super's apartment, it was the only street facing, below-grade unit on the block. There was a private entrance under the stoop with direct access to the basement where he stored almost everything he trucked in from Vegas.

Comfort wasn't a big priority for Chip, but an unobstructed view of David's apartment building across the street was. Standing at the window, Chip's chin cleared street level and the fire hydrant at the curb guaranteed a clear line of sight.

Until this morning.

He turned back to the bed and found his pack of Camels, now crushed from a night of tossing and turning. Shuffling a few feet toward the kitchenette, he dropped the mangled pack in the sink and reached in the overhead cabinet for a fresh one.

Lighting a cigarette, he went back to the window. To Chip the car looked to be government issue. The man in the passenger seat held a coffee cup in one hand and gesticulated with the other. In the driver's seat, his partner's hand was draped over the steering wheel. In his grip, he held a pair of binoculars.

There was movement in a second-floor window across the street. The two men shifted in their seats and the binoculars moved up to the driver's head. *There's no doubt about it, they're checking out the second-floor windows above the building's green canopy.* Chip decided his scheme would have to wait. The government was interested in the same person he was—the college kid who lived with his grandfather in apartment 2D across the street.

His little stepbrother, David Greenberg.

⋙⋘

Jacob Goldstein entered the kitchen to find David sitting by the window with a glass of orange juice on the sill. He pulled his robe around him and moved past the kitchen table to where his grandson sat.

David turned around to face him. "Morning Gramps, you can start on your prunes, I'll get the eggs and toast."

Jacob put a restraining hand on his shoulder. "Look, I can see you're busy. I'll do it." Jacob stepped into the small, galley-like cooking area and found the eggs in a pot of water. He touched the shells with the back of his little finger. "Hot they're not," he mumbled. "And again, the toast is burnt. Not so bad this time, but still...."

"I'm sorry Gramps, I'll eat them myself. Start on your prunes and I'll make everything fresh."

"No need," Jacob insisted. "There's nothing wrong with hard boiled eggs. I'll scrape the toast; everything will be fine." Jacob poured two cups of tea, gave one to his grandson and sat down to eat his prunes. He watched David put his tea on the windowsill next to the orange juice and turn again to scrutinize the street below.

The boy changed drastically since moving in with him over three years ago. Reed-thin and pale then, David's physical transformation was uncanny. Looking at him now in his shirtsleeves, it was easy to appreciate his wide shoulders and the well-defined arms that gripped the windowsill. His once roundish face became squarer with subtle indentations under the cheek bones—a sign of character and steadfastness. Beneath a tumble of dark brown hair, the wide arch of his dense eyebrows set off a pair of magnificent blue eyes. If the young man decided to grow a mustache, he would resemble a young Omar Sharif.

His grandson finished his orange juice and continued to scan the street below. After a few sips of tea Jacob asked, "So, maybe now you can tell me what all the fuss is about?"

David shifted in his chair to face him and poked his thumb over his shoulder to point out the window. "There's a car parked across the street."

Jacob removed a pit from one of prunes. "I saw. And that's a problem?"

"Well, it's parked in front of the fire hydrant. Almost four years living with you, and I've never seen a car parked so long in front of the hydrant. It's strange."

He was well aware of David's uncanny memory. "I believe you, but what's so unusual? Someone's picking up a passenger maybe?"

"I thought so too, but no one has gotten in or out. The car hasn't budged for almost an hour. I'm getting a bad feeling."

"Oy, don't tell me." Jacob didn't like his grandson's bad feelings. He was convinced his grandson was a *mazi-kasir*—a fortune teller. Many years ago, David sensed tragedy would strike. A week later Jacob's wife Sarah, cut her wrists in the bath. Afterwards, Jacob thought the foretelling a coincidence, but through the years more of David's predictions came true. He had to admit, not only did David have a phenomenal memory, but second sight as well.

David looked concerned. "Maybe I shouldn't have said anything. I didn't mean to bring up—"

"Look, it's all right," Jacob nodded. "So tell me...how long before something, eh...unpleasant happens?"

"Oh, well, I never know for sure Gramps. But it's soon—within the next week at least. Don't worry though, it's not the same feeling I had back when... when, you know, grandma...."

Jacob nodded again, "I know. So, it's nothing terrible?"

"No, Gramps...nothing like that."

Silence.

To lighten the mood, Jacob tried humor. "So maybe this time it's only gas?"

David's smile was not convincing, and Jacob understood why. The mere mention of his grandmother's suicide called up precise images of her body floating in the blood-soaked tub. Reliving that horror in such detail, was tough. He made a come-hither motion with his hand. "Come, come away from the window. You should eat at the table like a *mensch*, not a rat."

ss

Twenty minutes later, Jacob was in his bathroom scrutinizing his reflection in the mirror. He removed his nightcap. Swaths of long hair fell over his right ear, and he swept the unruly mess back with his fingers. As usual, the image of the old man staring back at him was not pleasing. The white patchwork of stubble on his chin matched his mustache and eyebrows. On top of his bald head, the reflection from the light bulb above the vanity brought out the nicks and scrapes of his eighty-two years. Several large brown spots peppered the shiny dome.

Jacob fingered the wide patch of hair that circled halfway around his head in the shape of a crescent. Although the hair on the left was neatly trimmed, the hair on the right almost touched his shoulders. He reached for the Vaseline and smeared it along the length of hair. With the aid of a hand mirror, he placed the threadlike tendrils over his scalp to approximate the slicked-down-look of a full head of hair. Putting on his reading glasses, he trimmed his mustache and added a bit of color to his cheeks with some of his wife's blush.

Moving the ironing board out from his closet, Jacob set it up next to the bedroom window to give his pants a light press. He glanced down at the street—the Buick was still parked by the hydrant. Then, David appeared from under the green canopy and walked along 88th Street toward the bus stop on Broadway. About to turn from the window, Jacob saw the door to the Buick open. A man with sandy hair—short and powerfully built—stepped out onto the pavement. He turned around and leaned his head back into the car.

Holding onto the door frame, he talked with the driver until David was half a block away. Then, he shut the car door and took off in David's direction.

CHAPTER 2

The Snoop

David reached the middle of the block, and heard a car door slam. He was being followed. *Keep on walking,* he told himself. *Your only advantage is to let them think you're clueless about what they're up to.*

Before leaving the apartment building, he took steps to find out who they were. He viewed the Buick through the window of the lobby door. The two men in the front seat were clearly visible and he noticed how the car's rear-view mirror was tilted to spot anyone exiting the building without the driver turning his head.

He pushed the lobby door open and stepped out under the green canopy patting his pockets as if checking its contents. Stopping short of the curb, he pulled a pen out of his pant's pocket and clipped it to his shirt. Then, in one seamless motion, he looked up, blinked the car into his memory and turned left to head towards Broadway.

Reaching the bus stop, David joined the queue and eyeballed everyone as they lined up behind him. He recognized each passenger as someone he'd traveled with before on his morning ride to the university. No one looked suspicious, yet he could still feel an unknown presence. *The guy from the Buick is hiding somewhere. Maybe,* he thought, *in the entrance of a nearby store. If I'm lucky, I might catch him getting on the bus after me.*

But the plan didn't work. His seat was too far from the door and passengers stood in his line of sight. He would have to try again when he got off at 116th Street. David settled into the seat and closed his eyes. There was a change in air pressure—a hissing as the doors closed. As the gears shifted, and the bus lurched into traffic, David accessed his short-term memory. Section by section the first piece of the puzzle came together until the black Buick appeared on the inner surface of his eyelids.

No identifying marks or stickers on the car. Can't see the license plate. New tires. The driver's left arm is hanging out the window. Blue suit—a rectangular shaped watch—brown leather band. College ring. Clean hands.

He let the image go.

One thing's certain, they're professionals. Someone has kept tabs on me for years—watching and waiting. For what? Document my extraordinary ability? Convince some higher up I'm the real deal? And who is this higher up?

There was a ding—someone pulled the cord and David realized it was his stop. Passengers got up, jostled with packages; queued up to exit. This was his last chance to catch a glimpse of the guy.

Up on his feet, David found himself pushed down the aisle towards the exit door and, before he knew it, he was out on the pavement. He stood on the corner and glanced furtively around half-expecting to be grabbed, stuffed into a waiting van, and driven off to some secluded warehouse.

❧

From the shadowed entrance of a drugstore, CIA operative Frank Riley caught sight of a sandy-haired man slipping on his sunglasses to watch Greenberg cross the street. After the kid entered the Fine Arts Building, Riley watched the stranger pick up a paper at the newsstand, cross over to the traffic island and sit on a bench.

It was an ideal spot to set up surveillance. The corner building housed the Schools of Music, Theater and Visual Arts of Columbia University. The entrance to the classrooms and studios, the subway entrance and the bus stop were all in eyeshot of the sandy-haired stranger now hiding behind the newspaper.

Riley immediately pegged him as law enforcement and wondered which other agency might have an interest in David Greenberg. More importantly, he wanted to know everything the sandy-haired operative knew about his target.

He couldn't afford any mistakes.

❧

After Jacob spotted the sandy-haired man take off after his grandson, the Buick pulled out from the hydrant and followed him at a snail's pace. Deep in thought, Jacob laid his pressed pants across the bed and dismantled the ironing board. It was hard for him to imagine what David did to cause two men to follow him. Always thoughtful and level-headed, his grandson was not the typical, counterculture hippie he read about in the papers. Yet, it was obvious the boy was in trouble.

Jacob sat on the edge of his bed to wrap his shins with Ace bandages—something he did every morning in preparation for his morning walk to the newsstand. As he wound the elastic fabric over his arthritic legs, his glance drifted to the empty bed across from him and the photograph of his wife Sarah on the nightstand. After her funeral, it was David who helped him avoid the retirement home.

The family sat *shiva* at his daughter Ellen's house. The week of mourning was punctuated with heated discussions about Jacob's future. How, they asked, could an old man live alone? He remembered the visits to several retirement homes close to his daughter's house—the tasteless, greasy lunches and the depressing tours of the facilities. Just choose, they said. Ellen promised to visit regularly—he would be fine.

Did they expect him to spend his last days sitting in a room the size of a prison cell? And why should he mingle with strangers in a walled-in common area or take his walks around a barren exercise yard? He enjoyed his walks near the reservoir or meeting his friends in Riverside Park to feed the pigeons. Most of all, he loved the home his wife made for him.

Jacob felt fine where he was. He wanted to be nurtured by the people and places that defined his life. To be pampered by the familiar instead of adjusting to the unfamiliar. He needed to cuddle in his own bed and feel the lingering presence of his wife Sarah. If they forced him into a retirement home, he felt his life would be over.

It was David who saved him. "Gramps stay in your apartment, and I'll come live with you," his grandson insisted. "I'm going to Columbia University in the Fall. It's a short bus ride from your apartment. What do you say?"

"What are you talking...you want to live with me?"

"Sure," answered David. "Commuting to the city from Long Island, back and forth everyday would be a drag. It's simpler and cheaper if I stay with you during the week. I'll come home weekends. It's win-win."

Now it was Jacob's turn to help David. But what could an *alta kocker* like him do? Jacob decided to think it over during his walk. He finished dressing and, on his way out, passed his grandson's room. He stopped, and realized he knew very little of David's life. How could he help his grandson if he didn't really know him?

Jacob retraced his steps and entered David's room. The walls looked like an art museum. An eclectic mix of Jacob's antiques, David's paintings and childhood furniture. Sarah's antique bureau stood against an adjacent wall. On it lay a thick leather-bound folio. Against the opposite wall, the bed was made. A few novels and a checkbook rested on the mahogany nightstand.

David's work area was toward the back of the room. Ratty studio equipment brought from his home on Long Island was arranged near the window: an old folding table smeared with paint; a junky-looking stool and a rickety bookcase crammed full of sketchbooks.

The top of the bookcase held a strange Lucite paperweight in the shape of a hexagon. Encased inside was a small electrical component; the lettering around it read: "The Transistor, Invented at Bell Laboratories, A Result of Basic Research". Next to it were several photographs of David's girlfriend Nina, a transistor radio, and a saucer with loose change and bits of erasers.

On the folding table, he found pens and brushes stuffed in glass jars. A ceramic jug held drafting instruments, pencils and a magnifying glass. On a shallow butcher tray, dried puddles of watercolor paint lay next to a sponge reeking like an old dish rag—its dank odor attesting to years of use with little rinsing out.

Taped to the drawing board was a thick sheet of drawing paper. He bent down to look at it—his bald head missing the large overhead lamp. It was the beginning of a drawing. At first, Jacob thought it to be a scene from the Bible—Genesis 22—when the heavenly angel stops Abraham from sacrificing his son Isaac. Looking closer, he realized it was, yet it wasn't.

David changed the face of Abraham to look like his father, Sy Greenberg. Isaac's features became David's, and in a bizarre twist, David held the knife. The Angel of God was replaced by the Devil who, hovering behind David, urged him to plunge the blade into his father's chest.

Jacob was overcome with dread—the message was clear—David wanted to kill his father.

✌✌

The moment David got off the bus at Broadway and 116th Street, he was smack in the middle of Columbia University—a campus comprising six city blocks of the Morningside Heights district of Upper Manhattan. As he walked into Dodge Hall and up to the second-floor painting studio, he felt even here, amongst his fellow students and supportive faculty, he wasn't safe.

He pulled his painting from the stacks, placed it on an easel, and rolled it near the windows. As he angled the canvas to catch the best of the cool morning light, the image of the black Buick returned to him. He searched the figures of the two men in the car and realized they weren't thugs. David knew the type—his own father was one of them—a government agent.

David dragged a paint-stained stool before his canvas and sat, his mind wandering back to August 1961. He entered Columbia as a precocious young artist with a prodigious visual memory. Shortly after, he met Dr. Max, who said he had Image Adhesion—an unconscious ability to retain most everything he saw.

Throughout his college years, David used his indelible memory to develop a remarkable artistic ability. But success came at a cost. It set him apart from other students and brought him to the attention of his professors. One in particular—Professor Carl Haverstock.

Haverstock conducted David's entrance interview and was critical yet curiously helpful at the same time. It did not go well, and David felt there wasn't a chance in hell of his acceptance.

And yet he got in. During his first three years, Haverstock would pop into each of his studio classes. He'd talk with other instructors and always made an excuse to look at David's work. His interest seemed excessive, and David suspected the professor of being a government recruiter.

It was well known the CIA recruited Columbia's top students every year in February. A recent book critical of the CIA by David Wise, called *The Invisible Government*, was circulating on campus. In it Wise wrote, "On every large campus there is usually someone who serves secretly as the CIA's talent scout."

If the book came out earlier, he would have kept a low profile. Now, his artistic genius was well known around Columbia's Art School. It wasn't hard for David to imagine Haverstock informing his handlers of David's unusual ability. Hence, the appearance of the black Buick this morning.

David examined his painting. Every time he took up the brush, he faced disaster. The struggle was to put together the bits and pieces of pigment until the meaning of the painting became clear. Professor Haverstock, the men in the black Buick—these were pieces of another puzzle. A dangerous one. He needed to fit them together, or he'd be faced with a more deadly disaster than a ruined painting.

But there was nothing he could do now, so he willed himself to the task at hand. Placing his paints and brushes on a metal table, he squeezed colors onto his wood palette. The familiar ritual always cleared David's mind, and soon the reality of the paint surface took precedence over his earlier concerns.

The assignment was to use a recurring dream as the springboard for each student's senior painting project. Stapled to the back of David's stretcher was his typewritten summary of the painting's narrative:

Message from an Unknown Past
30"x 40", oil on canvas
David Greenberg, 1964

A young boy is depicted at a soda fountain in a drugstore. He's staring out the window at a stranger whose face is pressed against the glass. The man's mouth is open in a scream. With his elbows raised to shoulder level, the man is striking the glass with balled up fists in a desperate attempt to get the attention of the young boy. Other children are sipping their drinks, oblivious to what is going on.

We notice the confusion on the boy's face and ask ourselves the same question the boy might ask. Who is this stranger? What is he trying to say? When we scrutinize the figure of the man further, we see the painter has melded the landscape into his body. The man is transparent—an apparition—perhaps from the boy's past. Is he trying to warn the boy of something? If so, the boy isn't getting the message and his future remains unchanged.

David didn't agree with notational ekphrasis. Placing a descriptive commentary side by side with a painting belied his belief that a painting should communicate on its own. But with a dozen students in the class, he understood why the professor would insist upon it.

Several minutes were devoted to passing a critical eye over his under drawing. Satisfied with the composition, he began the dead-coloring stage. The scent of turpentine and oil drifted to his nostrils and, little by little, he became lost in the creative process. By the time the professor and other students arrived, David found himself deep into the painting.

Sometime later, he looked up from his palette to see his professor reading his summary sheet. Professor Haverstock nodded and walked around the easel to study the painting.

"I take it," the professor asked, "the young boy at the counter is you, as a child? The man outside the window is someone from your past. He's trying to tell you something of importance. Is that correct?"

"Yes, sir, that is it exactly." David answered.

"Can you tell me then, what warning the stranger is attempting to impart to your younger self?"

David's answer came in an instant. "The point of the painting is to motivate each viewer to ask themselves what such a warning might be if they themselves were the young boy."

A satisfied grin spread over the instructor's face. "Very good Mr. Greenberg. Very good indeed. You managed to side-step my intrusion into your personal life in a most ingenious way." He looked up at the painting for a few seconds, nodded again, and moved on.

After a long while, students eager to start Spring Break trickled out of the studio. Only David remained, and the professor once more came over to examine his painting. David noticed his head nodding imperceptibly, as if he made a weighty decision. The professor then wished David a happy holiday and left the studio.

Alone now, David wondered, *Strange, the look in his eyes before he left....* It took a while for his thoughts to settle down, until finally, he took up his brush. One brushstroke at a time, he became lost in the hush of the empty studio and the viscosity of the paint.

❧

Professor Haverstock left the studio in a hurry. As the subject of David's painting became clear, he realized the boy was ready for the final step in the long-awaited plan.

In his office, he picked up the phone and dialed. "*Herr Scholz?*" the professor asked. "*Carl hier, ist Der Chef dabei*—Carl here, is your boss in?"

The professor listened and then nodded. "*Gut, uch werde warten*—Good, I'll wait." *Three years of waiting for a breakthrough—what's another few minutes?*

"Yes, it's me." Haverstock replied. "David's ready, we need to make our move on the boy soon."

❧

Shortly after noon the rumbling in David's stomach reminded him of a lunch date with Nina. Putting down his palette and brushes, he moved to the studio window to look for her. Placing his palms against the pane, he pressed his head against the cool glass, rolled it back and forth to search the wide expanse of Broadway.

Below him, pedestrians strolled along the pavement. A group loitered around the subway entrance, and a queue formed at the bus stop. An intermittent breeze from the Hudson River brushed the tops of the trees to the left forcing his gaze toward the end of the traffic island. Sitting on a long bench, a group of students, college professors and secretaries ate their lunches from paper sacks.

Except one. Halfway down the bench, a sandy-haired man sat reading a newspaper. Alone and without any lunch, his dark blue suit, tie and aviator sunglasses made him seem oddly out of place. His glance pivoted between the subway entrance, the bus stop, and Dodge Hall.

No question—this must be the guy following me.

Then, David spotted Nina walking on the opposite side of Broadway. Her stride was assured and easily identified as that of a dancer. She looked younger than her twenty-two years, and her demeanor was one of understated elegance.

Born in Colombia, to a family of distinguished lineage from Popayán, Nina grew up as a member of the *abolengo*—landed patricians whose family members held some of the highest offices in government and the church. Her breeding was hard to miss. To David's parents, she was an elitist, but he knew underneath her aristocratic bearing was a woman who listened with her heart.

She approached the intersection and crossed over to the traffic island slowing her pace—hoping to find an empty seat on the bench. The sandy-haired guy shifted sideways. He moved the newspaper off to the side, giving him a clear view of her as she stepped into his line of sight. Suddenly, the man dropped all pretense of reading and watched her as she walked by.

There's no doubt about it, David reasoned. *He knows who she is and is checking her out....*

CHAPTER 3

The Whiz Kid

Nina Caldas strode past the crowded bench on the traffic island, ignoring the jerk hiding behind his newspaper. Stifling a smile, she crossed Broadway towards College Walk and spotted David moving toward her with alarming urgency. She waited at the gate's north pylon wondering what happened.

Agitated, David moved to her side and pulled her behind the pylon. "I'm being followed."

"What?" She glanced quickly around.

"Here, hold my sketchbook. Don't move."

He started to leave but she held onto his sleeve. "Wait...why would someone follow you?"

"I have my suspicions. Now I'm going to find out for sure," he tried to move past her again, but she blocked his way.

"Hey," she said, placing an open palm against his chest. "Talk to me...what's this about?"

"The guy on the bench, the one holding the newspaper up in front of his face," he explained. "He's following me and scoped you out when you walked past him."

She smiled, "That creep. Sure, I noticed him. It's no big deal, most men look at me when I pass by."

"This isn't a joke, Nina. Following me is frightening enough, but if he knows we're together there's a chance you might be in danger too."

She noticed the firm set of his mouth; his face flushed in anger and thought, *he's taking this very seriously.* "Okay fine. So, what are you going to do...punch him in the nose?"

He shook his head. "No. I'll demand an explanation."

"Oh, you're going to demand, are you? He may be short but there's a lot of muscle under that suit. You'll be lucky if he only looks at you like you're crazy and walks away."

David stared at her for a second, then deflated, leaned back against the pylon. "You're right, I didn't think of that. What should we do?"

She linked her arm in his. "Let's walk to Prexy's; we'll figure it out over lunch."

❧❦

Jacob sat on the stool next to David's drawing and stared again at *The Sacrifice of Isaac.* That his grandson wanted to kill his father was not too surprising. When Jacob first met Sy Greenberg, he thought him overly aggressive and secretive with all the hallmarks of a crude opportunist. But at the time, his daughter Ellen was desperate to marry, and Jacob was too involved with his own problems to pay attention. Sy Greenberg ended up in the right place at the right time.

Jacob scanned the walls. David surrounded himself with paintings of his mother, his girlfriend Nina and studies of Jacob and Sarah. There were none of his father.

He looked again at David's drawing. Despite the horror it portrayed, he realized the intelligence behind it and his respect for his grandson grew. Jacob stood and noticing stacks of cardboard leaning against a wall, went over and flipped one around. Although it was unfinished, he at once recognized William F. Buckley. On the bottom of the illustration, in blue pencil, a caption read: Client-Atlantic Monthly, Subject-WF Buckley.

He looked through more illustrations. Some advertising related, others medical illustrations for a Doctor Max Bruckmann. He found a savings book on the nightstand with dozens of deposits going back over two years.

It was all unbelievable. He never understood the level of his grandson's artistic ability until now. When David was a child, everyone considered him to be a dim-witted epileptic with a flare for drawing. No one in the family believed he got into Columbia on his own merits. Everyone thought Sy Greenberg threatened someone.

Jacob took up the thick leather-bound folio from the bureau and lifted the cover. Clipped to the top of a thick sheaf of documents, was a letter written on Bell Laboratory stationary:

24

February 8, 1961

Dear David,

Attached, please find the results of the perceptual tests we administered over the past few months. They document your astonishing ability at visual information storage and memory recall. These reports are proprietary to Bell Labs and, as we discussed, are for your use only.

As you know, our neurological team has confirmed that, despite what you were told as a child, you never had epilepsy. As of this date, you are perfectly healthy in every respect. What you experienced as a child, and continue to have now, is a rare condition known as Persistent Visual Memory Recall. The convulsion you experienced when you were ten, mistaken for a grand mal seizure, was psychogenic in origin. It was caused, not by any physiological malfunction, but by the brutal beating you received from your father. The childhood staring fits, with hallucinations, were past images spontaneously recalled from your memory. The prescribed Phenobarbital was unnecessary and kept you in a constant state of over-sedation.

Since discontinuing the drug, you have learned to control your memory recall by using biofeedback. You now have the ability to selectively retrieve any image from your past. You can either view it in your mind, or project it onto any surface as an aid to drawing. You have also shown a puzzling ability for Empathic Precognition. Although we know these premonitions to be triggered by extreme emotions, we have found no scientific basis for them.

As we discussed, I expect to see you back here every year to monitor these abilities of yours. The first article about you entitled "The Blink Factor", will appear soon in the <u>Journal of the Optical Society of America</u>. Naturally, your name is not mentioned and neither your parents nor college will be told about your time at Bell Labs.

If anything changes to your vision or memory, please call. The same holds true if you need encouragement, advice or just a friendly ear. My best wishes and kindest thoughts are with you always.

Blink on,

Max

Dr. Maximilian Bruckmann

Visual Perception Analyst

Cognition Science Services

Bell Laboratories, Murray Hill, New Jersey

Jacob flipped through the pages of charts, diagrams and test results, but didn't understand anything. He noted the date of the letter—written three years ago. He needed to read the letter several more times before he understood his grandson's genius.

David's some kind of whiz kid and he's hiding it from everyone.

✑✐

Nina spotted the sandy-haired man as she walked to the restaurant with David. Stockily built, wearing a dark blue suit, and aviator sunglasses, he was shouldering his way through the crowded street behind them.

Entering the restaurant, they passed by a long, solid wood counter crowded with lunch goers. On the way in, the stranger stopped to study the large, black and white photographs of Ivy League college campuses on the opposite wall. It was clear to Nina the man was looking to find an empty stool at the counter.

The couple continued to the dining room at the back and paused near an alcove of payphones to look for an open table. David directed Nina's attention to their friends AJ and Amanda who just finished lunch. Nina nodded and as David detoured to the Men's Room, she moved toward their friend's table.

Amanda greeted her, "I'm glad to see you so soon after my performance. What did you think?"

That morning, Nina attended a student performance at Juilliard, and she now took the opportunity to congratulate Amanda on her choreography.

"You really think it was good?" Amanda asked.

"Oh yes, far better than anyone else's." Nina remarked.

"I'd love it if you could critique it sometime."

Nina agreed, "Okay, we'll do that next time we meet."

AJ grabbed the check, got up and offered Nina his chair. "I've a history class in twenty minutes otherwise we'd join you for awhile."

Nina hung her dance bag over the spindle backed chair and noticed the stalker sitting on a stool near the end of the lunch counter, the newspaper hiding his face. He had a very good view of the dining room.

When David returned to the table, Nina noticed AJ's expression. "Anything wrong AJ?"

"Some guy's watching us," he whispered.

Nina nodded. "We know, the one at the counter with the newspaper."

"Uh, uh," AJ corrected. "It's the dude at the payphone."

David arrived at the table. "What dude?"

AJ gestured toward the alcove of payphones and both Nina and David focused on a tall man with his back against the wall of phones.

Catching their glance, the man moved the handset to his other ear and turned around quickly. His was the straightest spine Nina ever saw.

"Oh no," Nina exclaimed under her breath and turned to David with a questioning look.

David was incredulous. "Two of them?" He turned to AJ. "You sure he was looking at this table?"

"Not this table but you in particular," AJ explained. "Caught him tracking you as you walked toward us from the restroom."

"Thanks AJ."

"No problem," AJ replied. He and Amanda picked up their belongings. As they left, AJ turned around saying, "You need to watch your six—you're hanging too loose—you gotta stay engaged. You snooze, you lose."

The friends left and Nina sat down with her back to the counter so David would have a clear view of the two men now watching them.

"What did AJ mean by that?" Nina asked.

"Don't know. But it was a strange thing to say—almost as if...."

He drifted off somewhere and she needed to bring him back.

"David?"

"Hello, David." She waited and when his eyes fluttered, she said, "Welcome back."

David explained, "Sorry, I was thinking—maybe AJ knows more about me than he's willing to admit."

Nina nodded. "Maybe. I was going to ask you if you blinked in the guy at the payphone after you left the restroom."

"Actually yes...walked right by him. He gave me that knowing nod strangers give each other to pump themselves up with self-importance. But there was a hint of recognition in his eyes, so I captured his features."

"Well, that's good. But maybe AJ's mistaken about what he saw?"

"No, I don't think so. He used the word 'tracking' instead of watching—it's military speak—so is 'watch your six'. He's involved in countless civil rights protests. He's trained to keep his eyes open."

"I guess you're right," she agreed.

David closed his eyes. "Okay...I've called up the image of this new stalker. I'll sketch out a likeness—maybe at some point, we'll be able to figure out who the guy is." He opened his sketchbook. "Order for me will you please—you know what I like."

She did, and when the waitress came, she ordered a Post Graduate Burger with melted cheese for David and The Hamburger with a College Education for herself—both with fries and Cokes. Then, she leaned over the table to watch as David used thick black lines to delineate the man holding the phone to his ear.

As the sketch took shape, Nina thought about David's impulsive reaction to protect her earlier. Although secretly pleased, she was glad to have forestalled any confrontation with the powerfully built stranger on the bench. Now, two men followed him. The danger they represented was palpable and she wondered if David was up to the challenge. When she met him three years ago, he was rail thin. Since then, thanks to weekly work out sessions with AJ, he put on a lot of lean muscle. Still, he was no match for the bulldog at the counter or the ram-rod military type on the payphone.

Although David was still somewhat boyish looking, Nina considered him handsome. Given a year or two, she was sure the area under his jaw line would fill in and he would project a more mature image. She hoped his intense blue eyes would always remain as crystal clear as they were now.

David finished the drawing and his glance was darting between the two stalkers. She asked him what they were doing.

"First guy is talking to the waitress behind the counter. He's sitting kind of catty-cornered so he can keep an eye on us. The sunglasses are on the counter, but the newspaper is still covering his face. The guy at the payphone waited for an open stool, but none were available, so he left. He's probably hanging around outside."

"Be careful," she cautioned. "The expression on your face is too intense. Smile—make love to me with your eyes—don't be so obvious."

David looked into her eyes. "How's this?"

"Perfect," she said. "So now that you've got one of them sketched out you can do one of the guy at the counter—he's bound to drop the newspaper at some point, if only for a second. That's enough time for you to register his features, right?"

"Right. So, you're thinking these two have crossed my line of sight before?"

"Let's hope so."

David glanced repeatedly in the direction of the counter. Nina knew how difficult it was for him to hide his feelings and continued to remind him to smile. "Who would benefit from having you followed?"

"I've told you about Professor Haverstock. I think he works for the CIA spotting gifted students for their programs."

Nina was skeptical. "You're obsessed with this crazy idea that someone's out to use your gift for nefarious purposes. I can't buy it."

"Okay, have it your way. So, what about my father, he's always looking for ways to fuck me up."

Nina shook her head, "I know he's a bastard but why do that?"

"I'm not sure. You know my parents are on my case about you. You're a *shikseh*–marrying a non-Jewish girl is an abomination to my father. Gee...maybe one of the men is following me and the other one is following you."

"Me? Why would your father want me followed?"

"Could be he's hoping to find some dirt on you. Use it to persuade me not to marry outside my religion."

She smiled at the thought. "Fat chance of that."

"Hold on," David said. "A waitress is holding a bowl of soup in front of the guy. She's waiting for him to clear a space–the newspaper is about to drop."

Blink.

Their hamburgers arrived and David ate with his left hand and sketched with his right. Nina knew it was easier for him to pull details from his short-term memory right away. Accessing them at later date meant using his long-term memory–it took longer and was less reliable.

He finished the drawing and passed it across the table.

"Baby face under a mop of unruly hair," she commented. "Do you recognize him?"

David nodded. "I may have seen him recently. Give me a moment...."

To a casual observer it looked like he was having an absence seizure–a type of epilepsy. She first witnessed his strange behavior a few days after they met and would have dumped him if he hadn't explained.

Three years have passed...and it still looks weird.

CHAPTER 4

Warwick, New York, 1961
One Weird Summer

Nina thought it was a great idea. Two weeks in the mountains, all expenses paid, lots of rolling hills and a beautiful lake. She explained it all to her mother.

"Only five dancers are invited. It's a great opportunity to get away from this oppressive heat. The choreographer's going to put on a few performances in the camp's outdoor theater. There'll be some mentoring of high school kids, but it'll be like a mini-vacation."

Her mother agreed. A few days later, Nina drove her Fiat out of Manhattan and arrived in the cool mountains of Warwick late that afternoon. The house for the dancers was situated next to a lake; the smell hit her the minute she opened the door. *Wood rot. Maybe that's all I'll have to put up with—I really want to be on my own for a while.*

She found the women unpacked and sitting cross-legged on their beds. "Afternoon everyone," she said. They made her welcome and one of them pointed to a vacant bed. Nina placed her suitcase on the floor and dropped her purse on the mattress. She looked around. It was a large room, with the dancers' costumes and cosmetics spread out on every available surface. The room was okay, but it needed a good airing.

"How can you take it?" Nina asked. "It's stifling in here. You girls don't mind if I open a window to get some fresh air, do you?"

One of dancers looked up from painting her nails. "Don't bother, they're stuck. Won't budge...we all tried."

"I don't think I can stay here." Nina said it under her breath, but the second it came out she regretted it.

"It's not that bad," someone said.

"Better than staying in the city," another chimed in.

Nina asked, "Are there any other women's quarters on the property?"

"All full up, I expect," said the first girl. "Guess it wouldn't hurt to look around."

Nina's olfactory sensitivity was part of her compulsive need for cleanliness. If the room even looked unkempt, there was dirt somewhere. She apologized, grabbed her things and left. She would either find a clean alternative or head back to Manhattan.

The other women's lodgings were full and as she headed for the parking lot, she passed one of the men's quarters and thought. *Why not? If there's an empty room, I'll convince one of the dancers to bunk with me. We can clean it up....* She walked up the path to the house. A young man opened the door and stood on the front steps.

"Hi," Nina said. "Any empty rooms?"

"Sure...on my floor." He replied.

"Can I take a look?"

"Of course. Need some help with the suitcase?"

"No thank you, I can manage."

"Okay. Come on in," he said holding the screen door open. "It's up the stairs to the left."

The room had two beds. It was clean and bright with cross-ventilation from two windows. Across the hall was another room just like it and a common bathroom which looked spotless.

"I'll take it," Nina said, smiling.

"You do know...we're a bunch of guys here, right?"

"That's not a problem. I can get another girl to come in with me." He smiled.

He has the clearest blue eyes.

"Name's David," he extended his hand.

David?

She took his hand, "I'm Nina."

Those eyes....

Nina and another dancer settled into the room. The days passed and Nina encountered David in the hallway, outside the bathroom, on the stairs and at community functions. With each meeting, she couldn't shake the feeling they met before and after searching her past, she finally remembered.

After moving to America with her mother, they settled in Queens, New York where she attended Parochial School. It was there she noticed the boy with the clear blue eyes. She would see him most days after school sitting at the bottom of the stone staircase drawing in his notebook. He wore no uniform, so she guessed he was from a nearby public school.

He waited for her to come down the stairs, staring and blinking at her when she passed by. At first she ignored him, but on one occasion Nina turned her head toward him and the boy froze. When she gazed into his blue eyes, she felt as if he was looking into her soul.

Nina would meet him by "accident" outside her school, her cousin always close by. His name was David, and they talked politely about mundane things while their eyes seemed to acknowledge something deeper.

Then it ended. Nina's mother re-married and they moved to Manhattan. David was ripped from her life, in much the same way as her father had. There would be other disappointments with men—in each instance she was left alone.

David became a forgotten memory, until a few days ago, when she found an available room in a house by a lake. *Could this be the same boy I met ten years ago? I must find out.*

The next day, while she was swimming in the nearby lake, David showed up with one of the painting instructors. As he walked out on the dock, she swam toward him and held onto the edge of the decking. With the glare of the sun dancing all around him he just stared at her, blinking incessantly.

He never said a word.

That evening she spotted him again in the great room. Two young women hovered over his chair making a fuss. She came closer. He was complaining about the food.

"Do either of you know where I can get something to eat," he asked them. "Eggs...anything?"

Nina broke in. "I can make you some eggs."

David looked up at her. "Really...how?"

"There's a small kitchen at our lake house, remember?"

At *"our lake house"*, the eyes of the young women widened.

As it turned out eggs were unavailable. But by that time there was something else cooking between them. She could feel it. Yet she still wasn't sure if he was the same David from her past.

They were upstairs in the hallway. He wanted to show her his room across the hall—his roommate was called away unexpectedly—he was all alone. She was in his room...and then in his arms. She melted into him—not from passion, but a strange sense of familiarity. Unexpected tears pushed against her closed lids, and as she clung to him, there was an awakening.

She was lost and finally found her way back.

They spent every available moment together. Night after night they made love in his single bed, the lake breeze washing over their exhausted bodies. But there was more—a remembrance from a former life—and the depth of its intensity frightened her.

She told herself it was a summertime diversion. A summer fling with a nice Jewish boy who seemed familiar and undemanding. But there was no denying it—she was caught in the strong undertow of something uncontrollable and she panicked. A dancer and a painter, both from different cultures and social classes. When he became serious, she put him off. She tried to harden her heart and searched for a reason to give him up. She tried not to fall deeper, but he was the boy with the blue eyes from long ago and her heart found a home.

Yet the more time they spent together the more she realized how weird he was. There were times she caught him staring into space without any expression. At first, she thought he was daydreaming, but her stepfather was a doctor, she knew what long lapses in awareness meant.

Epilepsy.

One night after they made love, she asked him about the seizures, but David insisted he was perfectly healthy. He told her of his troubled childhood and the misdiagnosis. Finally, when he noticed how reticent she still was, he told her of his time at Bell Labs. The far-fetched tale was hard for her to swallow. Perceptual scientists at a world-renowned research facility discover a young man with near perfect visual recall? Nina now wondered if she was involved with a nut case. In the days that followed she became unresponsive and withdrawn.

David clung to her. He showed her his letter from Bell Labs along with the accompanying test results. But even in the face of such evidence, Nina was skeptical. Men deceived her before, and she insisted on a demonstration. Knowing he never set foot in the camp's kitchen, she dragged him there and watched as he took it in with a casual glance.

There was the vacant stare, at which time David said he absorbed everything he focused on. A slow blink followed to etch the scene into his memory. Somehow, he explained, he would know when his mind catalogued the information, and his eyes would open.

After two minutes, they left the kitchen. She stayed with him for three hours until she told him to retrieve the image from his memory. David closed his eyes. He later described it like scrolling through a roll of microfilm. Remembered images would flash in front of him until he recognized a pattern of shapes, a person or setting. Then, he'd slow the scenes to a crawl until he found the exact image he needed.

He told her he could hold the scene in his mind's eye and how when his lids opened, a ghostly image materialized in the air. How he could overlay it on any surface for however long it took to trace it.

Inside of an hour a light sketch of the cooking area was indicated: types and numbers of pots and pans; placement of fryers, stoves, exhaust fans; wash sink, spigots; knives in racks; stacks of dishes; warming lights and columns of serving trays. He built up the details of each item: strengthening a line; adding shadows; making one object appear closer than another. When Nina realized it would take another hour or two to refine the drawing, she relented and took it to the kitchen.

The kitchen and the drawing were the same. And in the days that followed, she realized another truth. About a boy she met and lost a long time ago.

He had clear blue eyes.

His name was David.

And she found him again.

CHAPTER 5

1964
The Note

At Prexy's, Nina looked on as David put aside what was left of his burger to search his memory for the sandy-haired man. Since their meeting over three years ago, hardly a day went by that he didn't disappear into his memories to watch a replay of his past. For him it was a marvelous gift, for her it was a curse.

She understood his disengagement from the present was critical when accessing the past. But when his eyes fluttered to a close and his jaw went slack, he shut her out and she felt abandoned. He would go where she could not follow, and she was left alone.

"Got him," David said, and described the image he pulled from his memory. "It was last week. The same baby-faced guy who's at the counter sat at a window table in Moe's Deli. Someone else sat there with him. A stack of folders, a camera and binoculars were on the table. Both men were looking out the window at the Food Mart, across the street."

"That's it?" Nina asked. "He and another guy were watching Mike's store?"

"Looks that way." David avoided her scrutiny by glancing at the counter again. "He doesn't look like the gangster type. Cop maybe. Yeah... the guy's a cop. That explains the other one who was sitting with him at Moe's. They work in twos."

"Oh great...so they were what...staking out the Food Mart because Mike's in trouble? He didn't get you involved in illegal betting, did he?"

"I don't gamble, you know that."

Nina thought his answer came too quickly. *David seems anxious...he's holding something back. I hate it when he does that.*

She waited....

A moment of silence, then he said. "Maybe they're investigating the gangsters who are harassing Mike."

Nina frowned. "Okay, so now gangsters are harassing Mike. Why didn't you tell me that before?"

David demurred. Then, sheepishly, answered her, "You advised me to stop hanging around the grocery, but I couldn't walk away. I knew you'd be angry, so I didn't say anything."

The oil from the French Fries turned rancid in her mouth. "Well, I *am* angry. How can you lie to me? You know how I feel about lying." She stood up and fumbled for her dance bag and purse. "You can eat by yourself."

David was up on his feet. "Wait, wait please!" he pleaded. "You're right...I'm sorry. I just couldn't stay away. The more I learn about my father's shady past, the more justified I feel about breaking into his file cabinet. I needed to stick around the Food Mart."

She could see the regret on his face and sat down to hear him out. "Okay, I know Mike's stories are important to you, but you knew he was involved in a numbers racket. You should have distanced yourself from him. Now it looks like you're involved in illegal betting."

"I know," he admitted. "It occurred to me too. I'm sorry."

"I can see that. But remember to be up front with me. I won't spend my life with a liar." He nodded, and the expression on his face told her he meant it.

Nina changed the subject. "What makes you so sure there's compromising stuff in your dad's file cabinet?"

"He never leaves it unlocked. Keeps the key with him all the time. Puts it on his night table before going to sleep. Even takes it into the bathroom. There's no spare. I've looked."

"So, you're still going to break into it?"

David was adamant. "I am, no question. I graduate in two months. I'll be out of the house for good and won't have another opportunity. It's gotta be done this weekend."

Nina was skeptical, "Are you sure you can open it?"

"I told you, he used to keep his girlie mags in the top drawer. When I was a kid, I would yank on the top drawer until the catch slipped.

Once that top drawer is open, I can get into the other drawers. No problem, I simply need you there as lookout."

"Okay," she agreed. "I'll be there Monday. But I've got to ask you to do something, and don't get mad when I ask."

"Okay, what is it?"

"You won't get mad?"

"I just said I wouldn't."

She took a breath. "I want you to look for your birth certificate."

"I have my birth certificate."

"That's not a real birth certificate," she insisted. "You have a court document. It says you were born 1941, in New York City. It also says the original birth certificate is on file at the Department of Health."

"So, it's perfectly legal," he countered.

"Yes, it's good enough to get a passport. But a real birth certificate has the child's weight, the mother's name, time of birth...*the father's name.*"

"So?"

"So, you suspect your father's a crook, and I think he's not your real father."

"What?" he snapped. "That's crazy."

"You promised not to get mad."

"I'm not getting mad. I can't believe this! Why would you think that?"

"You wanted a passport, right? Your parents said they lost the original birth certificate and gave you that court document dated 1954. Why not an official copy of the actual certificate that's on file? And besides, you're an only child, I've never seen your baby pictures. There isn't anything from your baby years: cups, rattles, spoons, albums...."

"So?"

"You keep saying 'so'. That's not an explanation. Parents save keepsakes of their child. Besides," she reasoned, "you look nothing like your father."

"Keepsakes can get lost. And I take after my mother. You're wrong about this."

"I'm not wrong. For someone with super observation skills you're so blind to the obvious. He can't be your real father. No father would keep his child drugged like that."

"The doctor misdiagnosed me, that's all."

"I don't believe it. He arranged it somehow."

"Why would he do that?"

"He wanted you doped up to control you."

"How can you know? There's no way you could know that. This is crazy."

Nina couldn't let it go. The question nagged her for years. She lived with a stepfather—she felt the detachment—knew the signs. "I know the man is evil and controlling...just like my stepfather. Now that you're staying with your grandfather, he's keeping your mother drugged too."

"She's on Valium for menopause, for God's sake."

"It's an excuse to keep her drugged. My mother's going through menopause without taking Valium. My aunts too."

"That's different." He was quibbling now.

"Why?" she insisted. "Why is it different?"

"I don't know. It just is, that's all." His shoulders slumped, "It's all too much. I can't deal with all this: Professor Haverstock, the two guys following me, my father, your suspicions. Why can't people leave me alone?"

Nina recognized David's old self pushing through the new persona he carefully built during the last few years. "Remember you asked me to warn you whenever 'little Davie' reappeared?"

David was slouched down in his chair, looking away from her with his arms crossed. He dropped his chin to his chest. "I'm regressing again?"

Nina nodded and noted a far-a-way look in his eyes. A painful memory was playing out in his mind's eye, as if it happened five minutes ago. The curse of an eidetic memory.

"Don't be sad for 'little Davie'," she said, reaching for his hand. "What happened to him is in the past. You're David now and you're here with me."

"Sorry." He took a shaky breath and shook his head as if throwing off a demon.

She waited.

"You're right." He sat up in the chair adding, "And I'm very grateful for your love."

"I know you are." Her endearing look elicited a small smile from him. "I'm sorry I dumped all this on you, but I thought you'd feel better knowing you didn't have his genes."

"If it were only true, but I think you're wrong," he scoffed.

"Please. Look for your birth certificate. Do it for me."

Resignation showed on his face. "Fine. If only to prove how wrong you are."

Every emotion David felt played out on his face. It was his worst handicap when dealing with his father. She knew he worked hard to control it, but he didn't with her.

David removed a piece of paper from his pocket and handed it to her. "If you can buy some film and flash bulbs it would be a big help. Once I find something in the file cabinet that can incriminate him, I'll need to photograph it. What I need is all written down there."

Nina scanned through it. "Okay, I'll drive out to the Island Monday morning to help you." She put the note in her purse and looked up at him—self-reproach was written all over his face. "What's wrong now?"

"I screwed up. The cop saw me pass you that piece of paper."

"What's wrong with passing me a list?"

"Mike's writing markers for bets. I could be passing you a list of today's markers...or worse. I don't need the cops questioning me. Not now."

"If they do, what will you say?"

He shrugged uncertainly. "I don't know...I really don't know."

It occurred to her the cops might think she was involved too. "Well, if they question me, I'm telling them the truth—all of it."

She locked his gaze firmly in her own—she wanted to make herself perfectly clear.

"I won't lie David, not even for you."

⁊⳩

They walked back to campus and found the Limo from Bell Labs waiting outside Dodge Hall. Nina said goodbye and headed for the corner bus stop. When David phoned that evening, she found out he never made it to the lab.

"But I saw you get into the Limo," she said into the receiver.

"Yeah, but there was a note on the seat from Dr. Max. After reading it I told the driver to take me home."

"Why, what did it say?"

"I'll read it. 'Your identity compromised. Can't get away until Thursday. Meet me at the Met, 11A.M., Egyptian Exhibit. Be careful, you're being watched. M.'"

"Oh God. Do you think it has something to do with the two stalkers?" she asked.

"I hope so. Maybe now we can get some answers. Are you free to drive me Thursday morning? I need to make sure I'm not being followed."

"Can't. I've got an early rehearsal Thursday."

"No problem, I'll ask AJ."

"Good. Sorry I can't help." There was a pause and then she added, "I thought you were getting paranoid about the professor and these stalkers. I guess I was wrong. Now we have to wait a day to find out what this is about."

"I've suspected people were watching me for years. Now it looks like they're watching you too, because the guy on the bench recognized you. They may use you to get to me. I don't want you snatched."

"Snatched? Now you're really over-reacting. Whoever these people are they're probably scoping you out like the football recruiters do with AJ. They watch you for a while and when they decide you're the real deal they offer you a legitimate contract."

"I hope you're right, but still...I have a bad feeling about this. Like AJ said, you've got to keep your eyes open.

"Fine, if it makes you feel better, I'll be careful...I promise." She hung up the phone.

CHAPTER 6

Day 2
The Tunnel

FBI Special Agent in Charge, Alan Hunter, tossed the case file on his desk and leaned back in his chair. Perpetually warm in all kinds of weather, the twenty-five-year veteran sat in his shirt sleeves while the drone of a metal fan did it's best to cool off his temper. Hunter, usually fair and easy going, demanded quick results and an unflinching adherence to protocol.

Neither was happening in the recent investigation into racketeering on Manhattan's Upper West Side. Hunter pushed against the desk to wheel his chair closer to the fan. With hands clasped behind his head, he closed his eyes to mull over the report he just read.

Agents Jim Hawkins and Tom Keyes were staking out Mike's Food Mart—a known numbers "parlor" on Columbus Avenue between West 86th and 87th Streets. Hawkins reminded Hunter of himself twenty years ago—tall, lean and ruggedly handsome. His partner, Keyes, was the exact opposite. Short and stockily built; his boyish good looks were topped by a mop of sandy-blond hair.

The agents identified David Greenberg as a person of interest going in and out of the store all week. Agent Keyes, fresh out of the Academy, became convinced Greenberg was a runner. He insisted the young man wouldn't spend his free time in a dilapidated grocery, unless there was something to gain. A background check found Greenberg wasn't on payroll nor was he related to Mike Trozzo, the owner. What made it more confusing—the boy's father, Sy Greenberg, was law enforcement.

Agent Hawkins thought it unlikely the son of an IRS investigator would get involved in anything illegal. Keyes disagreed. His initial report said Greenberg's behavior looked suspicious: the kid showed up at the grocery at odd hours, sometimes he stocked shelves or swept up; other times he was in the store but didn't work. He was seen carrying packages through the back door, but never made deliveries.

Hawkins's report laid out the results of an early morning stakeout at Greenberg's apartment building. It explained how Keyes left the car to tail Greenberg, yet Keyes didn't file his surveillance report. Hunter was not at all pleased. From the outset, he pegged Keyes as a loose cannon. No disciplinary measures were taken against the agent—there was nothing Hunter could do—the rookie agent was the nephew of his Division Chief.

He wheeled the chair back to the desk, pressed the intercom and asked his secretary to send in the two agents. Hawkins and Keyes entered and settled into two swivel chairs in front of him. Hunter moved around his desk and leaned against it.

He addressed Keyes. "We're meeting this morning because you failed to file your surveillance report. I want to see it by the end of the day. What I want to know now is if Greenberg is involved or not?"

Slumped down in his chair, Keyes looked up at his boss. "Looks like it."

"I'll take that as a yes. What corroborating evidence did you find?" questioned Hunter.

Keyes avoided Hunter's eyes and fiddled with his aviators. "Well, there are a number of things."

Hunter decided to urge him on. "Such as?"

"Caught him slipping his girlfriend a piece of paper."

"A bunch of markers or a slip of paper?" probed Hunter.

Keyes looked uncomfortable. He had a habit of talking with little movement of his lips—as if hiding the real meaning behind everything he said. "Slip of paper. Maybe folded up. I'm not sure."

"Walk us through it," ordered Hunter.

Keyes removed a small notebook from his pocket and thumbed through it. "In the middle of lunch, Greenberg passes the girl a piece of paper. I'm thinking, okay, it's not flimsy like flash paper, but could be a list of Mike's markers. So, I figured: the kid phones Mike before lunch; writes down a list of morning bets; at lunchtime he passes the list to his girlfriend; later on, she calls Mike to get the additional afternoon bets and adds them to the list. She either drops it somewhere, passes it on or delivers it herself."

Hunter pursed his lips and sighed, "Sounds a little far-fetched. What do you think, Jim?"

Hawkins looked skeptical, "Anything's possible. It all hinges on what was written on that piece of paper. Could be anything."

"Right." Eager to explain, Keyes swiveled his chair to face Hunter. "But then it gets weird. I follow them out of the restaurant and spot someone else tailing them from across the street."

"Mob related?" asked Hunter.

"No, ex-military—arrogant looking too."

"Military?" Hunter repeated under his breath.

"So, listen to this—after lunch they reach campus and Greenberg hops into a waiting Limo and disappears."

"License number?" Hunter asked.

Keyes shook his head, "Too much traffic, but it was a Jersey plate."

Puzzled, Hunter's first thought was the Limo might belong to the Manhattan crime family, but the New Jersey plate threw him off.

"Okay, what did you do next?" Hunter asked.

"I decided to follow the girlfriend. She grabs a cross-town bus and I tail her to a doctor's office on Park Avenue. She's in there five maybe ten minutes—plenty of time to call in a list of bets. She comes out yapping in Spanish with a blond older woman—a real exotic number by the way—and enters the adjacent apartment building. So, I keep an eye on both the doctor's office and the apartment building. Nothing until," Keyes flipped through his notes, "1:55. That's another ten minutes she can use to phone in more bets."

Hunter stopped in front of Keyes and glared at him. "Where's this going Tom? There's no hard evidence—"

"Wait," Keyes held up his hand and grinned, "it gets better. Then the girl zips around the corner to the 92nd Street Y. Inside, I find a bunch of sweet looking broads in tights. It's some kind of rehearsal. So, I hang around—not a bad way for a guy to spend an afternoon."

Keyes's arms were spread out, palms up and a disagreeable smirk on his face. Hunter exchanged a quick glance with Hawkins, before closing the office door. He turned and leaned against it with his arms crossed.

Before Hunter could reply, Keyes continued. "Anyway, when I'm sure the girlfriend's stuck on stage, I walk back to Park Avenue and talk to the doorman. I find out the doctor is a neuropsychologist by the name of Martin Broder. According to the guy who cleans his office, there's a room with a steel-clad door that's always locked—"

"Tom please..." interrupted Hunter, "all this doesn't add up to a hill of beans."

"But it does, it does," Keyes insisted. "Did you know that in 1925, a doctor by the name of Cheney operated a small numbers bank out of his Park Avenue office? The only reason he got caught was his girlfriend tried to kill him. Otherwise, no one would be the wiser."

Hunter moved away from the door to circle Keyes's chair. "Are you suggesting this Doctor Broder is bankrolling the numbers operation on the West Side?"

"Exactly." Keyes kept swiveling his chair left to right, trying to keep his boss in sight.

Hunter stopped and placed both hands on the back of Keyes's chair. "Why would a respected physician get in bed with the Mob?"

Keyes affected an air of relaxed indifference and looked at him. "It's the Colombian connection."

Incredulous, Hunter whipped the chair around and leaned into Keyes—nose to nose. "The Colombian...are you out of your mind?"

Keyes was undeterred. "It's simple, the good looking blond—the doctor's second wife—is Colombian. Greenberg's hot girlfriend is her daughter—also Colombian. Could be the famous doctor is in deep—drugs maybe, or gambling—probably needs a lot of cash."

Hunter straightened up, "You're jumping to conclusions. We can't make assumptions based on some obscure forty-year-old case."

Keyes was defiant. "A loser like Greenberg doesn't ride in Limos, hang around with mobsters, and bang a swanky piece of Colombian ass unless there's something fishy going on."

"What!" Hunter glared at him. "Keyes, I don't care who your uncle is, I'll put you on desk duty if—"

"But wait," interrupted Keyes, "you haven't heard the corker. Remember the other guy tailing Greenberg—the ex-military dude—well I caught him coming out of the doctor's office. Waltzed right by me."

There was a prolonged silence as Hunter moved behind his desk and dropped in his chair. Pushing against the desk with his foot, he wheeled the chair around to face the fan, loosened his tie and ran a finger around the inside of his collar.

Three oscillations later, he spun around again and addressed Hawkins.

"Chances are the girl's father is worried. Greenberg's from the other side of the tracks. Could be he hired a private detective to follow David around. It's the Limo from New Jersey that doesn't fit." He addressed Hawkins, "You need to do a 'knock and talk' with that kid and straighten this whole thing out."

Hawkins nodded. "We'll tag young Greenberg either at the restaurant or his grandfather's apartment." The two agents got up to leave. They were halfway through the door when Hunter called out.

"Agent Keyes, close the door and take a seat."

≈≈

That same morning, David arrived at the studio to find it deserted. Neither students nor the professor showed up for class. Then he remembered—it was a few days before Easter Break. Called Spring Break after the movie *Where the Boys Are*, the Holy Week turned into a string of parties, drinking and sex, with most students rushing down to Ft. Lauderdale to claim their spot on the beach.

David never got involved with the ritual because his parents wanted him home for Passover. Going home every weekend was stressful enough, but the thought of spending an entire week trying to fool his father into believing he was still a sickly epileptic was not his idea of a vacation.

There was much on his mind and it took a lot of effort to re-focus on his painting. The pictorial composition was based on the way it looked in his recurring dream: a drugstore's interior, obfuscated by gloomy shadows and soft-focus. On the left side of the painting, the sunlight came in from a display window and broke the hazy atmosphere of the store. The diagonal shaft of light ran parallel to a long soda fountain which led the eye to David as a young boy of ten. Sitting on a stool, his head was turned sideways looking at the backlit shape of a man outside the drugstore window.

The man was screaming at him.

Usually, David could tell the difference between recalled memories and dreams. He thought this particular dream was a re-packaged memory. It was certainly strange, and its narrative always a puzzle. He knew the young boy was himself but could never identify the man behind the store window. The man seemed desperate to impart some warning to him. If he worked it out in paint, perhaps he could find the hidden meaning behind the dream.

David set his palette, thinking about color, brushwork and the small passages of light he needed to lead the eye through the painting. He mixed a deep, cool red for the top of the stool and set the indigo of the boy's blue jeans against a dirty orange he laid in for the front panel of the counter. The effect of off-white marble was troweled on to indicate the countertop, lessening in value as it trickled off to either side. And so, it went for the better part of the morning, until the hairs on David's neck stood on end and an inner voice suddenly whispered in his ear.

Behind you....

He turned. A man with a gun. A muffled crack and his left arm rose to cover his chest.

Thwack—something embedded itself in his wood palette.

The man reloaded. David rushed from the room swinging the palette around to deflect any incoming projectiles. He bounded down the stairs and bumped into AJ.

Startled, AJ blurted out, "I was just coming to see...."

"I'm being shot at."

They heard someone on the stairs....

"Follow me," AJ said. They scrambled down the staircase to a basement storage area where AJ opened a door with a "No Admittance" sign. Inside a muffled hum surrounded them as they ran down a long corridor, the hollow sound of their footsteps reverberating around them. Eventually the space opened up, and David could see large boilers with steam valves, dials and wide diameter pipes of different colors running along the walls. Careening down some metal stairs, the duo rushed through a rusty gate and made their way along a brick corridor.

They passed under a huge ventilation shaft and turned the corner to come up against a rusty steel door. A red fire extinguisher was attached to the wall. There was a hole where a doorknob use to be and a flimsy latch. AJ worked the latch while David ran his gaze over the door. Splotches of reds and oranges with areas of clotted white paint surrounded two frightening signs. One had two symbols—a skull and crossbones and the trefoil—both international radiation symbols. The sign underneath announced in blood red letters, "Warning! Ionizing Radiation, Keep Out!" It scared the shit out of him.

AJ jammed his shoulder against the door and pushed him through.

David was frantic. "Wait—don't..." They were in and the door slammed behind them cutting off the light.

"Jesus! Are you out of your mind?"

"Don't mind the sign, we're perfectly safe." AJ reached into the darkness. There was a brief click as he switched on a flashlight and led the way forward. "Come on we better move further into the tunnel where it starts to branch off."

"Tunnel? What is this place?"

CHAPTER 7

Mob Muscle

They were hunkered down in the semi-darkness of what looked to be an old, abandoned command center. Office furniture from the 1940s, and several rolling black boards with remnants of strange equations were scattered around the room. Old maps and faded documents littered the floors. It was cold, damp and terribly dusty.

David's wood palette lay on the floor between them—its pattern of colored pigment repeated on AJ's shirt. "Sorry about your shirt." His whisper reverberated off the walls.

"At least it's paint and not one of those." AJ pointed to the dart embedded in the middle of the palette. "Whoever the guy was, he sure meant business."

"He's the same person you pointed out in Prexy's—the one at the payphone."

"Christ!" AJ exclaimed. "You gonna tell me why this guy is after you?"

David wavered. "There are some things you don't know about me—"

"You think I don't know?" AJ broke in. "Of course, I know—you've got some unusual talents man."

"Well, it's more than that."

"You mean like knowing when somethin' 'bout to happen?"

"So, you do know."

"Hey, didn't you warn me to keep away from certain demonstrations. You kept me out of jail several times—probably saved my black ass too. Then there's that photographic memory of yours."

"That too? But I've never told anyone."

"Didn't have to. Whenever you study with Amanda and me you either know the answers—or the page it can be found on. That's not normal."

"I had no idea."

"Man, you may think you're careful," AJ continued, "but you can't be on top of it twenty-four-seven. Know what I mean?"

David looked at his friend. "How come you never said anything?"

"Wasn't my business—a man has his reasons. But if I caught on, I figured it'd only be a matter of time 'til someone else did too. It's why I'm sharing my hideout with you. It's a nifty way to dodge anyone following you. I use it all the time to lose those football recruiters."

"So, where are we?"

"You know the university was built on the old location of Bloomingdales's Insane Asylum, right?"

"Yeah, something about Buell Hall being the original building."

"Exactly. These underground tunnels are also part of that asylum. They connect most of the buildings on Columbia's campus. This room is one of many used for war-time research by the Manhattan Project. Someone told me there's a dismantled atom smasher somewhere under campus."

"A cyclotron...here?" David was incredulous, "There could be radiation, those signs...."

"Yeah, yeah, I know. I borrowed a detector from the physics department and checked out the route we're taking. Don't worry, it's safe. But I'll tell you one thing—I'm not interested in exploring any other tunnels."

"So, you're telling me there are other tunnels?"

"Uh-huh, several," AJ answered. "You could go underground from one building to the next and emerge outside of campus at multiple locations. Even if someone followed you in here, they wouldn't know which tunnel you took. With food, water and a good book, you could stay down here a long time. No one would ever find you."

❧

Agent Keyes drove around the block twice before dropping Hawkins off in front of Moe's Deli. "If I keep circling the block our cover will be blown," Keyes said. "Set things up in the deli while I find a parking space a couple of blocks away."

"Good idea," agreed Hawkins. "You want some lunch?"

"Yeah. Order me a corned beef sandwich and some coffee."

Hawkins entered the deli nodding to Moe's wife at the checkout counter. His glance fell on the tall stack of greasy order slips impaled on a six-inch spike. Despite the increased crime in the neighborhood, business looked good.

He continued passed a long display case on his right and a low partition which separated the takeout area from the dining room. Whiffs of steamed pastrami and other delicacies hit his nostrils, and by the time he reached the dried salami hanging near the kitchen, saliva pooled under his tongue.

Fed up with the unsavory characters loitering outside his restaurant, Moe gave the agents exclusive use of a window booth. Hawkins took down the Out of Order sign and sat down, removing a pair of binoculars, camera, and several file folders from his bag. To stave off his hunger, he grabbed a pickle from the bowl on the table, and scanned the decaying store fronts lined up across the street.

Located in the middle of Columbus Avenue, between 86th and 87th Streets, Mike's Food Mart was the nexus of illegal gambling between West 76th and 96th. Originally a meat market, Mike's father bought it in the forties as a means of keeping busy after retirement. A year later, he became bored with running the store, and handed it over to Mike and his brother Vinnie. There was a catch. Old man Trozzo wanted to bankroll a small numbers operation out of the back room of the store. Mike's brother, Vinnie became his right-hand man. Mike was pressured to act as a part-time enforcer. After their father died, the Food Mart passed on to the two brothers. Mike still ran the store and Vinnie took over the numbers operation with the backing of an unknown policy banker.

Hawkins put the binoculars down. There was nothing going on across the street. Flanking the Food Mart were the corner Drug Store with Al's Barber Shop on one side, and a Laundromat and the boarded up West Side Social Club on the other. Above them, apartment windows were stacked one upon another, the checkerboard pattern broken up by the zigzag of a rusted fire escape running up and down the front of the building.

From his pile of folders, Hawkins removed the directive initiating the investigation of Mike's Food Mart for racketeering. It outlined the massive urban renewal program that was pushing out many West Side residents to make way for public housing and new schools. Many businesses closed around the area and several boarded-up stores were now used as drop points for processing bets.

The drop points changed periodically. What didn't change were the fixed locations where bets were placed. Mike's Food Mart was a known betting parlor. Numbers salesmen, known as collectors, would write a bettor's three-digit number and bet amount on a piece of flash paper called a "marker". Sometime around mid-day, markers would be hidden inside a purchase, such as a pack of cigarettes. The purchase would then be handed off to a "runner" during a seemingly innocent retail purchase.

The runner delivered the markers to a drop point run by a Controller—in this case Vinnie Trozzo. Inside the drop point, Vinnie's clerks would tally the markers to figure the daily take of each betting parlor. If a better was lucky enough to choose the right number, another runner would deliver the winnings back to the betting parlor for the next day's payoff.

Hawkins had little interest in nailing small fry like Vinnie, his clerks or runners. He wanted the person bankrolling the entire Upper West Side operation—the policy banker who handled the money and made the payoffs. Nabbing the banker would not only wipe out the numbers racket but it might implicate the Manhattan Mob *Capo*, Benedetto Moretti.

Hawkins's plan was to uncover a runner at the Food Mart and follow him to the drop where Vinnie and his men processed the bets. With warrant in hand, the team would raid the drop and arrest Vinnie and his crew. Evidence would be collected and those arrested would scramble to finger the policy banker for a lighter sentence. If they nabbed the policy banker and Moretti, it wasn't a stretch to get them to squeal on the Manhattan crime boss himself—Anthony Salerno.

Hawkins looked up as his partner sat down. Keyes was in a foul mood after the unexpected dressing down he received from his boss that morning. As the SAC, Hunter frowned on fanciful speculation and was a stickler when it came to treating people with respect—especially women.

The waitress, Agnes, passed a damp rag over nearby chairs and then wiped down their table—with the same rag she used on the chairs. Keyes put a restraining hand over her wrist.

"That's disgusting," he told her. "You're spreading germs from the seats over our table."

She pulled her arm free and straightened up. "You gonna arrest me?"

Her Afro was backlit by the sun streaming through the window, which changed its color to an electric blue. Wayward tendrils hung limply around her neck framing homely yet warm features. Shaved eyebrows accentuated with eyebrow pencil hovered in asymmetrical arcs above bluish eye makeup and a ton of mascara. The effect was more funeral home cosmetologist than beauty parlor.

"I'm not going to arrest you," Keyes said finally. "No federal statute for that. It's just more sanitary if you use a separate rag for the tables."

"Yeah, well okay...maybe you're right. Don't pay me no mind—big lunch crowd today. I'll be back in a jiffy." Agnes turned and flounced back to the kitchen.

Hawkins shook his head in disapproval. "You know she doesn't like us. I hope she doesn't spit in your coffee...or mine."

"She'd do it anyway because she's afraid we're really after her son, AJ. He's sitting over there with his girlfriend Amanda." Keyes's nod pointed to a young black man, tall and well built, sitting with an attractive girl at a nearby table.

"What kind of name is AJ?" asked Hawkins.

"Short for Andrew James. He's a good friend of the Greenberg kid so I ran him through the system. Goes to the same university as Greenberg and is known on campus as a Civil Rights Activist. He and his girlfriend took part in the Southern Christian Leadership Conference last year and was involved with the Nation of Islam movement of Malcom X."

Hawkins looked the couple over. The girl's textbook was open and she was quizzing her boyfriend. "His hair is cropped short, and her Afro is discreet. They're conservatively dressed and look like the studious type. Just two peaceful protestors—that's their right."

"Maybe," Keyes said doubtfully. "But he's on an athletic scholarship. I don't know where he gets the dough to travel to these out-of-state protests. Thought maybe he's picking up some fresh cash from Greenberg by helping him run the numbers."

Hawkins gave him a wan smile. *Keyes just can't let up on Greenberg. But his uncle is the Division Chief and Hunter told me to play nice.* He replied dryly, "We'll find out when we interview Greenberg today."

Agnes returned with their order and a clean rag. She sprayed down the table, placed the food in front of them and disappeared into the kitchen. Hawkins brought out his binoculars and they settled in to watch the Food Mart across the street.

They snapped photographs and made notations. Finally, after endless cups of coffee, Hawkins spotted Greenberg entering the store around three o'clock. He followed his movements through the store window as David disappeared into the back and brought out a handcart stacked with cartons to the front of the store.

Time passed slowly, with Greenberg pricing cans and the agents discussing the scheduled opening of Shea Stadium in Flushing Meadow Park.

Suddenly, Hawkins's tone changed, "Hold on, something's going down."

"What's up?"

"Two suits on their way to the grocery," he said. "Typical enforcer types—dark suits, black shirts, minus the white ties. Big guy has a scar down the side of his nose."

The two agents watched the thugs drop their cigarettes on the pavement and enter the Food Mart.

☙❧

Snap–thwack–click. Snap–thwack–click. Snap–thwack–click.

The binaural beat of his pricing gun put David in an altered state. He didn't realize how long he was unaware of his surroundings until the last carton of cans was priced and placed on the shelf. David found himself bent over the two-wheeler, his hand reaching down into a box for the next can of soup, but the box was empty. He reached for the box cutter to slice open the next carton, but there were none. Empty cartons were scattered up and down the aisle.

He glanced at his watch—*where did the time go?* Disoriented, he looked around the small store: refrigerated display cases lined the left wall; on the right, old wooden shelves were packed with paper products and detergents. A short, back-to-back gondola stood in the middle of the floor with spinners on both ends. Cigarettes, candy and various snacks were displayed on angled shelves near the register. The aisles were deserted. No one was at the magazine rack or soda cooler. The store was empty.

David stood still; his eyelids fluttered. *Trouble coming. Two men, one of them a stack of bones, the other a chunk of blubber.* David put the pricing gun down and waited.

The bell above the front door jangled and two thugs stepped inside the store. The skinny one motioned his obese partner to stay put and made his way down the aisle towards the back. He leaned over the counter and pushed his chin forward to search the hallway leading to the back office.

His overfed partner leaned against the front door with his arms crossed and took in the store with wide sweeps of his goitrous head. The pockmarked face had a ragged scar over a broken nose. His half-crazed look shot down the aisle and locked on to David.

David recognized the look. He'd seen it countless times on his father's face—the slight tremor of the lips and a stoic calm concealing the slow boil to a maniacal outburst. At once frightened and fascinated at the same time, David shuddered and blinked involuntarily—the fearful image etching itself into his memory.

Mike appeared from the back room. Looming a full head over the two goons, Mike swung a baseball bat up in his meaty hand and cracked it down against the counter. As the skinny thug jumped back a few paces, his muddle-headed partner left the front door to lumber down the aisle. As he passed by, David caught a whiff of stale beer and body odor. The man was big and blubbery, but there was no way the doughy gangster was going to steam-roll over Mike, whose massive, heavily muscled body towered over him.

Caught up in the raw drama of the moment, David became startled when Mike's free hand rose to point at him.

"Out...now!" ordered Mike.

Leaving his jacket, David grabbed his sketchbook and rushed to the front. Once outside, he stood with his back against the door and listened.

No gunshots.

He turned to look through the window. Mike was clearly in control. With both feet planted firmly on the counter, Mike swung the bat over their heads. The goons made a poor show of standing up to the onslaught and when Mike jumped from the counter to the ground, they backed up toward the door.

Lest the thugs took their frustration out on him, David rushed across the street to Moe's Deli.

CHAPTER 8

Knock & Talk

David reached the deli and turned around to look across the street. Mike was out on the street brandishing the bat at the two goons, who just stumbled out of the Food Mart. As the thugs limped away, Mike went back in the store, turned the "Open" sign around and drew the window shade down. A smile of satisfaction crossed David's face as he continued into the deli and made his way past the takeout area toward the dining area. He almost bumped into Agnes.

"What's wrong Davie? You okay?"

"Oh, Agnes...a little preoccupied that's all." He gave her a weak smile and side-stepped around her.

But Agnes caught up with him and touched his arm. "Davie, wait. Those men at the window booth—the cops—they're watchin' Mike's place. Heard them talkin' 'bout askin' you questions."

It didn't come as a surprise. David nodded his thanks and took a quick glance in their direction: *nice suits, one of them could be about thirty, the other in his early forties. Stocky guy with the sandy hair was the one following me. His partner with the buzz cut has a great square face with high cheek bones. Probably the guy in the driver's seat of the Buick parked in front of the hydrant. They look honest...no real way to tell though.*

"If you ask me," Agnes continued, "they're watching you. You leave, they leave. Don't take no rocket scientist to work out you may be in some kinda trouble."

"Thanks for letting me know," David said.

"AJ and his girl are sittin' over there." Agnes added, tilting her head in their direction. "I'm afraid for him. You know I don't like my son hanging around with the likes of that Malcom X fella. You'd tell me if he was up to sometin' right?"

"You don't have to worry about Malcom X anymore," David informed her. "He broke away from the Nation of Islam at the beginning of the month. As far as I know, AJ and Amanda are not planning to join any protests. I'll let you know if I find out otherwise."

"Thanks, I'll bring ya a nice roast beef sandwich with some Russian dressing," Agnes said.

He thanked her and continued into the dining area, winding his way through the dozen or so tables covered in red and white checkered oilcloths. Bowls of pickles sat on each table along with chrome paper napkin holders, salt and pepper shakers and sugar dispensers. AJ and Amanda waved him over to their table.

"I see you changed your shirt AJ. Hope your mom wasn't mad."

"It's all good Dave."

"Nice to see you again Amanda." David said, shaking her hand.

"You too," she replied. "What was all that with AJ's mother?"

"Agnes warned me about the cops at the window."

"Oh, gee whiz," AJ said. "And I thought they were after me."

Amanda teased. "Yeah, I bet that's real disappointing."

"Nope, it's me they want," David said. Then, turning to AJ, "I forgot to ask you earlier if you can play cops and robbers with me Thursday morning?"

"Gotcha covered, what do you need."

"A lift to the Central Park Zoo."

AJ scoffed. "Doesn't sound very dangerous to me."

"I can't be followed."

Amanda looked alarmed, "It's not the guy with the dart gun is it?"

"You told her?" David asked.

"She wondered about the paint on my shirt. Figured you were involved," AJ answered. "Besides, she knows I've watched your back for a long time."

David was stunned. "Watching my back?"

Agnes placed three Cokes on the table. "He's watchin' his own back for years—those football recruiters follow him around all the time."

AJ nodded. "Look man, problem is you walk 'round like you're invisible or somethin'. There are people out there who hunt down and exploit achievers like you—the two guys at Prexy's and those cops over there. If you got a special talent everybody wants a piece of you—that's the way it works."

Amanda stood up and grabbed her coat. "I've got to make a class."

AJ too got up, asking, "What about Thursday?"

"Pick me up at ten outside Salters Bookstore."

"Okay man, see ya then."

His friends left and David took a long, deep breath to calm down. He looked at his paper place mat and an image of the fat gangster from the Food Mart appeared on its surface. As he studied the brutality of the scarred face, the once frightening visage became a study of facial muscles in extreme contraction. He turned the placemat over and in five minutes, an image of the man's crazed appearance was sketched out. David folded the placemat and slid it into his sketchbook.

Mike chased them out this time, but what about next time? It's getting too dangerous. Nina's right, I need to stay away. Good thing I'm going home for Easter Break. He heard the scrape of a chair—*any moment now.*

The baby-faced cop stopped uncomfortably close. The barrel chest puffed up a few inches from David's shoulder—a posture meant to intimidate. David used his legs to push his chair back causing the cop to spread a lop-sided grin across his face. The asshole withdrew a wallet from his inside breast pocket and flipped it open.

"FBI. Agent Tom Keyes, we—"

A memory intruded and time slowed to a crawl for David. The agent's mouth moved but all David heard was an incessant mumbling somewhere in the distance. Then reality slipped away....

He was ten years old shopping for school supplies: *Dad's pulling me into the alleyway. Afraid he'll hit me, but he's reaching into his coat instead. It's a wallet—he flips it open. Gold badge. Dad's picture—his name—"Simon Greenberg". He's telling me it's a secret....*

"Hey...Hey kid," Keyes was saying. "I'm talkin' to you. Greenberg, right? David Greenberg?"

Time reset itself.

"Sorry. Oh, FBI, huh? What's going on?"

"Investigating the Food Mart across the street. Hoping you can help us out."

"Okay, I'll try."

The agent dropped into a chair and leaned in. David caught a whiff of dry-cleaning fluid.

"Why don't you start by telling us something about yourself."

"Sure, what do you want to know?"

"The basics—where you live, go to school, your interests. That kind of thing."

The man's lop-sided smile was back. David didn't like the agent's calculated smugness but forced himself to remain calm. He remained expressionless and didn't shift his gaze from the agent. *He's trying to establish a base-line response so he can tell if I'm lying.*

"I'm a senior at Columbia majoring in art. I live with my widowed grandfather on West 88th off Riverside Drive. My parents live on Long Island. My mom runs a sportswear shop. My father's a criminal investigator for the Internal Revenue Service."

The FBI guy was writing stuff in his notebook. David paused and tilted his head toward the man's scribble.

"What's the point of taking notes if you know all this already?"

The agent's pen stopped moving. "What are you talking about?"

"You've followed me for days."

"What the...you made me? When?"

David exaggerated, "Since the beginning—stuffing your mouth with doughnuts by the fire hydrant, hiding behind the newspaper on the bench—watching me at Prexy's—I thought you guys were professionals."

The agent's bravado disappeared. He dropped eye contact and looked at his partner sitting at the window. He faced David again. "How?"

"Faces fascinate me. I observe people—memorize their expressions—collect them in sketchbooks. Why don't you ask me something you don't already know?"

First flustered, the agent managed to recover. "Okay wise guy, explain why you spend your free time hanging out at Mike's Food Mart."

"That's easy. I help out in the store and Mike pays me with groceries. Nothing wrong with that is there?" David was back on the defensive. He was beginning to think it was a mistake to tell the agent he spotted him.

"You help out huh?" The disbelief in the agent's voice was obvious. "That's hard to swallow. Why waste time sweeping floors just to score some free groceries?"

"It's the truth." David shifted back in his seat as the agent leaned in further. "I wasn't looking for work, but Mike gave me a break on groceries, so I started to give him a hand now and again. Mike's a generous guy. I'm reciprocating that's all."

"Okay, so you're reciprocating. How long have you known Mike and his wife?"

"About three years now."

"Three years," the agent wrote it down. "Didn't know that," he said under his breath. "Okay, let's say I buy your explanation. That kind of thing gets old fast. I can't see you playing stock boy year after year, unless Mike was offering you something you couldn't pass up. Something else is in play here."

Agnes appeared and slid the roast beef sandwich in front of David. "Here's your sandwich, hon." She looked at the agent and scowled. "Why don't you let the boy enjoy his lunch?"

"It's okay, we're just talking," David said. "These guys are FBI, Agnes, they're supposed to be a lot more polite than cops."

"Sure, they are." Agnes eyed the agent's close proximity to David. "I'll bring you more Coke in a bit. You want anything Mr. F-B-I?"

The agent shook his head. "Not right now." He watched Agnes swivel her hips back into the kitchen and then focused again on David. "That woman should be more respectful of law enforcement. Especially since her son is involved with civil rights extremists."

David lost it and raised his voice. "Wait a second, AJ never did anything illegal."

The other agent watched the confrontation and strode over. "Special Agent Jim Hawkins." He did the flip thing with his ID. "Sorry we interrupted your lunch. We can wait if you prefer."

"I'm okay with it, but not with his remark about AJ," complained David. "He's not an extremist."

The agent lifted an admonishing eyebrow at Keyes. "We're not investigating your friend. We're looking into illegal gambling. As far as we know, your friend isn't a person of interest to law enforcement."

"Good of you to say so," replied David. *These two agents are polar opposites. Either it's an act or they're really like that.*

Agent Hawkins pulled over a chair and sat down with his legs crossed. "We're looking for some information, son. It's a friendly chat not an interrogation. But you're within your rights to refuse to answer any or all of our questions."

David thought about it. "So, I can just walk away?"

Hawkins nodded. "Yes, but you should understand, your behavior looks suspicious. At some point you may have to answer our questions in a less informal situation. Telling us the real reason why you frequent the Food Mart will help us eliminate you from any wrongdoing—it's up to you."

"It's personal," David told him.

"As long as it's nothing illegal, we'll keep it in confidence. We do this all the time...there's nothing we haven't heard."

David thought it over. *Don't want to get Mike in trouble, but there's no other way to explain myself.* He decided to take Nina's advice and tell the truth.

"Okay, what your partner said is true—after a while, it did get old. But then I found out Mike knew my father when they were kids. I hang around the store to hear stories about my dad's childhood."

"Why not ask your dad?" Keyes asked.

"We don't get along...and he's secretive about his past."

"So, he doesn't know you're talking to a childhood friend of his?" Hawkins asked.

"No. It would be a disaster—especially because I'm learning stuff, he wouldn't want anyone to know. I doubt if even my mom knows the whole truth."

"And what truth is that?" Hawkins asked, raising his eyebrows.

"My father's a gangster with a badge."

Hawkins looked surprised. "Really, what makes you say that?"

"True stories from Mike's lips. One in particular...."

CHAPTER 9

Summer, 1925
Murder Incorporated

For young Mike Trozzo, escaping the summer swelter of the city was never an option—especially to the Catskill Mountains. So, when Allie Tannenbaum landed him and his best friend Sy Greenberg summer jobs at his father's exclusive resort, it was a dream come true.

By 1925, the Loch Sheldrake Country Club, was the summer retreat for many of Manhattan's underworld figures. With the city only two and half hours away, it was an easy drive if ever an operational problem needed attention.

Beating the heat at Sheldrake that summer was eighteen-year-old Mike Trozzo, his best friend, Sy Greenberg, and Harry Greenberg, a younger kid who was no relation to Sy. All were friends of Allie Tannenbaum. Allie worked in the kitchen alongside Harry, while Mike and Sy helped set up chairs by the lake, served bootleg drinks, and waited on tables in the dining room.

One afternoon in mid-July, Mike and his pal, Sy Greenberg, walked up from the lake toward the country club's main building. A covered porch ran the entire length of the hotel's front facade. Most of the Adirondack chairs were lined up along the porch wall, with a few placed around small tables.

As the young men approached the porch, Mike noticed six well-dressed gangsters in golfing knickers and jackets pushing tables together to make one large one. As they dragged the heavy wooden chairs to the makeshift table, Mike caught a glimpse of the shoulder holsters under their Norfolk jackets and realized who they were.

"We better get up there and give 'em a hand," Mike said.

They sprinted up to the porch, placed several tables together and arranged chairs around them. As the gangsters sat, Mike noticed how careful each man was in deferring to those of higher rank; with each man making sure they sat next to their most trusted friend.

After placing ashtrays, Mike and Sy took their orders and headed for the kitchen to give them to Harry. They then brought out bootlegged booze with glasses to the porch. After pouring out the gangster's drinks, they went back inside to stand behind the screen door and watch the six men. Shapiro broke open a new deck of cards and passed them to Dutch Shultz, who cut the deck several times and dealt a hand of Pinochle.

Mike whispered, "This is a gathering of Who's Who in gangland crime. The guy next to Shultz is Bugsy Siegel—he's kibitzing with his pal Meyer Lansky. Across the table from Lansky is Lepke Buchalter. The guy wearing the Panama is Albert Anastasia."

"How the hell do you know these guys?" Sy asked. "I thought you only stole cars and moved bootlegged liquor?"

"My old man's an enforcer for Lepke, he knows everyone."

Harry came out from the kitchen with a platter of finger food and six plates. The three of them passed everything around the table.

Dutch Shultz pulled the cigar out of his mouth and stabbed it in Sy's direction. "Hey, ain't you the Greenberg kid, the one Abbadabba promised to send to college?"

"Yes sir." Sy responded.

"Harry, right?" Dutch queried.

"No sir, Harry's the big kid over there—holdin' the tray of food—I'm Simon, everyone calls me Sy."

The Dutchman looked around the table, "Well dat's fuckin' confusin' ain't it? We got us two Greenbergs makin' their way into the family business. Can't have no mix-ups, can we? Tell ya what...big Harry over there...we'll call him Big Greenie and this here college kid we'll call Little Greenie. How about it boys?" Dutch encouraged everyone's agreement by bobbing his head up and down. Grunts of approval were heard around the table. The young men could do nothing more but grin and nod enthusiastically as well.

Dutch waved his cigar in the air and the inch-long ash fell to the porch's decking. "It's settled. You kids hang around in case we need somethin'."

Harry went back to the kitchen. Mike and Sy moved onto the lawn some distance away. After a while, the porch door opened and Otto "Abbadabba" Berman stepped out into the afternoon air.

Dutch spied him and motioned him over to the table. "Hey Otto, grab a chair and we'll deal you in." The ash fell again as Dutch moved his chair to make room.

Over on the lawn Mike said, "So what's with this guy Abbadabba? I never seen him hanging around the neighborhood. How does he fit in?"

"Mob accountant," answered Sy. "Cooks the books, gives financial advice and fixes odds at the track. He's big into the Manhattan night life, so he stays in the city."

"Why did he promise to pay your college tuition?"

"Met him four years ago at the barber shop over on Sutter Avenue. I'm waitin' my turn at the chair and this short, chubby guy opens the back door and holds it open while he talks into the room. 'Deal me out I'm getting a trim,' Abbadabba says. So, I'm looking through the door and I see Dutch Shultz. He's got his jacket off; sleeves rolled up. His shoulder holster swinging under his arm pit as he's dealing cards.

"Anyway, Abbadabba comes over and sits next to me. He opens the sports pages and begins writin' calculations on a sheet of scratch paper. Then he pulls out a scorebook and starts figuring percentages. I'm lookin' over his shoulder at his equations and boom, the fuckin' answer pops into my head. So, like an asshole, I blurt it out."

"Holy shit," exclaimed Mike. "You're kidding?"

"Nope. Pretty stupid huh? Then, he turns his head and says, 'Hey *boychik*, that's real impressive. What...you sixteen, seventeen? Wheredja learn to do algebra in your head?' So, I tell him I stole a book from school, looked at it once or twice, that's all. So, he makes a little grimace with his fat face and writes down a couple of equations. Hands them over with those pudgy fingers of his and says, 'Let's see you solve these big shot.'

"So, I spend a couple of minutes giving him the answers. Then, as an expression of respect, I let him take my turn in the barber chair. One thing leads to another and after a month or two he decides to put me through accounting school. Said some guy did it for him and it was payback. Who's to argue?"

"I'm happy for ya," Mike said. "Only talent I got is in my fists. My dad wants me to be an enforcer like him. Looks like I'm gonna be stuck doin' shit I don't wanna do."

Sy sees a hand waving them back to the porch. "Geez, Dutch is calling us back, we better hustle."

The young men reach the porch and Dutch points to Sy. "Get over here kid, I gotta see this trick of yours for myself."

Sy moves over next to Dutch's chair. "I'm sorry sir, what trick is that?"

"The phone book trick—the one Abbadabba taught you. Hey Mikey, go get a phone book."

Mike brought back a phone book. Abbadabba flipped through it and pointed to a random page. "Okay Sy, show the boss how it's done."

Sy ran his finger down the right-hand column stopping a second or two at the last digit of each phone number. He got to the bottom of the page he wrote a number and started adding the next digit and so on. When all four digits of each phone number were added up, he wrote the total on a piece of paper and gave it to Dutch Shultz. Abbadabba then added up the same numbers and wrote his total on a separate piece of paper.

Dutch compared both. "I'll be damned," he marveled. "They match—the kid did it!" He turned to Abbadabba. "Better keep an eye on him. This kid is gonna give you a run for your money."

CHAPTER 10

1964, Prexy's Restaurant
Forgotten Truths

David finished telling Mike's story and waited for the agents' reaction. Hawkins was the first to speak, "Great story, really. But who knows if it's entirely true? But let's say it is. It's still a stretch to think your father's Mob connected because Mike's friend has the same last name as your father."

"It's more than that," David said. "The math trick Abbadabba taught his young protége...it's the same trick my father tried to teach me when I was a kid. It was his signature *shtick* at parties. Also, the name of Mike's childhood friend was Simon Greenberg, but they called him Sy. My father's real name is Simon and for as long as I can remember everyone calls him Sy. Before joining the IRS, my father studied accounting. I told you he's secretive—always locks his papers away in a file cabinet—carries the key with him everywhere."

"So what?" said Keyes. "My real name is Thomas, but everyone calls me Tom. And what about the name Greenberg? Your last name is the same as Mike's friend—Mike should have picked up on that, but he never commented on it did he?"

"I never told him my last name was Greenberg. My full name is David Asher Greenberg. I sign my artwork David Asher. I'm legally changing my last name to Asher. Mike thinks my name David Asher."

"Why are you changing your name?" Keyes asked.

David pushed his sandwich away. His distaste for Keyes was increasing by the minute. "I'm the subject of discrimination—excluded from certain groups, bullied because I've got a Jewish last name. I'm tired of it and I'm getting married soon. I don't want to inflict that reality on my kids."

"What does your father say about it?"

"He doesn't know and I'm not telling him. He can go to hell as far as I'm concerned."

Keyes jumped on it. "Now we're getting closer to explaining why you're accusing your father of being a criminal. He's cramping your style and you're looking to get even."

"It may look that way," conceded David, "but even if we discount Mike's stories, I've got a few of my own—things I've seen and heard. They all point to the fact my father is on the take."

Hawkins ran his hand over the stubble on his cheek. "Your serious?"

"Yes, sir, I am." David insisted. "Once, while the family was on vacation, I overheard him threatening to audit the hotel owner unless he gave him a set of golf clubs. I've seen rolls of cash bundled up with rubber bands in his sock drawer. He never takes a phone call unless it's in his office."

"Doesn't prove a thing—coincidence," mumbled Keyes.

David balked. "I could sit here all day and tell you the stories—there are too many damn coincidences."

Keyes rolled his eyes. "So, you wait until today to come forward with all this? If it's so damn important why sit on it so long?"

David threw up his hands in disgust, *I'm sick of this asshole.* "Why is it so hard for you to believe me? My dad's IRS—not some auditor—but a Criminal Investigator. If I talk to the wrong kind of cop my dad will find out. I finally stumble upon two FBI agents I think are honest and what happens? They figure I hate my dad and I'm lying to get him in trouble." David grabbed his sketchbook and got up. "I should have left with my friends. This is going nowhere—no wonder the bad guys always win."

Hawkins got up to stop him. "Okay, okay...just calm down."

David faced up to him. "I don't appreciate being treated like some strung out hippie trying to stick it to the man. You guys came to me, remember? I said I would cooperate. But I'm not so sure now...."

"I understand, and now that you've explained yourself, I'm inclined to believe you. We're almost done. Just tell us what went on in the Food Mart today and we'll call it quits."

David sat down with sigh. "The store was empty; Mike was in the back room. Two goons came in looking for trouble. One of them..."

He opened his sketchbook and gave him the drawing on the back of the placemat. "This one here—looked at me like a rabid dog. Mike came out from the back of the store with a baseball bat. He motioned I should leave. That's when I came over here."

The agents shifted in their seats to examine the sketch of the fat thug.

"When did you sketch this out?" Hawkins asked.

"Just before you guys came over to my table," answered David.

"Nice," Keyes remarked, "but does it look like him?"

Tired of the agent's arrogance, David flipped through his sketchbook and stopped at the sketch he made of Keyes at Prexy's lunch counter. He passed the sketchbook to the agent. "Who does that look like?"

Keyes was astonished. "How is this possible? The newspaper was only down for two seconds."

Hawkins took the sketchbook and studied the drawing. He eyed his partner with an amused expression and shook his head. "This is unbelievable. In my fifteen years with the Bureau, I've never seen any sketch artist able to knock out a drawing so life-like without any preliminary work." Hawkins flipped through the sketchbook. He found a doodle of Agnes's backlit head with the fly away tendrils of her Afro and the penciled-in eyebrows. Hawkins recognized other drawings: pimps from the hotel on Broadway and 86th Street; two thugs accused of picking up protection money from store owners and several sketches of small-time enforcers.

"These sketches are nothing like the stiff, frontal, and outlined drawings of the Bureau's sketch artists," exclaimed Hawkins. "They really capture the breath of life. Look at the subtle tilt of this head, the twisted smile, the raised eyebrow. Every drawing shows some characteristic expression. How many of these sketchbooks do you fill up in a month?"

"Three or four I guess."

Hawkins sounded earnest now, "If you can come over to headquarters with your sketches of people from around this neighborhood, we might be able to match them up with mug shots—see who the players are."

"No problem." David flipped to his drawing of the military looking guy at Prexy's payphone. "How about putting a name to this guy?" he asked, tapping the drawing with his finger.

Hawkins asked, "Why?"

David stood, dug a hand into his pant's pocket, pulled out a glass cigar tube and rolled it over the table toward them. Keyes picked it up and held it out to the light—there was a tranquilizer dart inside.

"Okay, tell us about the dart?" Hawkins asked.

"Some guy ambushed me while I was painting. I stopped the dart with my wood palette and ran away."

Keyes raised his eyebrows, "Oh, so now people are after you, and you're Captain America with a shield?"

Hawkins held up a hand. "Hold on Tom, let's hear him out first." Then, turning to David, "Why would someone want to tranquilize you?"

"All I can tell you is I'm involved in sensitive research at Bell Laboratories."

Keyes was shaking his head. "Look, you gotta understand how all this looks. You're a college kid who's got an unstable relationship with his father. At lunch, I watched you space out in the middle of a sentence like someone on drugs. There's a research lab studying your superpowers, and to top it all off—some evil entity is out to tranquilize you."

Hawkins cut in. "Keyes is not trying to insult you. We're trained to recognize the symptoms of mental disorders. You're exhibiting all the signs of a pathological liar."

"What about the tranquilizer dart?" David asked.

"It's a dart," said Hawkins. "We don't know what it's laced with. For all we know you carry it around for kicks."

"So, you think you're being played?"

Hawkins gave him a nod. "I'm sorry son, but that's the way it looks."

David contemplated his uneaten sandwich and pulled it toward him. He took a few bites to give himself time to think. If he wanted the FBI to investigate his father, he'd have to tell them the whole truth. There was no other way. "Everything I say can be verified by calling Dr. Max Bruckmann at Bell Labs in New Jersey. Ask him about 'The Blink Factor'. Here's the number." He wrote it down on a napkin.

"New Jersey?" Keyes repeated. "You go there often?"

"Several times a month."

"How do you get there?"

"They pick me up by Limo."

Keyes nodded at his partner. "Well, the Limo's explained."

David looked from one agent to the other. "Oh, I get it. Agent Keyes was there when the Limo pick me up the other day. Suspicious behavior for a college kid, right? Well, I've told you guys the truth, and that proves it."

"We'll check it out with this Doctor," Hawkins said.

"'The Blink Factor'...what's that?" Keyes asked.

"It's a code name used to refer to the Lab's research into my ability. I have an exceptionally good visual memory. It's a secret program—I signed nondisclosure documents, so keep it between yourselves. What you types call 'need to know'."

Keyes rolled his eyes again. "Code names and everything very hush-hush, huh? Do you actually think we're going to buy into this cloak and dagger stuff?"

Hawkins frowned. "That's enough Tom. There could be some truth in what he says. How else could he draw such a perfect likeness of you after a single glance." He held the phone number up between his fingers. "Tomorrow we're going to follow up with this Doctor Bruckmann at Bell Labs. If he verifies your story, you can come down to headquarters sometime next week and we'll discuss this business with your father. What do you say?"

"I'll be going home this weekend. Call me Monday at my parents' house and tell me when." David wrote the phone number on another napkin and passed it to Hawkins.

Hawkins handed David his business card. "Leave the dart, we'll have its contents analyzed. Right now, I'm trying to figure out how to explain all this to my boss. It's too fantastic to believe."

෴

Across the street at the Food Mart, Mike stood in front of the large wash basin in the back room. With the bat under the faucet, he ran his hands up and down its length coaxing the blood off the polished wood and down the drain. He rinsed his forearms up to the elbows, cleaned the sink and put the bat back behind the door.

At 63, he felt as strong as he did when he was forty. The only difference was stamina—his recovery time was longer. When he was younger, violence was a way of life. Big guys like him were expected to step up and do whatever it took. But no matter how huge a guy was most didn't last long, so pumping up became his obsession. If that was the kind of life he'd lead, he'd make damn sure he would keep it. After his father died and left him the Food Mart, Mike bowed out of the rackets. Vinnie didn't like it, but Mike was a force of one and his brother left him alone. But when the city started to bulldoze the neighborhood everything changed.

He heard the back door open and made a move for the bat.

"Mike...you okay?" David came in through the back hallway.

"I'm fine, you're the one who looks like shit."

David put the key ring back in his pocket and sat down on a folding chair. "The FBI is watching the store. They really put me through the wringer."

"Yeah, AJ dropped by and gave me a heads up," Mike said. "Let's pop a few beers and you can tell me about it."

Mike listened as David, between sips of beer, outlined the confrontation with the two agents. At first Mike thought David was spooked by the interrogation, but when his young friend reached for a second bottle, he sensed David was struggling with something else.

"Just spit it out," Mike advised and listened in silence as the words tumbled out of David's mouth.

"There's something you should know. My real name is David Asher Greenberg. I'm legally changing my name to David Asher and began using it when I met you. At the time, I didn't know my father was your childhood friend until I got hooked on your stories. It was the trick with the phone book that clinched it."

Mike was surprised but simply nodded, waiting for him to continue. David was doing the thing with his eyes—scanning his features to figure out his reaction. He tried to give the boy a neutral look.

David leaned forward in his chair. With his eyes downcast, his thumb traced little squiggles on the wet surface of the beer bottle. "I was afraid to tell you the truth because I needed to find out why my father treats me so shabbily."

Oddly, Mike didn't feel betrayed. Sy's pathological need for total control ruined his friendship with him and he understood David's need to get at the root cause of his father's treatment.

David continued. "You're the closest thing to a real father I've ever had. I owe you. My father's going down. I know he's taking bribes as an IRS investigator and I'm looking for proof. I don't know if he's still connected to the Mob, but if you two are still in contact, I suggest you cut all ties with him.

"I've explained to the agents you wanted out of the rackets and how Vinnie pulls you back in. They told me they're willing to give you immunity from prosecution if you testify against Sy. It's all over for him, but you have a way out."

Mike's mind was in turmoil. He knew David was trying to help him, but he was asked to do the unthinkable—break the code of silence.

David pressed on. "Look, we're in the same predicament. He was my father for twenty years. He fed me, clothed me and paid for my education. I understand how you feel about betraying him...I really do. But he's rotten to the core. He uses people and destroys them. He treats my mother like shit and, before I met you, well, you remember how I was. You changed my life."

Mike downed the last of his beer. He thought of his wife—she too wanted him to put things right. "Thanks for being up front with me. And you're the son we've never had. I still feel that way—nothing's changed—we're still tight. And you're right about Sy and I won't let on I know you. But I've got some thinking to do. I'll let you know what I decide."

Minutes later, David grabbed his jacket and left. Mike opened another beer and thought about his situation. *I should've known it would come to this. If my brother left me alone, I would've led a nice, quiet life.*

The handwriting was on the wall—if he didn't help the FBI by turning state's evidence, he'd probably go to jail. But what David didn't know was, by helping the feds, Mike would rat out on the policy operator bankrolling the numbers racket between West 76th and 96th.

His childhood friend, Sy Greenberg.

CHAPTER 11

Day 3
Painful Revelations

Shortly before ten the next morning, David left the painting studio for Salters Bookstore. He waited inside the entrance until AJ pulled his '57 Chevy to the curb. David surveyed the street, and seeing no one suspicious, walked to the car and slipped into the passenger seat.

They drove aimlessly around Morningside Heights, David keeping an eye on the rear-view mirror. At 116th Street he asked AJ to turn east to Third Avenue and then head downtown. As they did, David told his friend about Dr. Max and his note.

"Wow, Bell Laboratories," AJ said. "Just as I thought, I always knew there was something special about you. I mean you told me about your father and how he sedated you and stuff, but this—it's straight out of *The Twilight Zone.*"

Twenty minutes later they turned at 65th Street and, wishing him luck, AJ pulled the car to the curb on 5th Avenue, across from the Central Park Zoo. David thanked him and disappeared into the park.

David found the long succession of iron and concrete cages depressing. It was a squalid place with most animals pacing back and forth like prisoners inside bare, confined spaces. He weaved his way through the crowded pathways and exited the zoo, emerging into Central Park itself. Glad to be rid of the incessant noise and fetid smells of the animals, he mingled with the crowds, sometimes walking, other times joining groups of joggers. Heading north, he passed Glade Arch Bridge and exited the park on 79th Street near 5th Avenue.

Up ahead was the Metropolitan Museum of Art. Usually, a mass of people could be found congregating on the grand stairs leading up to the museum's entrance. Today a nippy March wind kept most people off the steps, and he realized how exposed he would be while climbing up to the museum entrance.

He waited and eventually joined a group of students as they emptied out of a bus and trekked up the stairs. As the group entered the building, he slipped behind one of the double columns and checked behind him. Satisfied no one was following him, he made his way into the museum and found the Egyptian Wing.

Dr. Max was waiting in a crowded corner of the gallery. The doctor made eye contact and David gave him a slight nod. They circled around the exhibit and positioned themselves near a staff elevator.

Clearly worried, Dr. Max dispensed with pleasantries and rushed headlong into what he wanted to say, "The CIA knows you're 'Subject X' of 'The Blink Factor'–they're after you."

"The CIA?"

"Yes, seems they're funding a lot of clandestine research at Bell through the NIH. They're poking around all the departments."

"NIH?"

"National Institute of Health. A government agency that sometimes acts as a proxy for some of the CIA's more questionable research projects. Word is, they're after anyone suspected of having paranormal abilities. Some military type tried to pressure me into giving you up. In the name of National Security, he said. I refused. That night my files were broken into."

"My folder?"

"Safe."

"Thank God."

"Well, you're not off the hook by a long-shot. They're not asking for volunteers. I've read reports of food being laced with LSD at soup kitchens and mental hospitals. I suspect their operatives follow their victims around hoping to observe paranormal reactions. They're looking for the perfect subject for their mind experiments. Here–take this," he handed David a paper sack. "Empty jars to collect urine samples."

"Come on, you're kidding?"

"Have you felt kind of wonky lately?"

"No, I'm fine."

"Good. I was afraid they may have slipped you something at the Bell cafeteria. Whatever you do, don't eat or drink anything questionable. If you feel even a little off-center, lock yourself away—somewhere safe—for twenty-four hours. Piss in a jar and have someone send it to me. I'll get back to you with the damage." Dr. Max looked at him through haunted eyes, "I'm sorry David, I should have taken your premonitions seriously."

David was flipping through his sketchbook. "It's not your fault." He stopped at two drawings. "You need to know—these two FBI agents, Hawkins and Keyes—are coming to see you. Tell them everything. Include your visit from the CIA. Wait..." He searched through more drawings until he came to the military type at Prexy's payphone. "Was this the man who came to see you—the CIA guy?"

"Yes, that's him."

◈◈

David's father was at the IRS Regional Office catching up on paperwork and filing reports. By 11:30, everyone left for the Easter/Passover weekend. Sy decided to stay. He waited a quarter of an hour to make sure no one returned and then broke into his boss's office. Interdepartmental investigations were ongoing and Sy needed a look at his personnel file to see if any of his cases were red flagged.

Careful to replace everything he touched, he rifled through his boss's desk. He felt the underside of drawers for taped envelopes, rifled through the trash bin and looked behind picture frames.

Nothing... Then, he thought. *What about this file cabinet?*

He tried the key from his own file cabinet at home. It wouldn't turn. Frustrated, he slammed his fist against the side of the cabinet. On top, a small potted plant rattled in its saucer. It was one of those miniature cacti plants some people buy in gift shops—stupid, unobtrusive and dwarfed by his boss's humidor and collection of pipes.

What's with this puny plant?

Sy looked around, it was the only plant in the office. Wrapping his handkerchief around his fingertips he pinched the stem of the plant and pulled up. On the bottom of the pot, he found a key.

In his personnel file, Sy found two cases red flagged for review and removed them. Making sure there were no additional references to them elsewhere, he returned the file to its rightful place. It was something he was good at—cooking the books or white-washing a report—it was the same thing.

At one o'clock, Sy left the office and walked a few blocks to Maxwell's Pub for a sandwich and beer. While he ate, he studied the postcard he received a few days before. Disregarding the message, he turned the card over. There was a photograph of the Ferris wheel at Coney Island. The wheel signified a location—St. Peter's Church. The passenger chairs suspended on the perimeter of the wheel denoted the hours on a clock. In this case, a small red dot next to a suspended rocking chair in the three o'clock position gave the time. Sy scrutinized the photo's caption: 'Coney's Famous Wonder Wheel'. The letter "F" was underlined indicating the day—Friday.

Three o'clock, today—St. Peter's Church.

The church was a few blocks from the IRS Regional Office. Sy admired its Greek Style structure, yet despite its beauty, he never ventured in. There was always something foreboding about a house of the gentiles, and as he walked the few blocks down Church Street, his felt his pulse quicken.

He paused before its facade to take in the six Ionic columns before walking up the steps and entering the cathedral-like interior. Feeling lost, he scoped out the sea of dark wood pews and scanned along the marble walls for a familiar face. Next to the bank of red curtained confessionals was the pockmarked face of Tony Gambino above a white collar. The mobster nodded and turning to place a "Closed for Repair" sign in front of a confessional, disappeared inside.

Sy walked over, unhooked the rope in front of the confessional and entered the tiny enclosure. He sat and placed his briefcase next to him on the seat and accustomed himself to the gloom. He was uncomfortable with the sanctity of the small space. The smell of candle wax made him nauseous, and the sweat trickled down his neck. Then, he heard his mother's disembodied voice. *A shanda fur die goyim!* –Shame on the Jew in a house of Christ!

A hard thumping banged against his chest, and he moved around nervously, his shins bumping into the kneeler. Something heavy fell to the floor—he bent down and felt around—it was another briefcase. He tasted blood and found his nose was bleeding. The partition opened and the gruff voice of Tony Gambino rattled out from behind the latticed screen.

"Good ta see ya Sy. How long's it been?"

Sy held a handkerchief to his nose. "Since we seen each other or my last confession?"

"Ha. Da Jews got it easy—only confessing once a year."

"Too many sinners, too few Rabbis. So, we confess directly to God."

"Funny. Listen, the boss got a problem. Hope ya up for it, 'cause it sounds like ya gotta cold."

"Nah, a fuckin' nosebleed that's all."

"Jesus, you're not bleedin' in a church?" Tony couldn't control his laughter. "Ain't that rich—a Jew with stigmata."

"Stigmata huh? You're a regular comedian. What does Moretti need?"

"A month back, Norman Feldman's in the middle of taxes, and boom, he drops dead—natural causes—great loss. So, we calls in some favors from out of state. Dey send us three bean counters ta finish up. Ya got copies in the briefcase on the kneeler. Boss says dere's stuff... redacted I tink the word was—for yer own protection. Anyways, Moretti don't trust no one from anudder outfit. Wants youse ta give the tax stuff the once over."

Sy bent down to pick up the briefcase and blood splattered on his hand. "Too bad about old Norm—*sniff*—he was one of the best. How many returns?"

"Five."

"It'll take a couple of weeks. We'll have to file an extension."

"The boss figured. Dere's two hundred in the briefcase. Another three when you're done."

"Nice briefcase, mine's old and beat-up."

"Really? Da boss collects a lot of old stuff. Tell ya what...keep the new one and I'll give him yer old one when I pick up the returns. Lemme know when they're ready."

Sy grabbed hold of both briefcases and got up to leave. *Shit, now the briefcases are smeared with blood.* "Okay, I'll uh, send you a postcard."

"Wait, before you leave, dere's more...it's personal shit."

"Whaddayamean personal," Sy said, wiping the handle of the new briefcase with his handkerchief.

"It's about the broad you knocked up in Vegas."

"I told you a thousand times, I'm not giving her any more money," Sy felt a trickle and dabbed his nose. "The goddam city is demolishing my betting parlors to build projects. There's no money coming in."

"Yeah, we heard—that's tough. She's not the problem. The dumb broad died from an overdose two months ago. It's your bastard son Chip—he's disappeared."

"Shit." Sy's fingers felt slippery. "I thought he was in tight with the Vegas outfit?"

"Yeah, was. Probably in Manhattan now because he knows you're his father. His mother told him before she died."

Christ, how much blood is on my hands now?

"Okay, so he knows. Big deal." Sy said, cleaning his fingers with the handkerchief. "Why should I care?"

"Some Vegas loan shark is after him. You need to take care of it—Moretti doesn't want no trouble."

Sy looked angrily at the shadow behind the latticed screen, "What kind of crap is that, huh? Whatever the kid does is his own business—I'm not responsible for his shit."

"Boss's orders Sy. If the kid shows up, ya gotta handle it and dat's dat."

"Jesus, tell Moretti not to worry. If the kid shows I'll deal with the little bastard. Anything else?"

"Nope that's it—gotta be going."

The partition slid shut. Somewhere in the chapel a choir of heavenly voices started up. The music drifted into the enclosure and wrapped itself around Sy's stone-cold heart. The blood caked under his nose and its metallic smell fused with the confessional's musty odor. His nostrils cleared and for a fleeting moment he was breathing free and felt a strange sense of peace.

Then from the darkness, the sweet voice of his mother snatched it away.

Far shod! —for shame!

⋙⋘

Dr. Max's note worried Nina ever since David mentioned it a day and a half ago. The note was short and ominous—David's secret was comprised. At first, Nina thought the two stalkers were government recruiters that showed up every year at college campuses.

But after thinking it over, she became concerned. Finishing rehearsal that morning, she rushed back to Park Avenue to meet David for a late lunch. Nina found him in the kitchen talking to her mother, Elsita. The sketch of the stalker lurking at Prexy's payphone was on the kitchen table. The mood was somber.

"Mom, David, what's wrong?"

Her mother tapped her fingernail on the drawing, "This man *mijita*—he has made many visits with your father this year—always after the office hours."

Nina hated it when her mother referred to Martin Broder as her father. He wasn't, and could never be, a father to her. Even though her mother was a self-styled feminist, she abdicated much of her independence by marrying manipulative men. First to her biological father and then to Dr. Broder.

"Well good," Nina said, "since he's a patient we can find out his name."

"He's not a patient," David said. "You know I met with Dr. Max this morning?"

Nina nodded. *Here it comes—the answer I'm waiting for.* "What did he tell you?"

"Max told me someone came to his office wanting to know all about me. When he refused, the man insisted it was a matter of national security."

"What?" Exhausted, Nina sat down. She was hungry and sweaty from rehearsal and now felt a headache coming on.

"I showed Max this drawing of the payphone guy," David pointed to the open sketchbook. "He identified it as the man who came to see him."

"We waited for you *mi amor*," her mother said in a heavily accented voice. "David, he allows me to look through his book. I see this face," she slid the sketchbook away in disgust. "At once I know him."

Nina was confused, "I still don't understand. What's the guy at the payphone got to do with my stepfather?"

"I too want to know this," Elsita said. "I ask, and David tells me everything."

One glance and it became instantly clear. *She knows,* Nina thought. *For whatever reason, David told her about his ability.*

Nina turned in her chair to look him in the eye. "You told her?"

He nodded.

Incredulous, she turned again to her mother. "*¿Y le creiste?* –and you believed him?"

"*Por su puesto, mijita,*" her mother replied. "Because I remember someone with a memory like David's."

Nina was really confused now. "What, when, who?"

"In Bogotá, *mijita*, before you were born. *Por ahora, no importa*–it's not important right now."

David explained, "I confided in your mother because both of you have to know who Dr. Broder is involved with."

"Okay, so who did Dr. Max say the payphone guy was?" Nina asked.

"CIA."

Nina removed the rubber band from her ponytail and rubbed her temples. "Why would the CIA be following you?"

"The government wants to weaponize my ability."

"Dr. Max told you that?"

"No, the CIA guy made it crystal clear yesterday–he shot a tranquilizer dart at me."

"Oh God...."

∽❧

Riley drove out to La Guardia to catch an hourly shuttle to DC. As much as he hated interrupting his pursuit of David Greenberg, he needed sanction from Langley to use extreme measures to capture and turn Greenberg into a CIA asset.

So far it had all gone very wrong. The discovery of another government agent interested in David Greenberg raised the stakes. He spotted the sandy-haired man watching Greenberg at the university bus stop several days ago. Then again at the hamburger joint during lunch and yet again that same afternoon as Greenberg drove away in the Bell Lab Limo. If that wasn't enough, when Riley returned to Park Avenue to pick up Dr. Broder's copy of "The Blink Factor", the unknown agent was there again—outside the doctor's apartment building.

It was only after reading his copy of the article, that Riley concluded the college kid was more useful than he originally thought. Greenberg's abilities were unique and could be a crucial asset to a branch of the CIA responsible for human intelligence gathering.

The NCS–The National Clandestine Service.

Project Paperclip was not just another assignment for Riley. It had deep ties to the occult going back to Nazi Germany, the Italian occultists and recent satanic practices. Riley was an ardent believer; hence his manic obsession with capturing David Greenberg and turning him into a CIA asset.

Here was an unassuming young man who could insinuate himself into situations where cameras or recording devices were impossible to deploy. Not only would he be able to remember everything he saw, but he could document everything through a series of drawings as valuable as photographs.

But it turned out Greenberg was not an easy mark to snare. Riley's attempts to tranquilize him with a dart filled with Dr. Broder's LSD concoction failed. The scientists at Bell described Greenberg as displaying intuitive flashes of second sight. "The Blink Factor" article summarized it:

"...We found no empirical evidence to suggest such phenomena exist. What we have witnessed, however, suggests a willingness of the subject to be guided by what can be described as, a quiet voice within. There are many inner voices, and they all shout out to us, but the loudest does not always offer the correct path. More often than not, it is the quiet voice, and it may speak only once. 'Subject X' is able to listen and trust it."

Riley realized his mistake. He should have never attacked Greenberg. Winning his trust now was out of the question. Riley would have to isolate him and, with the help of Dr. Broder, make him chemically dependent. To capture his mind, Broder would use a system of "psychic driving". He would bombard David's mind with auditory messages in a drug-induced coma to turn him. Ultimately David would be re-programmed and controlled by "trigger phrases" to accomplish missions for the CIA.

As David's handler, Riley's career would be assured.

CHAPTER 12

Confrontations

Sometime after four in the afternoon, Sy Greenberg weaved his way past the swarm of newspaper hawkers on Thirty-third Street and descended the Seventh Avenue staircase leading to the Pennsylvania Train Station. One year ago, the historic above ground portion was demolished to make way for a new Madison Square Garden. The train hub, now confined to a warren of underground tunnels, reduced commuters to the indignity of scurrying around like rats in a maze.

He traversed the length of the urine-soaked passageway and turned toward the concourse overlooking the tracks. He descended the stairs heading to the lower-level and track five. As he did, he heard the 5:25 train to Long Island burst out of the tunnel and begin its long metallic screech to a standstill.

The minute Sy stepped on the platform, he spied a familiar face. He remembered meeting Judge Scarpello at a function the year before. His Honor pumped him for tax advice, and after getting what he wanted, abruptly ignored him. Sy suspected the judge worked for the Genovese Family and dug into his relationship with Mob boss Antony Salerno. It took a year, but he learned the judge was signing warrants then warning Salerno's Capos of impending raids.

The good judge is on the take. Probably looking for ways to hide all the bribes he's taking.

Sy recalled the recent rumors—the judge had issues with his taxes again. Never one to miss an opportunity, he followed him into the coach and found a seat where the judge would be sure to notice him. Sy reserved the empty seat beside him with the extra briefcase.

Nothing like a discreet chat on a noisy train to ask an IRS agent for some tax advice. Good, he spotted me...he's trying to make up his mind.

There was an inherent distrust of IRS agents and Sy knew many people, who wouldn't give him the time of day during the year, suddenly get in touch with him during tax season. They wanted a few minutes of his time, maybe meet for drinks to "catch up" and then ask a few questions.

For something more complicated, he might be invited to a small dinner party where he'd be asked to take a quick look at the host's returns. Sy understood these were not overtures of friendship, but veiled agreements to exchange favors.

Sy liked collecting markers more than accumulating wealth. Money gave him the security he never had when he was young. But he didn't need money anymore. Financially secure, he could now feed his greatest pleasure—demeaning others. When an honorable person owed him a favor, Sy felt he stole a large measure of the man's dignity.

Soon, the influential judge would find himself in Sy's pocket.

❧

Meanwhile, out on Long Island David's mother was shopping for the coming Passover week. Although Ellen hated the atmosphere of hypocrisy that pervaded the house during religious holidays, she took comfort in knowing David would be home for an extended stay and wanted to make it special. The first Seder on Saturday night was to be hosted by Sy's brother. On Sunday, Ellen would drive her father in from the city for the second night of Passover at her house in Woodmere. Both David and Jacob would stay the week—she'd be surrounded by the two people she loved most.

Ellen finished her shopping and headed home thinking of her loveless marriage. She tried to remember when she stopped loving her husband. Unburdened by both principle and self-control, Sy proved to be indistinguishable in character from his Mob friends. She wondered if she would ever screw up the courage to tell her son the truth about his father. If there was some way to end the marriage she would, but Ellen knew divorce would leave her penniless. Sy was funding her sportswear shop and he was sure to close it down and kick her to the curb. It all seemed so hopeless.

On the way home she noticed a hardware store and turned into the parking lot. Once inside, she explained her problem to the clerk. There was a big rat in the house, and she needed to get rid of it. The man listed her options, and she chose the tried-and-true method women have used for centuries.

It didn't take Ellen long to make the small purchase. Leaving the store, she put the box of rat poison in the trunk of her car and covered it with an old sweater.

∽∾

Nina spent the rest of the afternoon with David and her mother. There was a long discussion about her stepfather: her mother's disillusionment with the marriage, Dr. Broder's continual secrecy and the long hours he spent locked away in his laboratory at the office. They made a quick dinner after which her mother excused herself, and Nina cleared the dishes from the kitchen table.

David sat hunched over, his chin resting in the palm of his hand. He poured a fourth glass of wine with a forlorn expression on his face.

"This is like a bad movie," he said.

"What are you going to do?" Nina asked.

"I don't know. I just want to disappear."

"You've got to face this, David; it's not going away."

"It's all too much: the FBI wants me to help them break up a gambling ring; thanks to Professor Haverstock, the CIA wants to use me for espionage; my father wants to destroy my self-esteem and your stepfather, the great Dr. Broder, wants to stick electrodes in my brain.

"If that isn't enough, I'm going to have to sit through *Seder* this weekend with a bunch of hypocrites. Oh wait...let's not forget breaking into my father's file cabinet to look for my birth certificate because you have this crazy idea my father isn't my real father."

Something snapped inside Nina, and she slammed her hand down on the counter. "Oh no...don't you dare do that to me. You're the one who wanted to break-in—not me—you wanted to find evidence against him. I only asked you—for your own peace of mind by the way—to look for your birth certificate while you were searching through his stupid file cabinet."

She continued to glare at him. "I think I'm very supportive. Any other woman would walk away from all this, but I happen to love you. You're not the only one who's tired and scared. To make it worse, you're lumping me in with the bad guys."

Nina started to walk out of the kitchen but turned at the door. "Well, since I'm making your life so miserable, I'll be the one to disappear. That way you'll have one less problem." It wouldn't be easy, but she would manage to continue without him. "You can see yourself out...."

She stormed out of the kitchen.

"Oh God, wait...." David followed her to the bedroom, but she slammed the door in his face. He heard the click of the lock. "I'm sorry, I didn't mean anything by it. Please open up, we shouldn't leave things like this."

"Go away," she said through the door. "You won't miss me—you've got three years of memories to live with."

"Nina please...."

He waited.

"Nina?"

He slid down to the floor and sat.

❧

David felt like a fool. He sat by Nina's bedroom door for an hour, and she still hadn't opened it. She already ate; had her own bathroom—she could stay there until morning.

Her mother came by and shook her head. "My daughter, she is stubborn. Let her sleep. Tomorrow it will be better."

David stood up. "I have to go to my parent's house for an entire week. I don't want to leave like this."

"Yes, it is the right way, but not always so easy. Sleep here tonight. The guest room it is always ready. Tomorrow speak with her—it will be better—you will see."

❧

Since Sy seemed to be in a good mood at dinner that night, Ellen thought she'd broach a difficult subject. She served Sy's coffee with a slice of cake and gave him a timid smile.

"Can you pick David up at the station tomorrow?" Crumbs accumulated around her husband's mouth.

Sy wiped his lips with the back of his hand. "Yeah, fine."

Ellen proceeded cautiously. "I uh, thought maybe you could speak to David on the way home?"

"About what?" He took another forkful of cake and swished it around his mouth with some coffee.

"Well, he's way over eighteen now and about to graduate. I thought it's a good time to tell him the truth."

"The truth? Again, with the truth? What the hell are you trying to accomplish?" Coffee-stained cake crumbs now stuck to his lips. "We made a decision. Why do you insist? I don't understand you?"

She found it difficult to sustain eye contact. His face was turning red—a bad sign. "But we changed our minds later on. We said we made the wrong decision and decided to tell him when he was older."

"We?" Specks of cake shot out from his mouth. "We never agreed. If I've told you once, I've told you a thousand times. We're not going to tell him."

"But Sy, you promised...."

"Promise? I didn't promise. You promised—you're the one who promised. I have nothing to do with your stupid promises."

Her heart was pounding. *So much for his good mood.* She screwed up her courage. "I remember distinctly we agreed to tell him when he was eighteen."

It was beginning: the trembling of his lips; the eyes widening in their sockets; his voice raised a few octaves and his hand gesticulating wildly in the air. "I never agreed. Did you ever hear me agree? You're the one who thought we should tell him." He was showering her with his spittle now. "When we took him to the doctor you mentioned it; after his Bar-Mitzvah you mentioned it; you mentioned it when he turned eighteen, and now you're mentioning it again. So, you mentioned it, but I never agreed to anything."

"The judge thought it was a good idea," she whimpered.

"Jesus Christ, what does the goddamn judge have to do with it?" His tongue scooped up the crumbs clinging to his lips. "It's not his kid."

"Even so—"

"For crying out loud, will you once and for all stop with this stupid thing."

"But he has a right...."

Sy exploded. "A right? A right? He doesn't have any rights—he doesn't have a right to a goddamn thing." He stood up and leaned over her, poking his chest repeatedly. "I decide who has the rights in this family and no one's going to find out about this or anything else. Is that clear?"

Silence.

"Well, is it?"

She was beaten again. "Yes."

"Yes, *what?*"

"It's clear."

"Good." He blew his nose into his napkin, threw it on the table and left.

Sy locked himself in his office. Ellen cleaned up from dinner trying not to think about what he was up to—she knew too much already. Although she played the part of the compliant wife, Ellen was nobody's fool. She turned a blind eye to his shady deals, the rolls of cash wrapped with rubber bands, the card games with his mobster friends, and the mistress in New Jersey.

And all the "white lies" she was forced to tell—one piled on top of another. *If I didn't agree to that first lie, there would be no need for the others. But after the horrors of World War II, Sy's tiny deception seemed so innocent it would hardly have raised an eyebrow. Besides, Sy said, it was no one's business. Didn't people have a right to live their lives anyway they pleased?*

She understood now how his belligerent nature turned a simple lie into something more complicated and damaging. After their marriage, Sy Greenberg proved to be a man obsessed with a pathological need to dominate, humiliate and accumulate wealth. As time went on his maliciousness was so great, he would allow nothing to stand in his way. As reasonable questions were asked, facts were altered. When lips wouldn't stay sealed, bribes were given, or threats were made. In the end, laws were broken, documents were falsified, and spirits broken.

Ellen thought about the rat poison and a life free of her husband's abuse. No more would she hear him scurry around his office hiding pieces of paper or scratching through ledger books. Never again would he gnaw at her son's self-esteem or snatch away every shred of her own happiness.

Best of all, the disgusting creature would never crawl into her bed again.

Nina continued to ignore David as he knocked on her bedroom door. That she complicated his life by insisting he look for his birth certificate, was a slap in her face. If she was right, finding out Sy was not his father would go a long way in freeing him from the man's hold over him. It was for his own good. Hopefully, David would come to realize how hurtful he was. Meanwhile, if Nina opened the door now, she might say something she'd regret, so she slipped into a hot bath of Epsom salts to ease her troubled heart and aching muscles.

Dancing the role of Simon Legree, the evil king in *The Small House of Uncle Thomas*, necessitated a strong, menacing mindset, which she found emotionally exhausting. The narrated ballet from the musical *The King and I,* in which the wives and court musicians of the Siamese

King stage their own version of *Uncle Tom's Cabin*, was to be part of the opening night gala for the newly built New York State Theater at Lincoln Center.

The warmth of the bath soothed her nerves, and as she lay there, she realized her love for David was absolute. But the past three years were not easy. She encouraged his self-imposed struggle to reinvent himself—to bring to the surface the nobility she knew lay buried within him. But the progress was excruciating slow. Sometimes he could be very charming—other times brooding and aloof—disappearing into his own world of recalled images, revisited thoughts and reinvented dreams. His was a world she couldn't visit nor understand. At any moment a memory might bubble up and steal his attention away from her. She pleaded with him to stop living in the past—to face down his demons and master them.

For Nina, mastery was all about creating perfection through movement. The struggle to achieve it meant a strong will and an uncompromising dedication to creating a life that would nurture excellence in her body, mind and spirit. In contrast, David was raised in an atmosphere of complacency and mediocrity. His medicated childhood and the demoralizing influence of his father led him to develop a bunker mentality. The result was pessimism and insularity—an attitude she found abhorrent.

Nina found it hard to compromise. She loved David, but he would have to change to fit into the life she envisioned for herself. It was the only way she could live.

CHAPTER 13

Day 4
Lifeline

Soothed by the bath, Nina fell into a much-needed sleep until a childhood memory mixed with present-day fears turned into a horrific nightmare. Shaken awake early Friday morning, Nina found herself in the consoling arms of her mother.

"Tell me your nightmare, *mijita*," her mother insisted.

"You remember the slaughter of *El Bogotazo, Mama?*".

Her mother nodded and held her close. "*Por su puesto, mi amor.* You were seven when it happened." In 1948, week-long riots in Bogotá called *El Bogotazo* began after the assassination of then, liberal party leader, Jorge Gaitán.

Nina continued. "I was playing with my dolls in my room and I heard the sound of rifles. I looked out the window. A mob was coming past our house carrying knives, axes, and pitchforks. Some soldiers had rifles with bayonets attached.

"Then, my remembrance turned into a nightmare—a twisted version of what actually happened mixed with passages from my dance solo. Leading the angry mob was a man dressed in a Siamese costume of black & gold velvet penangs, a shirt with jeweled sleeves and gold winged epaulets. His face was hidden by an ornate mask with a pagoda headpiece."

"Like the ballet for the *King and I* you're rehearsing?" Her mother asked.

"Yes. Yet in the dream David's father was Simon Legree. His arms were spread out—as I do in my solo—beckoning the insurgents to follow him. But then Sy duplicated himself—making multiple Simon Legree's. The evil is everywhere. I become frozen to the spot, squeezing my doll to my chest as all the Simons removed their masks. Their faces, mama. Their faces were Sy Greenberg's and my stepfather's, Martin Broder. They had hideous smiles. Their long black fingernails were pointing in my direction. They surrounded me."

❧❧

Nina and her mother talked until the sun came up. Nina confessing her love for David and Elsita sharing her misgivings about her marriage to Dr. Broder. He wasn't the man she thought he was, and she felt something terrible was going on behind her back.

Then, Nina learned David spent the night in the guest room.

"He waits in the kitchen *mijita*," she said. "In the middle of the night, I come for milk and hear him. He tosses and turns in his sleep. I think perhaps he is very much sorry for what he said."

Nina entered the kitchen to find David haggard and pale. He stood up from the table and moved closer. Hesitant to touch her, he simply looked into her eyes, and she could read the regret that lingered there.

He was sorry, explaining he reached a breaking point and was thoughtless to insinuate she was part of his problem. If he wasn't soused with wine and at such a low ebb, he would have never said what he did.

"I too am to blame," she admitted. "I didn't want to tell you. Rehearsals are grueling, and with a costume fitting coming up, well, I'm taking amphetamines. You know—to curb my appetite and give me endurance. I'm afraid I was strung out and nervous."

"Oh Nina," he responded. "I'm sorry I wasn't there for you."

"Don't apologize. I should have told you."

They held each other for a long while. She could tell how tired he was. "I'll make you something to eat and then drive you to Jacob's so you can shower and change. It will make you feel better."

He nodded and said, "Hey, what if we spend part of the day together and you can take me to the train station afterwards. I can pack my duffle after I shower and dress."

Later, they walked along Fifth Avenue, popping in and out of stores and dreaming about all the wonderful things they would buy to furnish their first home. It was a day to chill out and relax, and they managed to forget both the danger they faced and their foolishness of the night before.

During lunch, they talked about their honeymoon. Nina wanted to take him to Europe to see all the museums and then to Greece to swim naked in the Mediterranean. When they left the restaurant, they browsed the stacks at Barnes and Noble for a very pleasant half-hour until, for some unknown reason, Nina became agitated.

"Let's go," she said.

"Fine," he agreed, and they left the store.

After walking out onto the street, David could sense something was wrong. He asked her about it, but she walked on in silence for nine blocks until she stopped.

"I'm sorry David, I won't marry you."

He was stunned. "I thought you forgave me—what did I do now?"

"Nothing and I did forgive you. It's not because of last night. It's because I love you so much."

"Your joking?" David said.

"I'm serious. I've decided and I'm not changing my mind. I can't marry you."

"Why are you saying that? I thought we were okay—we're having a wonderful time. What happened?"

Nina answered through a stream of tears. "I was looking at this book on palm reading. It pointed out the lifeline—I looked at mine—it's very short. I don't want to hurt you by dying early. I don't want to leave my children motherless. I won't marry you. We can continue seeing each other until you find someone else to marry."

David couldn't believe it. In desperation, he dragged her back to the bookstore and found the book. She turned to the page and he looked at the illustration.

Then he read the caption next to it and smiled. "Look, it says right here, 'The length of the lifeline does not indicate the length of a person's life'. You didn't read that did you?"

"It doesn't say that...you're lying."

David handed her the book. "Read it for yourself."

Nina read it. Tears of relief followed. A minute ago, she reconciled herself to living her life without him. She was willing to let him go for the sake of his future happiness, and it made her realize how very much she loved him. They left the bookstore and hailed a cab to take them back to Park Avenue. It was the middle of the afternoon and they found themselves alone in the apartment. She went to her bathroom and when she came out, he was standing next to her closet looking at a portrait he painted of her.

He turned and smiled at her. "Are you feeling better?"

"Yes. I'm sorry about what happened at the bookstore," she offered. "I love you and didn't want you to suffer if I died early."

"I would have suffered more living without you—even for a short while. Every moment I spend with you is precious to me."

Nina came beside him and looked at the painting. "You made me look very beautiful."

He put his arms around her and drew her close in a protective embrace. "That's because you are." He lowered his head, so his lips nuzzled the nape of her neck.

She felt him stirring and the thought of it sent a flame of desire through her. Nina pulled her head back and removed the rubber band from her ponytail. "It's still office hours; my mother is downstairs working."

His hand snaked around her waist and pulled her against him so she could feel the extent of his hardness. She clung to him, her pelvis rising in reply to his insistent caresses.

He whispered in her ear. "What if she returns?"

Nina broke away, moved a chair into her closet and turned on the light. Shooting her a lop-sided grin, David followed her into the closet and sat facing her. She closed the closet door and leaned against it. Eyeing him seductively, Nina gathered her skirt up from behind and pushing down her panties, wiggled her hips. They dropped to her ankles.

Stepping out of them, Nina hiked up her skirt exposing herself to him. She moved forward, straddled the chair and hovered above him, her long hair caressing his cheek. As his hands roamed over her thighs and buttocks, she reached down to free his erection and gripped the length of him. He let out a long groan and grabbing her waist with both hands, tried to push her hips downward. She teased him, bulking up her thigh muscles, denying him entrance as he strained upward to meet her.

Then she stroked him. He gave up his struggle to enter her and moved his hands under her blouse to cup her breasts. He buried his face between them, his grunts of frustration exciting her. She could no longer hold back. Her thighs gave way to her passion and Nina lowered herself onto him, rocking back and forth, savoring the deliciousness of the moment.

She could feel him—he was on the edge of release—waiting for her to join him. The idea of it pushed her further toward a climax; her uncontrollable moans sparking his own floodtide of pleasure. They shuddered together, jolting their bodies against each other until exhausted, they collapsed on the closet floor.

⚮

Late that same afternoon, Ellen was in her basement folding the last of the laundry. When she finished, she sat quietly on a stool in front of the folding table. Shoved back in a dark corner of the overhead cabinet, the box of rat poison waited for her decision.

Yes, or no?

She heard a scratching of shrubs against glass and raised her glance to the small window near the basement's ceiling. The wind picked up and she heard the far-off rumble of an approaching storm. Outside, a dramatic shift in the weather turned the sky dark grey and a sinister gloom engulfed the laundry room.

A warning?

Refusing to believe it, she dug deep to find new resolve. Through the rapidly fading light, she opened the overhead cabinet and thrust her hand deep inside, her fingertips searching for the cardboard box.

I'll put it in his borscht. He'll slurp it up in his usual disgusting manner and I'll finally be rid of him.

But then, realizing she would have to mop up the red and white slime from his lifeless mouth, a wave of dizziness followed, and her resolve faltered. A crack of thunder and Ellen withdrew her hand from the cabinet. The lights flickered, then died, bringing a creeping blackness into the room. Splatters of rain struck the building's siding, and a downpour began. Amidst bright flashes of light, and deafening claps of thunder, she awoke to the reality of the terrible thing she was contemplating.

I can't do it.

Soon the storm fell silent. An orange glow filtered through the window bathing the laundry room in the amber hue of the setting sun. The holy day of rest was fast approaching. Preparation for tonight's dinner needed to be made. The *Shabbos* table prepared. She must light the candles before sundown and pray for a *shalom bayit*—a domestic peace—to descend upon her family.

She thought again about the box in the back of the overhead cabinet. It was waiting for her.

Just in case.

❦

Sometime before sunset, Sy arrived at the Woodmere train station ten minutes before David's train. He parked, closed his eyes and drifted off. At the rumble of the train, Sy awoke with a start and glanced up just as David stepped out onto the platform. The boy looked around briefly until he spotted the car and then made his way through a light rain toward the parking lot. As the rain increased, his son quickened his pace—weaving in and out through the parked cars like a linebacker.

Sy's stomach twisted into a knot. David looked like any normal twenty-two-year-old: the stooped shoulders were gone; the kid seemed more alert; his complexion was good and the uncharacteristic assurance his son exuded both stunned and worried him. In truth, Sy wasn't paying attention and became sloppy. He reminded himself that control was the key and fear the only way to keep it. He was losing control and needed to re-assert his dominance over the boy.

David opened the back door and threw his duffle on the back seat. It landed on Sy's newly acquired briefcase. The young man's voice was deeper than Sy remembered.

"Hi, Pop."

It irked him how puffed up with confidence David seemed. Almost as if he scored big in the sack. Sy plastered a smile on his face and pulled out of the parking lot. He'd begin gently and ambush the kid later.

"You ready for a home-cooked meal?"

"You bet," David said. "How's mom?"

"Good. Real good. So, tell me, how are things?"

"Okay. Finals are coming up; I'm getting my portfolio ready. I'm planning to look for a job after Easter break."

"Nice to hear." Sy nodded and waited a few beats before asking, "What kind of work are you looking for?" David turned to face him. Sy kept the smile going. The hook was baited—he needed to give the kid time to bite.

David continued enthusiastically. "Well, here's what I'm thinking. I recently got paid seventy-five bucks for twelve hours of free-lance work. That's not bad. They were really impressed too. So, I thought I'd look for some free-lance illustration jobs."

He glanced at his son. "Well, I'm also impressed. Over six dollars an hour is fantastic. Shit, you'll be making over twelve thousand dollars a year. You can begin to support me."

"Very funny Pop. I wouldn't be working forty hours a week. This would be free-lance work. I'd get paid by the piece."

"Oh, so let me understand," he began innocently. "If you work on salary, you get paid less per hour for doing the same work?"

"Right, that's the whole point. It's why I don't want a full-time job. I can make more money per hour freelancing. That way I can pick and choose the jobs I want, and I don't have to work a nine-to-five day. Of course, the bottom line depends on how many jobs I get. But I'm good. I'm sure it will work out."

Got him...

"I see, so what you're telling me is, you plan to live from hand to mouth?" Sy's eyes started to burn. "That's it, huh? So, this is why I break my back to pay for your education—so you can play the dilettante—pick and choose when and how long you work?"

Outside the thunder was moving away. Sy saw his son implode like a trapped animal. The boy twisted in his seat to look out the window. The last flicker of lightning was far-off in the distance.

"I'm talking to you, David."

"I'm s-still in c-college. Give me a ch-ance," he stuttered.

Good, the stammer is back.

"Listen up big shot. The income from free-lance work is unreliable. Ya gonna want to move out into your own place. Rent is due every month. You gotta pay for food and health insurance. It's time to man up to your obligations."

Silence.

He's probably stalling until we get home. Sy eased his foot off the accelerator. "I'm waiting," he prodded.

"Wuh-what obligation?" David asked.

"Whaddayamean what obligation? What are you stupid? I'm talking about supporting yourself. You don't expect me to do it, do you?"

"No, no...Don't worry about it, P-Pop. I'll take care of m-myself."

"Don't worry? What makes you so sure you can pay your bills, huh?"

"I d-don't have any bills."

"You're damn straight you don't." Sy's knuckles turned white from gripping the steering wheel. "I pay your bills. I pay your bills. Hey—maybe I'll stop paying your tuition—how about that wise guy? Then we'll see how goddamn high and mighty you are."

"Wuh-why would you...Oh, fa-fa-get it... 'snot important." David's forehead was leaning against the window. The sky was turning dark again.

"Forget it? How can I forget it? You know, you make highfalutin plans for the future. You've got fancy ideas about what you're gonna do with your life—then you screw up. Don't expect me to pay for your mistakes. And if you think for one moment, I'm going to allow your mother to coddle you. You've got another thing coming."

There was a bright flash—a violent crack of thunder reverberated through the car.

Sy raised his voice, "And by the way mister, when did it become a crime for a father to give his son some advice?"

David didn't respond. The wind started up again. The rain splat hard against the windshield.

"Oh, so now you're not talking. You know, when you start with your know-it-all attitude, I could spit in your face."

"Sorry Pop, I didn't mean—"

"And what the hell is it with you? 'Pop' this, 'Pop' that? Stop calling me 'Pop'. Pop was *my* father. I called *my* father 'Pop'. You don't get to call me that—understand?"

After a few deep breaths, David's words tumbled out of his mouth. "Okay, suh-sorry."

Sy looked across at the cowering shape of his son. His leverage was back, and he was going to keep it that way.

CHAPTER 14

Day 5
Morbid Fixations

Central to his father's control of him was the strict observance of the Sabbath as a day of rest. While David's friends spent Friday and Saturday partying, he was forced to "rest" in observance of an outdated religious custom. Of course, nothing stopped his father from disregarding the religious laws. A fact that prompted David to complain to his mother at breakfast Saturday morning.

"So, I've got to stay home all day?"

"Yes, it's expected. We're Jewish and we follow our religious customs...you know that."

"Dad left early to play golf, didn't he?"

She shifted uneasily in her chair. "Well, yes he did."

"Kinda hypocritical isn't it?"

"Now Davie, let's not start this again."

"Why not?" David leaned over the table to make his point. "Playing golf on the Sabbath is not allowed—you know that. Why can't I follow Dad's example and enjoy my day off?"

Playing golf on Saturday was considered work. The Rabbis reasoned the golf swing and resultant divot, mimicked the whacking motion of the scythe used to mow grass in the eighth century.

"Well, it is a crazy throwback to ancient times," Ellen responded. "But still, it is Jewish law."

David took a different tact. "Okay, putting that silly comparison aside, Dad still violates other traditional laws of the Sabbath. He's doing it this morning: he drove to the club; he'll ride around in a golf cart; pay his green fees with cash and eat a non-kosher lunch. Not to mention the—"

"Why are you so against religion?" she interrupted, clearly annoyed at where the conversation was heading.

"I'm not, I'm against hypocrisy."

"Because he drives on the Sabbath?" She pointed at herself. "I drive on the Sabbath; does that make me a hypocrite?"

"It's different with you—you have a moral compass."

"Oh, so that's it," his mother glanced down at her lap. "Your father tries his best."

"Next you're going to tell me 'He's a diamond in the rough', well I'm sick of hearing it."

She shot him a hurtful look, "Davie..."

David held his palm up to her. "Okay tell me, where's the spiritual commitment of his Jewishness? There's none—his belief is a sham—a clever way to deceive people. I've never seen him make an effort towards any kind of moral transformation. He's as bad as his father—worse maybe."

"What are you talking about? Grandpa Pop was a *Kedoshim*—a holy man," she insisted.

David was flabbergasted, "Oh, so he could do no wrong, correct?"

"Exactly. He was very learned in the Torah; very orthodox in his religious practice," she insisted.

"Wrong," David said shaking his head. "I myself saw him fondling the breasts of my young cousins—the 'holy man' was nothing more than a dirty old man."

She didn't respond. He watched her micro-expressions—they gave her away. She knew all along. "You're constantly sweeping stuff under the rug," he pointed out. "You forget, I've got a long memory."

For a brief while, she was silent, as if searching for something to say. She conceded the point by raising her eyebrows and removing a pack of cigarettes from her apron.

"You're a man now and I'm very proud of you." She searched for her lighter.

"Mom don't. I thought you're trying to quit?"

She frowned and put the pack aside. "I'm going to the store for a while. Come with me. You can study in the backroom and we can go out afterward for a nice lunch. We can talk some more."

David smiled. "I'd like that." She had no idea, nor would he tell her about the CIA, or his hope the FBI would take down her husband. Tractable and scared of her husband, his mother couldn't always be trusted.

He gathered his things and thought, *where is this God she prays to?* Last night wasn't the first time he witnessed her pray for a peaceful home. But despite her prayers, she still lives with an evil man. David believed in her God once, but as he grew older, he couldn't put up with the constant reminders of how a Jew should act and think. He didn't want to meekly take his place as part of an aggrieved minority. To wallow in their history of marginalization so it would always define who he was and what he would always be—a victim. He had no desire to suffer passively for a religion—he suffered enough.

On the way to the store, he asked her, "What time are you driving into the city to pick up Gramps for tomorrow's *Seder?*"

"I want to get there before eleven," his mother replied. "Spend some time with him; maybe take him to lunch; do some shopping for his apartment. I'll start back by three before the traffic."

"Perfect," David said. "Nina invited me for Easter Brunch at eleven. You can drop me off and I'll meet you back at Gramp's apartment after two."

"That will work, but don't tell your father you're having Easter Brunch."

"Okay, fine. But remember Nina's driving out here on Monday."

"I remember," she said. "But you never told me why."

"She has no rehearsals the day after Easter and we want more time together."

"Are you two getting serious?"

"It's past that."

She looked at him sharply. "Marriage serious?"

"Yes, we've already decided."

Silence.

"But she's not Jewish," his mother reminded him.

"That's not an issue."

"It's going to be a problem for your father—a big problem."

"I'm sorry if it's going to put you at odds with him. It can't be helped. I hope you're okay with it."

"Nina's a nice girl and I think she's good for you. But it won't matter to your father. If you insist on marrying her, he'll want her to convert."

"Really? Well, that won't happen."

"Your father will hit the roof. He'll blame me for encouraging you."

"I'm sorry Mom, I really am. I just don't see any way around it."

"Well, we'll deal with it somehow. As long as you're happy. That's all that counts."

"I wish there was a way to make *you* happy."

She smiled. "Seeing you happy will make me happy, Davie."

∽৵

Meanwhile, Chip drove out to Woodmere to snoop on his father again. On each previous occasion he followed Sy, not to the Golf Club as he expected, but to the International House of Pancakes where Sy met once a month with his numbers crew.

Chip perched himself at a nearby table to eavesdrop on his father, Mike, Vinnie, and the controllers running the five drop points. Although they worked for Sy, Chip knew they were all part of Genovese's Manhattan crime family. The unorthodox setup was explained to him many years ago by old-time mobsters in Las Vegas. How, in the mid-1940s, an IRS agent poked around the construction site of the Flamingo Hotel off Route 91 outside Las Vegas.

Chip never knew the IRS agent was his father until two months ago when on her death bed, his mother told him. The affair took place while the agent was the lead investigator dispatched to ferret out the truth surrounding the financing of the hotel. Publicly, the money seemed to come from out-of-town investors, but rumor had it Jewish gangster Bugsy Siegel surreptitiously funneled the money through Mormon-owned banks and was convincing Meyer Lansky and other mobsters to invest along with him.

It turned out Bugsy, Lansky, and the others weren't worried about the IRS. Agent Sy Greenberg had deep connections with Jewish mobsters that went way back to his teenage years in Brownsville. In fact, Bugsy was there in 1925, when Dutch Shultz gave Greenberg the nickname "Little Greenie". Sy Greenberg was one of them: a landsman, a friend of Murder Inc., and best of all, a crooked IRS agent.

Every mobster's dream.

The way the story was told, Sy deflected inquiries into the financing of the hotel and smoothed the way for his old pals to reap big profits. When the Flamingo Hotel opened in 1946, the Syndicate owed Sy a big debt of gratitude. That's why, when Sy returned to New York, he became an auxiliary *Consigliere* to then Mob *Capo*, Anthony Salerno. "Fat Tony" as Salerno was called, eventually rose to become underboss and made Benedetto Moretti, *Capo*.

As underboss, Salerno was too busy, so he made Moretti Sy's handler. Going through Moretti, Sy advised Salerno on financial and tax matters. In return, Salerno allowed him to buy a small numbers operation from old man Trozzo and set himself up as an independent. In those days IRS agents could do no wrong, agent oversight was very slack—Sy's superiors hadn't a clue as to what was going on.

After a while, Sy acted as the de facto underboss of his territory with the Food Mart as his headquarters, Vinnie Trozzo as his *Capo,* and Mike Trozzo a reluctant enforcer. Normally, Moretti wouldn't have stood for it, but Sy was IRS, and his value to Tony Salerno was incalculable. As long as Sy kicked up a percentage of his take every month, Moretti let the insult slide.

Chip knew *Capos* like Moretti—insults were tolerated but never forgiven—they just festered. Moretti would bide his time until Sy fell out of favor. Then, he'd take his revenge without mercy.

Meanwhile every week, Chip watched as Sy walk away from meetings like this one with a Manila envelope full of cash. Chip guessed his father kept a huge stash somewhere in his house. But today the Manila envelope was very thin and Sy was not happy. The beet red face, the spittle flying from his mouth, and the accusatory finger admonishing each of his men, said it all.

Now and then, some of Sy's harsh words floated over to Chip's table. "Uncle Sugar's poking around...Food Mart...Feds set up shop... Moe's Deli for God's sake...."

Chip knew the city was tearing down the neighborhood around Sy's operation. The feds were, as Sy put it, "poking around" the Food Mart. He was losing money and beside himself with anger.

Jack hammering his fingertip against the tabletop, Sy browbeat each controller as he went around the table. No one ate or looked him in the eye; everybody nodded their heads. All except Mike who looked to be on a short fuse.

Sy's spittle stopped flying when he jerked his finger toward his childhood friend. Mike's face turned to stone and his eyes tracked Sy's finger like a bird of prey. When confronted with his old friend's angry face, whatever was on Sy's mind floated unsaid in the air between them, and he backed off.

The men relaxed as his father wrapped up the meeting with what looked to be a bit of false bravado. The crew scoffed down what remained of their breakfasts and left. Sy, Mike, and his brother Vinnie stayed behind.

Chip continued to hear snatches of their conversation.

Vinnie: "...Mikey's not pulling...weight."

Mike on offense: "You asshole, no way...involved."

Sy broke in: "...ing Christ...pain in the ass...piss or...off the pot...."
The finger jabbing continued. Mike's palms went up in front of his
heaving chest. He was shaking his head—*no way*. Vinnie leaned back
smug-like and lit a cigarette.

Chip could tell Mike knew it was a classic setup. His huge hands
curled into sledgehammers and as he stood, his knuckles dug deep
into the table.

Mike leaned his massive frame over Sy. "You owe me...some friend...
treat me...shit." Getting up, Mike trampled through the empty chairs
like they were balsa wood and headed toward the front door. All the
commotion—the banging of chairs, Vinnie yelling after his brother—
made nearby customers uneasy. Mike's anger was palpable and there
was a collective sigh of relief as the door slammed behind him.

Vinnie shook his head in mock disgust, got up and exchanged a few
words with Sy before leaving on the heels of his brother. Left alone, Sy
finished his coffee and headed for the men's room.

Chip asked for the check so he'd be ready to follow Sy to the golf
course. He stifled a yawn but stiffened when two hands gripped his
shoulders.

"You dumb fuck. You look exactly like me when I was your age." His
father moved around from behind and sat down opposite him. "Did
you really think I wouldn't recognize my own son?"

Chip rolled his tongue. "Uh—"

Sy shook his head in disgust. "You've been following me around
for weeks. I'm tired waiting for you to make your move. Where are the
balls I gave you, huh?"

Chip finally found his voice, "And who the fuck are you to talk about
balls—leaving my mother to die like that. I guess "Little Greenie" refers
to the cocktail sausage you hide between your legs."

Sy grinned. "That's more like it—now you're talking like a son of
mine should."

"Like you care."

"I don't care. I know nothing about you. When I do, I might care.
But it depends."

Chip passed his fingers through his long black hair. "On what?"

"On whether or not you've got what it takes to follow in my
footsteps."

"Follow in? What the fuck are you talking about?"

"I'm talking about my legacy, dumb ass. Tell me, who's going to take over everything I've built up all these years—make it an empire?"

Chip made his disdain obvious. "I figured you're gonna pass it on to David."

"That ineffectual pansy. He was ten when I decided he'd never be able to handle it. You should have shown an interest then. Now you gotta prove yourself."

Chips eyes lit up with attention. "What the fuck? You're just going to hand over everything to me?"

"Exactly. You're planning to take it anyway, right? That's why you sneak around—to size me up, get the lay of the land; try to dredge up the courage to take me on."

"I, uh—"

"Well don't bother, one way or another I'm on my way out. I'm getting old and slow. If I don't get out now, either the feds will get me, or I'll die from a heart attack. So, stick around awhile, learn from me and I'll be out of the picture before you know it."

"You're saying team up?"

"Team up? Where the hell do you get 'team up'? Did I say anything about teaming up? Do as I say and stay available that's all. Learn the fucking ins-and-outs and when you prove to me you're ready, it's all yours."

"Just like that?"

"It's not as simple as you think. There's a lot to do to get my operation up and running again. First, we need to wiggle out from under Uncle Sugar's thumb. When the feds leave, we move in again. I've got the money, contacts, and the know-how. From what I hear, you've got the cunning, strength, and guts."

Sy jack-hammered his finger against the table again. "But you're going to have to wing it until the city finishes with their rebuilding program—move your drop points from one empty building to another—that kind of thing. I'll give you enough seed money to get it going after the feds clear out. As your advisor, I get twenty-percent the first year and ten every year after that."

"Okay, what do I do first?"

"You gotta get rid of Mike Trozzo."

"What?"

"You heard me. I gotta know you've got what it takes. You in or out?"

Chip paused a moment before responding, "I'm in."

"Good, you need to fix up his van with a pineapple—set it up like they do in Vegas—do it on the weekend so he goes up in smoke next week."

"Okay."

"Also, keep an eye on David for me. Tell me where he goes, who he sees. Here..." Sy dug in his pocket and took out a key ring. "The key to Jacob's apartment—just in case."

Chip put the key in his pocket. "Where am I supposed to pick up a pineapple?"

"You got a pencil? Good, here it is." Sy wrote the address of an explosives guy who owed him a favor. "I'll call him to expect you. Don't play wise guy with him, he's got a short fuse."

"Very funny," Chip said.

"I'm giving you five-hundred bucks." He dug into his Manila envelope. "Pay him and get one of those new pagers. Set it up so I can reach you. Gimme your phone number."

Chip wrote it on a napkin and handed it across.

"I phone *you*. You never call me, understand?"

"I understand, it's no big deal." Chip fingered the bills—a celebration was in the air.

"Listen dumb ass, this is a big deal. More money than you ever dreamed of. Power and influence like you've never imagined. True, you won't have the muscle of the IRS behind you, but the amount of dirt I've got on people guarantees your success."

This was news to him. "I had no idea...."

"Of course, you didn't. That's why you need to listen up. The seed money I'm going to give you isn't play dough. It's operating capital. I phone you, tell you what to do and you spend it on the operation. Use it on booze and broads and you're toast. Both here and in Vegas. There'll be no place you can go. You'll end up washing dishes."

Chip tried to illicit some fatherly concern. "I just want to belong somewhere—make some real money. I've been kicked around my whole life."

"Christ, am I talking to David, or my own son?" His father leaned in on him to drive the point home. "Forget about all that touchy-feely shit and man up. I'm making you my right-hand man. Do as you're told and don't get any ideas of your own, otherwise, you're out on your ass. Understand?"

Chip tried another approach, "Sure, thanks...thanks a lot."

"I don't want your goddamn thanks. I want your loyalty. Whacking Mike goes a long way in winning it."

It took a while for Chip to respond.

"Hey, wake up! Is all this too confusing for you?"

"No, you have a nosebleed that's all."

❧

It was late in the afternoon when David and his mother left the sportswear shop and arrived home to find a delivery truck in front of the house. A man in overalls was off-loading a tall carton and placing it on a two-wheeler. David got out of the car and approached him.

The man wiped his hands on his overalls and picked up a clipboard. "Delivery for Greenberg. Sign here please."

David looked at the invoice and his heart sank.

Shit, a new file cabinet...How the hell am I supposed to break into this?

CHAPTER 15

Day 6
The Hideaway

During the early part of 1955, Sy "found" several tax code violations in the returns of a construction company. The frightened builder facing stiff fines and a ruined reputation, was willing to negotiate a manageable price for a three-bedroom, two-bath home—if Sy looked the other way.

Sy made him sweat it out by haggling over details. By the time a deal was struck, the builder agreed to a handful of off-the-books upgrades—among them a hidden closet to be built in an empty space across from the air-conditioning unit in the attic. He instructed the builder to put in shelving and leave room for a five-foot file cabinet.

The hideaway was to be Sy's command center. A secret space where he could hide everything to do with his nefarious empire. But Sy never used it. On moving into the house, his wife decided to put David in the two attic bedrooms. An exhaust fan was installed in one to make a small studio, while the other became David's bedroom. The kid was up there day and night. Sy could only access his attic hideaway when David wasn't home.

But now David was graduating and moving out of the house for good—the hideaway could be used in earnest. Legitimate files would stay in his office in the new file cabinet. Records pertaining to his gambling operation would be transferred to the old file cabinet he would move to the attic hideaway.

And he couldn't wait to get started. Sy thought about it during Saturday night's *Seder* at his brother's house. He could hardly sleep that night and he woke up Sunday well before breakfast to lock himself in his office. He emptied the old file cabinet, dumping the household stuff and other harmless files on the couch. Then, he piled his bookmaking and Mob related folders on the desk and the credenza next to it.

Across the hall, he heard his wife get up to use the bathroom. He had to hurry. Close to three dozen rolls of cash remained in the file cabinet. He dumped them in an overnight bag along with his fake driver's licenses and passports, locked the office and went down to the garage to put the bag in the trunk of his car. With the feds snooping around he wanted to be able to move at a moment's notice.

By the time he came up from the garage, breakfast was on the table and the family ate in silence for a while. Soon, Ellen and David would be gone most of day to pick up Jacob from the city. Sy asked his wife for more coffee and turned to David. "After breakfast, give me a hand with the large box in the garage."

"Sure," David said, "no problem."

Twenty minutes later father and son dragged the huge box into the house in preparation to move it up the stairs. Sy positioned himself above David on the upper end of the box leaving David to lift from the downward, heavier end. He always took every opportunity to undermine his son's self-confidence and he couldn't wait to see his son falter under the weight of the file cabinet.

"Tilt it toward me," he ordered. "I'll grab it and you lift from your end."

David leaned the box against the steps and hoisted the box from the bottom. Sy took his time lifting his end, and when he did, he fudged a little to make David's side even heavier.

To his surprise, David took the additional weight without difficulty. He had expected the boy to drop his end or, at the very least, struggle under the weight.

By the time they reached the first landing, Sy was winded.

"Gotta pee," he said, and went to take a breather in the bathroom. When he came out, David already moved the box up the last set of stairs—by himself.

He couldn't believe it. "How did you manage to get it up the stairs by yourself?"

"Simple, I leaned it over the stairs and pushed from below—it slid up on the carpeting."

This was not what Sy expected. David's quiet display of strength on the first set of stairs and his quick ingenuity pushing it up the second set was worrisome. To make matters worse, as they moved the box into the middle of the office, David glanced covertly around the room and blinked.

Sy watched his son and thought, *again with the goddamn blinking?*

The first time David blinked like that he was ten years old. Sy caught the little brat standing on a chair in front of his open file cabinet. David's little hand gripped the top drawer. He was peeking inside.

Blink, blink, blink...

He gave the boy a beating. The crybaby dropped in a heap to the carpet and convulsed. For weeks afterward, David experienced a series of fits with fainting spells. Ellen was beside herself with worry, but the boy never mentioned the beating.

The first specialist said the seizures were psychogenic events caused by mild trauma. They would pass. David was put on a short-term dose of mild sedatives. He became quiet, withdrawn, and less inquisitive. Sy preferred him that way and arranged for another specialist to make a different diagnosis. One which required David to be permanently sedated.

Over time, David's fixation with the file cabinet never disappeared. Now, with all his secret papers strewn around the room, David's presence was a liability. He put a hand on David's shoulder, thanked him, and ushered him out of the room. The sooner he transferred the files up to the attic the better.

A half-hour later, Sy heard the garage door open and close—Ellen and David were gone. He climbed the stairs to the attic and entered the storage closet. At the back wall, he switched on the overhead light over the air-conditioning unit.

Moving around the unit into the semi-darkness, Sy stopped before a studded wall. He moved some boxes aside and peeled the insulated batting from the wall to reveal a sturdy padlock. Keying it open, he pulled on the latch and opened the camouflaged door to his hidden closet. Inside, a box of cash was stacked up in the middle of the floor. Shelves held more money in Manila envelopes.

It took three trips up the stairs to relocate all his secret files and one more trip to bring the empty boxes up from his car. Then, leaving the hideaway open, he went back to his office to move the old file cabinet up to the attic.

It's only one flight of stairs...If David can do it, so can I.

Grabbing hold of the cabinet in a bear hug he tried to lift it. Too heavy—heavier than the new one. He tipped it over toward the office door, laying it down on its side. Getting on his hands and knees, he pushed it out the door. Near the stairs, it got hung up on the rug. He crawled around to the front and straddling the cabinet with his feet, pulled up on a drawer handle to free the snag.

His back went out.

Fuck, fuck, fuck!

Sy's fist came down on the side of the cabinet.

More pain. A drop of blood fell from his nose onto the cold steel.

He sniffed back the flow of blood and ran a hairy forearm under his nose. He lay on top of the cabinet, his arms draped over its sides. There was no one to call, he was all alone.

After twenty minutes, the pain subsided enough for him to crawl back into the office. Still on the floor, he leaned against the front of the sofa and reached up behind him for a throw pillow. As he placed it behind the small of his back, he caught sight of a bottle of scotch on the side table. Keeping his back braced against the sofa, he slid himself painfully toward it. Reaching up he grabbed hold of the bottle and after catching his breath, took a long swig.

Everything is fucked up—work—the numbers racket—fuckin' family—now my back.

In time, he got woozy from the scotch. His mind drifted and the episode on the stairs came back to him. David—the little piece of shit handling the file cabinet with hardly any effort at all. Sy's own breath coming fast and short while his arms felt like they were being pulled out of their sockets.

In Sy's alcoholic haze, a vision of his old age crept slowly into his mind. He saw himself in a wheelchair; drool dribbling down the side of his mouth. David had the key to the file cabinet and was swinging it back and forth in front of his face. Ellen carried boxes of money down from the attic and put them in her station wagon. All the while Sy's parents looked on, his mother weeping while his father, wrapped in *Tefillin* with a large *Tallis* around his head, recited the mourner's *Kaddish.*

Yis-gah-dal, ve-yis-ka-dash, she-mei ra-ba....

Sy shook his head to throw off the nightmare—the pain now a dull ache. He took another sip of scotch and pulled down the old photo album from the sofa. As he turned the pages the memories came flooding back: his boyhood in Brownsville, the gangsters, the gambling, the money and the girls.

His trip to Vegas.

At twenty-six, he was assigned lead investigator into the alleged takeover of the Flamingo Hotel by the syndicate. He met Brooke and became obsessed with her. Blonde, sultry, stacked, and completely uninhibited. She was forbidden fruit, yet he couldn't keep away from her.

The stupid *shiksa* got pregnant, and no way would his father allow him to marry a non-Jew. He cut a deal with her and asked one of the Vegas boys handle it. He sent money, and later more money for Chip's education. But by that time Brooke was into drugs and the money disappeared.

That's why he married Ellen—he was hemorrhaging money—he needed a leg-up. Skimping and saving wasn't his style. He wanted to live large; Ellen could introduce him into society. He could garner influence and favors that would open up endless opportunities.

Another swig. Maybe he could have done it without Ellen? And what about Brooke, would she have turned to drugs if he hadn't left? He had the hots for her—her smell—the long blond hair—the young body. If he was capable of loving anyone other than his mother, it might have been Brooke.

But God wouldn't allow it.

ও৵ৎ

Ellen knew little about Nina's parents other than her stepfather was a renowned neuropsychologist and her mother married him a few years after her move to the States. It seemed an odd match—a Jewish doctor and a divorced Catholic celebrating Easter Sunday. That David was invited to brunch was also strange, and Ellen attempted to learn more about Nina's parents as they drove into the city.

According to David, Elsita Caldas was a woman of contradictions. She gave the impression of being a strong, independent woman. Yet, her decision to marry Doctor Broder was one of convenience and David thought she was trapped in a loveless marriage from which she could not escape. The description struck very close to home. Ellen's own decision to marry Sy was much the same, and as she dropped David off in front of Nina's Park Avenue apartment, she wondered if her son thought the same about her own marriage.

Ellen drove across town to Jacob's apartment and found a parking space along 88th Street. She entered the familiar lobby, and when she approached the old elevator, a host of painful memories returned. For her, the tiny cage was like a time machine. She stepped in, closed the rickety gate and pressed the button for the second floor. With a whir and groan the ancient pulleys lifted her into a world of yesterdays.

It was 1946 when she slipped into this elevator to sequester herself in her parent's apartment. There, she hid her shame from society until, a year later she left to begin a life of lies and compromise with Sy Greenberg. Although the ride took less than half a minute, the horrible years of war and disillusionment rushed towards her from the past. With it came the remembered promise of her youth—the pangs of young love—all lost to time.

On the second floor, the dark gloomy hallway bore no resemblance to the mirrored corridor that once led to the Goldstein's opulent nine room apartment. After the war, the building's owner divided it into two separate units. As her father's fortunes fell, her dreams of happiness fell with them.

Now, standing in the hallway, she tried to imagine her mother opening the door. Smiling, caressing her cheek, and telling her all would be well. Instead, the memory of her mother's blood-soaked body floated in the bathtub before her. She choked back her tears and rang the bell. When Jacob opened the door, she noticed the redness under his eyes and the past dissolved in an instant.

"Dad, is something wrong? It looks like you were crying."

"What cry? All right, a little maybe." Jacob gave her a nod and weak smile, "Listen, I'm okay. Don't worry yourself. Come, I'll tell you the whole *magillah*."

Ellen followed Jacob into the living room and sat down next to him on the couch. "What's going on Dad?"

"Foist, you should know—I'm all right. I see things clearer now, and listen, it's not such a bad thing to see your mistakes before you die. But before that happens, I need to tell you...how sorry I am."

She put a hand on his arm. "Dad, you're worrying me. You're not dying?"

"Oy no, not yet. But I need your forgiveness—for what I didn't do for you, for the family—I'm sorry."

"Oh, Dad, I've never heard you talk like this. I don't think you should do this to yourself."

"No? Then when? When should I make amends, after I'm dead? No—a *gemeyn foter*—that's what I was—a lousy father and a rotten husband. I thought of nobody else. It was always what I wanted—

everybody suffered. David also—right under my nose all these years—my own grandson. And what did I do? *Bupkis*, that's what. *Bupkis*."

She saw the tears roll down and disappear into the creases etched into his face. Her stomach knotted up. What happened to precipitate such a reaction in this once self-possessed, self-centered man?

"Okay Dad, take a couple of breaths and calm down, I'll get you a tissue."

She got up and came back with a box of tissues and a glass of water.

"Water you give me?" he said, dabbing his eyes. "A little scotch is better. And I'm thinking also, maybe you should have one too."

She went over to the sideboard and poured the drinks with a trembling hand. A lifetime of parental indifference skidded to an abrupt end, and she was ill-prepared for it. She listened as her father recounted his sins of omission. Never had she witnessed such a genuine display of contrition. Not even when, as a youngster, she went to Synagogue on *Yom Kippur* and watched from the women's section as her father beat his chest in atonement.

Afterward, sadness was in his eyes. "So, now you know and God willing, with what little time I have left, maybe I can help you and David."

"Help? Dad I—"

"What, you think I don't see how unhappy you are? And David—such anger he carries. Come..." he got up. "We'll go into David's room. I'll show you what I found."

Ellen couldn't believe it all: *The Sacrifice of Issac* with the knife at Sy's throat, the illustrations with the Asher signature, the savings book, and the letter from Bell Labs. Like her father, Ellen needed to read it several times before understanding its full meaning and her part in letting it happen.

She put the letter down and closed her eyes against the weakness that defined her life. Before her lay the still-born dreams of her childhood—thrown away for the sake of appearances. That, and her inability to struggle for the things she believed in, all led to the dead-end life she lived.

Ellen looked up at her father and caught the pained look on his face and she stifled a cry. She realized it all had to end, and remembering the rat poison in the laundry room, she held her father in a steely gaze.

"So, help me Dad, this time I'll kill him."

∽๛

It was almost two when Sy awoke from his alcohol-induced nap. Getting up slowly, he twisted his torso from side to side and found it easy to move around. But he would have to be careful—another strain and he would be out of commission again.

In the bathroom, he took a bunch of pain killers, and put on his back brace. His stomach grumbled, and he went downstairs to raid the refrigerator. As he ate, he realized everything needed to be put in order before his wife returned with David and Jacob. If he asked David to help him move the old file cabinet from the hallway floor back to his office, embarrassing questions would be asked. He'd have to do it himself.

Fifteen minutes later, Sy was pulling the drawers out of the old file cabinet. Then, careful not to sprain his back again, he managed to move the cabinet back into the office. Still strewn around the room were household files, inventory sheets from Ellen's sportswear shop, IRS bulletins, a cash box and two old photo albums. Sy dumped them all back in the old file cabinet and locked it.

The good news was every compromising piece of paper was now in the attic hideaway. The bad news was both the old and new file cabinets where now in his office. He'd have to find another opportunity to move the old file cabinet.

He trudged up the stairs one last time, padlocked the door, stuffed the insulation back into the false wall and stacked the boxes up in front of it. After shutting off the lights and moving out to the hallway, he noticed the open door to David's bedroom. He wandered in and poked through the kid's duffle bag on the chair. Packed amongst the clothes was a small watercolor kit, a Polaroid camera with extra film and a sketchbook. He flipped idly through its pages, the drawings holding little interest for him.

He stopped. There was a name and phone number scribbled in one of the margins.

Hawkins, PE6-8732 ext. 4676.

CHAPTER 16

Day 7
The Break-in

Early Monday morning, Nina slipped behind the wheel of her Fiat. She planned to arrive at the Greenberg home no later than nine-thirty to give David enough time to break into his father's filing cabinet. During the drive, she thought about David's toxic relationship with his father.

She met Sy Greenberg several times. No two personalities could be any different. Where David was gentle, sensitive, and caring, his father was heartless and crude. As hard as she looked, she couldn't find any physical resemblance they had in common. It was one of the reasons she encouraged David to look for his birth certificate.

If she was right and Greenberg was not his father, she wondered how David would handle it. Everyone in his family believed David was calm and reasonable—sometimes bordering on the compliant. But she met him after he weaned himself off the phenobarbital. The new David was nothing like the old one. If David found out he was lied to there was no telling what would happen.

It was an hour later when she turned onto Woodmere Boulevard. Woodmere was one of the more affordable of the Five Towns. It attracted middle-class Jewish families like the Greenberg's, who aspired to hobnob with wealthier homeowners living in the neighboring townships of Cedarhurst and Lawrence. She entered Greenberg's neighborhood and pulled into the driveway of their split-level home. The first time Nina saw it she blanched. It was the only house on the block with a tacky turquoise colored siding. Inside the drapes were also turquoise, and the rug had yellow pee stains from a now-deceased family dog.

As David came out to greet her, she gathered the supplies he asked for and got out of the car.

After a long embrace he said, "I've missed you."

She smiled. "And I you. Are you ready for this?"

"I guess. My dad was in his office all day yesterday transferring stuff to the new file cabinet. The old one is in the middle of the floor now. It might be empty."

"Well, let's hope it isn't." Nina handed him the bag of supplies.

"Thanks. I'm all set then. All I need is for you to stand outside the door and let me know if my mom comes back or Gramps walks up the stairs for his nap. By the way, he doesn't like being here. Don't be surprised if he asks you to drive him back to the city."

Several minutes later, Nina stood in the hallway outside Sy's office and watched David line up his tools and other supplies on the floor next to the file cabinet. Its dull, battered surface attested to decades of use, the gold-like finish covering the handles worn away.

She noticed a childlike fear cross David's face. Was it the fear of being discovered or a fear of discovering an unknown truth? Whichever it was, she knew he was confronting the demons of his childhood and needed to be alone. As she closed the door, she thought she heard the pounding in David's chest.

In the hallway, she realized the thumping was her own.

Alone now, David stood in front of his father's dilapidated file cabinet and pictured himself the day when he was ten. As a child his head barely reached the third drawer. He felt small and powerless, but even then, he suspected his father's darkest secrets were hidden inside.

They were still living in the apartment at the time. His mother was out and Sy took him to the corner drugstore. He left Davie at the lunch counter and wandered over to browse the magazine rack. While the boy sipped his soda, he recognized a man peering through the drugstore window. Sy too saw the man and turning beet red, dashed out the door to confront him. An argument ensued with Sy pushing the man away from the window. In time, his father came back in, paid for a magazine, and whisked Davie out of the store.

Back at the apartment, Davie spotted his father stuffing the magazine in the top drawer of his filing cabinet. Later, he snuck into his father's office while his father was watching the football game. The file cabinet was unlocked, and pulling over a chair, he stepped up and opened the top drawer. A stack of girlie magazines lay inside. On the cover of one, a naked woman smiled at him.

Blink, blink, blink.

He felt a presence and turned his head to see his father's huge frame filling the door. The wild eyes were on him. A red splotch broke over his father's forehead and spread into the adjacent skin until his entire face was beet red. The cruel mouth twitched and in two long strides, the beast was upon him.

"What did you see!" yelled his father, "What did you see!"

Uncontrollable fear made Davie freeze on the spot. The boy's head swam, his heart pounded, and the room tilted. "Nuh...nuh-thing, nothing." The room kept moving to the left. There was a horrible taste in his mouth and, all at once, the floor wasn't there. Davie held onto the ledge of the cabinet drawer as if hanging from a precipice.

"You're damned right you saw nothing," Sy bellowed. "I'm the only one. I'm your father... you think you can sneak...you're not...I'm going to teach you...."

The slaps came in rapid succession. Face, ears, neck, and shoulders. Flecks of spittle flew from the creature's mouth. The boy was a rag under the man's bulk.

Then a ringing began in Davie's ears. Terrible whirling lights and oscillating colors obscured his vision as a dark curtain descended over him. He dropped into a void and careened down an unending tunnel of pulsating sounds and violent tremors.

Sometime later he was diagnosed as epileptic. He was never the same again.

David shook off the memory. It was twelve years since he saw the man behind the drugstore window, and he still didn't know who he was. The childhood memory became a recurring nightmare which ultimately formed the basis of his senior painting project. This was the moment he waited for since his childhood—there could be no turning back now. Would he finally unearth his father's secrets? Or would he find he was obsessing over the wild imaginings of a ten-year-old boy?

He grabbed hold of the top-drawer handle and pulled.

Nothing.

He pulled again.

A loud snap and the drawer rolled open. He tried the others, but they wouldn't budge. David rolled the top drawer all the way out and using a flashlight, looked inside at the locking mechanism. He found a hook at the opposite end of the lock with a long rod attached. He figured once the lock cylinder was pushed in, the rod moved down and locked all the drawers. To reverse the process, he undid the cotter pin holding the rod to the lock cylinder. He lifted the rod up and the remaining drawers opened.

He was in.

The top drawer had all the stuff he'd seen as a teenager: adult magazines; two Crown Royal bags filled with old silver dollars; a box of fake army medals which wowed him when he was a kid; American Legion stuff; a metal plate engraved "Internal Revenue Service, Official Business" and various keepsakes from another life. The remembered musty smell was still there.

Oddly, the other drawers were practically empty with hanging folders thrown in haphazardly. The subjects on the folder tabs were varied: tax forms, IRS Bulletins, household papers, and inventory sheets from his mother's sportswear shop. The medical folder held three smaller Manila envelopes: Medical (Sy), Medical (Ellen), and Medical (David).

He removed his medical file and inserted a screwdriver to mark its place. There were medical bills, x-rays, and doctor's reports. The neurologist's report confirmed the diagnosis of grand mal epilepsy. It described a recommended daily medication and the need for follow-ups and further testing.

The next report, written at an earlier date was from a different neurologist. His diagnosis described a pseudo-seizure of psychological origin. It indicated a short-term regime of phenobarbital and the prognosis: "with time and understanding the child will most likely stabilize and the seizures will disappear."

So, Nina was right after all—his father was keeping him drugged. The first diagnosis describing a non-epileptic event was the truth. His father deliberately arranged for a second diagnosis to keep him permanently sedated. What had he ever done to make his own father hate him so much? How could his mother not know? Why did she allow it to happen? He wanted to scream. He saw himself tearing into the couch with the screwdriver, gauging the wood furniture, destroying everything in the office.

But he held himself back. There was no time for anger now. The goal was to find the evidence that would put his father away for a long time. He returned the medical file and opened another drawer to discover two photo albums and a metal cash box. He flipped through the first album stopping at a photograph taken from under an elevated subway station. It featured a group of his father's friends in their early twenties standing in front of a candy store. Along its deckled edge his father wrote, *Midnight Rose's*. He lingered long enough to etch a few photographs into his memory and went on to the second album.

It contained his parents' wedding pictures. The usual black and white photos of family and friends celebrating the union of two happy people. *Odd*, he thought, *I've never seen these pictures before*. As he turned the pages, the door opened, and Nina stuck her head in.

"Find anything yet?" she asked tentatively.

"Well, you were right. My misdiagnosis of epilepsy was intentional. I'll explain later. Meanwhile, there's this," he handed her the album.

She looked through the album and said, "Your mother's not wearing white."

"Oh, well it was the war, maybe the dress was too expensive."

"I thought your grandfather was rich?"

"Yeah, they said he was. That is strange."

"Let me know if you find anything else." She went out and closed the door.

He returned the albums to the drawer and picked up the metal cash box. It was locked, but the hinge was on the outside. He removed the long hinge pin with a needle nose pliers and the lid popped off. Inside were some stocks and bonds, a sealed brown envelope, and a yellowed copy of a marriage license application.

He gazed over the document, found a date, and panicked.

✌︎❧

Nina opened the door again. She took one look at David and her heart skipped a beat. "What's wrong, you're white as a sheet?"

"I found this," he said, pushing the paper onto her. "Read it—under date of marriage."

Nina took the document and closed the door behind her. It was a marriage certificate and gave the year of his parents' marriage as 1947. David was born in 1941, months before the attack on Pearl Harbor.

She was right after all—Sy Greenberg was not David's father.

"Oh David, I'm so sorry." Yes, she was sorry. But deep inside she felt a wave of relief. He was not the offspring of that horrible man. She returned the certificate to him and sat down on the couch. "Sit next to me for a moment, you look like you're going to faint."

He sat with his head in his hands. "My whole life's one big lie. Who the hell am I? Some kind of bastard? How many people knew the truth? How many times did friends and relatives pile lie on top of lie with those condescending smiles of theirs?" He leaned back against the cushions, his eyes darting around the room like a lost puppy.

She held his hand, her eyes wandering over the contents of the cash box. "What's that thick brown envelope?" she asked.

He removed it and turned it over. "It's says "Last Will and Testament".

She saw him waver a second before putting a finger under the flap of the envelope. "What are you doing?" Nina protested. "You can't do that—opening a man's Will is wrong."

"Shut up!"

She was shocked. This was David at his rawest and it frightened her. Yes, he was impolite at times, but only when alcohol loosened his tongue. There was no wine to blame this time and she looked at him sharply.

"I'm sorry, Nina, but it's gone too far. They lied to me and I'm going to do this."

Nina knew he was right. The magnitude of the deception was immense. "Wait, we'll steam it open. Boil some water, ask Jacob if he'd like a cup of tea."

Within minutes, the water was boiling, and the envelope opened. She placed it in a kitchen drawer. "I'll pour the tea; we'll look at it later." They sat sipping tea and making small talk with Jacob until he finally thanked them and left the kitchen. Nina removed the envelope from the drawer and they both went to the office where they sat on the couch again. With the envelope now open they could see something written on the inside flap.

Nassau 84659098630-3.

"What does it mean?" She asked him.

"I don't know. Maybe a file number for the court—we live in Nassau County. Hard to say." She saw him blink briefly before removing the Will. He flipped through the pages scanning each until the page turning stopped. His breath came heavy, short, and once again he became pale.

"What is it? What did you find?"

David passed the Will to her.

"My real name is David Aschbacher."

CHAPTER 17

Stench of Truth

Nina scanned the page and found the passage: "...and to David Aschbacher, son of my wife Ellen by a former marriage, I bequeath..."

The shock of David's discovery weighed heavily on them both. It was one thing to have suspicions about David's parentage, but to face the naked truth of it—the immense implications were hard to grasp. They sat together in silence for a long while until they heard the garage door open.

David jumped up, resealed the envelope and returned everything to the file cabinet. "Go downstairs and keep my mom occupied while I finish up. I'll join you as soon as I can."

Nina scrambled down the stairs as Ellen came in from the garage with a shopping bag. "Can I help you with that?" Nina asked.

"No, I've got it," Ellen answered. "But why don't you make some iced tea while I put the sandwiches out on plates. Where's Davie?"

"Upstairs, I'll let him know you're back." Nina lingered outside the kitchen to make sure Ellen stayed put and bounded up the stairs.

"It's me," Nina announced. "Your mother brought lunch. Hide the tools and other stuff. We'll return them later."

"What will I say to her? How am I going to get through this?" David asked her.

"I'll take care of it," she answered. "Just watch what you say and try to keep your expression cheerful."

At lunch, Nina monopolized the conversation, asking a half dozen questions about Ellen's sportswear shop and her newest lines of clothes. Jacob chimed in with stories from his days in the dress business. Ellen seemed incredibly happy to have her family around.

But David withdrew into himself, and Nina could tell his mother noticed. "All this talk about women's clothing is boring him," Nina said, and changing the subject, mentioned they planned to go to the World's Fair.

David put his fork down and looked up from his plate. "Oh yeah, they're going to have Michelangelo's Pieta on display, and a reproduction of—"

The phone rang and Ellen got up to answer it. "Hello. Yes, he's here. Just a moment." She stretched out the cord and gave David the phone. "It's for you...a Jim Hawkins."

David put the phone to his ear and as he listened, his face fell. "Certainly, no problem...tomorrow morning. Thank you. See you then." He hung up and looked at his mother. "Uh, sorry mom, a client wants a project a week early. We have to go back to the city."

"Oh, I'm going in on Wednesday," she said. "I can drive you in then."

"Thanks, but I need at least two days to finish the assignment," David replied. "I'll be finished Wednesday afternoon. Pick me outside the Met Museum and we can drive back together."

✌

David slumped down in the passenger seat while Nina backed her Fiat out of the driveway and headed back to the city.

"The call was from the FBI right?" Nina asked.

"Right."

"And they want to question you tomorrow morning?"

"Yes, and am I glad they called. It gave me an opportunity to get away."

"So you lied." Nina said.

Annoyed, David snapped at her, "Okay, so I lied. I would think you could let it slide this time. I had to get away. Under the circumstances, I think it's justified."

She paused slightly, "You're right, but so you know—your mom looked disappointed."

"Oh really? Well, I'm kinda disappointed myself. She's the one who lied to me for over twenty years. Why is she allowed a free pass, but I'm not?"

Nina understood his anger and drove on in silence while he sat still as a stone with his head dropped to his chest. After driving several blocks, she pulled over to the curb and faced him. "I'm sorry I mentioned the lying," she said feebly. "It's kind of automatic with me. Forgive me for bringing it up."

When David looked at her, she saw the pained expression in his eyes. "She lied to me... my own mother." Tears welled up and he looked away, "God, oh God...my whole life—one fucking lie."

As they headed down Peninsula Boulevard, he straightened up in his seat and let out a long sigh. "All this time I thought I was the devil's spawn. Now I'm finally free of that bastard. I'm sorry I was so stubborn about looking for my birth certificate."

"Don't worry about it," she said. "What's important is you have time to think about your reaction. Whatever you feel you can't hurt your mother. You're the only family she has."

He looked out the window. "I never suspected—not even once. I feel like such a fool."

"You're not a fool," she said. "You were a child. And you were drugged. I know it's an easy excuse, but it's the truth and you've got to accept it—put it behind you—move on."

"Easier said than done—especially for me."

"I can only imagine what it's like for you—remembering every terrible moment of your life in such detail. What I don't understand is, you've got this super-duper memory, yet you can't remember your real father—this guy Aschbacher?"

"I tried to figure it out during lunch," he said. "You're familiar with the Orwellian concept of the Memory Hole, right?"

"Wasn't it like a trash bin for inconvenient truths?"

"Exactly. So, the way I see it, anything having to do with the identity of my real father was dumped into this memory hole—figuratively speaking—and was forgotten."

"How?"

"I think it was a combination of the Phenobarbital, the lies my mother told me, and his constant browbeating. I don't think the memories disappeared—they've just become twisted, incomplete; hazy."

"Like your painting of the drugstore dream?"

"Of all my lost memories, it's the most persistent, but there are others."

"Tell me one."

"Well, it's always the same. I'm in a highchair. Several beads are strung along a ridged wire running along the edge of my tray table.

My fingers are sliding colored beads back and forth. The beads are all mixed up and I'm trying to put them in order. Reds with the reds, yellows with the yellows, and so on. But they won't come off the wire. I'm slapping my hands on the tray in frustration. I need to put them in order.

"I look up and a man is sitting in front of me with a bowl of food in his hand. I see a uniform with shiny metal stuck to his collar. His long fingers hold a spoon out in front of my face. I sense his kindness, but I can't make out his features. They're all fogged over. But there's something special about the man because when he speaks, I feel good inside. 'Davie', he's saying. 'Open wide, Davie.'"

"Did you ever ask your mother about it?"

"Sure. I recall how flustered she became—didn't know what to say for a while. When I told her the man's face was blurry, she relaxed. I asked, 'It's gotta be dad, right? But how can that be when he was still in Australia during the war?'" David shook his head. "She ended up telling me it was Uncle Marty home on leave.

"It was a good enough answer when I was kid, but as I got older I thought about her answer and it didn't make sense. I reasoned if it really was Uncle Marty, I would have recognized his face. After all, I could remember my mother's face from the same time—before she got her nose job."

"You never told me your mother had a nose job."

"Didn't seem important I guess," he replied. "My Aunt Rose had one too."

"So grandpa Jacob really was well off," she mused.

"Well, that's what they say. But, given what I found out today, I don't know what's truth and what's fiction."

Nina agreed and they became lost in their own thoughts until she broke the silence.

"David, if the man in front of the high chair was your father, it means the man you saw outside the drugstore was your father."

"You're right," David said. "Both faces were blurred out in my memory. If I can find a photo of my real father, I can finish my painting."

"Well, at least you don't have to feel guilty about changing your name anymore," she added. "Have you heard from the lawyer?"

"Yes, I forgot to tell you. The name change went through the court and they're finalizing the documents now. I should have the papers in enough time to get a diploma in my new name. So, it's official. I'm no longer David Greenberg."

"Turns out you never were," Nina said. "You changed your last name from Greenberg to Asher before knowing your real father's name. I hope you don't decide to change it again."

"Why?"

"Don't you think Nina Asher, has a better ring to it than Nina Aschbacher?"

"That is a mouth-full. Don't worry David Asher is well known on Madison Avenue. It's foolish to start my career with another name. You can count on being Mrs. David Asher for a long time."

"David Asher. From now on that's how you should think of yourself," Nina suggested. "It's time to bury little Davie Greenberg for good. That identity was foisted upon you by cruel circumstance. Mr. Asher is who you were meant to be. Thinking of yourself that way will help everyone see you the way I do—smart, strong, confident, and very handsome."

"I, David Asher, take this woman...."

"And I take this very handsome man."

After driving on for a while, they crossed into Manhattan on the Queensborough Bridge. The aroma of freshly baked bread from the Silvercup Bakery made her mouth water. "What do you say we go out for dinner; get some comfort food. Then well, we've got your grandfather's apartment all to ourselves."

She gave him that look.

❧

They decided on Chinese takeout. It was fast, convenient and they wanted to be alone. It was too late for Nina to arrange an overnight alibi her mother would accept, so they had only four hours before she would need to go home.

At Jacob's apartment, Nina emptied the food onto plates while David opened a bottle of wine. They sat in the small kitchen drinking, nibbling on egg rolls, and talking about the next morning's interview at FBI headquarters.

"Are you going to tell the FBI everything?" she asked. "How Mike is being harassed by his brother and why you spend so much time at his store?"

He looked idly out the window. "Yes everything. Mike, the gangsters, the truth about my father. Wait, I should call him by his name now. I'll tell them about Sy's childhood, that he's not my real father—maybe try to get them to find out what happened to Aschbacher. They should be able to identify him through a marriage license."

"Aschbacher," Nina repeated. "Not a particularly Jewish name, is it?"

"Doesn't seem so," David replied. "Maybe it's how I got my middle name. Asher could be a derivative of Aschbacher. What do you think?"

Nina nodded. "Probably. Could be your mother intended to tell you the truth and wanted you to carry something of your father's name. I'm sure your father...I mean Sy...wouldn't let her tell you. Stepfathers are like that."

David's blue eyes turned to ice. "Fucking bastard. There's no way he's going to get away with this."

"Don't wallow in hate David. You can walk away from him with a free conscious now. Forget him. Everything's over and done with, it's in the past. Dredging it all up, again and again—it's not healthy."

He reached for the wine and poured out two more glasses. "I know you're right," he paused and drank half the glass. "But I can't stop remembering—it's not as if I can shut it off—everything comes back—so fresh, so real."

More wine was poured until David's mood mellowed. She loved him like this. The anger was gone, his blue eyes turned calm again, and she was drowning in them. She felt herself slipping deeper into the very core of his being.

Nina covered his hand with hers, "I love you, David Asher."

They held each other's gaze in a timeless awareness of what they meant to each other. Still holding his hand, she got up from the table. "I feel like having dessert first...."

Falling into bed he held onto her like a drowning man—the tiny mattress their whole world. It was a different kind of love making than other times. He seemed lost and vulnerable. Willing to let her take him somewhere where he could escape the terrible reality of the deception he faced.

And when she finally drew him into her, it was an intimacy of a shared oneness that excluded everything else. All they had was the moment and their release was absolute. Afterwards, their bodies limply entwined, they floated on the sea of an uncertain future—minds adrift.

CHAPTER 18

Day 8
The Bomb

A quick taxi ride down Park Avenue placed Nina at 69th and Park before one o'clock the next day. She paid the cabbie, turned left, and headed toward FBI headquarters, a plain limestone and brick building located off Lexington Avenue.

She met David in the lobby, "Nervous?"

"A bit," he admitted. "I trust Hawkins, but Keyes is another story. I really don't like the man."

"Well, keep your cool. If I think you're losing ground, I'll give you a signal."

"What kind of signal?"

"I'll pull on my ear like Carol Burnett."

In the lobby, David gave his old name of Greenberg and received two passes. When they turned around David drew her attention to a man leaving the elevator.

"That's Hawkins."

The man approached with a smile on his face. "Sorry to have kept you waiting," the agent said, as he extended his hand. David grasped it and then introduced Nina. She gripped the agent's hand and found it as warm as his smile and could immediately understand why David liked him.

At the elevators, Hawkins asked David about his weekend, which gave Nina the opportunity to assess the agent. She recognized the man's chiseled features from David's sketch of him. But what fascinated her were the agent's expressive hands. He moved them through the air as if they had a language of their own. Despite their obvious strength, there was a lyrical quality about them.

Hawkins continued. "You understand this is an informal chat, right? No need to be nervous or guarded. You're not in any trouble. It'll be like it was at Moe's—without Agnes putting in her two cents worth."

Nina felt grateful for the agent's good humor but reminded herself to be on her guard. "So, you've met Agnes," she commented. "She's a force to be reckoned with."

"That she is, and very protective of David," added Hawkins.

"I'm glad to hear it."

After arriving at their floor, Hawkins ushered them through a network of long, featureless hallways with nameplates on office doors. When they came to the end of the maze, Nina could hear the rattle of typewriters. On turning the corner, they emerged into a huge space dominated by a typing pool of at least a dozen women.

Hawkins made a gesture with his arm. "Not a very cheery place to work, is it? But it's a challenging job and my boss is a great guy. I think you'll both like him."

Nina followed behind David, who was making a wide sweep of the room, something he did every time he found himself in a new environment. She followed the arc of his gaze, taking in the worn-out linoleum, the unmatched chairs and desks under the buzzing fluorescent lights. Two glass partitioned areas flanked the room. A long conference table could be seen in one, and across the room, a private office had its shades drawn. As they approached the office, another agent looked up from the spill of the teletype and nodded at them.

"That's my partner, Agent Keyes," Hawkins told Nina. "No doubt you've heard about him."

"I've seen him before. He was sitting in the theater during one of my rehearsals," she said. "Of course, I had no idea he was FBI. At the time, I thought he was some creep off the street—we get them sometimes."

Hawkins seemed embarrassed. "Uh, right...well, it's standard procedure in an investigation."

They were introduced to Special Agent in Charge, Alan Hunter. David shook the man's hand. "Actually, it's David Asher now. Two months ago, I petitioned the court to change my name and it finally came through."

"Asher then," Hunter repeated, "and a pleasure to meet you, Ms. Caldas." He motioned to the chairs in front of his huge oak desk. The two agents sat on the sofa against the wall while Hunter leaned informally against the edge of his desk.

To Nina, Hunter looked like an older version of Hawkins. What was a well-muscled physique had now gone soft. A slight paunch pushed against Hunter's belt. His was a pleasant face that caught her in a steady gaze and disarming smile. Nina felt immediately at ease.

Hunter addressed David. "Agents Hawkins and Keyes have filled me in on the substance of your conversation at Moe's Deli. The whole thing sounded fishy to me, but my agents verified it with Dr. Bruckmann at Bell Labs. As fantastic as it all seemed, it turned out to be true.

"The doctor told us the CIA leaned on him to disclose your medical history. We suspect he's the man Agent Keyes spotted following you and Ms. Caldas last week, and probably took a shot at David in the studio. We analyzed the dart. It contained a strange compound of both tranquilizer and hallucinogen. Dr. Bruckmann identified him as CIA from the sketch you showed him. Do you still have it?"

"I do," said David, as he flipped through his sketchbook. He tore out the drawing and handed it to Hunter.

"We have almost no leverage with the CIA," Hunter admitted. "If he's one of theirs, I'll figure out how I can best protect you from their abuse."

"Thank you," David said.

Hunter passed the drawing to Keyes. "Find out if he's CIA."

Keyes cocked his head to one side. "Geez, that's the guy—no question about it."

"Now," Hunter ordered. "Get someone on it right away."

"Yes, sir." Keyes got up and left.

Clearly annoyed, Hunter continued, "We're hoping you can give us further information to assist us in our investigation into the Mob's activities around the Food Mart. You're under no obligation to answer our questions, but I assume your presence here indicates your willingness to do so."

"Yes sir."

Nina looked at David. He seemed very much at ease.

Maybe too much.

❦

Hunter had seen it before. A protective family member on high alert for any suggestion their loved one could be railroaded into saying something incriminating. Ms. Caldas sat with her hands folded in her lap and, like an attorney, watched for pitfalls in the interrogation of her client.

Keyes returned to the room and sat. "I've got a team negotiating with our CIA counterparts. No telling how long it will take to get an answer."

Hunter nodded. "Fine. Meanwhile, we can listen to what David has to say." He moved from the edge of the desk and placed a folding chair between David and Nina. When he sat, he deliberately cut off Nina's view of David.

"Have you seen or heard anything around the Food Mart that might connect Mike Trozzo or his brother Vinnie with organized crime?"

"That's hard to say," David answered. "I see guys who look like gangsters come and go during the week, but I don't know if they're connected to organized crime."

"I see," said Hunter. "Have you ever witnessed an exchange of money or slips of paper which weren't part of a normal sale. Like adding something extra to a purchase or slipping a piece of paper inside a pack of cigarettes?"

"No."

"Has anything unusual happened around the store that didn't seem to be an ordinary occurrence? Anything at all?"

"Oh sure," David answered. "Once I heard a phone ring, but it wasn't the regular store phone. I followed the sound and discovered it was coming from behind a picture of Mike's mother. The phone was hidden behind it, jammed in between two wall studs in the back room."

"Did you ask Mike about it?"

"Yes, he told me it was installed by his father when he owned the store during the 1940s. Mike wanted to remove it, but his brother wouldn't let him."

Hunter was confused, "What kind of leverage does Vinnie have over Mike that he can tell him what to do with his store?"

"Well, strictly speaking, it's not just Mike's store. The brothers own it jointly. Since the city's re-urbanization of the neighborhood, it hasn't done well. Vinnie agreed to make up the shortfall in rent each month, but only if Mike made certain concessions. Mike doesn't like most things Vinnie tells him to do, so some months Mike has to scrape up the additional rent himself."

"Anything else you've seen or heard?" Hunter asked.

"Well, once I found flash paper in the desk drawer and an old safe stuck inside a refrigerator in the back room. Found out they all belong to Vinnie. He comes in once or twice a week to use the phone and meet with people. If I'm in the store, Mike tells me to take a hike."

Hunter nodded, then asked the question uppermost on his agents' minds. "Have you ever delivered or picked up anything for Mike, his brother, or anyone else connected with the store or organized crime? Anything—groceries, a package or box, mailed a letter, passed an envelope or a piece of paper."

"No, all I do is sweep up, stock, and break down boxes for the trash. Sometimes I cover the register for Mike when he goes out. That's it."

Agent Keyes broke in, "Really, then why have I've seen you sneak packages in and out of the back door?"

David frowned. "With all due respect sir, you're the only one here who wants to catch me doing something wrong. Well, sorry to disappoint, but I don't sneak in and out. I have an easel in the back room. The packages are art supplies and paintings."

"Can you explain that?" Hunter asked.

"Four, maybe five months after Mike and I became friendly, he asked if I had any problems living with my grandfather. I told him I quit painting in the apartment because Jacob was bothered by the smell of turpentine.

"Mike showed me a large room off the back of the store. It had high windows along one wall with gym equipment in the middle. He said he'd move the equipment off to a corner, so I could paint there. But there was a condition—I needed to work out several times a week. He said it was for my own good."

Keyes smirked. "You don't look all that buff to me."

David chuckled. "You should have seen me before I started. Anyway, I got my friend AJ to train with me twice a week. He's on the football team at the university. Afterward, we'd sit and have a beer with Mike, and he'd tell us stories about being a kid in Brooklyn. He said his father was an enforcer for a Mob hit squad the press later called 'Murder Incorporated'. It seems Mike and his friends hung out at a candy store that was the outfit's headquarters."

Hunter knew the history. Beginning in the 1920s, Murder Inc. was established as a group of Jewish and Italian killers on retainer for the exclusive use of the National Crime Syndicate. In 1939, a woman called Brownsville Rose was arrested for using her candy store as the hangout for its members.

He got up and moved to the coffee machine. "Does anyone want some joe? Ms. Caldas, what about it? It's Colombian. I picked up some samples at the Colombian Center last week."

"Thank you," she said.

He poured two cups, put one on his desk, and brought the other cup to the young woman. "What was your signal going to be?" he asked good-naturedly. "A touch to the nose, the ear or perhaps scratching an itch?"

"Thank you." She took the cup, then answered with a smile, "The ear. Was it that obvious?"

He shrugged. "Well, after all, I am a trained investigator."

"It's very comforting for me to know David's in such good hands."

Hunter gave Nina a wide smile and sat behind his desk. "Well, now that all of us can relax, we'll continue." He took a few sips of coffee and addressed the next thread of his inquiry.

"I'm aware of the story Mike told you. It was outlined in the field reports: the high-ranking mobsters playing cards, your assertion Mike's childhood friend Sy, was your father and why the math trick proves it."

"Right," said David. "My stepfather's name is Simon, even though everyone calls him Sy."

"Wait a minute," Keyes interrupted. "You never told us he was your stepfather."

"I just found out Monday."

Keyes shot back, "Really? So, you decided to change your name two months ago, but didn't realize Greenberg wasn't your father until the day before yesterday? Cute story—"

Hunter interrupted, "Hold off Keyes." He noticed Ms. Caldas's reaction and gave her a reassuring look. "Let's hear Mr. Asher out without comment. We'll decide later if anything he says has relevance to our investigation." Hunter paused to let the reprimand sink in.

He turned to David and continued, "We've checked the facts and all the card-playing mobsters were real. Mike's young friends, Allie 'Tick Tock' Tannenbaum and Harry 'Big Greenie' Greenberg ended up as top hitmen for Murder Inc. From all accounts, Mike himself was a reluctant street enforcer until the fifties.

"Otto 'Abbadabba' Berman was indeed a math whiz who worked for Dutch Shultz. After the two of them were murdered in 1935, rumors surfaced that someone with the nickname "Little Greenie" took Otto's place. Seems he played it very low key—no one knew his name. You're speculating it was your stepfather, Sy Greenberg?"

David gave a slow nod.

"But" continued Hunter. "Despite all the truthful elements in Mike's story, there's no definitive proof your father was 'Little Greenie' or is now involved in anything illegal. To go forward with an investigation, we need physical evidence or the testimony of a reliable witness."

"I'm that witness," David told him. "And I'm trying to find the evidence—that's how I found out he wasn't my real father."

"Unfortunately, you wouldn't be considered a reliable witness. A photographic memory can be a valuable investigative tool, but it's not reasonable to expect any judge to issue a warrant based on snapshots a college student takes with his mind. Too many kids are strung out on drugs these days."

Hunter's phone rang. He picked it up, listened briefly, then hung up.

"A car bomb went off in front of the Food Mart."

"A bomb?" David stood up and the two agents rose with him.

Leaning over the desk, Hunter said, "You and Ms. Caldas go with Hawkins and Keyes. I know you're both concerned about Mike."

Hunter got up and followed everyone to the elevator, "Jim, officially both are ride-a-longs—civilians with close personal ties to a person of interest in our investigation—that's it. Unofficially, I want David to soak in the scene with those camera eyes of his." The elevator opened and Hunter put a hand on David's shoulder. "Given the circumstances it might be difficult for you but try to sweep the crowd hanging around the scene. Blink in everyone you see.

"Sometimes the perp hangs around to gloat."

⁓ॐ⁓

As Keyes turned the Buick onto Amsterdam Avenue, David could see black smoke billowing up between the buildings. The street was cordoned off with police cars at one end and a fire truck on the other. Firemen rushed around with equipment, shouting over the cloud of smoke. A small crowd accumulated across the street outside Moe's Deli. Hawkins flashed his credentials and Keyes pulled off to the curb. Ahead, surrounded by a blanket of chemical foam, a hulk of metal smoldered in front of the Food Mart.

David's heart sank, "Oh my God, it's Mike's van!" Beside him, Nina reached for his hand.

Keyes got out of the car and rushed up to the scene with his ID in his hand. Hawkins twisted in his seat. "It looks bad. If it's something either of you can't stomach, we'll understand." But David was out on the pavement before Hawkins. He ran up behind Keyes, who was talking to an NYPD Sergeant.

"Who's in the van?" demanded David, as Hawkins arrived with Nina.

The Sergeant looked at him with some confusion, but Keyes gave him a nod. "Witnesses said the guy came out of the grocery store. Last name Trozzo, first name Mike."

David blurted out, "How do you know?"

The Sergeant looked up from his notes. "His store, his van; people in the deli saw him get in. You know any different?"

"No, sir. I, uh, just can't believe it."

"Well, I'm sorry, son." Then the Sergeant addressed Hawkins. "The firefighters speculate a car bomb. What's your interest in this?"

"We're investigating a gambling operation in the neighborhood and got the call," replied Hawkins. "We'll liaison with your precinct later."

David shuddered. "My God, Mike...."

Nina put a hand on David's shoulder. "How was he identified?"

"Body was burnt beyond recognition," said the Sergeant. "But we found his wallet with the driver's license still intact. You folks next of kin—you both seem broken up by this?"

"No, but he has a brother, Vinnie and a wife, Margret." David said. "She's at her sister's house in New Jersey somewhere."

The Sergeant scribbled some notes, after which Hawkins led the couple across the street to the deli and sat them down at a table. Hawkins left to say a few words to Agnes and then returned to the table.

"I'm awfully sorry David—I know how much Mike meant to you. Agnes will bring both of you something to take the edge off. Sit tight for a while—I'll be back as soon as I can."

David nodded. In his memory Mike was still alive—laughing, joking, and telling stories. Images of his friend pushed themselves into his consciousness and he slipped gratefully into the past.

CHAPTER 19

Day 9
Irrefutable Facts

Slightly reminiscent of a squatter's shanty, Jeremiah Koop's ramshackle newsstand on the corner of 86th Street and Amsterdam Avenue, was a patchwork of newspapers, magazines and comic books. Its colorful facade of reading material was stacked, clipped, and wedged into every available corner of the wooden structure. Koop, known as Jerry to his friends, debated the news of the day with anyone who would listen, especially during the early morning hours when news was fresh.

Sometime after nine Wednesday morning, Jerry sat on a stool inside his dinky stand checking the metal coin changer hanging from his belt. Seeing it half empty, he loaded it with quarters, dimes, nickels, and pennies from jars he hid under the counter. Then, cutting the strings on a third batch of morning papers, he lugged them out the dwarf-sized door to pile them on a plywood plank at the front of the stand.

As he straightened the last stack, a station wagon pulled up to the curb and the passenger door opened. Jacob Goldstein stepped out onto the pavement and retrieved his overcoat and thin-brimmed fedora from the back seat. As the old man approached, Jerry greeted his friend warmly. "Mornin' Jacob haven't seen you lately. You been feeling okay?"

"And why shouldn't I be?" Jacob responded. "I was with my daughter for Passover but couldn't take my *paskudnik* son-in-law. My daughter was driving in today, so I asked her to take me back."

"*Paskudnik?*"

"Scoundrel. The worst!"

Jerry nodded and pointed to the overcoat. "Kinda nippy out this mornin'."

"Eh, here...not so much. You want cold, come for a visit. By the Hudson you got cold."

Jerry smiled and folded a newspaper. "Here ya go Jacob, a nice fresh off the press *New York Times*. Sorry I didn't have time to iron it out for you."

Jacob's silent response to Jerry's good-natured ribbing was not what he expected. He was focused on one of the periodicals pinned to a cord above him. His already pale complexion quickly drained of its remaining color.

Jerry followed Jacob's gaze to a front-page photo on the latest issue of the *Columbia Daily Spectator*. Known as the *Spec* to its readers, the broadsheet was the campus newspaper for Columbia University.

"Looks like you've seen a ghost."

Jacob pulled the Spec off the cord, handed Jerry some coins, and slipped the *Spectator* between the folds of the Times.

"Not a ghost," Jacob replied. "Someone from my past."

❧

How, David thought, would he confront his mother about her hidden first marriage. He could understand the pressures which might make her lie to him. Even forgive the unforeseen consequences resulting from that lie. But since the truth was out, he expected a full disclosure of the facts. Only her complete honesty would wipe the slate clean so they could start anew.

One thing was certain. Now that he knew about his true parentage, he would cease to think of himself as Greenberg. Unknowingly, he changed his last name to Asher, an Americanization of his real father's name. He was David Asher now. And as he discovered at FBI Headquarters yesterday, referring to himself as David Asher gave him a freedom and confidence he never felt before.

The doorbell rang and David opened it to find his mother with a small bag of groceries and Jacob's suitcase. "Gramps is back, how come?" He moved the suitcase into the foyer.

"Your father didn't make him feel welcome," his mother said.

"I'm not surprised." David took the grocery bag from his mother and headed for the kitchen.

Ellen straightened her scarf and followed him in. "We did a little grocery shopping and I dropped him off at Amsterdam Avenue. He wanted to buy a newspaper and walk home."

As David put away the groceries, he smiled to himself. It couldn't have worked out any better. "Please sit down Mom, we need to talk."

Ellen moved closer to the kitchen table. "You sound serious. It's about you and Nina wanting to get married, isn't it?"

"I told you, we do plan to marry, but that's not what I want to talk about."

She placed her handbag on the table and sat. "What's wrong?"

"I know, Mom."

For an instant, a dark cloud of dread crossed her face. Ellen turned away to look out the window. "I don't know what you mean."

"I know about Aschbacher."

⊰⊱

It was the moment Ellen hoped for, and the one she dreaded the most. After two decades of waiting, and with the truth finally out, she found herself totally unprepared. Her relief was mixed with an extreme fear of both her husband's and son's reactions. She studied David's face—no anger, no hurt—just frank, open curiosity.

She wiped the tears trickling down her cheeks. "Who told you?"

"No one, I broke into Dad's file cabinet and read his Will."

The shock doubled. *The Will? He saw the Will....* "Oh my god Davie! What did it say?"

"It said, 'To David Aschbacher, son of my wife Ellen, by a previous marriage I bequeath....'"

"That's all, nothing else?" she asked.

"What do you mean, 'that's all'? Isn't it enough? I discover you're lying to me my whole life and you're interested in what else is in his Will? What's going on here?"

Oh God, what's wrong with me. How can I ask him now? "I'm sorry, you're right. It's just so...shocking. I mean that you broke in, opened his Will. Why would you do such a thing?"

"Nina suspected he wasn't my father. I was looking for my birth certificate."

"Your father... what will he do?"

"Don't tell him. Nothing can be gained by it. Both our lives would be a lot easier if he didn't know. As long as he thinks he's in control, he's happy."

"Not tell him..." She thought about it. *Of course, that's the answer.*

"It's our only protection against his anger. What would it accomplish if he knew? It's for the best."

"Yes," Ellen said. "Yes, you're right." With the passing years, he looked more and more like his father. He had Leo's piercing blue eyes. She couldn't help wondering what else he found in the Will and searched the kitchen as if the answer was written on the walls.

"Mom?"

He was waiting for an explanation, but she couldn't go on. Ellen fumbled for her cigarettes, her hand shaking as she put the cigarette between her lips. She picked up the lighter and spun the wheel against the flint, but there was no flame. David took the lighter and put it in his pocket.

"No more smoking and no more lies. Now's the time to tell me the truth."

He sounded like Leo. The edge to his voice, the quiet insistence. *I can't press him anymore about the Will. I'll have to wait. As long as Sy doesn't know...* She took a deep breath and began. "All these years I've wanted to tell you—I couldn't—I was frightened of what your father would do. Sy, I mean." The unsteady words caught in her throat, and she willed herself to continue. "So many lies. I didn't like lying to you, Davie, but I did." She turned sideways and gazed absently out the window again.

"So now you know," she continued, "and I'm so relieved, but afraid. Afraid of Sy. Afraid you'll never forgive me. Afraid I'll never be able to forgive myself."

David sat beside her and held her hand. "I forgive you, Mom. I understand how hard it is for you. Just tell me about my father. Tell me everything."

"Well, his name was Leo Aschbacher. I loved him very much..." *Did I? Did I really love him?*

"Aschbacher...what kind of name is that?" David asked.

"His family came from a town in Germany called Aschbach."

"So, my middle name—Asher—comes from Aschbacher?"

"You never had a middle name until I married Sy. I felt you should retain something of Leo, so I gave you the middle name of Asher."

"Okay. So now we're getting somewhere," he said. "Did you meet him before or during the war? Was he American born or a Jew escaping the Nazis? Wait, he didn't die in the war did he?"

She shook her head no as he spoke and held up her hand to stop his questions.

"We met in 1935. He was an American citizen for ten years and made a lot of money selling European art. I married him two years later—four years before the war.

"Leo was very cultured, had impeccable manners, and very handsome—like you. All these years, seeing you grow up to be just like him. It was hard for me. His first language was German, and he had a photographic memory. During the war, he worked for Army Intelligence as a translator. Then he was assigned to process the survivors of a concentration camp. When he came home, he was different, a shell of his former self. He'd get these terrible moods; become depressed—stop working and leave the house for days. I never knew where he was or when he'd come home. I couldn't cope. My mother practically moved in with us. Leo said she interfered. It was a mess."

Ellen couldn't go on; it was all too much. She got up from the chair, walked to the window, and crossed her arms. "So many years ago," she said softly. "Oh Davie, Davie... he... he was the love of my life, and I was weak and selfish. God, I'm so sorry! I just couldn't find the strength to fight for him."

David came to her and put a consoling hand on her shoulder. "Fight for him? What do you mean—what happened?"

"I can't..." she shook her head, "No more, it's unraveling too fast." Without warning, Ellen began to sob. In her despair, her head fell against David's chest and she clung to him. The inconsolable grief she carried for decades broke under the weight of her mistake and her entire body shook.

"It's okay, I forgive you." David kept saying.

The soothing words calmed her, and Ellen relaxed. It was a familiar remembrance—the voice—the same wiry frame as Leo's. *This is Leo's son, not Sy's. I've deceived everyone—myself included. How could I let this happen?*

She felt a hollowness in her heart, and it all became too much to bear. Turning away, she clamped a hand over her mouth and rushed from the kitchen in tears.

✒

Back from his walk, Jacob met Ellen in the foyer. "What's going on?"

"He knows, Dad," she cried. "He knows everything." She rushed down the hall and disappeared into his bedroom.

Stunned, Jacob entered the kitchen and found his grandson staring out the window. "How did you find out?"

David turned to face him. "I broke into his personal files and read his Will."

"*Oy yoi yoi...*" Jacob pulled out a chair and sat down. "*Ir zent in tif dreck*–when he finds out you're in deep shit."

"He won't. Mom and I agreed to keep it secret."

Jacob breathed a sigh of relief. "Ah, *Zeyer klug*–very smart."

"She clammed up on me Gramps."

"Listen, your mother went through a lot of *tsoriss*. You know this word, *tsoriss*?"

"Sure, it means suffering."

"Good, so you understand why she can't talk about it?"

"No, not really. She kept me from the truth. I need to know why."

Jacob nodded then pointed to the chair across from him. "Sit; we'll talk."

David sat and ran his fingers through his hair.

"Something happened a long time ago," Jacob said. "It's a scar that's never healed. She's fragile, my Ellen, like her mother." Jacob picked up a napkin and dabbed his eyes. "Who do you think cleaned up the bathroom after they took your grandmother away. My daughter has nightmares. She's still afraid of ending up like her mother."

"I'm sorry, I really am," David said. "I still see grandma in that tub as no one else can. It breaks my heart, but nobody worries about me. If I can deal with all the detail I still see, Mom should be able to deal with a normal person's recollection."

"Still, some secrets are none of your business," Jacob said. "You should respect the privacy of other people."

"I see. So, when everyone dies, I'm left clueless. Great." David slammed a fist on the table. "I'm supposed to suck it up and go on my merry way like nothing happened? It's my business too."

Jacob noticed Ellen listening at the kitchen door. Her mascara smeared around her eyes, giving her a haunted look.

"He's right, Dad, it is his business, and he shouldn't be left in the dark. I can understand how he feels—after all these years—to find out. It's like unreal." His daughter avoided eye contact and seemed to be in a daze as she moved to the kitchen table. She picked up her handbag and rummaged through it.

"So now he found out." She continued searching. "He wants to know who he is. Oh, here it is." She pulled a compact out of her bag. "I have to freshen up for my appointment." She moved toward the door, stopped at the threshold, but didn't turn around. "He has a right to know about Leo, Dad. But I have to leave. Tell him what you can. I'll pick him up at the museum after three to take him home." She disappeared down the hall.

The front door closed.

Jacob bobbed his head. "All right, I'll tell you everything, but the story...it's not so good and I'm not so blameless. Once I was a wealthy man, but to my shame, not so smart—I lost my business. In the end, I was forced to rely on Greenberg financially. I was under his thumb. Otherwise, I would have told you a long time ago."

"I understand, Gramps."

"Okay, so it started in 1935 when we lived out on the Island in Cedarhurst. That's where your mother met Leo and came under his spell. My wonderful Ellen—so obedient, helpful, loving—became rebellious and stubborn. Business wasn't so good so I figured we'd move away, downsize, and at the same time, it would end their relationship.

"So, we moved here, to this apartment. Back then it was eight, nine rooms—very fancy. Your mother then, she wasn't so good... If you know what I'm talking? In those days, unmarried women, they didn't, um, set up house with a man. But we found out she did—with Leo. My Ellen, so talented she was, I was giving her money to study piano at New York University. Too late, we found out Leo moved into the city and she was using the tuition money to pay for an apartment."

"You mean they were shacking up," David said.

"Okay, not so nice, but yes." Jacob shook his head, "And if that wasn't enough, she was carrying on with a German."

"Mom mentioned he was from Germany."

"You should understand, we heard terrible things about the Nazis— the things they did to the Jews. We didn't trust Germans. Maybe if Leo was a German Jew—but listen, he wasn't. He was German—worse, a *goy*. It was unacceptable."

Jacob saw the questioning look on David's face and nodded sympathetically, "All right, so maybe today, it's not impossible." He gave his grandson a weak smile and continued.

"Where was I? Yes, 1935, I mentioned my business was failing. I was struggling financially, while your mother lived in sin with a German. Then, in 1937, she announced they were getting married. He wasn't Jewish, so naturally we thought maybe he wasn't even American. We questioned her and found out he became an American citizen shortly after college."

"So, despite Leo not being Jewish they got married anyway in 1937?" David asked.

"Right. But then in 1938, there was *Kristallnacht,* and we became worried again. You know about this—the night of the broken glass?"

David nodded. "A mob stormed Jewish shops, smashing windows."

"So, like I said, we were concerned. We read about German American spies. We asked Ellen if Leo's parents had anything to do with the Nazis. Her answer was to keep our noses out of her marriage. It continued like that for three, four years—always keeping us at arm's distance. Ellen modeled for my dress business. Leo sold European antiques and paintings at...what was it...Bernet, yes, Parke-Bernet Galleries.

"Then, we heard talk about Leo's father being held in a South American detention camp. Again, we became worried. Everyone heard the rumors—the shipments of paintings confiscated by the Nazis—first to South America; then to art dealers in New York."

"And you thought the entire family were Nazi spies?"

"What else to think?"

"Geez, Gramps, this is unbelievable."

"That's the way it was for us. Young people today have no idea what we went through during the war."

David shifted in his chair. "So, what happened next?"

"Next, you were born." For the first time since beginning his story, Jacob smiled. "Suddenly, we became a family. Your grandmother babysat. I came over to their apartment and played with you. It was a happy time—until America entered the war."

"Leo was called up?"

"No. He enlisted. He spoke German, so naturally the Army sent him to Europe as a translator."

"When was this?"

"1942, summer—June, July—I can't remember." Jacob got up and went to the sink. He poured himself some water and continued. "So, all of a sudden, everything was peaches and cream. I realized, all right, so he's a *goy*, but at least he's not a Nazi." Jacob paused to drink some water. "Leo strutted around in his army uniform for a week or two and then left for Europe."

Jacob came to the table and sat down again. Telling the story became too distressing for him. He rushed through to its conclusion. He explained Leo was a broken man after the war, with recurring nightmares, and vivid flashbacks during the day. The doctors talked about hallucinations and persecutory delusions.

Pills were prescribed but when electro-shock therapy was mentioned Leo disappeared. He loitered outside Ellen's apartment but never went in. Her feelings went from compassion to anger to fear. She worried Leo would snatch her son away from her and finally moved in with her parents. In time, she sued for divorce.

In those days, grounds for divorce were few. At first, Leo refused to agree to an infidelity plea. Jacob enticed him with a lot of money, and he agreed to be photographed in bed with a prostitute. They took photographs at a local hotel and Ellen's attorney presented the case. The divorce was issued, and custody of David was awarded to Ellen.

"Legally the marriage was over, but my Ellen wanted more," Jacob said. "She wanted a *get*. You wouldn't know, but a *get* is a religious bill of divorce. Without it, a Rabbi can't perform a second marriage. According to Jewish law, a *get* is obtained only through the good graces of the husband. Leo refused. So, I offered him more money and my Ellen got the *get*."

But even that wasn't enough.

Ellen wanted the marriage wiped clean—as if it never happened. Shunned by polite society, she needed to prove her innocence in the failure of the marriage. She wanted an annulment. Arguing she was unaware Leo was mentally imbalanced when they married, she obtained a rabbinical annulment at Jacob's further expense.

The payoffs ate into Jacob's nest egg, and after his business failures, it became a devastating blow. Realizing he could never recover his losses, he filed for bankruptcy.

Leo disappeared.

CHAPTER 20

Offshore Banking

Thanks to Jacob, David now knew the history behind his mother's first marriage. As he waited for her to pick him up outside the museum, he was sure she'd be forthcoming with the rest of the truth during the drive home.

When his mother pulled the car over to the curb shortly after three, David slipped into the passenger seat. "How was your afternoon?" he asked.

"Fine Davie, I ordered what I needed for the store and it was good to be in the city for a change."

"Okay, I'll rephrase. How are you feeling after what happened this morning?"

"I'm fine."

"That's all you have to say?"

"Try to understand. After all these years, it's hard for me to talk about Leo."

"Gramps told me the facts. There's no need to rehash the painful stuff. I understand. But at some point, I'd like to find out what he was like."

"A lot like you Davie. It's been so difficult watching you grow up. You both had the same interests—art, classical music—a crazy memory."

"My memory? What are you talking about?"

"I may have kept things from you, but you're not upfront with me. I know about Bell Laboratories and your alter ego as David Asher."

"How did you—"

"Your grandfather was worried about you," Ellen interrupted, "so he poked around your room. He showed me the letter from the doctor and that horrible drawing—the one where you're about to stab your father—Sy. Why didn't you tell me?"

"I was afraid you wouldn't be able to keep it secret."

"Well, it was the same with me. I didn't tell you about Leo because I was afraid your father—sorry, let's call him Sy—I was afraid he'd find out. He has a strange ability to smell deception. You have no idea how many times I tried to hide things from him—he always knew something was up—always."

"For what it's worth, I'm sorry," David said. "Let's agree to let it go. We lied to each other out of fear. From now on we need to stick together. That being said, you should know two months ago I contacted a lawyer to change my last name to Asher."

"You hated your father—Sy—that much?"

"Yeah, I hated him. Still do. But it's more than that. With all the discrimination I've experienced, I couldn't see giving my children the name of Greenberg. It wouldn't be fair to them."

"So, you're David Asher now."

"Yes."

"Will you tell Sy about the name change?"

"No, he'll just get angry."

"That's good. If he learns you changed your last name, he'll think I encouraged you. He told me if I betrayed him in any way, he'd divorce me. I'd be penniless."

"Mom you're kidding?"

"No, he's made it very clear what would happen if I went against him in any way. I'm trapped."

"What about the store?"

"Forget it. Any obvious profits went to pay for your tuition. He never used a dime of his own for your education. Anyway, more money comes in than I can account for, then it disappears. I think he's using my store to move money around."

"You mean laundering dirty money?"

"Yes, that's what I mean. There's so much you don't know."

They drove on in silence. David never gave any thought to how secure his mother was financially and understood her unwillingness to go against Sy's wishes. There had to be a way to free her from his grasp and safeguard her financial future.

Driving down Peninsula Boulevard his mother broke the silence.

"I have to apologize about this morning, I know I made you angry when I asked you if you saw anything else in the Will, but it was important. It still is."

"I was upset, forget it. What is it you want to know?"

"I'll tell you, but first let's get some takeout. It's late and I'm in no mood to cook tonight."

ৰ্জ্ঞ্ঞ

CIA operative Frank Riley found a parking spot on Cedarhurst Boulevard and watched mother and son walk into the Kosher Maven.

More than I hoped for, thought Riley. He walked past the restaurant's window several times and spotted them standing next to the checkout counter looking at menus. *Takeout–this can't get any simpler.*

His previous role with the CIA was a dangerous and bloody one. Now in his late forties, Riley wanted to hold on to this type of limited fieldwork. If MKUltra was scuttled, his next job would be behind a desk. He had to make this work.

A sliver of light spilled into the adjacent alleyway. He stole toward it and saw the partially opened kitchen door. Hiding behind a dumpster, he watched the progress of the takeout order. *Fifteen-seconds max to slip inside and dump the LSD into the soup container. The Greenberg's are going to take a trip tonight.*

ৰ্জ্ঞ্ঞ

David chose a table in a far corner of the dining room to wait for their takeout order. His mother ordered a cup of coffee and David a Coke. When the waitress moved away, Ellen explained why she was so interested in her husband's Will.

"That vacation we take every year to Florida, Mexico, or the Caribbean," Ellen said. "Well, before we leave, he stuffs money in the lining of a custom-made golf bag. I don't know how much, but wherever we end up, we always take a side trip to Nassau. During the two or three days we're there, he deposits the money in a bank account in my maiden name. We both have signature. He says it's our nest egg, but I doubt it."

"You think he plans to disappear with the money?"

"Yes, eventually, I'm sure of it. Probably with the hussy from New Jersey."

"Hussy from New...?" David stammered for real. "He's got a mistress?"

"For a long time now."

"What a piece of shi...sorry," David said. "I'm beginning to see the whole picture. So, what was it you were thinking?"

"It was a daydream really. I'd tell him Aunt Rose was going in for surgery and I needed to go to Florida for a couple of days to help her out. I'd do it during tax season so he couldn't come along. From Florida, I'd fly to Nassau and transfer the money into another account—one he wouldn't know about. But that's where the plan falls apart."

"Why?"

"He's the only one who knows the account number. Whenever I must sign a bank form, he puts his hand over the account number and holds it there. He says to play dumb, stick with him, and do what I'm told. When he dies, I'll find the account number with his Will. It's why I asked if you saw anything else written in the Will."

"I see. Well, there was the Will, the envelope, and some other papers in the cash box. Give me a moment to search my memory."

David pictured the open file cabinet. *Practically empty, the magazines, keepsakes, store accounts, medical files, and old albums. The cash box held stocks, bonds, and a marriage application. The Will was in a brown envelope with the words Last Will & Testament. Nina steamed it open; put it in the drawer. I opened it after tea. I saw numbers.*

Nassau 84659098630-3.

"You said Nassau–in the Bahamas–that's where the bank is?"

"Yes."

"I know the account number."

"What, how?"

"It was written on the inside flap of the envelope. I didn't think anything of it because we live in Nassau County. I assumed it was some sort of file number for the court."

"How do we know it's not?" Ellen asked.

"It makes sense. After he's gone, you'd find the envelope; see the word Nassau. Immediately trips to the bank would come to mind. Eventually, you'd realize it had nothing to do with the Will itself."

"I guess you're right."

"It's tax season. You need to take a trip to Nassau now." David wrote the account number on a piece of paper torn from his sketchbook and handed it to her.

"How can you remember all these numbers?"

"You've read the letter from Bell Labs, believe me, the numbers are correct."

"It's hard for me to imagine. I guess you're not the person I thought you were, Mr. Asher." Ellen smoothed out the piece of paper on her lap as though it was a precious heirloom.

David smiled, "I'm beginning to think the very same thing about you." He watched her tuck the account number in the zippered compartment of her purse.

"Set things up with Aunt Rose today. Get a plane ticket to Florida and leave tomorrow. Buy your ticket to Nassau when you get there. Buy it with cash."

"Why tomorrow?"

"You have to get to the bank before they close for the weekend. You'll need an extra day just in case something goes wrong. Before you deposit the money in another bank, take out enough to help you live on your own for a few months. Find out how much cash you can take back to the States without raising any alarms or making a paper trail."

His mother looked at him, "How do you know all this?"

"It doesn't matter. What matters is the timing. Contact your lawyer before you leave. Tell him you want to start divorce proceedings because you found out your husband is involved in racketeering. Your son is talking to the FBI and you're going to stay with your sister because you're afraid of him. Don't tell him about Nassau."

"A divorce..." she repeated.

"That's what you want, right?"

"It'll be for the second time," she said.

"This time it's different, Mom."

"I guess this time it is."

❧❧

Held up at the office and then tied up in traffic on the freeway, Sy didn't get home until five. He understood the hidden closet was a liability. He must destroy it. But with Ellen and David due back from the city at any moment, dismantling the hideaway would have to wait. The key now was to pack up the rest of his money so he could cut and run at a moment's notice.

Sy already separated his cash into fifties and hundreds and dumped them in a cardboard box. Anything lower than a fifty he spent. The hundreds he divided between a beat-up leather satchel from prohibition days and the Callaway Weekender bag he used at the golf club. He put his fake driver's licenses and passports in the outside pockets of the satchel and chose a small overnight bag for a change of clothes and personal items. Sy slung the satchel around his neck, picked up the Weekender in his right hand, and the overnight bag in his left. He paced back and forth and found them very manageable. Taking them to the garage he stashed them in the trunk of his car, just as Ellen's station wagon pulled into the driveway.

As his wife parked in the garage, he wondered how he was going to get her out of the house so he could dismantle the hideaway. And if he had to cut and run, it would be nice to do it in Ellen's station wagon—in case he needed to sleep off road.

"It's about time," Sy said, as they got out of the car. "Now you're gonna take your time cooking something. I'll have to wait even longer—I'm starved."

David got out of the car and pulled a paper bag out from the back seat. "Nope. Mom picked up dinner at the Kosher Maven. She got your favorite—borscht."

They all went into the house and as Ellen heated the food and set the table, she told Sy her sister was about to have an operation.

"She has no one and asked me to fly down for a couple of days. A week at most," she said.

Sy couldn't believe his luck. "So, you're leaving?"

"You're not angry, are you?"

"Nooo...not at all. When's your flight?"

"I'm hoping to get a shuttle out tomorrow. If that's okay?"

"Sure," Sy said. "You know how busy I get during tax season. Better call for flight times now...we'll eat afterward."

He gestured for her to get going and moved into the dining room where he sat and watched her at the phone through the connecting door. She seemed puzzled at his benign acceptance and kept glancing at him—like an animal not sure of his master's wishes. This was exactly the kind of break he needed. Under normal circumstances, he would have made her squirm before consenting. But with Ellen out of the house, he could empty the hideaway and burn the evidence in the back yard.

She hung up. "Tomorrow morning at 10:00. I'll have to pack tonight."

Perfect. Now all he needed was her station wagon. "Fine. I'll drop you at the airport on my way to work."

"Really, you'd do that?"

"Why not? We'll take the station wagon. Gotta leave at eight sharp though, so I can make my appointment in the city."

Ellen smiled. "I'll be ready."

"Can we eat now? Sy demanded, I'm famished." It was true. He hadn't eaten since breakfast and was eager to dig into the container of borscht.

❧

Sy was unusually quiet while he finished the bowl of borscht. When Ellen moved to take the empty bowl away, he put out a restraining hand.

"Is there more?" Sy said.

Ellen nodded. "There's plenty, but we have pastrami sandwiches next."

"Give me another bowl."

Unaware the borscht was laced with LSD, his wife served him the second helping. He dropped in a dollop of sour cream, broke off a piece of pumpernickel bread and slurped up the orange-red soup. With each successive spoonful, he was taken back to the squalor of his childhood in Brownsville: the tiny kitchen with clotted paint peeling off the walls; grimy windowpanes; sodden rags draped over the radiator and the terrible chill in his bones.

And the bugs. One in particular—the deathwatch beetle.

A superstition of the *Shetel* warned the beetle's nighttime ticking presaged someone's death. And death was everywhere in Brownsville. Ellen and her son had no idea what he went through. They were self-indulgent and ungrateful. What really irked him was how peaceful David seemed.

Well, he'd take care of that. "Pretty handy having your girlfriend around to drive you back last Monday. You never told us why she was here."

"It was the only day we could spend some time together."

Tic.

"Eh?" Sy nodded absently and looked around the floor.

"She's busy with rehearsals." David added.

Tic.

Again, the ticking sound. He felt woozy. Then, the hallucinations started. David's head changed shape. It became darker, hard, shiny; more beetle-like by the second. He glanced at his wife and found she too had morphed. Mother beetle got up and stood at her son's side to fuss over his plate, her antennae bumping into David's.

Sy shook his head to erase the sight. "Uh, right..." *What was I going to say?* "So, you can't stay away from her for a couple of days, huh? This doesn't sound so good. You told me it was a college fling—'nothing serious' you said. Don't tell me you've fallen for this girl?"

David's mandibles opened to speak. "I'd rather not discuss it," he ticked. "I'm getting a bad feeling this is not going to end well."

It's a bluff, Sy thought. *He's trying to put me off with another one of his weird hunches.* "No, it needs to be discussed...and right now. You better not be thinking of marrying her."

Click, tic.

"What? Hey, don't think you're going to get away without answering me again. Are you planning to marry her or not?"

"I'm going to leave the table—*tic*—I feel something terrible is going to happen." The beetle moved his chair back.

Sy got up and stood behind David's chair. Holding his head back so as not to brush against the antennae, Sy reached out and clamped down on top of the bug's shoulders, pinning the shell-like casing to the chair.

"You wanna know what's terrible," Sy began. "I'll tell you what's terrible. She's not Jewish!"

David shook his head; his segmented antennae wobbled back and forth. "I don't have a problem with that."

Sy jerked his head back. "Whaddayamean, you don't have a problem?" Sy's borscht-stained spittle landed on the boy's reddish-brown exoskeleton. One of David's arthropod legs came up holding a napkin and wiped Sy's spittle from under the shirt collar.

"You want to know why it's a problem?" Sy said softly. "I'll tell why." He leaned over the chair and placed his mouth inches from what looked like David's left ear.

A foul smell caught in his nostrils, and he pulled away. "She's a goddamn *shiksa.*"

Ellen's lilting voice didn't match the way she looked. "What your father is trying to say is—*tic*—Nina's a nice girl but she doesn't share our beliefs. Your father's hoping Nina will convert. Isn't that right Sy?"

Sy didn't expect it. *It's a fucking ambush. They're trying to manipulate me into accepting her.*

"You shouldn't get upset right now," beetle boy clicked. "Take some deep breaths and lie down. You don't look so good."

"Lie down? What are you, a wise guy?" He was gasping for breath now. "We're going to discuss it, understand?"

David the beetle placed the napkin back on the table.

"You better realize right now—no son of mine is going to marry some *shiksa* spic."

Beetle boy whipped around in his chair. "Why do you continue to treat us like this—what have we ever done to deserve such a total lack of compassion?"

Sy found himself looking into a pair of compound eyes—electric blue with orange reflections. "Oh, I'm sorry, did I hurt your feelings?" The shell-backed creature moved to get up. "Are you going to your room to cry?" Sy tried to squash him down, but his hands slipped on its slimy surface. *The deltoids are like slabs of granite.*

The beetle lurched up from the chair. "Get your hands off me!"

Click, tic, scrape.

Sy struggled to hold on but the bug's bunched up biceps were rocklike under his grip. When the creature turned to face him, Leo Aschbacher's smiling face was now plastered below David's antennae. He was winking at Ellen whose face lit up like a schoolgirl in heat. The dining room stretched out lengthwise—with red, pink, and orange flowers. Beets hung from the chandelier like bloody testicles.

Sy's hands fell to his side. His whole world was falling apart. The room tilted. It became very hot. The drilling in his skull made his heart skip beats.

"I don't believe this..." Sy said it out loud, then thought—*Heart attack? No. It couldn't be...not my heart...There's nothing wrong with me, I'm fine.* Holding onto the backs of chairs, he moved down the table to keep himself from falling. *No way I can lose control.*

"This is all because of that Park Avenue floozie," he continued weakly. "Well, don't think for one moment you're going to bring that *shiksa* into this house again."

It was David on his feet now. With his hands balled into fists, he headed towards him. "You have no right—"

"Oooh, I have a right. I have every right," Sy admonished. "This is my house, and that fucking whore will be part of this family over my dead body."

A knife found its way into David's hand.

"Davie. No!"

Surprised, piss leaked out into Sy's underwear.

David came at him screaming, "You fucking piece of shit!"

Sy pushed the chair toward David in a feeble attempt to stop him, but it toppled to the floor. "Oh, so now you're gonna kill me huh?" Raising his chin Sy spread his arms out. "Well, okay bring it on big shot—right in the gut. Do it, slice me up good."

His stepfather laughed, taunting him. "What, lost your nerve? Here," pointing to his stomach, "I'm wide open. Come on...where are your balls, huh?

"Kill me!"

The boy blinked and seemed to come to his senses. The knife slipped from his hand and clattered to the floor.

"Your nose is bleeding," David said, as he walked into the living room.

Sy passed his hand under his nose and looked at his blood smeared index finger. A wave of nausea caught him. He was in a cold sweat. "You get back here." He stumbled into the living room and knocked into the sofa. "I'm...not done with—"

"Well, I'm done with you," his son yelled back.

Sy collapsed on the sofa. He saw multiple Davids walking up the stairs into a haze. "Don't you people walk away...."

"Go to hell old man!"

A black shade descended in front of his eyes. As he licked the blood from his upper lip a warm wetness spread over his crotch. His hand reached down to squeeze his penis shut while the other pinched his nose. Neither action could stop the flow.

He was still hallucinating, his wet crotch reminding him of when he was sixteen. The *shiksa* splayed out on his father's butcher table. The gangsters entering through the back door, and little time to stuff his dick back in his pants. Dragging the drunken slut into the darkness of the ice safe.

He was leaking all over the place.

Looking through the window of the ice safe....

The mobsters laughing; sounds of shattering bone.

Beet juice everywhere.

And an acrid smell of tarnished copper.

CHAPTER 21

Brownsville, 1919
The Butcher Shop

The hallucinations took Sy back in time. He was sixteen, scanning the Manhattan skyline from the overlook of the Ridgewood Reservoir. His first trip into the land of the Gentiles was not a happy one. The fine clothes displayed in the shop windows; the fancy cars passing him on the street, all fueled his anger toward the life of poverty he was born into. Reluctant to return to the ratty tenement above his father's butcher shop, he chose to spend the rest of the afternoon walking in the park.

He followed the flight of a Red-Shouldered Hawk as it circled lazily in the updraft above him. Its seemingly innocent flight between air currents belied the bird's presence at the reservoir. Sharp-eyed, ready to dive and pounce on its prey at a moment's notice, the hawk was looking for an easy mark.

To Sy, the bird mirrored his own way of life. Growing up amongst the Jewish and Italian gangsters in Brownsville, he never thought about success—it was always a question of survival. He learned to steal, to lie, to manipulate and bully and found great enjoyment in frightening people—in making them feel bad about themselves—in crushing their dreams.

He met survivors of the Holocaust, listened to their pathetic stories, and stared at the numbers etched into their arms. One-third of the

Jewish population of Europe wiped out by the Nazis. Jews were an easy mark.... *Survival is everything. Never trust. Never assume. Everyone's against you. If you have it, they want it. You're either predator or prey.*

The stories he heard of the Pale of the Settlement—the toilet of Russia. The Jews, relegated to the ghetto, spit upon because of their noses, accents, strange ways, and greedy fingers. They were persecuted, shunned, and excluded. *The chosen people against the rest of the world.*

His mother's tales of the Cossacks: how they stomped over the floorboards above his grandfather's cellar where he, barely two years old, hid with his mother for a week. Their passage to America to join his father in Brownsville. Mother and son languishing in the bottom of the steamer for over a week. No sanitation, starving from a lack of kosher food, allowed an hour a day of sunlight, then hosed down with disinfectant before reaching Ellis Island.

Survival.

But along with the passage of these innocents to America came the predators looking for a quick score. Instead of Cossacks, it was the Italian and Jewish thugs who fed on the poor and honest people escaping the ghettos of Europe.

He recalled playing outside Midnight Rose's, the Brownsville candy store that was the headquarters of Mob hitmen. It was there, along with his best friend Mikey Trozzo, that he slipped into the life.

"Hey *Boychik*, wanna make a shekel?"

"Sure."

"Okay, listen. You and your friend here, take this package over to the synagogue on Chester Street. Give it to Moshe Zimmerman. Only him, understand?"

"Sure, sure...gee, thanks!"

It was so simple, so innocent.

The hawk seemed to stop in midair before falling into a dive. The free fall continued for several seconds until he disappeared in the foliage below. Sy wanted to fly away—free himself from the poverty his family traveled an ocean to escape only to find again.

Brownsville—just another Shtetl.

Getting out was easy. Staying out took dough. If you got in good with the outfit you could pick up some serious cash. And Sy had dreams—big dreams. He was tired of sleeping on the threadbare couch while his younger brother Eli slept in a real bed. He wanted out.

It was getting dark and Sy left the park to take the subway home. He wandered the streets of his Brownsville neighborhood until nightfall, stole a bottle of wine, and hung around the social club for an hour where he picked up a pretty young thing.

He led her into the alleyway behind his father's butcher shop. They drank and made out until she became plastered. He opened the back door with a copied key and led her inside. The girl was slurring her words and could hardly stand up.

Ripe for the picking.

Sy splayed her out on his father's butcher table. Too drunk to resist, she let him lift her dress and push her panties aside. She was weak and fresh meat. He was strong and there was no stopping him now. He pushed himself into her and went at it with a brutal force that released all the morning's frustrations.

Sounds at the back door....

He stopped and hauled her into the darkness of the ice safe where she crumpled to the floor. Through the small window, he saw three hoods from Midnight Rose's carrying a rolled-up rug into the shop. They unrolled it and dumped a body on the butcher table.

His father, Tovi, rolled in two beer barrels and handed out aprons, saws, cleavers and bundles of old newspaper. Then, the holy man retreated to the sink, turned around, and lowered his head. Was it fear, shame or was he praying—it was hard to tell?

The sounds of laughing, hacking, and sawing seeped into the ice safe. Sy saw his father finger the blue and white *Tzitzit* strands of his *Tallis*. A *Chazzan* of the synagogue and a righteous man, Tovi wore his *Tallis* beneath his clothes—the tassels poking out of his waistband were splattered with blood.

While the men wrapped body parts in newspaper and dumped them into barrels, Tovi pulled the *Tallis* out from under his shirt and faced the sink to scrub out the blood. It wasn't until the gangsters lifted the barrels and filed out of the shop that his father turned around. The last man out tossed a package on the counter next to the sink and slammed the door behind him.

Tovi put on an apron, wired down the wooden butcher table and rinsed it off along with the tiled walls. After sweeping up the blood-soaked sawdust, his father dumped the pile into a bin and spread a new layer over the floor. He dropped the aprons in the wash bin and picked up the paper bag from the counter.

At the table, his father counted out the bills, sorting them into smaller piles. After wrapping them in little packages of newspaper, he inspected his *Tallis* and left with his money.

That's right holy man—more money in one night than you make in half a year. Not a bad night's haul for a little wet work.

Who's to know?

God, maybe....

But once a year you can repent....

So, it's not a big deal.

CHAPTER 22

Woodmere, 1964
A Scratch on the Floor

David cast his glance down into the living room from the second-floor landing. His stepfather was passed out on the couch.

His mother joined him. "What should we do? It smells like he released his bladder, but he's breathing okay. He really got himself into a state this time."

"I think he's out for the night," David remarked. "Why don't we get the suitcases from the storage closet so you can start packing the clothes and jewelry you want to hide in the store." They headed toward the attic stairs and David noticed a snag in the rug outside the office. He pointed at the carpet, "Mom, do you know what happened here?"

She turned the lights on. "I have no idea."

They both leaned down to scan the carpet for other signs of disturbance. David pointed out two parallel indentations stamped into the pile on the edges of the first few steps.

"Maybe it's a trick of the light?" Ellen suggested.

David bent down and ran his finger over them. "Nope, there are two ridges here and it looks like they would match the width of a file cabinet," he said. "And see there, how the carpet is flattened. Like something heavy was on top?" With his mother following, he moved up the stairs. "The marks repeat on each step—and they continue on the landing as two long furrows. Look, they disappear in front of the storage closet."

"You think he moved the file cabinet up here?" his mother asked.

"Could be." David opened the door to the storage closet, turned on the light, but didn't see anything out of the ordinary. "Warn me if he wakes up," he said to his mother. He entered the closet and made his way towards the back passing a jumble of boxes, old books, beat-up lampshades, and his mother's ivory mahjong set.

Ellen stood inside the door. "Anything?"

"Nothing," replied David. "If you can get the flashlight from the kitchen, I'll pull out the suitcases. Check on him. Make sure he's still zonked out."

His mother met him outside her bedroom with the suitcases and gave him the flashlight. "I shook him slightly. He's going to be out for a long time," she said. "I had to hold my breath from the stench. I guess the couch is ruined."

David took the flashlight, "I'm going back to the attic. Check on him now and again. Come and get me if you think he's waking up."

She nodded and moved the suitcases into the bedroom. He went back to the storage closet, switched on the flashlight, and headed toward the gaping blackness at the back. As he continued deeper, he swept the beam of light over the sloping rafters with its insulation, ductwork, and the large air-conditioning unit beyond.

Then the attic flooring ended. Ahead of him, a narrow bridge of plywood decking offered a tenuous walkway over the exposed joists. One false step and he might put a foot through the ceiling.

David aimed the flashlight at the decking. It was torn up as if something heavy was dragged over it. He ventured further in, swinging the light into the murky corners on either side of him, expecting to see the old metal cabinet loom up before him. But it didn't appear.

A few more steps and the path split. One led to the A/C unit in front of him and was smooth and dusty. The other veered off to the left. It was splintered; the dust disturbed. He stood at the crossway and penetrated the darkness on the left with the flashlight. The path led to a pile of boxes stacked up against a wall.

It was a dead end.

৵৹

Outside on the street, Riley watched as lights in the Greenberg home went off and on several times. The family should be dreaming heavily from the strong tranquilizer mixed with the LSD. Instead, there seemed to be a lot of activity in the house.

It was eight-thirty, and he was hungry. He'd give the sedative some time—drive into town; pick up a bite to eat. When he returned, the lights would be out.

∽∾

David left the attic thinking to check on his stepfather. When he reached the second-floor landing, he heard Sy's snoring and went into his mother's bedroom instead.

"I've got the suitcases all packed," she said to him from across the bed. "Since he's still out cold, I should take it to the store. While I'm there I'll clean out the register and petty cash."

David put the suitcases in the station wagon and his mother drove off. He snapped off the lights and went back to the attic. If his stepfather woke up, he would stumble around in the dark—the noise would give him plenty of warning.

He went into the storage closet and closed the door. Leaving the overhead light off, he turned on the flashlight and headed towards the wall of boxes. If his stepfather looked up the stairs, he'd see nothing but darkness. He poked through the boxes against the wall. They held hangers from his mother's store, outdated tax bulletins, and broken picture frames.

Squatting on his haunches, he passed the flashlight aimlessly around. A film of dust covered the tops of the boxes, but there was little on the floor. A small arc could be seen etched into the plywood beyond where the boxes were stacked—as if the edge of a door scratched the wooden planking. Looking straight ahead, he noticed two studs in the attic wall were spaced wider than the others.

A hidden door?

∽∾

Riley picked up a sandwich and headed back to the Greenberg home. Preoccupied with eating and driving, he took little notice of the station wagon that passed him in as he entered Greenberg's neighborhood.

Parking near the house, Riley stole around to the patio door, jimmied the lock and entered the family room. Removing the tranquilizer gun from his waistband and holding the flashlight in his left hand, he cradled his gun hand on top of his other wrist. Opening the door to the basement, he slunk halfway down the stairs and swept the room with his flashlight. There was no one.

He turned back and headed up to the first floor where he was surprised to see Sy Greenberg splayed out on the couch. It was a good sign, and he hoped the LSD would have the same magic on the rest of the family—especially David.

Taking the next set of stairs up to the living quarters, he made a quick search of two rooms off to the right—an office and spare bedroom. They were empty. The master bedroom across the hall was unoccupied as well.

Where was the mother?

Wary now, he headed up the last set of stairs. It made sense a loner like David would isolate himself from the rest of the family. He found three rooms in the attic. The one on the left, a makeshift studio, was empty. So too, was the one on the right, a storage room. With one room left, Riley moved quietly down the hallway and slowly turned the knob to David's bedroom door.

෩෨

David stepped back a few paces and blinked in the location of the boxes piled in front of the wall. Moving them aside, it didn't take long for David to peel down the insulated batting stuffed between the right and left studs. Cleverly disguised as part of the attic wall, the door had three hinges on the right side and a padlock on the left. Since the hinges were on the outside of the door, it would be easy to knock out the pins to gain entrance.

He heard a noise. He killed the flashlight and held his breath to listen. Had his stepfather wandered up the stairs looking for him? Sleeping in an attic bedroom, he was familiar with the creaks and groans of the house at night and was sure his stepfather was still asleep. Even so, Sound carries at night. Knocking out the hinge pins would be noisy—it could wake his stepfather. David put everything back the way it was and decided to wait until his parents left for the airport the next morning.

෩෨

Riley moved into David's room with his finger poised on the trigger of the tranquilizer gun.

The room was empty.

He looked under the bed. In the closet. No one was in the house, but the old man. He left the room and backtracked down the stairs to the Family Room. Riley opened the door to the garage—a car was missing. While getting his damned sandwich, mother and son took off.

Riley left the house the same way he entered. On the way back to his car he recalled the last time he tried to nail David. *The boy seemed to sense danger and turned in time to stop the dart with his wood palette. Maybe he experienced a similar premonition tonight and convinced his mother to leave the house. Maybe they were in the station wagon that passed me on my way back to the house. Damn.*

He got in his car to start the long drive back to the city. There was no doubt in his mind the kid was something special. According to the Bell Lab article, the boy could not only project mind visions onto a piece of paper, but he had an unexplained pre-cognitive ability.

It wouldn't be a stretch to assume Greenberg could also be adept at remote viewing. Perhaps he's not even aware of it? After all, to him, it would simply be another one of his visions. Remote viewing was something the government was very interested in, and Riley was more determined than ever to snag David.

If he couldn't sneak up on him, there were other ways of bringing him to heel.

CHAPTER 23

Day 10
The Ledger

Early the next morning, Ellen slipped quietly out of bed and moved through the darkened room to her walk-in closet. Closing the door and switching on the light, she rummaged through her belongings for the third and last time. Was there anything else she'd regret leaving behind? *Jewelry in my handbag, my best clothes are in a suitcase at the store with some old photos of Davie.*

She dressed and tiptoed downstairs to the hall closet. Her fur coat was toward the back hanging in a garment bag. It was the one extravagance Sy conceded to during their marriage—only because his brother's wife had one. She remembered when he came home and dumped the large box on the bed.

"Here," he said, "make sure you wear it to the Epstein wedding this weekend."

She modeled it for him in front of the mirror. It was not her style, but she gushed over it none-the-less. The old-fashioned cut and musty smell told her it was second hand. Looking at it now, she saw how it lost its sheen and the seams came loose in places.

Like her marriage.

The recent tidal wave of change picked Ellen up and tumbled her along an unknown course. There was no turning back now. Once her husband dropped her off at the airport, she'd be on her own for the first time in decades. With the money from the Nassau account, she would survive comfortably, but the change would be drastic, and she feared losing what little family life she had.

As daylight filtered through the windows, she went from room to room in a desperate attempt to find some meaningful memories to take with her. Small pockets of happiness came back to her, but they were crushed by the cruelty and deceit of her husband and her ultimate failure to stand up to him.

In the kitchen, she stood at the coffee maker and decided. If her father could change from a cold, selfish man, she too could re-dedicate her life to repairing the damage caused by her silence.

David and Nina would be her life now.

And then their children.

❧❧

Ellen was on her third cup of coffee, when David entered the kitchen. "You timed it perfectly," she said. "Sy is in the shower. He'll be down for breakfast soon, so we should talk now." She noticed the dark circles under his eyes, "You were asleep when I got back from taking the suitcases to the store. What happened?"

"I found a hidden closet in the attic," he said. "It's where he's hiding everything. I'll bet the old file cabinet is up there too."

She put her coffee cup down on the table. "What do mean 'everything'?"

"Everything like evidence, Mom. Proof that will put him away for a long time."

"You mean jail?"

"More like prison," he said.

She gave a brief shudder. "Did you open it?"

"Too noisy. I'll do it after you both leave."

A door closed upstairs. He was coming....

"Here," she said taking some large bills out of her apron, "from the petty cash at the store—to pay your tuition."

David took the money. "I'll pay you back. Have a good trip and call me from Aunt Rose's."

Ellen nodded and turned toward the coffee maker to refill her cup. Her husband walked into the kitchen, picked up his wife's fresh cup of coffee, and leaned his back against the counter. David started to leave.

"Where are you going?" Sy demanded.

"Back to bed," David told him. "I wanted to say goodbye to Mom."

"That's it, no apology for last night, huh?" he complained. "Who do you think you are coming at me with a knife like that?"

"I'm not the one who began to—"

"Listen, don't you mouth off to me," Sy exclaimed. "Whatever you got to say, I don't want to hear it. In fact, I don't ever want to see you again—I'm throwing you out—for good. We'll drop you off at the train station on our way to the airport. I'm finished with you."

"Not necessary, I can walk to the station," David insisted.

"Don't get fucking cute with me, I'm not in the mood. You're going now. And fork over the key to my house."

David went upstairs to get the key. Ellen turned to her husband, "Really Sy, is that necessary?"

"Oh, so I should just let him get away with it?"

"You've already said you wouldn't pay his tuition—isn't that enough?"

"It was punishment for something else—this is for trying to stick me with a knife."

David seemed deep in thought when he returned with his key. He handed it over and Sy left the kitchen with the cup of coffee. Ellen heard the office door slam and reached into her handbag. "Here's my key David. I want you to find out what's behind that door in the attic."

Her son took it from her as if in a daze—she saw him shudder slightly—it was what he did when he felt something wasn't quite right.

"What?" she asked.

"He's going to come back here. Why else take away my key. Its forty minutes round trip to the airport. It'll take half that for me to walk home from the station—I don't think I have enough time before he gets back."

She picked up the phone. "Call a taxi for an 8:10 pick up at the station. We're leaving at eight sharp."

⋘⋙

Sy waited a long time to say those words. He wanted to throw him out a long time ago. No one could argue with him now. After all, the kid threatened him with a knife. He had every right to disown him.

If that wasn't enough, he saddled the boy with his last tuition payment, and now he would make it even harder for him to pay it. Upstairs in his office, he placed the coffee cup on his desk and removed a small piece of paper from his wallet. On it was the phone number he copied from David's sketchbook days ago—some client named Hawkins. He decided to call him, put the pressure of the IRS on the man to make sure David would never work for Hawkins's ad agency again.

He took a sip of coffee and dialed. A practiced voice crackled through the receiver, "Federal Bureau of Investigation. How may I direct your call?"

Sy slammed the phone down. "Shit, fuck, piss! That fuckin' little turd!"

He couldn't believe it—David and the feds? But what did the little shit know? Nothing, that's what. A bunch of suspicions—nothing he could prove. Best case scenario the FBI would dismiss everything as some counterculture bullshit. But still, better not take any chances. If David was raising questions at the FBI, he needed to get in front of it—find out what the snitch was saying.

He called Chip.

"Yeah?"

"David's up to something," Sy told him. "I need you to keep an eye on him—tell me where he goes, who he sees."

"Already on it," Chip replied. "Your stepson's a sneaky little bastard. Spotted him going into the FBI building a few days ago."

"Fuckin' shit."

"Yeah, but it gets worse. I found out he hangs around the Food Mart. Usually eats over at Moe's after classes, then strolls across the street to schmooze with Mike."

"Are you kidding me—how the hell did he get involved with Mike?"

"Beats me. But the word is they were good friends. David and his squeeze showed up with two FBI agents an hour after the bombing. After the cops identified the body, he needed to be led into Moe's to recover from the shock."

Sy's mind raced. Mike must've known David was his son. During the years of their friendship, how many stories about the good old days did David listen to? All this time, Mike was getting even with him through David—setting him up—maybe even snitching to the feds.

"You see or hear anything else going down, let me know right away."

"Okay, so what about a little bonus for clipping Mike and keeping an eye on David?"

Sy thought it over. "Sure. Meet me today after two—McSorely's, on seventh across from Cooper Square. You'll get your bonus, and we'll talk about your future."

He hung up and picked up the coffee.

It was cold.

❧

Arriving back at the house at 8:20, David went up to the attic with a flashlight, tools, and the Polaroid. He knocked out the hinge pins on the hidden door and squeezed through the opening. Groping around in the dark, he found a hanging cord and snapped on the light.

The closet was roughly five by seven feet. A wall of shelves held empty Manila envelopes. A small built-in desk was in one corner. There was a lamp, an adding machine, legal pads, a bottle of Scotch, and a whiskey tumbler. On the shelf above was a large ledger with a light-grey cover. The old file cabinet was to the left of the door frame and an empty box stood in the middle of the floor.

David backed up as far as he could and blinked the entire section of each wall into his memory. Then, he opened the old file cabinet. Relatively empty the day he found his stepfather's Will, today it was crammed with papers, files, and old tax returns. Sifting through it all would be too time-consuming. He only had forty-minutes.

He looked over to the shelf above the scotch...*Maybe the ledger?* Flipping through it, he realized the ledger was a running history of his stepfather's crimes. This was more like it. Everything the FBI needed was spelled out in it: a list of Sy's scams and shakedowns as a young man in Brownsville; fraudulent tax returns he prepared while working for his brother's accounting firm on Pitkin Avenue. The money he made after taking over Abbadabba's lucrative position as an accountant for Manhattan's Mob boss. A long list of government officials on the take followed. Deals made and favors granted while a revenue agent for the IRS: bribes he took; gifts received; blackmail information on friends, and Mob associates.

Then, David hit the jackpot. Payments to Mike's father when he took over the numbers operation at the Food Mart. Summary pages of illegal profits from each year since Sy bought it. There was a gross profit column labeled "Actual", and another labeled "Adjusted". The last column was labeled "Kick up to Moretti".

It was all spelled out. Moretti's monthly kickback was calculated on a reduced amount of Sy's actual profit. As long as the monthly decrease was figured on the same percentage, Moretti would never become suspicious.

David took Polaroid shots of key pages and scanned many more into his memory. His decision now was a hard one. The ledger was the definitive proof Hunter needed. If he took it, his stepfather would discover it missing and disappear before the FBI could act. He looked at his watch—he must decide now.

David tore out two pages he thought most useful to the FBI—Sy's involvement in tax fraud, racketeering, money laundering, and his connection with the Mob. He put the ledger back on the shelf and accessing his memory, replaced everything he touched. He put the hinges and insulation back in the wall, then shoved the boxes in front of the hidden door.

He shuddered—Sy was coming. Grabbing his duffle, he stuffed it with the tools, flashlight, Polaroid, and ledger pages and ran down the stairs. Outside on the front steps, he spotted the station wagon turning down the street and took a dive into the bushes.

Sprawled out in the dirt off to the side of the house, David heard the garage door open. Soon, his stepfather shuffled up the steps. "Alone at last," David heard him say. And then the front door slammed shut.

৵৵

David sat amongst the shrubs and caught his breath. From the looks of the hidden closet, Sy was packing things up with an intent to flee. Scores of Manila envelopes lay scattered around the shelves as if they were just emptied. Flattened boxes were lined up against one wall. Now that his mother was away, it all made sense—his father was planning to disappear.

Crawling around to the back of the house, he hid behind a tall hedge and waited. Within a short while, he heard the patio door slide open and he moved down the hedge for a better view. Sy brought a bunch of boxes out to the patio filled with files. When the last box was positioned a few feet from the grill, Sy pulled out a handkerchief, dabbed his nose and inspected the red stain on the cloth.

This was not the first time David witnessed his stepfather's nosebleeds. Months ago, he recalled seeing a slight dribble and as weeks wore on, the blood flow became more profuse.

Sy sat in a lawn chair with his head thrown back and holding his nostrils together. In that brief instant, David noticed a childlike fear replace Sy's predatory look. Confronted by the fragile humanity of his stepfather, David was surprised to feel a twinge of compassion.

Five minutes later Sy was in front of the barbecue grill dumping reams of paper onto a feebly lit fire. Nothing happened so he squirted starter fluid on top. The resulting flash almost made him fall over backward. The the phone rang and Sy rushed into the house. David could hear him through the open patio door.

"Yeah, so what? Just because they haven't come to you for a warrant yet doesn't mean they went to some other judge...Uh-huh, okay, so call me...Make it every fifteen, twenty minutes.... Well, that's too bad—you owe me.... Okay, now that's more like it. And don't double-cross me, I've got ways to get to you—even from jail."

He hung up, "Fuckin' asshole."

Sy fed the fire with file folders until one box remained. He put down the long-handled barbecue fork and went in through the back kitchen door, returning with a large container of soup. David recognized it—the leftover Borscht. In fifteen minutes Sy passed out. David moved from the bushes to stand behind his stepfather.

The phone rang again.

Startled, David slipped through the patio door and hid behind the wet bar. The ringing continued, yet Sy didn't budge. Figuring it was safe, David moved into the garage, leaving the door open so he could see through the family room and out to the patio. Sy was still sleeping in the lawn chair, his head resting on his chest.

David surveyed the garage. The two cars were there with the station wagon facing out for a quick getaway. The cargo hatch was open. Inside, a few bags were thrown into the space. The golf bag contained all the usual gear: golf balls, tees, scorecards, and two pairs of gloves. His mother told him it was custom-made to hold large amounts of cash, but it was difficult to understand how. He pulled out some clubs, thrust a hand down the bag, and discovered a series of zippers attached to the lining. Noticing also, how short the golf clubs were, he realized the bottom of the bag held a secret compartment. A clever piece of work.

There were three other bags. A satchel held one-hundred-dollar bills and the golf tote next to it was stuffed with more cash. A small overnight bag held a few clothes and was bottom-heavy—it felt like something hard was underneath. He moved the clothes aside. On the bottom of the tote was Sy's ledger. If he took it now, Sy wouldn't find it missing until it was too late.

It was now or never.

CHAPTER 24

Sleeping Dogs

David replaced Sy's ledger with magazines from the family room. He zipped it up and started to close the other two bags. He stopped. The bundles of cash beckoned. Here was more money than he had ever seen in his life. *So much money–I could take a thousand–maybe more. Who knows where all this cash goes after it's confiscated by the FBI? After everything that's happened–I deserve it.*

Yes, but...

This was how it began. Like his mother, one small departure from doing what's right—even if justified by an undeniable grievance—leads to one misdeed after another until your moral compass is eroded. After that, there's no turning back. David shook off the temptation and zipped up the other two bags. He retrieved his duffle from the bushes, put the ledger inside, and took off through the adjacent easement.

After a long walk, he arrived at the train station and bought a ticket to the city. There was time before his train, so David called Nina. She insisted he call the FBI.

"Ask them to pick you up at Penn Station. The sooner you give them the evidence the sooner you can wash your hands of this whole business."

He hung up and called the FBI. Hawkins was out, but Keyes offered to pick him up at the Station. David gave him the arrival time and hung up and boarded the train. Finding a seat, he jammed his duffle between himself and the window and powered down.

The commuters around him held newspapers in front of them, their heads bobbed with the movement of the train until their eyes closed and the papers dropped to their laps. Discarded trash shifted between the seats to the monotonous sway and incessant clackety-clack of the rails. Every so often the singsong call of the conductor would rouse a few sleepy commuters. Each, in turn, folded their newspaper, gathered their belongings, and joined the queue at the door.

Exhausted from the dramatic events of the past few days, David eased back into his duffle, and launched himself into a much-needed purge of his short-term memory. One by one the pages of Sy's secret ledger turned in his mind's eye. His chin fell to his chest and the overload of images transferred to his long-term memory.

Each page delineated Sy's secret life of crime: lists of taxpayers from whom Sy accepted bribes; falsified income tax returns; profits from the Food Mart's numbers operation, and names of runners, controllers, clerks, and enforcers.

As more pages flipped by, David followed along—an idle observer, dwelling listlessly on bits and pieces of information and then letting them go. As the day's images were purged from his active memory, he felt a soothing release.

The conductor called out, "Penn Station next. Last stop Penn Station."

The announcement intruded on David's memory dump, cutting it short at a ledger page of Mob informants. Half-awake, his inner vision focused on columns of names—lawyers, judges, prosecutors, paralegals, and police officers on the take.

Suddenly, David shook himself awake.

Six NYPD officers—one of them Detective Tom Keyes.

❧

Forty-five minutes after the call from David, Keyes was standing on the platform of Track 5 at Penn Station, waiting for the inbound train from Far Rockaway. Finally, his luck was turning. With Agent Hawkins breathing down his back and Hunter's unending scrutiny, it was difficult to acquiesce to Moretti's demands.

The street boss was furious. "So, this kid David, you say he's got some kind of super memory, hates his father's guts, and is lookin' for the goods to put Greenberg away?"

"Right," Keyes said. "I know it sounds crazy, but I swear this ability of his is legit. It won't be long until he finds something."

"Fuckin' douchebag accountants," Moretti spat out, "always writing things down meticulous like. Sy's probably got my name plastered all over some goddamn ledger. You better get me whatever the kid finds, 'cause if the feds get a hold of it, you're gonna have trouble breathing."

The train rumbled out of the tunnel, the blast of warm air mussing Keyes's hair. He ran his fingers through it while watching the commuters step out onto the platform.

Come to papa.

But David didn't appear. Keyes moved next to the stairs to make sure they'd connect. After a time, the train emptied and idled, waiting for its next run. He looked frantically around. The platform was empty, yet David was nowhere to be seen. The rogue agent ran up the stairs to the second level concourse and spotted David heading towards the passage to the IRT Subway.

Why is David avoiding me?

Keyes hurried after him, sprinting through the crowded concourse, down through the tiled passageway to the underground subway. *I have to stop him—David might board the first train he finds and disappear with the evidence.*

⁊∽⁊

"FBI, out of the way!"

David could hear Keyes shouting his way through the commuters behind him. As he ran, he realized all the evidence was in his duffle—torn pages, photos; the ledger itself. He should split them up—just in case. As he dodged through the crowd, David removed the ledger and slipped it under his belt at the small of his back. Long and narrow, the ledger was concealed by the overlap of his jacket.

Behind him, Keyes's badge was out parting an empty path toward him. David ran full out now, his duffle bumping back and forth against his ribs. The tunnel gave off a rancid smell of stale urine, filling his lungs as he sucked in one long breath after another. Breaking free of the passage, he was approaching the waist-high turnstiles and jammed his hand into his pocket for a token.

Keyes was shouting, "FBI, stop that man!"

A few yards away, two transit cops appeared and closed in on him. If he could get on the other side of the turnstiles, he might make it. People scrambled away from the entrance. His token went in. He pushed his hip against the arm of the turnstile, and it gave way, another turnstile arm coming up from behind hit him in the back.

As he moved out into the open, he was jerked back. His duffle strap caught in the turnstile. He tried to pull it loose and spotted Keyes.

His gun was out; the two transit cops were in position to hop over the turnstiles.

There was no choice. Shedding his jacket, David left the duffle jammed in the turnstile and moved forward. But his twisting motion dislodged the ledger from his waistband, and it fell to the floor. David swung around to scoop it up and noticed the astonished look on Keyes's face. The pursuit was far from over.

Get on a train—any train. David raced onto a platform. A train was filling up. As he sprinted toward it, the double doors began to close. His free hand went out and held one door, the other hand jammed the ledger against the opposite door. Driving a wedge between the doors with his shoulder, he was in.

The train pulled away. Keyes and the two transit cops ran by the side of the train. David backed up in the subway car and collapsed into a seat. The sign above told him he was on the West Side Line heading uptown.

David exhaled in relief—he was on his way to Columbia University.

The cabbie crossed Central Park at 86th Street weaving in and out of traffic on the way toward the East Side. Jacob held on to the strap wondering how long it was since he rode in a cab. Last time it was a quarter to put your foot inside a taxi. Today a dime more.

As they exited the park and headed down Fifth Avenue, Jacob asked, "Tell me, when did the fare change from twenty-five to thirty-five cents?"

"Gee Pops, I think ten years back," the man recalled. "Didn't have my medallion then. But now you mention it, I remember fares started going up soon after I started."

"1952, maybe?" Jacob mused.

"Yeah, maybe, but if them new tax cuts don't kick in, they're goin' ta have ta knock up fares again. What ya goin' ta do—politicians don't care nothin' 'bout nobody—ya gotta take care of yerself. Right?"

They turned down 63rd Street, and Jacob got out near Ashcroft Galleries. As he walked into the impressive gallery, a tall, gaunt-faced man in his late fifties turned on his heel and approached him. He was well built for his age and had an overbearing expression. A name tag identified him as Hermann Scholz, Gallery Director.

"May I help you?" Scholz asked. Except for one disdainfully raised eyebrow, his face remained expressionless.

Jacob asked to see Leonard Ashcroft. The man's lips hardly moved as he informed Jacob, Mr. Ashcroft saw people only by appointment.

"But tell me, he's here today?" insisted Jacob.

"Yes, however as I mentioned, you would need an appointment. If you'll give me your name and number, and a brief description of what you require, I will see to setting one up for you."

"Listen, you think it was easy for an old man like me to get here? This is a matter of extreme urgency. I must see him today."

"I'm sorry but—"

"If I need to wait for an appointment, who knows what could happen. I could get sick and never make it back. I might forget what I need to tell him—or also—I could drop dead."

"But—"

"Look, I'm not some old man off the street. Ashcroft knows me—way back to the 1930s. My business is personal and very important."

"But—"

Jacob became agitated. "Stop already with the buts! There are things he has to know. Now—today—before it's too late."

The man seemed surprised at Jacob's outburst and became more agreeable. He removed his hands from behind his back and motioned to a chair.

"What is your name?"

"*Sag einfach Jacob Goldstein, Leopold wire sidi erinnen.*"

When Jacob referred to Leonard Ashcroft's given name of Leopold, Scholz's eyebrow shot up again. "*Jetzt versterhe ich, du bist der schwiegervater.*"

The man's German was flawless. He knew Jacob was Ashcroft's father-in-law—back when Leo's name was Leopold Aschbacher. Before Jacob could ask, *Der Direktor* gave him an understanding nod.

"Please to wait," he said and disappeared into the back. In less than a minute he returned, with an obsequious smile, to lead Jacob toward the back of the gallery.

༒

David realized he was in deep trouble. Keyes would find the ledger pages and photos inside the duffle left behind at the turnstiles. It would be enough to whet Moretti's appetite to want the ledger itself. David's life was now at risk. With the FBI compromised, handing the ledger over to Hunter was out of the question. Keeping himself alive was his main priority and the only way to do it was to hide the ledger. As the train sped through the darkened tunnel, David searched his mind for a safe hiding place.

Tunnel...that's it.

The train would take him straight to Columbia's campus at 116th Street and Broadway. Once there, he could follow AJ's route through the vast network of abandoned tunnels from the Manhattan Project. A suitable hiding place might be found hidden behind an old piece of equipment or a niche between a confusion of piping.

Then, it would be the ledger for his life.

∽≥

Special Agent in Charge, Alan Hunter picked up his office phone. David was on the line. He sounded guarded, as if afraid someone else was listening in on their conversation. David explained how he was chased through the subway on his way back from Woodmere and lost the evidence against Sy Greenberg.

"Are you okay?" Hunter asked.

"Yes, but we need to talk."

"Okay, I'll send an agent to pick you up."

"I'm sorry sir, but this has to stay between us. You've got a breach in your organization and I'll talk only to you. That's the way it's got to be. Pick me up at Salter's Bookstore near the university and we'll meet Nina at her Park Avenue apartment. We'll talk there. I'm asking Nina to act as a witness to our conversation."

Hunter agreed and picked David up at the bookstore. One look at him and Hunter knew the young man was in danger. They drove in tense silence to the Park Avenue apartment where Nina broke the uneasiness floating in the air.

"Glad to see you again," Nina said cautiously.

"Likewise, despite all the secrecy," Hunter responded as he entered the large front hall. He took in the Spanish style furniture accented by dark wood furnishings and the many tapestries and paintings on the walls. They sat down in the dining room and Nina offered him some homemade lemonade.

Hunter held out his glass. "Thank you."

"No, thank you for coming," Nina said. "There's been...a lot going on."

Hunter knew when two people were braving it out. "Okay David, tell me what happened?"

"I was visiting my parents for a few days," he explained, "and found a hidden closet in the attic with Sy's secret files, and a ledger. I tore two pages from the ledger and took photographs. It's all the proof you need."

"And?" Something told Hunter there was a "but" coming.

"It was stolen from me," David said.

"How?"

David seemed to be more at ease now. "I left the house with the evidence and called Hawkins from Woodmere to ask him to pick me up at Penn Station. I wanted to get the evidence to you as quickly as possible. Agent Keyes answered—said his partner was out, but he'd come get me. Fast forward a half-hour and I'm on the train back to the city. My eyes are closing, and I lapse into what I call a memory purge. It happens when I overload my short-term memory—everything I've seen previously comes to the surface. That's when I found something out."

"You mentioned a breach," Hunter pressed.

"Yes, this is difficult for me. I don't know who to trust anymore—it's why I need a witness to this. You know a lot about me, but there's still something you don't know. In many ways, it will be just as difficult for you to accept as my indelible memory."

"I'm willing to listen," Hunter said.

"I'm capable of precognition. It happens when I'm put in a dangerous situation."

Nina interrupted. "I assure you it's true, I've seen it happen many times."

David continued, "So I'm on the train nodding off—in a kind of twilight awareness—turning the pages of Greenberg's ledger. I see lists of runners, controllers, clerks, enforcers—that kind of thing. Then I get the shudders—you know, like when a fingernail scratches across a chalkboard. It's a sign of impending danger.

"So, I become fully awake, and I see a page laid out in my mind's eye. It's labeled 'Informants'. There's one column for Sy and one for Moretti. I scan the list and find—I'm sorry sir—but Agent Keyes is on the list."

Hunter passed a finger under his mustache and smiled. "We know. Keyes is working undercover pretending to be crooked. He passes the information we want Moretti to hear and then keeps his ears open. It was a need-to-know operation."

David shook his head. "Then why, when I avoided him at Penn Station, did he chase me with his gun drawn?"

"Are you sure it was Keyes?" asked Hunter. "I know you've had issues with him in the past. Maybe your mind was playing tricks on you?"

"The past," David mumbled, "wait, maybe...."

David became silent and looked asleep. Hunter turned a questioning glance at Nina.

"Something triggered a memory," she said. "Give him a minute."

David's eyes were open; moving back and forth as if something was written on the wall. After a while, he snapped out of it.

"I read from Greenberg's ledger again—carefully this time. I know you have a hard time trusting me, so I'm going to tell you information I can't possibly know."

"Okay," Hunter said. "Go on."

"The ledger page listing informants had several subcategories: lawyers; judges; prosecutors, and paralegals. Keyes was listed under the category 'Law Enforcement' as NYPD Detective Tom Keyes, not FBI Agent Tom Keyes."

Hunter was stunned. *How in God's name did this get past me?*

David noticed Hunter's expression. "So, I've hit on something?"

"The truth, I'm afraid. Keyes was a Police Detective before he went federal. But that was two years ago. His undercover work was assigned last year."

David added, "So, he was on Moretti's payroll when he was a cop and became a mole in the Bureau after you hired him, I was right after all."

Hunter was thoughtful. *I've had disciplinary issues with Keyes, but never considered him a security risk. This explains why we've never made any headway in our undercover work.*

David interrupted Hunter's thoughts. "There's something else. My stepfather burned a lot of evidence in the barbecue grill."

Hunter responded, "Okay, I'll call the Nassau County authorities and get them on it. Have you had lunch?"

"No, I haven't eaten since last night and I've got to call my grandfather to see if he's okay."

"I've got to go back to the office for an hour or so," Hunter informed him. "Get something to eat, rest up and I'll be back later this afternoon to advise you on what to do."

CHAPTER 25

Leo

Jacob waited in the gallery for Herr Scholz to announce him to Leonard Ashcroft. He wondered how to address him—Leopold or Leonard? By the time Jacob entered Ashcroft's office, he settled on Leo. It was the name most used by those closest to him and he hoped it would lend a measure of intimacy to their conversation.

Leonard Ashcroft was already moving toward the door to greet him. There was an uncanny similarity to David in Ashcroft's look and demeanor. Jacob took a quick glance around the large, well-appointed office.

"I'm delighted to see you," Leo said. "Please, have a seat. I hope there isn't any confusion about your rent—I'll continue to remit the monthly amount to the new landlord. You needn't worry."

Jacob was taken aback. "Rent? I had no idea. I thought Greenberg was paying my rent. So, it was you all along. Thank you."

It was Leo's turn to be surprised. He sat in the chair next to Jacob and tilted his head—exactly like David.

"Jacob, forgive me. Of course, you didn't know. Naturally you have questions...."

"I do, but that's not why I came. It's something else."

"I see," Leo leaned back in his chair. "What can I help you with?"

"It's about your son David, denied to you all these years by the bastard who ruined my daughter's life and my grandson's happiness. By some miracle, David turned out to be a real *mensch*. Just this week he figured out that son-of-a-bitch Greenberg isn't his father."

The look of surprise on Leo's face didn't go unnoticed and Jacob seized the opportunity. "You're surprised they hid it from him? You thought, what, that David knew all about you yet didn't care? That he loved the piece of shit my daughter married?"

Leo pursed his lips and nodded, yes.

"He's a good boy—the best. Greenberg has always given David a hard time, but now he's out to destroy him. David needs help. What can an old man do? And my daughter, once so independent and strong, has changed into a doormat. She can't help him. You're the only one he's got. David's a talented artist—some kind of whiz kid with a special memory. He also looks a lot like you. Who knows, you might like him."

Leo's eyelids closed halfway as if looking at something on his desk. His silence prompted Jacob to shrug his shoulders and rise from the chair. "All right, I've said what I came to say. I'll go now. Thank you for listening." Jacob headed for the door and turned around. "I've done what I can. Maybe, finally, I can find some peace before I die."

Getting up from his desk Leo stopped Jacob at the door. "Jacob, please come back." He led Jacob into the office by the elbow, this time to the couch at the other end of the room. "Please, sit."

Jacob settled into the cushions. A wave of exhaustion swept over him. Leo sat down next to him. "First, let me thank you for coming here. It must have taken a lot of courage. Can I get you anything? Coffee? Have you had lunch?"

It was Jacob's turn to be surprised. "Perhaps a little tea?" Leo's manner reverted to the consummate gentleman he was before the war. As mysterious as his one-time son-in-law was, he remembered Leo as a gentle and sensitive man. It was his erratic and bizarre behavior after the war that prompted Ellen to divorce him.

"Tea, of course." Leo seemed attuned to Jacob's frailty and spoke kindly. "I can see you're tired. You must love David very much to make such an effort." He got up, switched on the intercom, and ordered tea with pastries. When he sat down again, he leaned forward and held Jacob in a steady gaze.

"Thank you, Jacob, for apologizing to me. I too have carried a lot of guilt over what happened. It was the war," he admitted. "The horrors I saw. Finding out my father was a Nazi. My mother languishing in an internment camp. It was all too much. I took it out on Ellen...on you and your wife Sarah. I'm so sorry."

Jacob found his handkerchief and dabbed his eyes. In time, the pastry and tea arrived and the two of them sat in silence for a few minutes. Leo still retained the aristocratic bearing Jacob remembered. Strangely, except for the beard, it was an older David sitting opposite him now. Leo had the same searching look in his clear blue eyes.

Leo broke the silence. "To be honest, in some twisted way, you helped me. After the divorce, I invested the money you gave me and disappeared into a monastery. Some years later, I started this gallery. Thanks to you I'm a wealthy man. That's why I'm paying your rent."

Jacob nodded his understanding.

"And you were right," continued Leo. "I put David out of my mind. After I refused Greenberg's request to adopt David, I had a visit from some thugs. They roughed me up a bit and told me the adoption would go forward without my consent. They said if I knew what was good for me, I would forget David.

Jacob shook his head in disgust, "Oy, the adoption. You should know it was illegal. Greenberg's *gonnif* judge arranged it without David knowing. Everybody kept quiet."

Leo's bitterness showed on his face. "If I had only known. You see, David was already thirteen then. I knew that for Greenberg to adopt him, David would need to renounce me as his father. But despite the birthday cards and presents I sent when he was younger, the adoption was still taking place. It meant David felt nothing for me. Shortly after, I opened this gallery. I didn't want any trouble from Greenberg's thugs or the IRS. I couldn't let Greenberg ruin my business, so I changed my name to Ashcroft. Thinking David chose Greenberg over me, I stayed away." Leo shook his head. "Adopted illegally you say—what a horrible thing to do to a young boy. Greenberg is a Machiavellian monster."

"A monster, yes, and that's why I'm here. David needs help, guidance. I do my best, but I don't have the resources you have. I need to know someone else will take his side."

Leo's eyes became glazed over, and like David, he recovered quickly from his remembrance, "My own grandfather was there when I needed him. You were right to come to me."

Jacob gave a knowing nod. "David's a lot like you—drifting off in the middle of a conversation. He was ten when they said he had epilepsy, but it was all a lie trumped up by Greenberg's unethical and crooked doctor. They gave him drugs he didn't need. Such a mess they made of his childhood."

Leo looked at him in disbelief. "He has the gift then. You must tell me everything."

"Better I should show you," Jacob said, as he handed him David's letter from Bell Labs. "First, you should read the letter. Then, if you have the time, go back to my apartment—I have more to show you."

⁓⁓

Agent Hunter caught a quick lunch, picked up what he needed from his office and returned to Nina's Park Avenue apartment later that afternoon. He handed David an official-looking form. "It's an application for employment as an FBI Consultant," he explained. "Once you fill it out, I'll push it through. There's no obligation for you to work for us permanently. I simply want you on the books in case you can help out from time to time. Meanwhile, you can carry this FBI identification card."

Curious, Nina asked, "Can I see it?"

Hunter handed it to her.

Nina took the card, asking, "Does it come with a badge?"

He laughed and said, "No, It's only an identification card. A temporary one. It's missing a photograph so David will need to drop by headquarters so we can take one. It's not much, but it might help his credibility with local law enforcement if he finds himself in a tight spot."

"I'm grateful," David said, as he looked through the application. "I'll fill it out before you leave."

Nina handed David the ID card. "I'm engaged to an FBI agent. Imagine that?"

"Not an agent, Ms. Caldas. An independent contractor hired to consult with us by using his special area of expertise. He would work out of my office at an hourly rate on a case-by-case basis. No strings. No guns."

"That's reassuring, thank you," she said.

Hunter continued, "As to what to do about Agent Keyes—well, it's going to be tricky. I'd like to keep him in play; feed him misinformation for a while. As you've figured out by now, I need concrete proof of wrongdoing. Agent Hawkins will be kept out of the loop as well. I need to ascertain if he's tainted too. I know it's asking a lot—can you handle it?"

"No problem," David answered.

Nodding his approval, Hunter continued, "We contacted the Nassau County Sheriff. They investigated and called us back. A dark cloud of smoke was reported coming from Greenberg's back yard. The Fire department arrived before the police. Large amounts of paper and cardboard were burnt in a barbecue grill. The Sheriff confirmed the hidden closet in the attic—it was cleaned out."

"Good thing my mom is visiting her sister in Florida," David added. "I told her it would be safer for her to stay away for a while."

"Sound advice," agreed Hunter. "I understand the house is a mess. Smoke drifted in through an open patio door and inundated two floors of the house."

"So, the house is empty?" David asked.

"Yes. Only one car in the garage. Chances are Greenberg took advantage of your mother being away to pack up and leave. If he's got any money with him, he'll have to stash it somewhere. A bank, storage facility, or with someone he trusts."

"He doesn't trust anyone," David said.

"Maybe," Hunter replied. "But his type always recruits some sycophant to do his dirty work. Not to mention a mistress or two."

"That's it," David responded. "My mom told me he has a long-time mistress living in New Jersey."

Hunter wrote it down.

"And if you're looking for Sy's sycophant, it's the bastard who killed Mike," David added.

"Why not Sy Greenberg himself?" queried Hunter.

"Can't put my finger on it," David explained. "Seems like my stepfather is wearing down. He's acting weird lately—not looking well. I don't see him running around planting bombs in the kind of state he's in. Just a thought."

"You're probably right." Hunter replied. "Hopefully, we'll get a lead on—"

David was spacing out. Hunter was getting used to David's habit of searching his memory in the middle of a conversation and gave Nina an amused smile.

She returned the smile and then said, "Now you know what I have to put up with."

David came back. "The ledger also has a list of banks in Florida and income from various business holdings: construction companies, pawnshops, and a bar in New Jersey."

"Addresses?" Hunter asked.

"I'll recite a list for you," David said.

Hunter grabbed his pencil and wrote it all down. "This is exactly why I'm hoping you'll consult for us. Something seen in passing could never be remembered with such detail by an ordinary agent."

"What happens now?" asked Nina.

"Now we liaison with the IRS, put the word out at airports and such. He won't get far. Meanwhile, we need a warrant—I need to use your phone to call Judge Scarpello."

"Of course," Nina said.

"You might want to rethink that," said David. "Scarpello is on Sy's list of informants. Let me give you a list of judges on the take. Then you can choose someone clean."

Hunter realized working with David was going to be a whole new ballgame.

⊰⊱

McSorely's Old Ale House on Seventh Street stood across from Cooper Square in lower Manhattan. Sy's go-to spot for unwinding, it was an easy taxi ride from the IRS building and a twenty-minute drive through the Holland Tunnel to Sy's mistress.

Entering the saloon was like a trip back in time. Brass and wood details could be seen everywhere. A coal-burning stove stood in the middle of the front room; artifacts and old newspapers hung on the wall behind the ancient bar.

There were no bar stools to sit upon, so Sy bellied up and waited for the manager, Harry Kirman, to notice him. Back in the day, Sy did some big favors for Harry. He owed Sy big time, and always gave him the VIP treatment when he dropped in.

A thin crowd of regulars stood at the bar, and it didn't take long for Harry to spot him. Harry hitched up his chin in a nod of recognition, pulled a tall, dark one and placed the mug in front of Sy.

"How are you, my friend?" he asked, slipping a plate full of cheese next to Sy's beer.

"Could be better Harry. Things are unraveling fast; I need a quiet place to think."

"No problem, I'll set you up in the back. Want a little dinner?"

Sy took off his hat and coat. "Got any pastrami?"

"The best—nice and lean." Harry picked up Sy's mug; the plate of cheese; a bowl of beer nuts and led him to the back room. He put him at a table near the fireplace, under the nude portrait of *Woman with a Parrot*. Sy gave it a leering glance and hung his coat and hat on one of the hooks under the painting.

He leaned back in his chair and scanned the walls above him. It was one huge man-cave. Its dark, honey-colored ambiance and sawdust-strewn floors usually put him at ease. But today the confusing patchwork of photographs, artwork, and surrounding memorabilia crowded in on his thoughts.

Sy drank the mug halfway down and leaned back in his chair to take stock. All the evidence from the hidden closet was burnt except for one box. Inexplicably, he fell asleep and missed the phone call from the judge. Not wanting to take any chances he packed up the remaining files and left the house.

Harry slid the sandwich and more nuts on the table. "Anything else you need Sy—anything at all," he said, moving away.

Sy dug into the sandwich. He had money and fake IDs. He hated to skip the country without settling the score with David, but it couldn't be helped. How the boy ended up hanging around with Mike was a mystery, but the friendship explained the connection between David and the FBI.

An FBI background check would reveal David's father was IRS. A smart investigator would speculate about a possible connection between Mike, David, and Sy. They would scratch around Sy's old cases to see if there was a slight stench. They'd also wonder why, during their investigation of David, Mike got blown up by a car bomb. If they decided to drill deeper, the FBI would eventually find Sy's connection to the Food Mart and the Mob.

He polished off the pint and took it to the front for a refill. Placing it on the bar, he told Harry he'd be stepping out for a few minutes.

Outside on the street, Sy spotted Chip leaning against the parking meter next to Sy's station wagon. Sy noticed Chip's preoccupation with Sy's bags in the cargo space.

"Hey Pops, you goin' on the lam? Your wagon's packed."

"Wife's gone for a week wise guy," Sy told him. "Thought I'd take a golf vacation." He took out his wallet and peeled off five one-hundred-dollar bills. "Here's your bonus," he said, giving him the money. "You still want to take over my operation?"

Chip folded the bills and put them in his wallet. "Yeah, where's the seed money you promised me?"

"It's set aside," Sy said. "When I get back, we'll talk about it."

Chip complained, "So this is what you call passing the torch? It's my fuckin' dough—my inheritance—whaddaya holdin' on to it for?"

Sy got annoyed. "Jesus Christ. How many times do I have to tell you it's not your money—it's for the start-up—so you can carry on my legacy. But two things gotta happen before you get it. First, the feds need to clear out of the neighborhood. Second, all the stupid construction must end so we can set up our drop points. When that happens, I'll give you the go-ahead and you get the dough."

"Some legacy," Chip shifted from foot to foot, his eyes darting to the bags in the back of Sy's station wagon. "It sucks. How do I know you're on the level?"

Sy turned on Chip. "What? After bringing you along like this I'm gonna cheat you—my own flesh and blood?" Sy pushed past him. "Don't break my balls, sonny boy," he called back to him. "I get enough of that shit from David." Sy paused before McSorely's and watched his son tear his glance away from the station wagon to walk back to his car.

Back in the bar, Sy went to the payphone with his bowl of beer nuts. People owed him and it was time to call in the markers. Like the smuggler from Fort Lauderdale who moved marijuana and other contraband across the Gulf Stream. And the retired hitman who spent the last year as caretaker of a cottage Sy bought on the island of Bimini.

He picked up the receiver and dropped in a bunch of coins. While it rang, he dug his hand into the bowl and shook the salt from the beer nuts in a loose fist. The smuggler answered and Sy confirmed a prior arrangement.

After stopping at the bar for a fresh mug, Sy sat at his table and gazed up at the nude painting. The woman's body was stretched out on a divan, knees up; legs opened suggestively. The nude was looking at the parrot, but to Sy, she was looking at him.

The ale mellowed his mood. Her flesh beckoned. At the stirring in his groin, he realized what he needed before leaving the country. He went back to the payphone and dialed an unlisted number in New Jersey.

"Marta, it's me. The shit's hit the fan and I need some downtime. I'm coming by later, make sure you've got the scotch I like."

⊰⊱

Chip moved his car down the street so Sy wouldn't spot him when he came out of the bar. When his father got into the station wagon, Chip put his car in gear and followed him as he pulled out into traffic. After a few blocks, Sy turned onto the entrance ramp of the Holland Tunnel.

On the New Jersey side, Chip tailed him for another twenty minutes, until he entered a residential area in Jersey City. Sy stopped in front of a small house with green shutters and backed up into the driveway. Chip parked a half a block up from the house and took out a pair of binoculars.

His father got out and unlocked the garage door with his own key. He rolled it up and looked up and down the street before pulling a box and an overnight bag out of his wagon. As he moved the box into the garage, a window curtain moved on the second floor. Chip lifted his binoculars to focus on a blonde woman wrapped in a white towel. She watched as Sy closed the garage door, locked the station wagon and walked toward the front door with the overnight bag.

CHAPTER 26

The Double-cross

Twelve years younger than Ellen, Marta Signorelli was vacuous, compliant, and available at a moment's notice. No questions were asked about the box Sy shoved in her garage. It was, after all, his house.

Sy followed her into the living room where she poured him a drink in front of a small wet bar. She dropped the towel and offered him the scotch, a smile and so much more.

He downed the liquor and took her with no preliminaries. Entering her, he immediately spent himself in the same off-hand way he swallowed his scotch—something to take the edge off a bad day.

Usually, he fell asleep afterward, while Marta smoked and thumbed through magazines. But today, too much was on his mind—specifically the morphing of Ellen and her son into black beetles during last night's dinner.

It was a reminder of how a deathwatch beetle showed up during his mother's illness and the relentless ticking before her death. He heard the sound again before the death of his father.

Now the deathwatch beetle was coming for him.

The craziness of last night was unnerving—the knife in David's hand, Sy's dizziness, the nosebleeds, and the pounding of his heart. If death was stalking him, he would face it down. It was the main purpose of all his frenetic humping—to put a strain on his heart—the ultimate stress test.

That's why he couldn't sleep. Oblivious to his anxiety, Marta picked up another magazine. There was the snap of her lighter and Sy lay awake in a cloud of tobacco fumes waiting for signs of cardiac arrest.

He marked the passage of time by the crinkle of turning pages, the tip of Marta's cigarette turning orange, fading, and then glowing again. The billowing smoke hung above his head like a huge question mark. Then, it drifted to the ceiling and dissipated into nothingness.

Sy looked at her. Marta was of Italian descent—forbidden fruit, a Wop, his *shiksa* whore. She reminded him of the fifteen-year-old he nailed in his father's butcher shop when he was sixteen. Now that he thought about it, she also resembled another *shiksa*—Chip's mom, Brooke.

After Brooke, Sy met another kind of forbidden fruit—Ellen. She embodied everything he ever dreamed of but couldn't have—a high society woman with rich parents and well-placed friends who could open doors no amount of cash could.

Sy thought the sex would be great. After all, there was nothing more exciting than boning an upper crust, oh so proper society dame. No dumpy wife for him like his brother Eli. He'd be the one pounding a high-class pussy. And with her nose job and dyed blonde hair, Ellen looked like a real *shiksa*.

He tried. Oh, he tried to make her his whore. After all, demeaning the little princess was the one thing that turned him on. But she wouldn't have it, so he looked elsewhere.

That's when he met Marta.

A few months after their meeting he set her up in business—a nudie bar in Jersey City. He figured it wouldn't bring in much, but he'd keep the broad happy and available. After a while, he checked it out and was surprised when Marta made all her girls available to him.

It was a revelation. Why struggle with a finicky wife when he had, at his very fingertips, a bevy of beauties to do his bidding. Then six months ago, it occurred to him he didn't need a wife.

He got a slow-acting poison from a black-market sawbones. With David still out of the house, he'd slowly poison her. By the time David graduated, Ellen would be dead.

After a while, Ellen started to feel poorly, and he thought the end would come soon. Then, inexplicably she felt better. Every time a refill of Valium came from the druggist, he made the switch, but still, nothing happened.

Now he was the one feeling like shit. Did anyone care whether he lived or died? No one, certainly not Marta. The only reason she kept her legs open was to hold onto the house. Well, she could have it. Where he was going, he wouldn't need it—or her.

Last year he bought a small beach house in the Bahamas. He finalized the purchase after reading how Congressman Adam Clayton Powell fled to Bimini to escape extradition back to the United States.

If Powell could escape extradition, so could he.

❧

Toward the middle of the afternoon, Marta stubbed out her cigarette and scooted down under the covers. After a while, the air cleared and Sy sat up. He felt fine—there was nothing wrong with his heart—he was going to survive. His island paradise was waiting, and he had plans to put into action.

The first order of business was to burn the box of files in Marta's garage. A quick firing up of her charcoal grill would take care of it. Sy slipped out of bed, used the bathroom, dressed, and headed for the garage.

❧

After Sy left the bedroom, Marta waited. When she heard the garage door open, she put on a robe and slippers and went to look out the front window. Sy lugged a box out of the garage and left it in the driveway. He went back in and came out with a bag of charcoal, put it next to the box, and closed the overhead door.

As she watched him move the box and charcoal around back, she recalled their beginning. She sold herself to Sy for what she could get out of him. Eventually, the depths of his depravity became too much. She wanted out. Knowing Sy wouldn't let her walk away, she went to Moretti for protection.

"Stay with him a little longer," Moretti said. "Uncle Sugar's messing around his neighborhood—chances are he'll be pinched—meanwhile, it looks like I gotta do some spring cleaning. You tell me what Sy is up to and I'll make it worth your while."

Marta went to the bedside phone and dialed Moretti's private number.

"It's Marta. Sy is here. He dragged a box into my garage. Looks like he's going to burn it. There's other stuff in his car." She hung up, removed a small-caliber gun from the nightstand, and placed it in her robe pocket.

The sound of the garage door opening.

Back at the window, Marta saw Sy coming out of the garage again. This time with a long-handled barbecue fork. He stopped beside his station wagon, made sure it was locked and disappeared out back. He was burning stuff. Whatever was in the box and his car was the leverage Moretti needed. She needed to stall him until Moretti's men showed.

Then, Marta noticed a tall, lanky man in his twenties walk toward her house. He was an arm swinger, loping forward with alternating shoves of his shoulders. As he approached the driveway, she saw him pause at the station wagon and look inside the cargo space with an annoyed, stone-like expression. The long, jet-black hair parted in the middle, framed a pair of mud-brown eyes that seemed dead as a fish— just like Sy's.

Who the hell is this guy? Couldn't be one of Moretti's crew, I just called.

The doorbell rang.

She went down the stairs and opened the door. Standing partially behind the open front door, she held the terry cloth robe tight over her chest. "Jesus," she said, "you're like the spittin' image of him—but younger."

"Hi, I'm Chip," the stranger said. "Yeah, I get that all the time. I'm looking for my dad, he said he might be here."

"He did?" She didn't like his look and became wary. "He never told me. Look, I don't know you so wait here—"

She tried to close the door, but Chip wedged his foot against it. "The bastard's got my money." He pushed past her; she lost her balance and the belt came loose. Chip reached out catching the terry sash in his fist and pulled it through the belt loops. The robe fell away revealing her flesh.

"What the fuck?" Scrambling to cover herself, Marta gathered the terry cloth over her chest and cowered away from him. He was staring now at her exposed crotch. Indignant, she pulled the robe over her thighs, and shouted, "Get the hell out of here!"

"Not a chance sweet cheeks," Chip said. "Sy owes me. He left my mother to die, and it looks like he might leave me too. But not before I get my legacy. I know it's in the wagon. I'm takin' it and anything else I can get my hands on."

Moving backwards toward the kitchen, Marta felt the hidden gun bouncing against her thigh. *If worse comes to worse,* she thought, *I'll use it.* Then, her backside bumped up against the kitchen counter and she realized—*the block of knives.* She reached back, pulled a chef's knife from the block and shoved it out in front of her. Chip lurched for her wrist and wrenched the knife from her grasp, causing it to fall with a clatter on the counter. She reached for it, but he grabbed her wrist again and twisted her arm behind her back.

Marta was pinned against him. Her free hand still holding the robe closed over her thighs. Disgusted, she could feel his hardness against the back of her hand. Moving her hand, she let the robe fall open. As he glanced over her heaving chest, her hand inched closer to her pocket. She felt the weight of the gun—just inches away.

Her breasts sprung free and wobbled beneath his gaze. Chip's eyes went wide, and he cupped a free hand under the soft flesh. "Not too bad bitch, if you're willing to take it from him, wait 'til you get a taste of what I can give you."

She dug her hand into the pocket and lifted the gun barrel. The shot rang out through the small house, and as Chip slumped toward her, she backed away the gun smoking through her blood splattered robe.

⊰⊱

Sy was out back when he heard the shot. He rushed through the kitchen door, holding the long-handled barbecue fork. Chip was doubled over the kitchen counter, one hand holding his gut and in the other hand a knife. Marta was at the opposite end of the counter; splashes of blood dotted her exposed flesh and stained the robe. Hysterical, she held the gun limply with both hands. Oblivious to Sy's presence, Chip dragged himself toward Marta, his abdomen brushing a swath of blood along the counter's edge.

"You bitch, it was my goddamn money."

Sy screamed at his son, "Money? You want to steal your own money? You stupid asshole—I told you to wait, now look what you've done!"

Chip turned painfully around. "You." He waved the knife in Sy's direction. "You're the one who murdered my mother...left her to die."

With surprising quickness, Chip slashed out with the knife. Sy backed up, holding him off with the barbecue fork.

Jesus...first David, now my real son...

The blood was everywhere. A wave of nausea overcame him—blood on Marta, the kitchen counter, his son—it trickled out of his nose.

He could taste it on his lips.

Tic...the deathwatch beetle.

No please...

"You fucking piece of shit!" the bloody beetle yelled.

Dizzy and disorientated, Sy held the long-handled barbecue fork out in front of him. The beetle kept advancing. "Again?" Sy mumbled. "You're fuckin' gonna do this again?"

The beetle could hardly stand up—it was teetering forward.

Falling...

Marta screamed.

There was a soft crunch. Sy stood in stunned disbelief as the beetle crumbled to the floor—the weight of his son's body pulling the barbecue fork from his father's grip.

✌︎

Leonard Ashcroft stood at his bedroom window watching the glitter of lights surrounding Central Park. The breathtaking views of the Manhattan skyline, always a great source of solace, did little to calm his mounting unease.

After their conversation at the gallery, Leo drove Jacob to 88th Street, where he was invited to see David's room. Throughout his career, Leo analyzed countless examples of artistic talent, but none came close to what he witnessed on the walls and stacked along the floor. David's nom de plume, David Asher, was well known to Leo and whenever he came across the artist's work, he was impressed. The idea David Asher could be his own son never occurred to him.

Before leaving the gallery, he read the Bell Lab letter several times. Now after examining *The Sacrifice of Issac*, the full weight of what Greenberg did to David's childhood struck him hard and he became riddled with guilt.

If it wasn't for the war, he wouldn't have abandoned his family. But he witnessed the unthinkable and it was impossible to erase what he saw. The recurring memories drove him mad.

I had to get away, but my years of isolation and shame drove my wife and son into the clutches of a sociopath.

After spending two years at a Rhode Island monastery, he opened the gallery and lived frugally in an upstairs storage room. He painstakingly built his business until, in 1956, when he married wealthy socialite Sonja Kroes. They moved into his present home at The Dakota, a prestigious apartment building on 72nd Street and Central Park West.

The gallery was a success, and his personal life became stable and rewarding. He never attained the level of artistic skill that David had, but he did possess a formidable visual memory. An ability enabling him to develop an encyclopedic knowledge of painting which led him to become one of the country's leading authorities on European art.

But three years later Sonja's untimely death broke him. In his grief, he secluded himself in The Dakota. He became a recluse, dining in the Dakota's large dining hall or having meals sent up to his apartment. He made use of the in-house laundry, the gymnasium, and tennis court. Monday through Friday, the doorman ordered a cab to take him to his gallery. His only friend and confidant the gallery director, Hermann Scholz.

But now he needed to face his past. Leo turned from the window, moved across the bedroom, and out into the hallway. With mounting trepidation, he approached the storage closet and placed a hand on the doorknob. Inside was his trunk and the memories it held were both sweet and terrifying. *Helping David means raking up the past. But I can't bury my head in the sand forever—sooner or later I've got to face my demons—it might as well be now.*

Opening the double doors, he flipped the light switch and looked around. There were a dozen or so boxes lying haphazardly around the floor along with some old frames from the gallery. The trunk was there—in the back corner—under his worn army blanket.

He slid the dusty thing off the trunk, revealing a weathered top that caught the light from the overhead fixture. The glint of an infamous bronze emblem seared itself on his retina.

Der Reichsadler—the imperial eagle of Germany. Its talons griped a repulsive symbol—one belonging to the blanched corpse of his past.

The Nazi Swastika.

CHAPTER 27

Day 11
The Gulf

The next morning, grandfather and grandson were at the kitchen table. David could tell something was on Jacob's mind. He was polishing his spoon with a napkin.

"What's on your mind, Gramps?" David asked.

"Nothing," Jacob said. He stopped polishing to push his prunes around the bowl.

Despite his grandfather's denial, David knew he had something to say, yet didn't know how to begin. All the tells were there: the stroking of his mustache; his head bobbing from side to side; the decisive nod after reaching an agreement with himself.

David waited.

Jacob gave him a quick glance from under his bushy eyebrows. "So, listen," Jacob began tentatively. "Maybe we should talk?"

"About what, Gramps?"

"Things...things."

"Okay."

Silence.

"So, we're close now? I mean, I don't want to be a buttinsky—but—as far as your real father is concerned, you might want me to put in my two cents."

"If you know more about Leo, please tell me."

"He's changed his name—he's now Leonard Ashcroft."

"You found him?"

"Yes."

"How?"

"It was the day your mother and I drove back to the city. You remember, she dropped me at the newsstand?"

David nodded.

"So, I'm at the newsstand," Jacob continued, "and who do I see on the front-page of your college newspaper? John Barrymore with a beard, that's who."

"Barrymore, the old actor—he was on the cover of *The Spectator?*"

"No, a look-alike," Jacob said. "'This can't be,' I said to myself, 'Barrymore died in forty-two and this here is a recent photo.' I'm telling you I could have *plotzed* right there on the sidewalk. There was only one man I knew with a Barrymore profile—Leo."

Jacob handed him the issue of *The Spectator* and David read the caption beneath the photo.

"He's the owner of Ashcroft gallery? I've been in many times. I can't believe it."

"Not only did I find him, but I spoke to him. He drove me home, came up to look at your work."

"What did he say?"

"He said you're a better artist than he ever was. He wants to see you. And David, the reason you never saw him again—it was Greenberg. The son-of-a-bitch kept you two apart. A real *mamzer* he was."

"*Mamzer,* what's that?"

"Take my word for it—it's not so nice."

"Okay, so he wants to see me; I want to see him. Did he give a hint of where or when?"

Jacob nodded, "More than a hint. And such a *megillah,* he made—very complicated. Leo and your painting professor, they're old friends. They set the whole thing up."

"Set what up?" asked David.

Jacob poked the newspaper with a crooked finger. "Judging the student painting exhibition. They did it so Leo could contact you. But now that you know he's your father, there's a conflict of interest and he needs to cancel. He told me he'd be meeting with your painting professor this afternoon at your college."

"Thanks, Gramps, you're the best."

The smuggler shoved off around four in the morning from a secluded beach outside Fort Lauderdale. At the start, the ocean was uncharacteristically calm, but the fifty-mile crossing to Bimini wasn't the straight shot Sy thought it would be.

The plan was to head north for ten, twelve miles to catch the Gulf Stream, where the current would push the craft over the increasing swells. By the time they reached the Bahama islands, the sun would be at their backs to help them navigate through the shallows around Bimini.

Yet twenty minutes into the trip, the knife-hulled powerboat was spotted by a Coast Guard patrol. To outwit his pursuers, the smuggler turned south toward the northern Keys and plunged his craft into the dark, shallow shoals at breakneck speed. As they wound in and out of the sharp coral, Sy clung to his three bags, fearing they'd run up on a reef and all his cash would be lost.

Almost three hours later the smuggler left Sy on the north beach of Bimini. Shaking from the ordeal, Sy stumbled along the water's edge and passed out on the sand with the three bags hanging around his neck. When he finally awoke, he found himself parched and weary with blood caked under his nose.

Blistered and raw from sleeping in the burning sun, he decided to change clothes and make his way to Alice Town. Tomorrow he would catch a puddle jumper to Nassau, deposit his cash, buy some clothes and check into a luxury hotel. From then on it would be the best of everything.

Sy reached for the overnight bag to remove his clothes and found the bag wet. His ledger was on the bottom and, worried it was damaged, he reached inside to remove it....

Magazines?

Stunned, he turned the bag upside down and shook it. *Magazines– just magazines.* They spilled out onto the sand and flipped around in the breeze. He grabbed a handful and threw them away in disgust. He screamed. "The fucking bitch. The goddamn little whore. I give her the house, set her up in business and this is what I get? Why the fuck would she take the ledger? What could she hope to accomplish?"

Sy grabbed two handfuls of sand and squeezed as if it was her neck. He was played. Why didn't he see it? Moretti must've recruited the cunt. She swiped the ledger from his overnight bag while he was in the bathroom. Probably called Moretti afterwards.

He looked around frantically for a payphone.

Christ, what was he thinking—a goddamn phone booth on an island beach? And with Mike and Chip dead, who the hell was he going to call? Everyone he knew was connected to Moretti.

He was going soft. Instead of killing the sniveling whore, he left Marta there, took her gun, Chip's car keys, wallet, and pager, and drove off in the station wagon toward Jersey's Liberty International Airport.

Sitting in the sand, Sy thought of Chip. It was Marta, who killed his son. After all, she shot him—erased the Greenberg legacy—cut short the dynasty Sy planned to create. To his credit, Chip realized his foolishness and at the last moment, took responsibility by falling on something sword-like. A ritual acknowledgment—a noble act honoring the lifelong accomplishments of his father.

All my fucking plans—for what?

Sy removed his damp clothes, changed, and threw the overnight bag in the ocean. He grabbed the two bags of cash, climbed up the sandy hill to the access road, and turned to look down into the hidden cove. His overnight bag was bobbing in and out with the tide, the magazines flapped around in the breeze next to his clothes. The blue of the ocean shimmered in the distance.

Paradise—lost.

This was the island of Hemingway. A man's island, where someone flush with money could fish, gamble, drink, and whore around with any number of island squeezes. It was all waiting for him a couple of miles down Kings Highway in Alice Town.

For Congressman Powell, the long arm of the law couldn't reach him in the Bahamas. But for Sy, there was another enforcement arm whose reach was longer than the feds. The minute Marta gave the ledger to Moretti, Sy was a dead man walking. It would take them time, but they would find him.

There was no escaping the Genovese Family.

More than a thousand miles north of Bimini, David was back in the studio with the photograph of Leo, torn from the *Spec*. The last unpainted portion of his painting was the face of the old man outside the drugstore window.

Tacked to the side of his easel, the black and white photograph was small, grainy, and washed out, suggesting little about his father's facial structure or complexion. All he could do was guess Leo's skin tone would be similar to his. Since he need to change Leo's features into a scream, there wasn't much to go on.

Forcing himself to make a start, he mixed some basic flesh tones and tried to imagine his father's face with his mouth open in a scream. What shape the nasal furrows would take; how wide the nose and eyes would become. Suddenly, he didn't care. The search for answers felt pointless as was his need to express it through paint. Why imagine anything when his father was with Professor Haverstock in his office across the hall.

His search would be over in minutes if he simply walked out the studio door and down the hall. Everything would be explained. He would know where he came from, what his genes would allow him to accomplish and what he could expect of himself as a man. He'd know how close he came on his own to match the qualities of the man who was his father.

You idiot. Go to him. Show him you've got the balls to confront him—accept him as your father no matter what kind of man he is.

David felt a tingling sensation and turned....

"If you're looking for a face to fill that empty space, use mine, it belongs there."

A slim man in his sixties, roughly David's height and coloring, but with gray hair and a short-cropped beard, walked into the studio. He looked fit for his age, and as he approached, his blue eyes held David in a searching look—an expression David saw many times in the mirror.

"I'm staring at myself!" David murmured.

His father smiled, tilted his head, and raised an eyebrow. "I feel it too, he said. "You're the young man I used to be."

Time fell away for David as all his senses worked in concert to absorb the impression of the man before him. There was no thought of blinking in an image; no internal dialogue to categorize his feelings. As thoughtless as a sponge, he took in the presence of the man who fathered him. The nape of Leo's neck felt like his. The macro-movements of his weathered hands mimicked his own. The physicality of his own resemblance to his father was overwhelmingly obvious.

Then, David gazed into his blue eyes. The world behind them seemed to hold a shuttered darkness—painful memories—aching to be brought into the light of day. Whether born of hapless circumstance or Leo's own failures, David could sense parts of his father's life lay in ruins.

Mere moments passed, and David, not knowing what to say, approached his father offering an outstretched hand. Grasping it, Leo drew him into a fatherly embrace, the scent of a familiar cologne sending David back in time.

In his highchair, little Davie's frustration with the jumble of brightly colored beads was over. Now, each of the three colors strung along the edge of the tray were grouped together. Davie looked up at the man holding the spoon—the long fingers—a beige uniform—the shiny metal on the lapels of the collar.

"Davie" the man said. The fog surrounding the man's features lifted and a kind face came into focus as Leo, now holding him close, whispered in his ear. "My son."

Wrapped in an envelope of safety, the lost memories of childhood broke through and spilled into his consciousness. Tears began and David was lost to time.

✄✄

Sy trudged half a mile, until a delivery truck picked him up along King's Highway and dropped him off at the Complet Angler Hotel in Alice Town. He asked for some water, lugged his stuff up to a second-floor room, and fell asleep.

He woke up groggy and depressed. Within days, a contract would be placed on his head, someone would remember his vacations to the Bahamas, they'd ask around; maybe find the smuggler. Sy showered, shaved, then slinging the two bags of cash over his shoulders, went across the road to the Red Lion for a late lunch. The chalkboard listed red snapper for the daily special. He sat by a window and tried to catch the attention of the blonde waitress wiping down the tables.

She wore standard beach wear—a crop-cut T-shirt, shorts and sandals. The T-shirt ballooned out from her breasts, showing a lot of midriff and Sy watched her from behind, as she moved from table to table, reaching over with a spray bottle and rag. As she bent over, her breasts swung out and hung inside the cutoff tee as if in a sling—her wiping motion causing them to bump against each other. The blonde straightened up, pushed in some chairs, noticed him and smiled.

She came over to his table.

"What can I get you?"

"The red snapper special and a beer," Sy ordered. "Also, can you tell me how to get to the Carter beach house?"

"Sure," she said, leaning a shapely hip against the table. "Just go out here to the road, make a left and walk a hundred yards or so. When you see a mailbox with the name Sloane on it, follow the path down to the beach. You can't miss it."

"Thanks."

"You know, Carter sold it about a year ago—it's Ray Sloane's place now," she said, "I rent his guest cottage with two other women."

Sloane was supposed to stay in the guest cottage. Renting it wasn't part of our deal. "Really, so Sloane lives in the main house, does he?"

"Of course, he's the main guy," her ponytail bobbed up and down. "Strange character, Sloane."

Curious, Sy took the bait. "How so?"

"Not many people know him—at least the way I do," she put a hand on the other hip and gave him a quick look. "Well, I mean, with me living right there and all. He gets visitors every so often, but they always stay at the hotel even though there's room in the big house. You don't strike me as the type he'd pal around with though."

"And what type is that?"

"Mostly military types. You know, guys with muscle, stubble and attitude."

"We don't pal around," Sy said. "Sloane works for me, it's my property—I'm the one who bought it from Carter last year."

"Oh gosh...so technically, I'm living in your guest house?"

"Technically, yes, but I haven't seen any rent money."

Her hand came off the hip. "Gee, I didn't get Ray in trouble, did I?"

"Not much I can do about it—I'm not the muscular type, am I?"

"Well, no, but still, being the owner and all. So, who are you anyway?" she asked.

He had three fake passports to choose from but couldn't decide who he wanted to be.

"No one really," Sy said, "no one at all."

CHAPTER 28

Buried Memories

At first, Leo held his son in a tentative embrace, but then David clung to him, released a sigh and uttered a single word.

"Daddy."

Hearing it filled Leo's heart. Denied his child for so long, he felt like a father again and all his fears of rejection melted away. He released David and stepped back, putting a hand on his son's shoulder.

"Once the connection is made, the missing memories fall into place. That's the way of this strange gift we share. You must have driven yourself crazy trying to remember me. I'm sorry."

His son wiped the tears from his eyes. "I need a moment to sort out these incoming memories—"

"Of course," Leo slid a stool over. "Here, sit."

As David's focus turned inward, Leo realized how much of his own gift he passed on to his son. If David was anything like him, he would sift through the lost memories and slide them into their proper time sequence for viewing later.

A striking young woman appeared at the studio door and strode toward them. As she put her hand supportively on David's shoulder, Leo thought how familiar she seemed.

She smiled at him. "Excuse my stare, but the resemblance is uncanny...."

Leo offered his hand. "Lionel Ashcroft, aka Leopold Aschbacher."

By then, David finished with his memory sort and stood up beside Nina. "Leo, this is someone very special in my life."

"It's a great pleasure to meet you, Leo. I'm Nina Caldas. I'm so grateful you both have found each other."

Leo was surprised. "Nina Caldas? I once met a little girl named Atonina Caldas. The daughter of Antonino and Elsita Caldas of Bogotá–they called her Nina."

"Yes, that's me. But how?"

"No sobe? Esta es una gran coincidencia," Leo looked from David back to Nina. "And you two are together? A couple? Married? You must tell me."

"We are engaged," Nina replied with the most engaging smile.

"Unbelievable!" Leo exclaimed. "This is wonderful news. I can't imagine a happier beginning to having my son back in my life. Your father was my best friend when I lived in Bogotá. We still keep in touch."

"My parents are divorced now. I haven't seen my father since I was sixteen."

"It's a shame. The last time I saw them was in 1953 when I flew to Bogotá to bury my mother. I could tell then their marriage was in trouble. Your parents helped me through a difficult time. You were perhaps ten. I remember you put on a little dance performance for me."

"I'm sure I did. I imposed myself that way on all my parents' friends," she replied.

"And you became a dancer. I'll wager a very good one too," Leo said.

"You can tell?" said Nina.

"Of course. You're a very self-possessed young woman. You glided over here as if directed by some unseen choreographer. It's obvious you, yourself, are the art form. That's not something that can be turned on and off."

"You're very kind to say that, but I think my dance bag tipped you off."

Leo chuckled.

Noticing how approachable Leo was, David decided to admit his prior apprehension. "I'm sorry I didn't seek you out the minute I got here; I was nervous."

"So was I," Leo admitted. It's why I stayed so long with my friend Carl."

"I'm glad he's your friend," David said. "I thought he was CIA."

"CIA?"

David nodded. "During my time at Columbia, he showed an unusual interest in me."

Leo explained, "Carl and I became good friends when we were at Columbia. After your mother divorced me, I told him about you and Greenberg. Years ago, he recognized the Greenberg name on your admission material. He called me. We confirmed it was you by the return address on the application. Carl has kept an eye on you ever since your freshman year."

David looked hurt. "Over three years and you never contacted me?"

Leo gave him a cheerful smile. "It's not what it seems. I promise to sort it out later."

"And you two have all the time in the world to do so," added Nina.

All tall, very Germanic man entered the studio. Careful not to intrude on the conversation, he waited patiently until his presence was recognized.

"This is my Gallery Director, Herr Scholz," Leo informed everyone, "an indispensable friend." He waved him forward. "Come meet my son and his fiancée, Nina Caldas."

Herr Scholz approached. "I am very glad to finally make your acquaintance. Carl and I watched over you for years. And very pleased to meet you Ms. Caldas." Turning to Leo, he continued, "I'm parked at a meter. Would you like me to add coins or are you leaving presently?"

Leo looked at them. "What do you say—shall I take everyone to an early dinner?"

⚭

Sy finished lunch and the waitress followed him out to the street to point him in the direction of Sloane's cottage. He walked on and glancing behind him, saw her strike a pose at the restaurant's door. She blew him a kiss, waved and disappeared inside.

It didn't take long for Sy to locate Sloane's mailbox. He veered off onto the adjacent dirt road and followed the smell of the sea down to the beach. Soon, the two-story Bahamian-style home came into view. Facing the ocean, it had a small guest cottage off to the side and an overgrown garden out back.

Ray Sloane was a retired hit man, who Sy knew from his early days with the Mob. A year ago, Sloane struck a deal to take care of Sy's property on Bimini. It was agreed when Sy retired to the beach house, the younger Sloane would stay on in the guest cottage rent free, providing security, maintenance and other duties. Sloane's other duties referred to chores Sy might need if he lapsed into poor health. It didn't cover any enforcement or wet work Sy might need to keep his territory running back in the States. With both Mike and Chip gone, that option would be on the table. But now, Sy was uneasy about Sloane's friends who visited the cottage.

Sy walked up the path to the main house and rang the doorbell.

"Jesus," Sloane said, opening the door, "you look like a wreck, I've never seen you look so bad. Welcome home."

"I feel like I look." Sy replied. "You got any scotch? All they have on this island is third rate stuff."

"Sure. Sit; take a load off."

Sy plopped down on a long sofa facing the ocean through open windows. The sea breeze circulated freely through the spacious living room from two fans turning silently from high ceilings. The soft lapping of the ocean against the shore could be heard in the distance.

"How was your flight?" Sloane asked, pouring the scotch and placing the bottle on the coffee table.

"Flight?" Sy repeated as he took the scotch. "Are you kidding me? I'm lucky to be alive. Took a powerboat out of Ft. Lauderdale—in the dead of night—it was a fucking nightmare."

"Christ, I had no idea things were that bad."

"Fucking broad I was humping turned on me—stole a ledger that puts me on Moretti's hit list."

"That's bad. You called someone to whack her, right?"

"No one left to call."

"I'd do it for you back in the day, but not now. I'm out. Wasting people turns my stomach. Besides, by the time I got there, the damage would be done. Maybe they won't find you here."

"Oh, they'll find me all right." Sy countered. "How many of your old pals have you entertained during the past year?"

"Well, I..."

"Exactly. At least one of them will hear about the contract on me and remember your sweet little setup here. I stay here, I'm a dead man."

"Sorry Sy, what are you going to do?"

"I'm gonna have to give all this up—live somewhere else, and you're gonna help me get there."

"How?"

"You're going to buy this property from me. Oh, don't look at me like that. You got a good thing going here with the sea breeze and the broads next door. Their monthly rent will pay the utilities and then some. I can't believe all this past year; I'm breaking my balls while you're living the life I shoulda led."

Sloane passed an open palm across his stubbled cheek. "Buy this place? Well, I dunno...I got some dough squirreled away, but not enough to—"

"Don't worry, I'm going to give it to you for a song."

"Why would you do that?"

"What choice do I have? You could kill me tonight, call Moretti in the morning; pick up a nice chunk of change. This way, if Moretti asks, you can tell him you don't know shit. I passed the title to you through a lawyer for chump change and moved on to Plan B."

"What prevents me from picking up Moretti's contract after getting the title to this place?"

"Nothing. I'm counting on your delicate stomach and that favor I did for you fifteen years ago. If word got out you didn't honor a marker, your reputation goes in the crapper along with your head. You owe me Ray."

∽∾

P.J. Clarke's, an old brick building squashed between two skyscrapers on Madison and East 62nd Street, catered to an exclusive clientele. Everything was old: the brick, the wood, the tiles and stained glass. There were old clocks and mirrors, even an old cash register. As they dug into tasty appetizers, Nina and David explained how they met and their plans to marry after David's graduation. Nina's warmth and engaging manner put Leo at ease, making it easier for him to answer their questions.

"Can you tell me how you came to live in Bogotá and became friends with my father?" Nina asked.

"I grew up in Germany at a time when its economic and military power was the greatest in Europe. My grandfather on my mother's side, was the inventor and industrialist Hugo Junkers, who developed the world's first all-metal aircraft."

"And your father?" David asked.

"His name was Martin. He was a student of Hugo's and then worked for him at the Junkers factory in Dessau, Germany. He eventually married Hugo's daughter Gabriel—your grandmother. Like you, my memory set me apart from others. Unlike you, I had an inflated opinion of my own worth—after all, my grandfather was a genius, my father was very smart—why shouldn't I be exceptional.

"The atmosphere I grew up in changed drastically after the war. I'm talking here about the Great War. Aircraft companies like my grandfather's had restrictions. They could sell planes for commercial use only. My father traveled a lot and sold two Junkers F-13 aircraft to the Colombian-German Air Transport Company–SCADTA. Eventually, he became one of five investors in the airline. It was when he was given the post of German Consul to Colombia, that we moved to Bogotá."

"When was that?" asked Nina.

"The early 1920s. It was a very closed society then, children only mixed with others of their own social class. Your father's family was an old aristocratic one. We met at the country club and became fast friends."

"That explains what my mother meant when she said she knew someone with a memory like David's." Nina remarked. "It was you."

"Yes," Leo said. "I didn't hide my gift the way David does."

David asked, "How did you end up in the States?"

"Everything conspired to lead me here. After February of 1920, there were increasing concerns about Naziism. The atmosphere in South America was tense; German expatriates were suspect. During that time, the US legation in Bogotá distributed pamphlets outlining opportunities for Latins to study in American colleges and universities. I wanted to get away, so I applied.

"After graduation, I became a citizen and built my career at an auction house in New York City. Then, I met your mother. Jacob and Sarah weren't enthusiastic. I was darkly enigmatic–a mysterious German who might be a Nazi spy. It was difficult for me. Courting a Jewess made me an outcast among my German friends. I found myself caught between two worlds. But despite the difficulties, we married and had a number of good years."

"Jacob told me a lot of what happened during the war and after," David said. "Was your war experience that painful?"

"Worse than you can imagine," Leo said. "Because I spoke fluent German, I was assigned to the 104th Infantry Division that liberated the Mittelbau-Dora concentration camp. I'm not going to dwell on what occurred there–the horrible, inhumane things I saw–it's not the time and definitely not the place."

Leo's eyes glazed over for several seconds...

Nina brought him back. "It's so strange for me to see the same sad, far-a-way look in your eyes, as I've seen so many times in David's." She smiled at him and waited for him to continue.

"Yes, well...Needless to say, the briefing we received before entering the camp did little to prepare any one of us for the nightmarish images we would see. But I was different than the others. Anything I saw remained as fresh as the moment it happened. Asleep or awake, the haunting visions plagued me until I suffered a massive memory overload—a memory quake. After spending some time in the infirmary, I couldn't go back to the camp, and I was transferred to a unit of The Monuments Men."

"What was that?" David asked.

"A group of art historians and museum experts charged with recovering art stolen by the Nazis. They needed a translator in the Bamberg District. Oddly, in a little town called Aschbach, where my ancestors were from.

"I arrived at Schloss Aschbach in early May of 1945. I remember a large manor house covered in brownish plaster, overgrown with wild grapevines. It was the residence of the local Nazi Party Leader, Baron Gerhard von Polnitz. The baron was hiding and crating artwork for Karl Haberstock, Hitler's private art collector. As a translator, I was assigned to take depositions from local Nazi officials and translate German documents and invoices found on shipping crates in the residence."

Leo composed himself before continuing. "I came across some shipping labels addressed to my father in Bogotá. It seems the Nazis were shipping stolen art to German sympathizers in South America so they could forward the shipments to major art centers. Once there they were sold with fake provenances."

"So, your father was a Nazi sympathizer and pulled you into the scheme without your knowledge." David speculated.

Leo nodded. "All the time I was living in New York, building a career and family, I was sustaining my lifestyle on Nazi plunder. The knowledge of my father's deception and what I had unknowingly participated in, pushed me over the edge into a nervous breakdown. I became incoherent. There was nothing anyone could do. I was medically discharged and sent home.

"What happened after that was a different kind of nightmare."

CHAPTER 29

Safe Harbor

Herr Scholz returned to P.J. Clarke's just after Leo paid the bill. Nina and David slipped into the back seat and the four of them headed toward Central Park West. When they reached 71st Street, Scholz slowed the van in front of a pale-yellow, fortress-like building on the corner.

"The Dakota Apartments," Nina said. "It's Manhattan's most prestigious address. Very exclusive. A lot of famous people have opulent apartments here: Leonard Bernstein, Rudolph Nureyev, Lauren Bacall and others. It's co-op—not everyone can get in."

Leo looked across at David as he craned his neck out the window.

"It has a lot of character," David remarked.

"German Renaissance," Leo said. "I've lived here since 1956."

Scholz pulled the van to the curb, and they got out in front of a large archway. A doorman opened the gate as they approached.

Leo addressed him, "How are you today Johnson?"

"Fine sir, yourself?"

"Today is one of the best days of my life, Johnson—this is my son and his fiancée Ms. Caldas. Please allow them access to the building and all services. My son will be staying with me for a while."

The doorman touched his hand to his cap, "Very glad to do that sir." Then turning said, "Pleasure to meet you both. Welcome to The Dakota."

As they continued through the archway David asked, "I'm staying with you?"

"Yes, given your situation, I think it's best."

Leo led them thru the center courtyard to one of the four entrances at the corners. He explained each entrance had separate lobbies and passenger elevators leading to the apartments in each section of the building.

Leo's twenty-two-foot-long entry foyer, also served as a picture gallery. It opened onto a thirty-foot living room with high ceilings and a wood-burning fireplace. Adjacent was a twenty-foot dining room with an attached butler's pantry next to the eat-in kitchen. The living room was also large, with a high, carved oak ceiling, inlaid marble floors and a fireplace that ran halfway up the wall. Despite its grand proportions, it offered a warm and cozy atmosphere.

Herr Scholz appeared with a tray of finger food and told David his grandfather was on the phone. David left the room to take the call and returned later to relate the conversation.

"Jacob got a call from my mom. She's leaving Nassau for Miami late tomorrow morning. The plane arrives in New York tomorrow night. She wanted to know if Nina and I could pick her up at the airport. When Jacob told her I was staying here, she sounded relieved and happy Leo and I connected. She gave the phone number of the hotel she's staying at, and Jacob gave her your phone number at the gallery. We'll have to decide what to do about picking her up."

This was the moment Leo thought about since reuniting with his son. Should he take the offensive or wait for something to develop naturally. His gut said he waited too long already.

"I'll pick her up," he said. "No sense in delaying the inevitable. Whatever our differences, we'll thrash them out in the car on the way back."

David gave him a smile. "Something she said makes me think it won't be difficult."

"What's that?" Leo asked.

"She said, '... he was the love of my life and I was weak and selfish. God... I'm so sorry. I just couldn't find the strength to fight for him....'"

Leo held his emotions in check and made a gesture of gratefulness to his son. "Thank you. I hope you're right. I'll call her a little later to set it up—I've got to think about what to say."

There was a brief silence as they settled in with their drinks. Finally, Leo's mood changed, and he raised his glass in a toast. "Here's to Jacob, thanks to him I not only have my son back, but I may be able to patch things up with Ellen. Life has taught us some sobering lessons these past twenty years. We may be able to excuse our frailties and find each other again."

"Here's hoping it happens," David said, raising his glass again. "She's read the letter from Bell Labs and understands we share the same ability. I think if you explain what happened to you after the war, she'll be in a better position to excuse your behavior at the time."

"Perhaps you're right," Leo said. "If I explained to your mother how my memory worked, she might not have understood then. It was the 1940s, people were not open to those kinds of things the way they are now. She never understood why the liberation of the concentration camp haunted me day and night."

"And that's why Ellen sued for divorce?" Nina asked.

"Yes, she thought I was mentally ill—she couldn't handle it. After that, I needed to disappear. I spent two years at a Benedictine monastery on Narragansett Bay in Rhode Island. I taught art history at their Priory School. When I left, all I wanted was to bring David back into my life. I sent David birthday presents but never received an acknowledgement. I wrote Ellen asking if I could see my son but there was never any answer. I was so desperate I took to hanging around Greenberg's apartment building waiting to catch sight of David. One day I followed him to a drugstore and tried to get his attention through the window."

David leaned forward. "You're the man I saw outside the window of the drugstore. It was an instant recognition—I was confused because the father I knew was standing beside the magazine rack."

Leo nodded. "In that brief moment, I realized you recognized me as your true father. But then Greenberg spotted me. He turned red as a beet, dashed out of the store and pushed me away from the window. People outside tried to help, but he flashed his badge. He slammed me against a brick wall and threatened to ruin me financially if I didn't disappear for good.

"Two years later I received a letter asking me to give up my paternity rights. I refused. Greenberg sent thugs to threaten me. But I found a way to avoid them. I put you out of my mind because I thought you preferred Greenberg over me. I was starting my gallery—busy making amends—I couldn't afford to be audited by the IRS."

"Amends...amends for what, to whom?" Nina asked.

"I needed to wipe out the shame of unwittingly helping the Nazis smuggle paintings out of Europe. While in the monastery, I cross referenced my old inventory lists. I found all the paintings were part of confiscations of French and Belgian Jewish collections by the ERR in 1940."

"The ERR?"

"The *Einsatzstab Reichsleiter Rosenberg*, a Nazi task force engaged in confiscating art treasures. It's one of the reasons I opened the gallery.

I'm contacting my old clients, buying back the paintings, and if I can, returning them to their rightful heirs."

❧

By nightfall, they were down by the beach—Sy, Sloane and the three girls from the cottage. The rhythmic sound of the waves lapped up against the shore and the bonfire Sloane built was snapping little orange sparks onto the sand. The girls were sprawled out half-naked on the blankets, drinking, eating and pawing each other in front of them.

This was a taste of what could have been if it wasn't for that New Jersey bitch. What a fool he was. He accumulated enough money to make all this happen years ago, but avarice and the need to control had a stranglehold on him and he couldn't tear himself away.

The girls worked themselves into a fever-pitch and moved in on the men. Two of them sandwiched Sy between their warm bodies and added their purring to the lapping of the waves. He tried to let go—to swim in the sensuousness of the moment. But his thoughts were caught in a loop. The word was going out tomorrow—Moretti's goons and contract killers wouldn't stop until they located him—he wasn't safe.

A wave of anger coursed through his body. Here was the dream he harbored for so long—the buxom girls, the fresh seafood, the balmy weather and the freedom to spend his money on any number of pleasures.

His one and only night in his Bahamian paradise and he couldn't get it up.

❧

Nina left for Park Avenue before eleven that evening, leaving father and son to talk late into the night. David related his difficulties living under Greenberg's thumb and his mother's own struggles in the face of her husband's cruelty. Then, slipping into the present, he explained the various forces threatening his life.

"The Dakota is like a fortress. You're safe here," Leo said. "You can breathe a sigh of relief now and concentrate on the matter at hand—your own survival."

"And those of the people I love," David added.

Leo agreed, "You're right, Sy Greenberg's much more than a belligerent step-parent who wants to destroy you for his own twisted pleasure. He's a lifelong criminal whose Mob connected. It won't be long until he discovers his offshore account is depleted. That kind of betrayal will put Ellen at risk. If not from him then his underworld contacts. We need to protect her—Nina too."

"How?"

"Well, let's think it through. Who can you trust?"

"You, Nina, Gramps, my mom and my friend AJ."

"Tell me about him."

"Big, strong and on the football team at Columbia. Had some involvement with civil rights demonstrations, nothing radical. He's my only friend now that Mike's gone. He figured out I had some special talents a long time ago but kept it to himself. He's the one who helped me get into some kind of reasonable shape during the last four years."

"The question is, will he'll be willing to put himself at risk to help you out?"

"Yes, he's the one who told me to keep my head on a swivel."

"It's interesting you didn't mention the FBI as a trustworthy asset."

"Yeah, I realized that myself. Finding out about Agent Keyes changed my mind about how much I can trust the Bureau. There's no telling who else is on Moretti's payroll."

"Okay, so we can count on AJ to lend some muscle to the solution. Nina offers you moral support. That's good—but her presence in the mix is a liability—she's the kink in your armor so to speak."

"I know. I've already warned her. But she has rehearsals and she's very self-reliant."

"I can see that. And let's not forget Jacob. No doubt he'll want to continue living independently. Maybe Herr Scholz can move in with him for a while?"

"Good, it will stop me from worrying," David said. "What about Nina?"

Leo pondered. "Can you count on AJ to keep an eye on her when she's out alone?"

"Yes. Good idea. He can take reasonable precautions for her safety—that's comforting—but it doesn't stop this madness."

Leo leaned toward him to emphasize his words. "I can see a way out of this, but you might not like it."

"Tell me."

"If Greenberg is captured, he'll testify for the state and give evidence against Moretti. Moretti works for Tony Salerno, who in turn answers to the Genovese Crime Family. Moretti is in a tough spot. He's got to contain the damage Greenberg's created. As of now, we can assume no one else higher up in the Mob knows what's happening. Moretti's going after your stepfather, that's for sure. When he finds out you've got the ledger, he'll come after you too."

"He already knows," David said. "That FBI agent I told you about is on Moretti's payroll."

"But you've got leverage—the ledger itself. Moretti's got two pages and some photos. So, he knows what's in the ledger and needs to destroy it. All you need to do is give it to him in exchange for neutralizing the people who are after you."

"Wait, you want me to make a deal with a Mob boss to get rid of my stepfather, his accomplice and the CIA operative? You've got to be kidding me? That's murder."

"Wake up," Leo said harshly. "Do you honestly think everyone's going to be rounded up by the FBI, sent to jail and you'll be safe?"

David took out his FBI identification. "They gave me this—I'm one of them now—they're the good guys. There's witness protection."

"It's a fairy tale. First, the CIA guy will never be taken down by the FBI, so you'll continue to live in fear of him. Second, Greenberg may never see the inside of a jail cell if he gives up Moretti. He'll be the one who'll be in witness protection and remain a threat to you, your mother and Nina.

"If Moretti is put away, the Genovese Family will take their revenge. They'll find Greenberg and his accomplice and kill them. You'll be next—then Nina, your mother, me, and just to make sure, Jacob. Probably Nina's mother too."

David fell silent. How did it come to this? It was impossible to contemplate, but Leo was right. Moretti was the only one who could make all his problems go away—permanently.

"What's your plan?" David asked.

"Tell Moretti you've hidden the ledger and no one else has seen it. Offer to exchange it for his help in getting rid of the people who are threatening you. Remember, he has to clean house. Sy, and anyone else who's seen the ledger will have to be eliminated. No matter what. That's everyone who's after you. If you don't make this deal, Moretti will kill them anyway."

"I didn't think about that... But I carry the ledger in my head. So, it makes sense that he'll want to kill me too."

"It's not a problem if you promise not to say anything."

David thought his father was crazy. "Moretti's a gangster—a killer. Even if we can set up a meeting, how do we know he'll make the deal? And if he does, why rely on my promise when he could shoot me along with everyone else and be done with it?"

"Because he helps friends who do him favors."

"Friends, what are you talking about?"

"I've known Moretti for years—he's one of my biggest clients."

CHAPTER 30

Day 12
Brush with the Mob

The next morning, Sloane drove Sy down the western strip of North Bimini to catch the South Island Ferry. It was Sy's last look at the coast and the laid-back life he would have to abandon. When they arrived at South Bimini, Sloane maneuvered his Jeep off the ferry and drove the mile and a half to the Bimini airport.

Sy's plan was to fly to Nassau with Sloane, hit the bank, deposit his cash and transfer the beach house to Sloane with a cashier's check. Sy was buying Sloane's silence by selling him the property for much less than he paid for it.

Fortunately, Sy had plan B—Israel.

No extradition and as a Jew, he was guaranteed admittance. True, life there was a little spartan, but money would soften the rough spots and, if he needed a break, he'd be a plane ride away from Greece, Italy and Monte Carlo.

Who knows, he might also find God.

∽❧

After landing in Nassau, Sy and Sloane moved through the terminal toward the taxi station outside. That's when Sy spotted her. Stylishly dressed in an expensive new outfit, Ellen was carrying a Louis Vuitton travel bag through the Miami boarding gate.

"My wife," he stammered, "Sloane, it's my wife..." Sy took off yelling, "Oh Christ, my money, I don't know how, but I think she's got my money...." By the time Sy got to the gate, the door closed, and Ellen was out on the tarmac on her way to the plane. He moved to the window and saw her walking up the stairs.

Sloane came up behind him dragging an airline attendant with him. "Do something for the poor guy," Sloane asked her.

When Sy pulled on the gate's door, the attendant interceded. "Step away from the door sir, we need to keep this area clear."

"Stop that plane!"

On the tarmac, the stairs were being rolled away.

"Sir? Sir, you can catch the next plane. Please step away."

Sy pleaded, then argued....

The attendant picked up a nearby phone.

Sloane was shaking his head.

The hatch was closing.

The aircraft jerked and started to taxi out.

Nooooo.

ॐ

"I told you, don't do it," Nina insisted for the third time. "I know it's Leo's plan and you want to do the father and son thing, but it would be a big mistake."

"There's no other way," David said.

"Ask someone like that for a favor and you're forever in their debt," she said. "You thought your stepfather's control was difficult to live with, wait until the Mob begins to pull your strings. You'll be sucked into doing all sorts of despicable things and end up wallowing in the gutter along with them."

They ate lunch around the corner from Nina's apartment building. It wasn't pleasant. David went over Leo's plan to enlist Moretti's help and asked her to go with him for the sit-down with the Mob Chief that evening.

"What choices do we have?" David argued. "Because of Agent Keyes, my involvement with the FBI is now known to Moretti. He knows I've stolen damaging evidence from my stepfather that implicates him in racketeering."

"The FBI will protect us," Nina said feebly.

"The only way is through Witness Protection. They'll expect us to up-root our lives and hide God knows where. You'll be teaching dance to fat little girls in some small midwestern town. I'll end up teaching art at the local high school. Our careers will be over before they even start. Not to mention we'll be looking over our shoulders the whole time—never knowing a moments peace."

"I'm willing to give up my dance career, that kind of life is very short lived anyway. You could still paint—change your style—use a different name."

"And how long do you think we can hide? Five, ten, maybe fifteen years? In the end, the Genovese Family will find us. Besides, you know the CIA's not going to give up on me. If the Mob has a snitch inside the FBI, they've got one inside the CIA. And then there's all the collateral damage. God only knows what Sy will do to my mother when he finds she's emptied his bank account. Then there's you and Gramps—everyone I love is at risk here."

"But to get in bed with the Mob? David, I don't know if I can live with that. It's horrible to even think you—we—would be part of that world."

"Give me an alternative. Anything that will guarantee your safety. I'm doing this for you too—for Gramps and both our mothers."

"I know, I know." She couldn't wrap her head around it. The whole idea was too repulsive. "It's wrong..." was all she could say. "Wrong, wrong, wrong and I'll have nothing to do with it."

"Again, let me explain what Leo told me. It's a favor Moretti would grant to him, not to me. Leo would be the one beholding to Moretti—not me. All our problems would disappear with one wave of Moretti's hand. We'd get our lives back."

"You're going to believe some twisted code of gangster ethics? Once you agree to this, you'll be in their debt forever. They'll weaponize your ability somehow—by pressing your father—or threatening me to make sure you do something terrible. We'll never know when they'll come knocking on our door and take you away to do God-knows-what."

"Nina please, we need to work this out. Our future is at stake."

"If you do this, we won't have a future. I love you, but I can't watch you turn into your stepfather."

"I can't do this without you."

"Why is it so difficult? You men always do whatever you want. You're a real man now—so take decisive action—just don't expect me to be a part of it."

"I don't think this will work if you're not with me."

"Why?"

"Moretti places a lot of value on family. Your presence there will soften him up. Two helpless lovebirds caught in a web of deceit and danger. He won't be able to resist a vulnerable woman."

"Leo told you this?"

"Seems Moretti is a big art collector. Likes to think of himself as having a sensitive soul."

"So that's it? That's what you need me for? As arm candy to turn the head of some grease-ball gangster. I don't know...I'm not sure I can do it."

Nina turned from him to hide the tears welling up inside her. Everything she believed in was now taken hostage to save him. What else would David ask of her before she didn't recognize herself? What else would he force her to give up before she could no longer love him?

Lives were at stake—she knew that. But dealing with Moretti was morally reprehensible. She needed to decide and there wasn't much time.

CHAPTER 31

Phoenix Rising

Outside the Nassau airport Sy hefted the bags in his hands. They held all the money he had. How much? Forty thousand at most. Enough for a frugal man to last eight maybe ten years. But that wasn't the plan—he was supposed to live large.

Sloane hailed a cab and they headed for the bank, "Maybe it's not as bad as you think, Sy."

At the bank Sy found his account empty. He shouted at the manager. He was blind sighted, swindled by his own wife. The manager explained—she used the right account number, and her signature was on file—there was nothing irregular about the transaction.

Fueled by his rage he made a scene. Security guards surrounded him. They asked him to leave. He was led to the door....

"Wait," Sy pleaded, "my safe deposit box?"

"What about the box?" the manager said.

"Did she ask for access?"

"Well, no she didn't, and the fee will be due soon. Will you be closing that as well?"

Sy emptied the safe deposit box and walked out with twelve thousand dollars in cash and a fake passport identifying him as a Canadian national. He opened an account at another bank, deposited most of his money and met Sloane at a coffee shop across the street.

"Plans have changed," Sy told him. "I need your help in New York. I can't let my wife's betrayal go unpunished. And the more I think about it the more I realize my stepson helped her. Marta too needs to be taught a lesson. Come back with me and you can have the damn beach house for half its worth."

Like all hit men, Sloane packed his passport and gear whenever he left his home turf. They taxied back to the airport and bought two tickets to Miami. Sy would have no trouble getting into the States with his Canadian passport and Sloane was off the grid.

Once in the air, Sy envisioned himself in Tel Aviv, living amongst the pious. Or in Jerusalem, walking in the steps of prophets. Spending a few weeks in the gambling casinos of Monte Carlo or on a yacht on the Mediterranean. An aging playboy, relaxing, expanding his world and taking his pleasures.

But he knew it wouldn't work until he took care of business. The insult would remain. There could be no enjoyment, no satisfaction without vengeance. No arbitrary accident or random kill shot from the shadows would do. When Ellen and her son faced their end Sy needed to see the fear in their eyes. The memory of it would sustain him. Amplify his everyday pleasures. Soothe him in his declining years.

Israel can wait.

∾

Nina waited with David in the lobby of her apartment building for Herr Scholz to pull up to the curb. She didn't want to be there. Yet here she was. Angry because she felt swept along by fate; fearful because she would put her future in the hands of an unscrupulous killer. They had spent the rest of the afternoon together, she sullen and withdrawn, he exasperated with her stubbornness. But after thinking it through, she reluctantly agreed to take part in "the sit-down". There seemed to be no clear alternative. If David had a better chance of success with her at his side, she should do her part.

When the gallery van arrived, she went to the curb. Herr Scholz held the side door open and, Nina, ignoring David's outstretched hand, lifted herself inside and slid across the bench seat to shrink against the far window. David followed and edged closer to her than she wished.

They headed east on 96th Street toward FDR drive, Nina glancing idly out the window. "Listen to me," David said. "There are lots of stories about the ruthlessness of mobsters—their very name conjures up some pretty horrific stuff. But Leo told me they think of themselves as businessmen because even respectable men of business play dirty. Other men may be pillars of their community, but despite their pedigrees and fine manners they're just as brutal in their business dealings."

"You really believe that?"

"Yes, take your stepfather, the esteemed Neuropsychologist, Martin Broder. Then there's the IRS Criminal Investigator, Sy Greenberg and Agent Keyes of the revered FBI. Not to mention the entire cadre of operatives working for a covert CIA program hell-bent on weaponizing my ability. All these so-called good people don't care about ruining someone's life to reach their own selfish ends."

"I'm still nervous," she said. "I wish Leo was with us. After all, he's Moretti's friend and knows what to expect."

David explained, "I told you, with my mom arriving tonight the timing is off. Leo's dusting off his Austin Healey for their reunion at the airport. He's probably as nervous as we are. Try not to worry, I have a good feeling about tonight. You've trusted my premonitions before."

"You better be right."

It was pushing four in the afternoon when Herr Scholz pulled the van outside Rao's, an Italian restaurant at 114th Street and Pleasant Avenue. Scholz got out of the van and walked around to slide open the van door for Nina and David. He extended his hand.

"Step out and take a couple of deep breaths. You'll feel better." They got out and Nina stood on the pavement and looked around. The street was rundown and deserted.

"I don't know about this," Nina said, fidgeting with her handbag. Across the street, steam wafted up from a sidewalk grate, otherwise the pavement was clean of trash and cigarette butts. The air was crisp with a faint hint of Italian spices. Nina heard the hushed voices of family life coming from behind one of the curtained windows above.

"It's not as ominous as it looks," Scholz observed. "Rao's is the go-to restaurant for mobsters and celebrities alike. This is Tony Salerno's home turf. Their headquarters, the Palma Boys Social Club, is around the corner. Leo and I have eaten here many times, the food is outstanding."

Two cars pulled up behind them—one of them a Limo. A large man exited the sedan and walked toward the Limo. The window slid down a third of the way and the man listened, nodded and walked toward them smiling affably.

Scholz moved forward to shake the man's hand. "Nice to see you again," the gangster said to him.

"Always a pleasure," replied Scholz. "Then turning to Nina and David. "I'll leave you in Vic's capable hands. After your meeting, you'll be driven back to The Dakota. Leo should be there by then with your mother." Scholz got into the van and drove away. Vic motioned the other vehicles to pull up closer to the restaurant's entrance and addressed Nina and David.

"Moretti welcomes you. He said to go on in, you're expected. Don't worry about ordering, it's all arranged. My boys will check out the restaurant for Moretti while you both have a light snack. Also, a friend of yours is waiting at your table with a tale to tell. He wanted you to be prepared—his name is Mike."

"Mike?" David turned to look at Nina and then back to Vic. His voice cracked, "Mike...Mike Trozzo—he's alive?"

Vic smiled and nodded.

Suddenly, a veil lifted, and Nina's spirits lightened. Somehow, Moretti scattered an aura of graciousness and good will before their meeting. She took a deep breath and exhaled. "I'm okay now. Let's go see Mike."

She let David guide her into the restaurant where the maître d' motioned to a table next to a wall of radiators.

Mike stood to greet them.

"Mike!" David rushed to meet the big guy and was caught in a bear hug. In a few quick strides Nina too was at Mike's side.

Mike gave her a wide grin. "As beautiful as ever."

"Boy am I happy to see you," David said, as he gripped the man's massive forearms in disbelief.

"I'm sorry I didn't tell you I was alive," Mike said," but I thought I should disappear for a while."

"Nothing to be sorry about," Nina said, "you're alive—back in our lives again!"

The three of them sat down. Wine was brought along with a huge platter of antipasto and bread. There were smiles all around as David raised his glass in a toast to Mike and their friendship.

"Tell us what happened," Nina asked.

"I was in the back of the store when I heard the explosion. One look out the window and I knew the bomb was meant for me. I figured Sy arranged it. I know it sounds crass, but I knew it was my chance to disappear. Under the cover of smoke, I threw my wallet into the van and circled around the block, entering Moe's Deli through the back door. Agnes agreed to keep quiet and hide me. She's broken up about not telling you."

"Who was in the van?" David asked.

"My brother, I lent him my keys."

Nina reached her hand out to him. "I'm sorry about your brother and we understand why you had to keep silent."

"Agnes let me stay at her place until I could figure out what to do. It was AJ who persuaded me to come out of hiding. He told me you were both in deep trouble but didn't say why. I couldn't let you down David, so I went to Jacob's apartment to see how I could help. When I got to 88th Street, I realized I hadn't thought the whole thing out. I mean showing up from the dead and all. I didn't want Jacob to open the door and get a heart attack."

"I understand," David said.

"So, I walked across Riverside Drive to the Soldiers and Sailors Monument and sat on one of the stone benches. You know, the ones looking over the buried cannon balls. I wrote an explanation of sorts—that I was alive—to prevent someone going into shock. I was going to leave it outside Jacob's door—ring the bell—wait in the lobby.

"But then the strangest thing happened. I saw Sy Greenberg, the way I remembered him in his late twenties, walking up 89th Street towards Riverside Drive. So, I followed him until he got into a car and took off. By then I knew who he really was."

"Who?" David asked.

"Your brother, Chip."

"My what?"

"Stepbrother. Sy had an illegitimate kid before he married your mom. Left him to rot. Drove his mother to the needle and an early grave. Looks like he's doing Sy's dirty work now."

"Like father like son," Nina mumbled.

"Yeah," Mike nodded. "The spittin' image of Sy in every way."

"So, Sy sent Chip to kill you with a car bomb," added David.

"But why, I thought you and Sy were old friends?" Nina asked.

"In my world it's always your closest friend who bumps you off."

There were eight tables in the dining room, but the place was empty. Three other waiters were busy setting up a round table towards the back. Except for the clinking of glasses, it was deathly quiet. A restrained expectation permeated the room.

The front door opened, and they glanced up. Five big men made their way through the dining room to the back. As they passed their table, Nina noticed the appreciative glance from an older man she took to be Moretti.

The gangsters sat, Moretti in the middle with two bruisers on either side of him. David seemed fascinated by the group and opened his sketchbook.

Mike gave a slight nod to Moretti and explained, "The boss will give us a while longer. He likes to have a little wine while he sizes people up."

Nina felt uneasy under the mobster's scrutiny and tried to keep from gazing at his table. Intrigued, David rapidly sketched the group of men. "I don't think that's such a good idea," Nina said, "put the pen down." It was too late. Moretti seemed keenly interested in what David was sketching. When David put the pen down, Moretti dabbed his mouth and got up from the table.

She lowered her voice to a whisper, "Oh God, now you've done it—he's coming over."

&〜&

David and Mike stood as Moretti strolled over to their table. The gang leader made an expansive gesture with his cigar as he approached.

"Sit, sit," Moretti insisted. "My curiosity got the better of me. Lemesee what you've done."

David handed his sketchbook to the gangster. "My apologies sir, it's a difficult habit for me to break. I didn't mean to intrude on your privacy."

"Nah, I'm flattered." Moretti cradled his cigar in an ashtray at the adjacent table and held the sketch out in front of him. "Hey, this here is good. Excellent in fact. And so quick-like. Kinda reminds me of *The Last Supper* with the boys surrounding me like that. I like it."

"Well, it yours," David tore the page out. "Keep it as my thanks for agreeing to see us."

"Ain't that somethin'," the Mob chief exclaimed. "Okay, but you gotta sign it right? For all I know you might be some hotshot artist. Maybe I should get it framed?"

David took the sheet back, signed David Asher, and returned it. "It's just a sketch but thank you for the compliment."

The crime boss looked at the signature and cocked his head. "Hold on a minute, I seen this signature before—David Asher—you do stuff for magazines, right?"

"Well, yes sir—"

But then Moretti's eyes settled on Nina. "Oh, my apologies, I never introduced myself, Benny Moretti—such a pleasure to meet such a lovely lady. What a smile—and with your dark hair pulled back like that—*veramente una bellezza italiana, eh?* Look at those eyes—it's enough to break someone's heart. Mike, the little lady's sittin' with an empty glass. Get a waiter to bring more wine and some more bread for this wonderful antipasto."

David looked over at Nina and back to Moretti. "Ah, yes, I neglected to introduce Nina Caldas my fiancée."

"Caldas—a good Spanish name. I heard about your upcoming performance at City Centre. I have my tickets and can't wait to see you perform. I'll bet you're dynamite on stage."

Speechless, Nina smiled.

An extra chair was brought for Moretti and he sat. The waiter rushed over with another bottle of wine and more bread. Her wine glass replenished; Nina took a few sips to calm herself. David remained standing, waiting.

"Do it again," Moretti asked. "I'll pose right here. I gotta see how you do this. Come on, whaddaya say?"

David pulled his chair in front of the gangster's large frame and sat. When Moretti took a Napoleon-like pose, David slid off his chair to sit on the floor. Nina realized the line of sight from below would make Moretti dominate the onlooker from above.

Despite the man's pitted skin and boxer's nose, Moretti projected a dangerous elegance. Nina watched as David enhanced his penetrating gaze, softened the edges of the protruding jaw and only hinted at the deep nasal furrows accentuating his cruel mouth. The finished sketch made him seem like any amiable businessman of wealth and prestige.

Moretti took the drawing and studied it for a long while—his head bobbing up and down in approval. Then the cruel mouth lifted at the corners. "It's terrific but there's one problem—ya didn't sign it. Ya gotta sign it. It ain't worth nothin' unless it's signed."

David got to his feet and signed the drawing. Moretti thanked him and stood up to address Nina.

"Ms. Caldas, your honey and I gotta talk business—man to man—you understand?"

Nina nodded.

"It won't take long," Moretti assured her. "Mike will escort you to a car and wait with you while I talk with David. Afterwards, a driver will take the three of you back to The Dakota."

"Three of us?" Nina asked.

Moretti put a fatherly hand on Mike's shoulder. "Mike's gonna help fix this mess David's in. He'll stay close to you both until the job is done. When he brings me that rare book I want for my collection, he's free to find a new family of his own with my blessing."

David extended his hand to Mike. "Congratulations, I know how much this means to you."

"The car's waiting outside," Moretti said. "Make the young lady comfortable Mike, and don't forget to take the leftover antipasto and a bottle or two of wine."

Steve Barry

CHAPTER 32

The Sit-Down

As Ellen's plane taxied to the gate, she thought about her earlier phone call from Leo. It was unreal. His voice was calm, punctuated by considerate pauses with the same respect for Ellen's opinions he showed her before the war. He made no apologies for the past but said they had lost their way when the rest of the world went mad during the war.

Reconciliation was never mentioned.

"Whatever happens between us now, we must present a united front for David's sake," he said. "Thanks to your care, he survived a difficult childhood with a good head on his shoulders. He deserves the best from us, not the worst."

Soon, she would see him again. Ellen had little idea of what he looked like now. All the photos she kept were destroyed by her second husband. Over the past decade and a half, his face faded from her memory.

Is this a bad idea or an opportunity for a new beginning?

Pushed along by passengers pouring out from the gate, Ellen did not see him. A barrel-chested man, much the same type as Sy, smiled at her as she turned her head in a futile search for Leo. She felt abandoned and panicked. Then, someone pushed past her causing her to bump into a gentleman with a short, cropped beard.

"Oh, pardon," she said automatically. One glance at the man's face and she was held prisoner by his eyes—those blue eyes she once knew so well. The shock of the encounter turned her numb and she became frozen to the spot.

Leo smiled. "Let's move away from all this, shall we?" he said, and guided her through the teeming crowd toward the baggage claim.

She was afraid to look at him again, lest she break down in tears, "I'm sorry, it's such a shock, after all this time."

He stopped and seeing the tears well up in her eyes, offered her his handkerchief. "If we're going to do this, you can't be sorry—for anything—anymore. We can heal past wounds with each present moment we spend together. The future will take care of itself."

On the way back, there was little she could say—Leo monopolized the conversation. He reminded her how his own father deceived him with the Nazis and told of his time in the monastery when he compiled a list of stolen paintings to return to their owners. He discussed his second marriage, Sonja's untimely death and his art gallery. How he watched over their son, guided his way into Columbia and checked on his progress through intermediaries.

"And when Jacob came to me for help," Leo continued, "I realized David hadn't rejected me after all. David was plagued by distant memories, searching for a father he was forced to forget. His struggle to reinvent himself convinced me it was time for all of us to stop dredging up the past. As our son discovered, the people we once were are gone now. We occupy the same skin, yet our memories lead us to believe we remain unchanged. Each day brings new insights into who we've become."

As Leo talked about David, she heard the pride in his voice and noticed the glisten in his eyes. She was touched by his kindness—he seemed to know how uneasy she was and gave her time to get used to him.

When he finished talking, she could have allowed the rumble of the car's engine to fill the silence, but she wanted to know more about the meeting he arranged for David that evening.

"Will they be safe?" she asked. "I mean these are gangsters...what if—"

"There is nothing to fear. You will see him tonight after he returns. Then I will take you to your hotel."

"My hotel? I planned to stay with Jacob."

"I don't think it's wise," he said gently. "Not with Greenberg still out there. I've arranged a suite for you at the Pierre on Fifth Avenue—you'll be very comfortable."

"Leo..." she began.

"Yes?"

"Thank you."

234

~⳼⳨~

Outside, four of Moretti's men surveyed the street as Mike led Nina to a waiting car. Two men stationed themselves on either side of the Limo and two more escorted Moretti and David out to the curb. One opened the Limo's door for Moretti on the pavement side and the another opened the opposite door for David.

David slipped into the leather interior next to Moretti, who then rolled the window down halfway. A file folder was passed through the window. Moretti tossed it on the built-in bar and picked up a decanter.

"Scotch?" he asked.

"No thank you," David said. "I think I've had enough for now."

The mobster nodded and poured the amber liquid into a heavy glass. A hairy hand protruded from his starched French cuff. A diamond cuff link in the shape of a letter M nestled within its folds. The Mob chief leaned back in his seat; the scent of his cologne lingering in the air. He shifted slightly and David heard a rustle of cloth. The sound of it whispered money and power.

Moretti turned to face him. "Your father and I go back to when he started his gallery. I was in the import-export business; he was trying to return stolen art to their owners in Europe—reparations they called it. We struck a deal. I'd help him send the paintings back to their rightful owners, if he helped me build a legit art collection. He did good by me.

"After I got to know him, he told me about you and your mother. Very sad. I never liked Greenberg. If I knew he was making your life a living hell, I would have tried to make it easier. As a courtesy-like to the professor."

"Professor?"

"Ashcroft, your father—that's what I call him—the professor."

"Oh. But why would you intercede on my behalf?"

"I don't like no one harassing my friends—especially their kids..." Moretti paused and looked at him meaningfully. "The Family is sacred; you never go against The Family."

David didn't flinch as Moretti drilled the message into him with a penetrating gaze. He took the opportunity to search behind the mobster's dark brown eyes. What he saw was rigid determination, an overriding self-reliance and a need for complete domination. David was convinced that, unlike his stepfather, a sadness ran parallel to every destructive decision the man made. He was in a brutal business, forced to do unspeakable things, but he wasn't bereft of a conscious.

Moretti continued. "The professor has a certain way of speaking—careful-like, so he doesn't mention things that may be misconstrued by others. I know he's busy tonight trying to patch things up with your mother, so he sent you in his place. That's okay.

"So, as you know, I'm looking to buy this rare book for my collection. We're talking here one of a kind. Other collectors might be snooping around. They could be using one of them parabolic microphones to listen in on our conversation. It could compromise everything, if you get my drift. So, if you can talk as careful as your father—obtuse-like—I'm willing to discuss the matter between us."

David knew Moretti was offering to "buy" Sy's ledger by performing a unique service. He was concerned the FBI might be listening. David nodded, saying, "I'm happy to help and grateful for your trust. That rival collectors might be monitoring our conversation is a real problem. You can count on me to be circumspect in my dealings with you."

A glint of a smile transformed the stubborn line above the gangster's unyielding jaw. "Good. I can see we understand each other. Your nothing like Sy Greenberg. He's a bum. Sometimes, in business, you come across some lowlifes—that's just the way things are. You have no idea the kinda people I have to put up with—they're like animals. You hang around them long enough, you risk becoming one yourself. As I understand it, Greenberg grew up with a bunch of lowlifes. How he was able to become IRS is a mystery."

Moretti leaned forward to add a finger of scotch to his glass. "After Sy picked up the Food Mart from old man Trozzo, he ran it like some kinda Kingfish. Certain people were overlooked. They didn't feel they got the proper respect, so to speak. But his position with the IRS, well, let's say he knew things—he was too valuable, so they let him play with his toys. But I understands things are different now, people are getting nervous. They don't like it. They don't like it one bit."

David nodded. "I had no idea what my stepfather was involved with until Mike told me about his childhood friendship with Sy."

"It's a cryin' shame what Sy did to him. Mike's a sweetheart—got a good soul. Too bad about his brother. What a fuck up."

"I'm glad Mike's okay," David said. "No matter what happens, Mike will always be part of my family. There's no way I can measure how much he's helped me."

"Mike knows what he has to do. After that, he's free to do whatever."

"That's great, no one deserves it any more than he does."

"And what about you?" Moretti asked. "Do you know what's expected of you?"

"Absolutely. The way I see it, my future is my family. Nina, her mother, my parents, Gramps and now Mike. Each one holds a piece of a puzzle that can never be put together. Our happiness depends on it—especially mine."

Moretti opened the file folder and put a finger to his lips. Then, he pointed to the pages David took from Sy's ledger—the ones Agent Keyes found on the subway floor. "So, this book I'm looking to buy—you've examined it?"

"Yes."

"Tell me about it?"

"Well, certain parts," David pointed to the two torn out pages, "describe a man's business dealings and how he cheated on reporting the profits. His business is listed—who he bought it from and how much he paid. It lists ten years of profits. How the profits were reduced, maybe as much as fifteen percent. Evidently, he held back payments to an interested party." David pointed to Moretti.

"Any names in this book?"

"Yes, one name appears in a number of places." Again, David pointed at the gangster. "Then there are names of other people, some in high places who, if pressed, might point in that same person's direction."

"You're a smart kid. So, here's what I'm goin' to do—it's very simple— so pay attention. Mike's a good friend to you—ask him what he thinks. Whatever he advises will be the way to go. Follow his advice and you won't have to worry about nothin'. Everything will be copacetic. Things will work out for the best."

"What if another party is interested in the book—what do I tell them?"

"You're the college graduate—figure it out for yourself. I know you're playing cops and robbers and you've got this little tin badge to flash around. It must be fun. But it's not going to solve anything."

"How do you know about the games I'm playing?"

"It's my business to know. Look, it's fine if you want to play nice with the other side as long as I'm not in the middle. Go and mess around in their sand box, I don't care. When it comes to playing in mine, make sure your shoes are clean before you jump in. That's the way it's gotta be. Do that and all will be right with the world—end of story."

"Everything?"

"Yeah, everything. Remember, it's like using an ointment. You got an annoying itch, you smear it on, and it's all gone. For good. On my word—one, two, three—that simple.

"Oh, and just so you know," Moretti's look burned his meaning into David. "If you use the ointment; you're committed to the treatment.

You get second thoughts; you don't follow directions and the itch comes back—with a vengeance."

⚮

Leo dropped Ellen off at her hotel and returned to his apartment to find David and Nina with a large man. Coming closer, he recognized the giant at once, but held his tongue. After the introductions, Mike seemed embarrassed and mumbled something about helping Herr Scholz with leftovers and headed for the kitchen.

Both David and Nina were surprised Ellen wasn't with Leo.

"Where's Mom?" David asked him.

"She was tired and begged off. Although things went well between us tonight, I'm sure it was an emotional drain on her. Call her before she goes to sleep. She wants to know how everything went with Moretti. So do I."

"I'll call her now and we'll talk after," David said.

"You can use my office," Leo replied. David thanked him and left the room.

By the time David returned, Scholz and Mike arranged a mixed buffet of sandwiches and left-over antipasto. Leo finished pouring the wine from Rao's and asked David, "Now, tell us about your sit-down with Moretti."

"He agreed to help in exchange for the ledger. After Mike gives it to Moretti, he's released from his oath. All my problems disappear—no one will bother us anymore. And there's a bonus. Nina's mother gets a divorce and lots of alimony."

"No strings, Nina," Mike added. "Moretti's instructions were clear. As long as David keeps his confidence, he would never pry into his relationship with the feds. David owes him nothing but silence."

Nina glanced at Leo. "Tell me this isn't a Spanish promise?"

Leo knew a Spanish promise was one not intended to be kept. "He may be a criminal, but for as long as I've known him, he says what he means and does what he says."

"Mike, how about you—what do you say?" Nina asked.

He looked knowingly at Leo and said, "I agree with Mr. Ashcroft." There was a strange tension between Mike and Leo. The two men looked at each other for a long while.

Leo broke the silence. "You remember, don't you?"

Mike nodded, "Yes. Can you forgive me?"

Leo smiled. "Of course, how were you to know?"

David did a double take. "What's going on? You two have met before?"

"We have—a long time ago," said Leo. "Remember I told you about Greenberg's letter asking me to give up my paternity rights?"

"Yes," replied David.

"After I refused, two huge men came to see me. Bruisers we used to call them in those days. They ruffed me up and threatened me with serious bodily harm if I didn't sign away my paternity rights. When I said no, the shorter one wanted to plough into me right away, but the other one said, 'We'll let you think it over—you've got a week.'"

"That was Mike?" asked Nina.

Mike nodded. "Sy called my brother to take care of a problem and I was forced to go along. That's who I was back then. Afterwards, Moretti found out we threatened your father and told us to keep our hands off the professor."

"It was the first favor Moretti ever did for me," Leo said. "All he ever asked of me was to curate his art collection. Which he acquired legally by the way."

"I'm glad to have the opportunity to say how sorry I am," Mike offered.

Leo got up and extended his hand, "For years it's been Scholz and me. I think we need to sign on someone with more muscle—what do you say Mike?"

Mike's face lit up with a smile and Leo's hand became lost in the big man's grip.

"If everyone will wait a few minutes, I'd like to discuss the particulars with Mike alone."

On his way out of the living room, Mike stopped by David's chair. "All these years we were friends and I never realized I knew both of your fathers. It's a strange world."

Leo took Mike into his office and they sat next to the fireplace. "First I want to thank you for your kindness toward my son. You did the job I should have done. You have a position with me for as long as you like."

"Thank you, I'm grateful."

"Where have you been staying since the bombing?" Leo asked.

"With AJ at his mom's apartment."

"Well, that's not acceptable. David will be staying with me until this mess is over. I suggest you stay at Jacob's for an indefinite period. He doesn't want to admit it, but he's frail and I'm worried about leaving him alone. What do you say?"

"Well, I have no business now, my wife left me, and I have very little money. My apartment is bundled in with the Food Mart's rent payment. Soon I won't have a place to live. I'll be homeless by the end of the month. So yes, that's a very generous offer."

"Then it's settled." Leo reached into a drawer and put some bills in an envelope. "This should hold you over until we can discuss terms. If you have any outstanding debts, let me know and I'll take care of them. I insist."

Mike nodded. Leo could see he was overcome with emotion. "Well, let's get back to them, shall we?" The two men, from totally different backgrounds, faced each other in a shared understanding of a mutual interest—David's safety.

When they returned to the living room Nina said, "I think I'll leave now. It's been a long, emotional day and I understand you're arranging a family brunch tomorrow. I want to look my best."

"Good idea," Leo said. "Herr Scholz was going to stay at Jacob's apartment, but I've asked Mike instead. Herr Scholz will drive Nina back home. Mike, you tag along so he can drop you off at Jacob's apartment. From there Herr Scholz will go back to his place over the gallery."

David got up and went to Mike, "You are part of my family now, so it's time you knew the truth about me. On my bureau is a thick leather folio. All the answers you need are inside."

CHAPTER 33

Retaliation

Sy and Sloane landed in Newark late that same evening. Although Sy's station wagon was parked at the airport, they decided to take a taxi to Marta's house. He still had the keys to Chip's car and apartment. Using Chip's car would be safer, and they could hole up in Chip's apartment to watch for an opportunity to grab David. The cabbie dropped them off two blocks from Marta's house and they walked to Chip's car. Sy gave Sloane Chip's keys and pager.

"You're driving and hold onto the pager," he told him. "If ever we get separated, I can send you a message." They loaded their bags in the trunk and Sy grabbed the tire iron before they headed toward the house.

Sy went in first through the kitchen with his key. A small light was on–something Marta typically did before going to bed. Sloane came in behind Sy and they both went into the living room and moved cautiously up the darkened stairs. They could hear a repetitive thumping coming from the bedroom. A sound Sy knew well–Marta was not alone. Sy turned to Sloane and made a fist, pounding it three times against the palm of his other hand. Sloane nodded. They hit the landing and Sy peeked through the open door.

Eyes closed, Marta was spreadeagled on the bed, as a man slammed his pelvis wildly against her. The rhythm increased in intensity as Sy entered the room and maneuvered himself behind the bed. He raised the tire iron, aiming for the back of the man's head.

Now!

The thud of the headboard against the wall, the squeak of the mattress and the slapping of flesh ceased. The man fell on his side. Marta screamed and scrambled from under the man's body, bunching the bedsheets up around her chest. Sy reached into the drawer beside the bed, removed her gun and switched on the table lamp.

"Oh my God, Sy...Sy I...I'm sorry. He forced himself on me."

"Shut up!"

Sloane checked the pulse of the sandy-haired man. "Out cold—probably concussed." The tire iron came down on the side of the man's head, lopping off an ear. Blood seeped into the mattress.

Holding the gun, Sy turned on Marta. "Where is it? Where's my ledger?"

Marta glanced furtively from Sy to Sloane. "Ledger...what ledger?"

Sloane rummaged through the man's belongings on a nearby chair. "Sy," Sloane said, holding up Agent Keyes's credentials.

Sy waved his gun at her. "Jesus, first Moretti, now the FBI. You've been playing both sides against the middle."

Horrified, Marta inched away from the gun, her hands digging into the blood-soaked mattress. "No, I...he...he works for Moretti."

"Like you, huh? You stole my ledger when I was in the bathroom. Switched it out for magazines so you could give it to Moretti."

"No." Marta's lips twitched in her effort to get the words out. "Keyes said your stepson stole it."

"Keyes?" Sy repeated.

"The name on this guy's ID," Sloane explained.

Sy cocked the gun between Marta's eyes. "You lie."

"No, no, no." Marta winced and cowered back against the headboard. Her blood smeared hands coming up in a desperate plea. "Don't shoot—please! You've got to believe me. Keyes was Moretti's mole in the FBI. He found out David stole evidence from your house. I had nothing to do with it."

"So, you and this Keyes work for Moretti?"

"Yes, I informed for Moretti. He gave me no choice. I didn't know what to do with your son's body, so I called Moretti. Keyes showed up. Stayed for days. Forced me to do things...."

"So, Moretti hasn't seen the ledger?"

"No, but he knows about it. He knows David has it. Keyes saw him with it in the subway. Moretti wants it bad."

"The truth?"

"Yes, yes, I swear...I swear." Marta sobbed.

It all makes sense. David must have hidden outside the house when I was burning the files. The ledger was in the open station wagon. David took it after I fell asleep.

Marta whimpered. The mattress looked like his father's butcher table and she a slab of meat to process. One bullet to the head ended the life of the woman who took Chip away from him. Sloane followed suit by finishing off the FBI agent with the man's own gun. He pocketed the gun along with the agent's badge while Sy placed Marta's gun in his waistband and grabbed the box of bullets. Then, they left the house.

Sy leaned back in the passenger seat with his eyes closed—the tortured look on Marta's face looming up before him. He held it there—the red, gurgling hole in her forehead—the unfolding flower of crimson spreading over the pillow beneath her head.

As Sloane drove out of the neighborhood he said, "I told you it might not be as bad as you thought."

Sloane was right and Sy couldn't believe his luck. *Moretti hasn't seen the ledger and doesn't know I cheated him. The FBI never saw it—David still has it. If Moretti wants it, he'll put a contract out on David. The solution is simple—I get the ledger from David; I can go back to Bimini.*

⤬⤬

At that same moment, CIA operative Frank Riley was outside Jacob's apartment building making another attempt at David. As luck would have it, both of Jacob's second-floor windows had faux balconies—a wrought iron railing without deck space. Riley figured the smaller of the two was the old man's kitchen, so he threw a hook rope onto the railing and hoisted himself up.

The window was unlocked and once inside Riley paused to remove a vial and flashlight from his pockets. The place smelled like a brewery, the flashlight's beam revealing three empty beer bottles on the kitchen table.

What's this? A thick folio of papers—one sheet detached—looks like some sort of report. He hovered over it and the words "Blink Factor" glared up from the page in the beam of the flashlight. He flipped through the pages of test results. *Here it is—all the documentation Langley needs to springboard their research. Why bother slipping LSD into David's food. This is the mother-load. What I need now is the kid himself.*

The vial loaded with LSD went back into his pocket. Riley removed the tranquilizer gun from the back of his waistband replacing it with the leather folio. Holding the tranquilizer gun out before him, he headed to the foyer and opened the front door. Once tranquilized, he'd carry the scrawny kid out to the elevator. Snoring came from the first bedroom and, opening the door, he could see the art equipment in the far corner of the room.

His room... He entered and pulled the trigger.

Thunk.

It was unexpected. A massive, half-naked figure lurched from the bed and rolled onto the floor with a thud. Transfixed, Riley found it difficult to move. The sculpted shoulders rippled as a beast of a man rose to his knees. A guttural roar reverberated around the room as a slab-like arm swung up from the floor and knocked Riley's feet out from under him.

Stunned, Riley scrambled on all fours toward the door and, holding onto the doorknob, pulled himself up in a panic. As the muscle-bound giant rose to his full height, Riley braced himself for the terrible onslaught. But the sedative seemed to take hold and the man stumbled forward. Confident now, Riley stood his ground and reloaded another dart.

But then someone appeared in the hallway holding a baseball bat. "You?" said Riley. Jacob held the baseball bat out in front of him. Shaking it with his two hands, the old man looked like a character from one of Dickens's novels. Riley fumbled with the dart while Mike and Jacob advanced toward him. One was weak as a feather, the other a massive hulk of a man teetering on the edge of collapse. The dart was in the chamber—Riley's finger moved to the trigger....

The big man first....

It came out of nowhere—one feeble whack from the old man's bat and the dart was deflected. The body builder was on him, crushing his gun hand and catching his neck in a vise-like grip.

Riley couldn't breathe.

Chapter 34

Day 13
Taken

Arriving at Chip's apartment around seven Sunday morning, Sy and Sloane took turns watching Jacob's apartment building. There was little to eat, the coffee was undrinkable and both men were uncomfortable in the close quarters.

"We're going to have to get some decent food. I'm starving," Sy said.

"Yeah, I'll leave soon," said Sloane. "Someone may recognize you. Hey, a van just drove up in front of the old man's apartment building."

Sy moved to the window. It looked like David getting out of the van, but then he spotted the man's beard. *It's that pompous Nazi, Aschbacher. I shoulda known she'd be sneaking around on me."*

"Who's the guy in the drivers seat?" asked Sloane.

"Damned if I know. Get the car—we need to follow them."

Sloane left. Sy grabbed his jacket, and stuffed Marta's gun in his waistband. By the time he returned to the window, someone else was in the van—maybe David—he couldn't tell. Aschbacher lead Jacob out the lobby door as Sloane drove up on the opposite side of the street. Sy hid in the apartment's forecourt until the van pulled away before sliding into the seat next to Sloane.

They followed the van to the Pierre Hotel on Fifth. Aschbacher got out and the van pulled away. The Nazi went inside and a few minutes later appeared outside the hotel with Ellen. She was dressed in something expensive and seemed to be hanging on every word the German was saying. They crossed 61st Street and walked east toward Madison.

"Get out and follow them," Sy said. "I'll drive around until I see you."

Sloane got out of the car and Sy pulled out into traffic. The area was full of one-way streets, forcing Sy to take 59th Street and circle around through the congested traffic. He turned north on Madison and spotted them walking ahead of him towards 62nd Street. Sy stopped at the light and spotted Sloane at the corner watching Ellen and Aschbacher enter an art gallery on Madison.

≈≈

"This is it," Leo said. He opened the door and held it for her. Ellen stood just inside the door and took in the large open space. "My gallery director came in earlier with some of David's friends to set everything up."

Leo was still holding the door open when Nina and her mother came up behind them. "So glad you're back safe and sound," Nina said, as she hugged Ellen, "David's been worried about you." Nina then introduced her mother, Elsita.

"Glad to meet you finally," Ellen said. "I was thinking of contacting you for the longest time, but my circumstances were…difficult."

"You have no need to explain. My own problems, they too are over," Elsita responded in her accented English. "You and I, we are free women now. We should, how you say, stick together."

Ellen felt a friendship in the making and she clasped Elsita's outstretched hand, "That's a great idea, let's get together sometime."

They moved further into the gallery and encountered AJ and Amanda. "You remember AJ?" Nina asked Ellen. "AJ's kind enough to be my bodyguard during this mess. And this is his girlfriend Amanda, she's given me a lot of support too."

"I can't thank you enough for your help," Ellen said, shaking both their hands.

Nina introduced AJ and Amanda to Leo, who extended his hand to AJ. "Happy to finally meet you. I'm grateful for your assistance. Because of you and Mike, we all feel a lot safer now."

"Anything we can do for David, he's a good friend," AJ replied.

They all moved into the center of the gallery space with Leo noting, "We've moved the sculptures aside so we could set up the food. There's a makeshift bar next to the piano with Mimosas or plain orange juice, whichever you prefer. Oh—and beer—Mike insisted on beer."

Ellen turned to Leo. "The flowers you sent to my hotel room were beautiful, thank you," Ellen said. "The suite is very luxurious. You shouldn't be so extravagant. A standard hotel room is fine. You're going to spoil me."

"I hope so," Leo replied. "From my conversations with David, I have a good idea of what you've been through. It's about time someone pampered you."

Jacob joined them. "So, tell me, who is this striking woman next to you?" he said to Leo. "Such a dress—and the height of fashion too. It's a long time since I've been in the business, but I still recognize couture. And the fabric—*boucle*."

"Thank you, Dad, it's Chanel; you still have an eye. I heard what happened last night. You're obviously all right because you look good," Ellen said, giving him a light kiss on the cheek.

"Wait," Jacob said, "you haven't heard the whole story. But we'll get to it later. Now tell me, you saw your sister Rose, how is she?"

"Rose is fine now; she sends her love. We had a wonderful visit."

David came from the back room and greeted her with a hug, "Welcome home Mom, we missed you."

This is what Ellen hoped and dreamed of—a close-knit circle of family and friends who were kind, supportive and loving. She was introduced to Herr Scholz and David's secret friend, Mike. Ellen knew he was Mob connected, and a childhood friend of Sy's, yet she could sense the deep affection the big man had for her son.

Leo made sure everyone had drinks and raised his glass. "It seems I can't stop toasting Jacob. As everyone knows, last night there was a break-in at his apartment. Everyone's fine—no was one hurt. Thanks in part to Jacob and of course Mike, who subdued the CIA operative who was pursuing David. So, a big thank you to Jacob and Mike. And to Ellen, a very warm homecoming."

Jacob was very pleased with all the attention and told last night's story twice over. He began to embellish it again when David broke in.

"*Oy, Gevalt*," David said comically. "Stop already with the story. We admit, you're the hero of the hour—we're all very proud of you Gramps. I'm just glad you survived in one piece."

Jacob smiled. "I would like also to thank Mike for trying to help."

Mike protested, "What do mean trying?"

"Well, you were a little *fertummelt* from the dart. So naturally you stumbled. When you fell on top of that CIA fella, well, to put it delicately, he couldn't move. It's nothing to be ashamed of—you tried, that's what's important."

Laughter all around.

All through the celebration Ellen couldn't help noticing the way Leo regarded her. Admiration was in his eyes. And hope. It was strange being with him again. He was everything she remembered him to be, yet different in so many ways. Whether it was a good thing or not remained to be seen.

Ellen approached Nina and her mother. "I have a little something I picked up in Nassau for you," she said to Nina. "Perhaps both of you would like to go back to my hotel afterwards. I can give you the present and we can all spend some time getting acquainted."

Both mother and daughter agreed.

At a restaurant across the street from the gallery, Sy and Sloane finally filled their empty stomachs. They were taking up a window table for going on two hours, and the manager came over to remind them of the fact.

Sloane took out Keyes's FBI ID and Sy followed suit with his IRS credentials. "It shouldn't be much longer," Sy said. "We appreciate your patience."

The manager nodded and left. When they focused their attention back to the gallery, part of the group was exiting the gallery—it looked as though the party was breaking up.

"Okay, how do you want to play this?" Sloane asked.

"David's got the ledger so he's the primary target," Sy said. "But, if there's an opportunity to snatch my wife, we should take it."

It was now after two o'clock. Ellen, Nina, and an older woman Sy took to be Nina's mother, stood outside the gallery saying goodbye to David and Leo. The two men re-entered the gallery and a young black couple came out to join the three women. All five of them started walking south on Madison.

Sy stood up. "They're splitting up, and David's out of play for the time being. Follow them, and I'll get the car. When you see me drive up behind you, snatch Ellen first then David's little whore. Give the pager I gave you to one of the others. Tell them to wait for a message."

Although it was a short walk from the gallery to the Pierre Hotel, AJ and Amanda insisted on accompanying Nina, her mother and Ellen.

They crossed the street, walked a block to 61st Street, and were heading towards Fifth Avenue when Sloane met them mid-block.

"Excuse me ladies," Sloane said, flashing Keyes's FBI identification, "a quick word please."

Nina caught a brief glimpse of the man's picture ID and recognized Agent Keyes's photo. "Move away," she yelled, "he's not FBI."

AJ quickly placed himself between the four women and the fake agent but came up against a gun. Sloane motioned him back, grabbed Amanda and placed her in front of him, the gun at her back. Nina retreated behind a mailbox with Ellen.

"Back off or she dies," warned Sloane to AJ. A car drove up, and Sloane waved his gun. "You two, out from behind the mailbox and into the car. Now!"

Nina helped Ellen step off the pavement. The passenger door opened, and Ellen was pulled into the front seat by Sy Greenberg. As soon as Ellen was snatched, the gunman shoved Nina into the back seat.

Sloane placed something in Amanda's hand. "There'll be a phone number, tell David to call it."

Sloane got in next to Nina and the car sped away.

CHAPTER 35

The Setup

Scholz had left the gallery soon after brunch to drive Jacob and Mike back to 88th Street. Leo and David were still cleaning up when Amanda stumbled into the gallery.

"They've been taken," Amanda said, out of breath. "Nina, Ellen... two men. Older guy in a car—younger one with a gun."

"AJ and Elsita?" asked David.

"Okay," Amanda gasped for air. "I ran ahead. AJ is bringing Elsita back."

"Come into the office, I'll give you some brandy," offered Leo. "Elsita will need some too."

Amanda sat trembling on the couch and handed David the pager. "You're supposed to wait for a message." She took a few sips of the brandy and as her color returned, AJ came in with Elsita. Leo led her to the couch. She sat beside Amanda, furious.

"People on the street, they did nothing," she complained. The car... it left. They turned their backs and walked away."

"I'm sorry David," AJ said.

"There was nothing you could do," David said, looking at the pager. "If it was my stepfather, maybe you could have moved fast enough to avoid their capture. The guy was a hired gun. You did the right thing."

"Even so..." AJ responded.

"Don't dwell on it," Leo insisted. "Now we've got to put our heads together and figure out what to do."

"Sy's going to want an exchange," David said. "For the ledger."

"How does your stepfather know you've got the ledger?" AJ asked.

"Keyes," said David. "Amanda told us Nina recognized Agent Keyes's photo on the FBI identification. That means Sy and his friend got a hold of Keyes somehow. If they have his ID, they probably killed him."

"Why take Ellen too?" Leo asked.

"Taking Nina guarantees the return of the ledger. And as long as he holds onto Mom, he can exchange Nina for the ledger and still retain leverage over me."

"Makes sense," said Leo. "In the meantime, he'll force her to transfer the money back to him."

They were discussing what to do when the phone rang. Leo answered it. "Stay put and keep an eye on the street. Call us back if there's any movement," he hung up. "That was Mike. He was at Jacob's window when he noticed two men manhandle Nina and Ellen into a ground floor apartment across the street."

⋙⋘

Hands tied behind their backs, Ellen and Nina stood captive in front of the kitchenette of Chip's grimy apartment. Ellen silent and crestfallen, looked on in wonder as Nina struggled against her ropes, hurling insults and complaints at Sy. He was an animal, she said, a brute; the room reeked of urine. To shut her up, Sy smacked her across the face, something Ellen endured many times during her marriage.

The hope Ellen held in her heart a scant three hours ago vanished. During the past few days, she lifted herself out of a twenty-year malaise to feel vibrant and confident again. Standing next to this defiant young woman, Ellen was horrified to find how easy it was for her to slip back into the role of the bullied and compliant wife.

Despite the slap, Nina didn't cower, and began a fresh round of taunts.

"You goddamn *shiksa* whore," Sy yelled back, tearing the bed sheet into pieces. "You're the reason David changed." He came up behind her and stuffed the filthy cloth into Nina's mouth. When Sy wrapped a strip of cloth around her head to hold the gag in place, Nina shook her head violently from side to side. Sloane had to hold her head.

Then, Sy pushed her down on the bed. "There, where a good little whore should be—bound, silent and on your back." Infuriated, Nina's eyes opened wide with indignation. If ever a woman could kill, Ellen was sure Nina was up to the task.

Sy found it difficult to stare down the young woman's fury and averted his eyes to pick up the phone. "If you feel humiliated now," he said, "wait until I get you in front of your sniveling boyfriend—he's as spineless as his mother."

He dialed Chip's pager.

⊷≈⊷

David knew this was the defining moment of all his years of struggle. His transformation was complete. He was no longer a naive and helpless boy fighting through a haze of barbiturates. For the first time in his life, he forgot the past, and was living in the present.

He was also envisioning the future. Playing various scenarios over and over in his mind. Trying to come up with a plan. Finally, sometime before four that afternoon, the pager beeped. He called the number and Sy answered.

"Yes, I have it," David responded. "It's hidden at the University. The Columbia Fine Arts Building. It will take me a while to get there. An hour... Well, because I'm still at the gallery and I have to find a cab. Meet me at the first-floor maintenance area—near the steps leading to the basement. Campus Security doesn't break for dinner until five, so be careful. Yeah, I'll come alone. Look, let me speak to—"

The phone went dead.

David dropped the receiver onto the cradle and sat on Leo's desk facing AJ. "Everything depends on you and Mike. If it was one on one with my stepfather, I'm sure I could handle it. But the rules have changed since he picked up the hired gun."

"I agree," Leo said. "What do you suggest?"

"I hid the ledger in one of Columbia's old tunnels. Where AJ keeps a flashlight. They're going to meet me at the basement entrance for the exchange. My hope is they'll let me lead them into the tunnel. AJ and Mike should be waiting for me in the shadows."

"Mike will need a gun," Leo said, reaching in his desk drawer to pull out a German, 9mm Walther P-38 and an extra clip. "Eight rounds each clip—it's pretty straightforward."

"AJ, you and Mike need to hide on the opposite side of the tunnel from where your flashlight is. You've got to be there before I arrive," David cautioned.

AJ pocketed the clip and gun. "We can do that through another entrance—they'll never see us."

"Good, I'll make a lot of noise, so you hear us coming. If they get spooked and send me in alone, it changes everything. Then you'll have to follow me out and confront them in the light."

The phone rang again. David listened and hung up. "It was Mike. Sy and the other guy just left the apartment."

AJ stood up, "We better leave now."

With Scholz driving, they headed toward Jacob's apartment, Leo in the front seat and David, AJ and Amanda in the back of the van.

Leo assured David, "Don't worry about your mother. Now that we know where she is, Herr Scholz and I will bring her back safely." Leo thrust his hand toward the back seat to grasp AJ's hand, "There are no words for what you're about to do."

Amanda touched David's shoulder, "You're doing everything you can...they'll be okay. Don't worry about Jacob and Elsita, I'll make sure they're all right. Call us as soon as you can—we'll be anxious."

Then she snuggled against AJ and looked meaningfully into her boyfriend's eyes.

ༀ

Mike was waiting under the canopy when they drove up in front of Jacob's apartment building. Leo, Scholz, Amanda and Elsita got out to go upstairs to join Jacob in his apartment. AJ moved up to take the wheel and passed Leo's gun to Mike in the back seat.

"Mr. Ashcroft wanted you to have it." AJ said, as he pulled the van away from the curb and headed for Columbia University.

Mike checked the Walther, put it away and withdrew a tranquilizer gun from his pocket. "This one's for you David, courtesy of the CIA. It's empty now so get familiar with it. We're going to smash the light bulb near where AJ hid his flashlight and hide the tranquilizer gun under the ledger. They're going to pat you down and when they find you're clean, they'll relax. Once you're in the tunnel, pull the dart gun and ledger out together hiding the gun behind the ledger."

David practiced with the dart gun until Mike nodded his approval. By the time the van arrived on campus, the sun was down, and Mike went over several possible scenarios with David.

"AJ and I will be hiding nearby. Remember, Sy thinks you're a pansy. Play it up from the beginning. You're scared—do whatever you've done in the past to deceive him into thinking your still a wimp. When you get in position, keep on telling him what you're doing—nervous like. Get him use to your indecision. Remember, the more you tell him what you're doing the better we can follow your progress. When the time is right, we'll take him out."

"What about the tranquilizer gun?"

"Insurance. AJ will grab Nina while I'll take care of Sy, but you may need to neutralize his hired gun. There's one dart in the chamber—it's your call—so make it count."

David was dropped off a block from the Fine Arts Building. Both Mike and AJ gave him the thumbs up and continued to the other end of the tunnel. As David walked on, he used guided imagery to imagine every possible scenario that could happen. It was something he learned at Bell Labs—projecting a series of future outcomes onto his mind's eye before following through on them.

By the time he arrived at the Fine Arts Building, he felt as though every conceivable move already happened.

༺⚬༻

Leo stood by and watched Scholz use his ring of keys on the Super's door—but there was no way in. They moved to the window and peeked in through the curtains. The room was empty, so they headed up the stairs and into the lobby. It was a small anti-room with apartments on either side. A narrow staircase led up to the other floors. A faint thumping was heard from the floor below. Finding a door marked "Basement", they opened it, and moved down a short flight of stairs. The thumping there was more intense, and they hurried along until they came up against a door marked "Maintenance".

Leo pounded on the door. There was a weak response. "Ellen!" Leo cried, "We're here, we'll get you out."

Scholz's keys wouldn't work.

"Ellen, get away from the door. Back up as far as you can. We're breaking down the door."

CHAPTER 36

Death Watch

David moved down the empty hallway toward the basement entrance. Deathly quiet, only a few subdued noises seeped out from behind studio doors. It was the tail end of Spring Break and the bulk of students had not yet returned. Stopping at the water fountain, he wet his forehead and the hair around his temples—perspiration would telegraph fear.

He entered the maintenance area and spotted Nina with the two men at the bottom of the stairs. The hit man eyed David and motioned with his gun to raise his hands. Hands in the air, David descended the staircase where his stepfather patted him down, snickering all the time. Sy flashed Nina a told-you-so glance—taunting her.

"Look how he's sweating—a real hero isn't he?" Shoving David against the wall, Sy held him there with a palm against his chest. "Where is it asshole?"

"There's a sss-sub basement through th-that door," David stuttered. "It leads to a tuh-tunnel. It's there."

"Tunnel? What kind of crap is that?" Sy's face was flushed—he was beginning the slow boil.

"No really, I'm t-telling you the truth. Honest." David said in a panic, his eyes darting back and forth from Sy to the hit man. "It's th-there from World War II—the Manhattan P- P-Project. Uh-underground research center. It's deserted."

"What do you think, Sloane?"

"Yeah, sounds okay. I heard about it sometime back. Scientists and shit. If he's lying about the ledger, I'll crush her windpipe."

David went ballistic, "No, no, no, d-don't—I mean, you'll see, everything's like I say—just leave her b-be." He slumped against the wall, hardly looking at Nina. While the two men laughed, David winked at her.

Nina closed her eyes in recognition of his intent.

Sy looked at her closed eyes, "Disgusted huh? Gee, you're not gonna cry, are you? I told you, all the pussy in the world isn't going to make him a man." Then to Sloane, "Didn't I tell you the kid was a pansy," and he pushed David ahead. "Go ahead big shot, lead the way."

David led them through the basement to a door with a "No Admittance" sign. "This goes to the s-sub-basement." They moved down another flight of stairs and through a long corridor. A muffled hum followed their progress. Dank, musty air assaulted David's nostrils as he moved along noisily. He was getting the men use to the sound of their footsteps reverberating around them. They entered a long open space with boilers and large diameter pipes running along the walls.

"Jesus," Sy said, "how much longer?"

"Got to p-pass through the steel door."

After clanking down metal stairs and squeezing through a rusty gate, they finally arrived at the yellow steel door. Sloane read the sign aloud, "Warning! Ionizing Radiation, Keep Out".

"Fucking shit," said Sy. "It's legit."

David pushed meekly against the door, but it wouldn't budge.

"Move pipsqueak," Sloane leaned his shoulder hard against the door. It flew open, hitting the opposite wall with a clank.

"How much further?" Sy demanded.

"About three or four yards from the d-door—where the tunnel begins to branch off."

"Okay," said Sloane. "I'm gonna wait here to make sure it's not a trap. You go ahead. If you need me call out." Sloane kept the door open, but what little light there was crept in for no more than a yard, then everything went black. David moved ahead with Nina behind him, Sy holding the gun to her back.

"Hey, hold up. It's fucking dark in here," Sy complained.

"No p-problem, I stashed a flashlight b-behind a boiler...it's where I hid the ledger." David explained.

"All right, no sudden moves," Sy insisted.

David moved into position. "It's right b-behind this equipment here," he felt around with his hand. "I've got the light." He switched it on behind the boiler and the beam shot up to the ceiling.

"The ledger...give me the fucking ledger," Sy demanded.

"It's here...it's jammed. I need both hands."

"Do it. Bring it out slowly and put it on the floor so I can see it with the flashlight. Any sudden moves and I'll kill her."

David took a deep breath—*now it begins.* "You're going to let her go right? I mean there's no p-point in—"

"I'll kill your little whore, if you don't fork over the damn ledger now."

"Okay, okay. I'm p-putting the flashlight in my armpit. Wait, wait... ah, got the ledger." He lifted the ledger up and out with his left hand; his right hand held the dart gun underneath. *Fumble with the flashlight,* he reminded himself. His left armpit turned with him—the light beam wobbled around in the dark.

"S-Sorry," David murmured. "I have to kneel down on the floor." He squatted down and removed the flashlight from his armpit. It flickered briefly over Nina. Sy's gun was out from behind Nina's back—pointing over her shoulder in the direction of the light.

"Hey!" Sy exclaimed. "What the fuck's going on?" The gun was moving erratically.

David locked-in Sy's position and held the image in his mind—*clocked at one o'clock.*

"You're stalling..."

"Got the ledger on the floor now."

"Lemme see it, goddamnit, shine the fucking light on it."

David laid the flashlight on the floor, aiming its beam at the ledger.

"That's it. Shove it over to me."

David pointed his arm straight out into the darkness and sighted down on the remembered one o'clock position—*recorded.*

"Come on, come on already," Sy insisted.

David took hold of the flashlight and extended his index finger along the side of the flashlight, saying, "Uh, not before you let her g-go."

"Bullshit, that's not going to happen."

Peering into the darkness, David aimed the flashlight to the one o'clock position.

❦

Blinded by the blaze of light, Sy released Nina from his grasp to shield his eyes. Something granite-like came from below and whacked his gun hand above his head. The gun went off, the sound reverberating against the boilers and pipes. Through the brightness of the muzzle flash, Sy moved his free arm back around her neck to hold on to her. He was too late. Enraged, Nina twisted out of his grip and brought her knee up into his crotch.

"Goddamn dirtbag," she shouted.

The searing pain traveled from Sy's balls to his gullet. His hand now went between his legs. He felt her tear away from him and fired the gun wildly in her direction, but Nina was already lost to the shadows. A second beam of light flickered in the dark.

Sloane stumbled into the tunnel. "Jesus Sy, where are you?"

"Over here!"

"Ow!" Sloane grunted. "What the fuck is this? Oh shit!"

David crowed, "I got him Mike, he's down."

A massive hand twisted the gun from Sy's grasp. *Mike?* His throat was seized in an iron vise.

The vengeful face of his dead friend pressed close to his. "But you're dead," Sy gurgled.

"Really?" said Mike in a grisly voice. "Then you can join me like the good friend you are."

Sy's hands flailed against the savage grip. He felt the vise clamp down with ratchet-like precision around his throat. As he lost consciousness, his mother appeared cradling Chip's lifeless body across her lap, her eyes burning with tears. Behind Sy's father unfolded his prayer shawl and holding it above them, chanted the mourner's *Kaddish*.

Yis-gah-dal, ve-yis-ka-dash, she-mei ra-ba....

❧

Ellen remained in Leo's comforting embrace long after her sobbing ceased. That she was frightened, and he saved her was part of it. But the bulk of her tears were for all the lost years without him, and she told herself she would never leave him again.

Leo tried to help her up, but she resisted and clung to him. "Don't leave me...promise you'll never leave me...I had no idea what I lost until you came back in my life. I'm sorry."

"I'm sorry too," he said, "for the people we once were. It's all in the past now and it should stay there."

"Come," he encouraged her to get up, "your father will be worried."

❧

Through the haze of his final moments on earth, Sy heard David pleading, "...don't do it Mike...please, you'll regret it. Mike?" A rush of air filled his lungs and he felt himself clawing out of nothingness—desperately clinging to every breath. He was going to survive.

They were mumbling now, the good-hearted fools, about calling someone to help him. Oxygen had saturated his brain and his mind raced with all the possibilities before him. They would take him to a hospital—he'd have plenty of time to work out a plan. Nothing would stop him.

Still on his back, Sy breathed easier now. A shadow moved in the tunnel and someone checked his pulse. It was dark and quiet; he felt safe and drifted off.

He awoke to a ticking....

Blood pooled in his gullet.

He gurgled, then coughed.

Splattered blood covered his face and ran down his cheek.

On his back; choking on his father's butcher table.

Drowning in his own blood.

More ticking....

Something crawled up his neck.

❧❧

Ellen answered David's call shortly after they arrived at Jacob's apartment. She listened with an expression of relief and regret then, gave the phone to Leo. Leo heard the news and told David to come back to the apartment as soon as he could. He hung up the phone and looked around at everyone. It was all over, he told them. Nina was snatched out of harm's way by AJ. Both Greenberg and Sloane were subdued.

"AJ stayed in the tunnel to watch over Sy and his hired gun," Leo continued. "Mike followed David and Nina out of the tunnel to phone Moretti."

Ellen stopped him. "Let me," she said. Leo nodded and let her continue.

"Mike was about to go back in the tunnel when AJ showed up. It seems my husband talked to himself about a key to something and started coughing. The coughing turned into a struggle for air—he was choking on his own blood. AJ turned him around. When my husband's airway wouldn't clear he tried CPR.

"There was nothing AJ could do. Sy is..." she hesitated "Dead." The tears began, and Leo moved to support her.

"You should lie down now," he said to her.

Ellen nodded and headed for her father's bedroom with Leo close behind. She sat on the bed and waited for him to close the blinds. She felt safer than she had ever felt before.

"Anything you need," Leo said to her before leaving.

"No. Thank you," she replied warmly.

He closed the door and she eased down on the mattress with a sigh. The day's ordeal and the finality of its conclusion spinning through her mind.

Sy's life is over. Mine is just beginning.

CHAPTER 37

Epilogue

Months after his stepfather's death, the memory of his cruelty still intruded into David's now happy life. Sy crept into David's mind during his graduation and again during his wedding to Nina. Ellen too, found it difficult to flush her husband from her mind. Eager to embrace autonomy, she moved in with Elsita on Park Avenue to rekindle her romance with Leo. David and Nina spent their honeymoon in Europe, visiting all the major museums and ancient sites. Upon their return, Leo gathered the family together for an announcement.

"For some years now, I have planned to open a second gallery. At the time David and I reunited, I had already purchased a home in Santa Fe, New Mexico. It's the third largest art market in the country. Now that Ellen is back in my life, my priorities have changed. I no longer want to disappear into the Southwest like some hermit. There will be plenty of time to retire later.

"But the house is beautiful, and Santa Fe is a wonderful place for a young couple to begin their lives. To put it simply, Ellen and I suggest both of you take a trip out there to see for yourselves. If you like it, the house is yours as a wedding present."

"That's an unbelievable gift, thank you," Nina said. "David, what do you think?"

David was ready to jump at the chance but had reservations. He looked at Nina, "Well, it's certainly tempting. Now that I've experienced the underbelly of the city, I'm not so keen on hanging around. It'll be like wiping the slate clean and starting over. I've read about the Taos Painters and the marvelous light out there... but what would we do?"

"That's the second part of our proposal," Leo said. "I have an option to rent gallery space on Canyon Road. If it appeals to you, I can go through with my original plan to open a gallery, but only if you agree to run it. What do you say?"

"Wow, first a house and now entrusting me with the expansion of your business. I mean, I'm grateful and excited at the idea, but there's Nina's dance career, my connections with New York ad agencies and the new consulting work for the FBI. And what about Gramps?"

Jacob piped in, "Go. Take a look. What would it hurt? Ellen and Leo are taking good care of me, you should start a life of your own without some *alta-cocker* to worry about."

"He's right, David," Ellen said. "Leo and I spent some time in Santa Fe while you were on honeymoon. Coming in from Albuquerque it seemed kind of desolate at first. But when we reached the top of La Bajada Hill, the view, the atmosphere, the serenity of the land—you have to be there to understand the feeling."

"It's called 'The Land of Enchantment'," Leo added. "Check it out. Think of it as an extended honeymoon."

The charm of Santa Fe was undeniable. David and Nina fell in love with the clear blue sky and clean fresh air. Leo's home in the North Hills sat on five acres situated on a mountainous ridge outside the city with miles of National Forest behind it. Sparsely populated and surrounded by magnificent views, the rambling adobe structure had a guest house and a large outdoor patio overlooking the city lights. The dry weather, the smell of piñon and the cool nights all worked in concert to entice the couple to stay.

A month later they moved in.

Situated along Santa Fe's famed Canyon Road, Ashcroft Gallery West included several exhibition galleries, a guest apartment, and a large storage area. Scholz arrived soon after them and moved into the gallery's apartment to begin renovations. Mike and his wife took over the guest house at the edge of Leo's five-acre lot a week later.

Within a few months, the gallery was ready to hang. Leo and Ellen planned to arrive for the soft opening. Moretti too, said he was coming with his wife. During the renovation, David carved out some easel time to complete a portrait of Moretti's wife. He placed the last brushstroke on the woman's gown when Nina walked into the gallery's studio from the patio.

"It's a beautiful painting David," she said. "You should be very pleased with it."

"I am," David said. "Also, very proud of what we've done with the gallery. Of course, without Herr Scholz to guide us, I'm afraid we would be lost."

"Mike and Margret too," Nina added. "And they both promised to help me set up my dance school at the beginning of the year."

"Did I hear my name mentioned," Mike asked as he entered the studio.

"We said we couldn't have done all this without you and Margret," Nina said.

"Our pleasure. After all, you've given us a brand-new life," Mike said. "Anyway, you've got visitors. Two men in dark suits would like to speak to you."

"No one wears suits in Santa Fe," Nina said. "Especially dark ones. Did they say what they wanted?"

"Someone in New York sent them. They're here to ask David a favor."

"Oh god," Nina moaned. "It's happening—I told you there'd be a price to pay with Moretti. We're going to be dragged back into that horrible world—I just know it."

"Don't rush to judgement on this," David advised her. "It could be anything."

Nina turned to Mike. "Tell them we're not here."

David shook his head. "They'll just return another time. Best to see what this is all about. Send them in Mike."

The two men entered. By the looks of them, there was a lot of hard muscle under their suits. One of them extended his hand, "Mr. Asher?"

"Yes, what can I do for you gentlemen?"

"I'm Agent Harvey and this is Agent Gallegos—FBI." They did the flip thing with their badges. "I'm out of the Albuquerque Regional Office and agent Gallegos is out of our Satellite Office here in Santa Fe. You've come highly recommended by Alan Hunter of the Manhattan district. He suggested you might be able to help us with an investigation."

"I see," David said, flashing Nina an I-told-you-so smile. He moved around the desk and leaned back in his chair....

Here we go again.

About the Author

Born in Manhattan, Steve Barry studied painting at Boston University, The Boston Museum School and the Art Students League of New York. After an early career in advertising, he left Madison Avenue for the Southwest where he worked as Creative Director for the Santa Fe New Mexican. After gaining recognition as a painter, he taught art at the Institute of American Indian Arts in Santa Fe before moving to Texas with his wife. Always attracted to the creative process, *Blink Factor* is his first novel.

www.ingramcontent.com/pod-product-compliance
Lightning Source LLC
Chambersburg PA
CBHW070519100726
47907CB00004B/896